Authors

Aaron Allston

Maxwell Alexander Drake

Janine K. Spendlove

Michael A. Stackpole

C.S. Marks

Donald J. Bingle

Kelly Swails

Jean Rabe

Jennifer Brozek

Daniel Myers

Bryan Young

Tracy Chowdhury

Gregory A. Wilson

Dylan Birtolo

R.T. Kaelin

Steven Saus

Sarah Hans

Bradley P. Beaulieu

Aaron Rosenberg

Brian E. Shaw

Maggie Allen

Timothy Zahn

From

Adventure of the Ghost Watch

Michael A. Stackpole

The brown-eyed boy slid a thumb under the flap and gently tore the envelope open. The notecard within matched the envelope's color. The initials FW stood out at the top, embossed as they were in gold. He scanned the note, and then read it aloud to his mother.

Dear Master John,

I request the pleasure of your company this evening, for a midnight tour of the Shippington Mansion. Doctor E. Everett Everson of the Everson Institute of Ectoplasmic Investigation is going to show us a ghost.

Yours sincerely,
Miss Flora Williams

Silence in the Library

Silence in the Library was founded by a group of authors with the lofty goal of reshaping the publishing industry, or at least our small corner of it. We seek to leverage the powerful tools and distribution networks universally available in twenty-first century publishing to ensure that all of the creative drivers, the authors, and artists, and graphic designers, and editors, involved in bringing a book to market have a substantive voice in the process. It is our firm belief that, as the rapidly changing publishing industry evolves, this will continue to be the correct path toward a quality product that keeps readers engaged and entertained.

This anthology is a product of our concept of how publishers, authors, and other creative drivers should work together. Most of the stories and illustrations you will find inside are the result of a collaborative effort to produce something that speaks to what readers desire in a manner that uplifts not only the readers, but all of those involved in bringing the book to them.

Please enjoy.

Acknowledgements

Silence in the Library would like to thank GAMA and Origins Game Fair for bringing together the diverse collection of talent found in these pages. We'd also like to thank Kelli Neier for the incredible cover design, and Matt Slay for the amazing illustrations. Finally, we'd like to thank Jean Rabe for the application of her unparalleled editing skills and her tireless dedication to this project.

Time Traveled
Tales

Edited by Jean Rabe

Interior Design by Ronald Garner
Cover Design by Kelli Neier
Interior Art by Matt Slay

The text for this book is set in Palatino
Printed in the United States of America
First Printing: June 2013

Table of Contents

Replay Value

Aaron Allston

China looked at the simple gold band with its diamond protruding, at the little hinged presentation box it occupied, at the noticeably trembling hand that held them. Wide-eyed, she glanced up at the face hovering over the box.

A good face. Handsome in a bland sort of way, soft brown eyes that reflected their owner's intelligence and sincerity, wavy brown hair always trying to defy its styling to become shaggy, a jaw so square across the bottom that it was obvious its owner would grow into feisty old age and laugh at his grandchildren.

And now he was talking. "China, would you make me the happiest man on the face of the Earth... by becoming my wife?"

"Uh, no." Inwardly, she winced. She hadn't meant to be so abrupt. Jerry was a nice guy. She didn't want to hurt his feelings. But he'd caught her off-guard.

Jerry took it well. He didn't recoil or look as though someone had just cracked a two-by-four across his face. He sighed and leaned back in his chair, but remained holding the ring out before him. Beneath it, the skewer of shrimp on China's plate continued to cool, waiting patiently to be eaten.

"I mean, Jerry, I really like you —"

He finished the statement for her. "— as a friend. You have no idea how much I value a co-worker who never lies, never throws you under the bus —"

"I would have said 'cherish.'"

"Sometimes you do."

"Don't make fun of me. It's true." China felt on the verge of tears. "I like you a lot. You're funny. You're smart. But —"

"— I've never thought of you that way. This is kind of a complete surprise."

"Get out of my head." She pressed her palms to her ears, blocking out his voice.

He shut up. Looking rueful, he snapped the ring box shut and withdrew it, setting it beside his own plate. It sat there, dwarfed by the mound of spaghetti on the dish. China fancied that the little box waited like a trap-door spider, ready to pop open if she ventured too near.

She pulled her hands down and looked around the restaurant, giving herself a moment to recover.

It was a nice, intimate little Italian place, white tablecloths and waitstaff in suits or little black dresses, dim overhead lighting, candles on the tables. None of the other diners had apparently noticed Jerry's proposal or China's distress. The violin player had; a few yards away, he continued sawing at something mournful from the old country, watching their table. China had never seen a violin player here on a Thursday night.

Finally she returned her attention to Jerry. "I'm not kidding when I say I want you to be my friend. It's —"

"— not a brush-off."

"You're doing that again."

"Sorry."

"How do you know exactly what I'm going to say?"

"I've heard you say it all before. Twenty-four times before."

She blinked at him, confused. "We've never had a conversation remotely like this one."

"This is the twenty-fifth time I've asked you to marry me. With the same results." He sighed and looked around. "I

4

thought maybe the violin player would help this time. Clearly not. Sometimes we're here. Sometimes we're at the table by the window. I have to slip the hostess an extra twenty to get seated there. Sometimes I wait until dessert to pop the question. You always choose the tiramisu."

"They have great tiramisu here."

"Wine or no wine, lobster or shrimp or rib-eye, casual or formal... it's always the same answer. 'I don't feel that way about you.' At this point, I'm usually choked up so bad I can't talk, so I drop some money to pay for dinner and make a dash for my car. You can't keep up with me in high heels, so I tear off for home before you can catch me. But this time..." He shook his head. "I guess I've been through it so many times that finally I can still function. So this time, you don't have to see me cry."

She shook her head. A strand of honey-blond hair came loose and flopped across her cheek. She brushed it back up over her ear. "Please explain that."

He shrugged. "Last weekend, on a whim, I went to an amusement park. You know, the kind where they rent a vacant lot and move in a bunch of portable rides for a few days."

"Sure."

"There was a tent, a fortune-teller's place. Madame Carla Reads Your Future."

"Carla. That's the name of our waitress, too. She hasn't refilled my tea."

"Well, this Carla told me I was doomed to a life of loneliness because I didn't know how to attract a woman. I knew she was right because that's the way it's been all my life. We got to talking, for an extra ten bucks, and she brought up the idea of a wager. Twenty-seven chances at winning your hand in marriage, but I'd live the same day over and over until I succeeded so you wouldn't feel, you know, like I was stalking you. If I failed, the clock would get reset, and I could vary the equation and try again. And again. And again."

She gave him a worried look. "What happens if you fail all twenty-seven times?"

"I think I'll find out two times from now. I'm pretty sure it's grim. I go away and I don't come back."

"Jerry, you *idiot*. I'm not worth that risk."

"I think you are."

Well, okay, it was nice to hear him say that. She struggled not to show him she was kind of pleased. Now wasn't the time.

He kept talking, though. "I'm surprised you even believe this."

"But I do." She thought it over. "I guess it's because you never lie. This would be a big, weird way to start. Why twenty-seven?"

"I asked that. Something about magic numbers. Three's a magic number. Three to the third power."

"So it's like the number of squares in a Rubik's Cube."

"I think the center square in a Rubik's Cube is the mechanism. So there would only be twenty-six."

She waved his objection away. "So what happens next?"

"At midnight tonight, it suddenly becomes midnight *last* night. I'm Cinderella in business casual." He indicated his dark slacks, light shirt, red-tinged power tie. "Then I have twenty-four hours to... fail again."

China took a deep breath as she settled her thoughts. "Okay, I'll marry you."

"*What?*" Finally Jerry did look like someone had gotten his attention with that two-by-four. "What changed your mind?"

"Nothing did. Here are my terms." She began ticking them off on her fingers. "You make all the arrangements. You pay for everything. Tomorrow or next Friday, we fly to Vegas. Two nights, three days. *Separate rooms*. We get married. No sex. Partying, drinks, gambling, sure. One show. Blue Man Group or Cirque du Soleil if you can get tickets. The instant we get back, we file for an annulment."

He stared at her for long moments, and then remembered to close his mouth. "You'd do that for me?"

"To keep you from going to Hell? I wasn't lying when I said I was your friend. Even when you're the *dumbest* man on the face of the Earth."

He took her hand. It wasn't a lover's gesture. It was an expression of gratitude. "Thank you."

"And I get to wear the ring at the wedding. You can trade it in after."

"Deal."

"No deal." The voice was female, hard.

Standing beside their table was their waitress, in the little black dress worn by female employees of this restaurant. China had barely noticed her before. Now she gave the woman a good look.

She was dark, petite, with facial features that claimed eastern European ancestry. Her hair was long and drawn back in a tail, a glossy shaft of black that swayed as she looked from Jerry to China. She seemed born to wear the red lipstick that made her mouth an erotic invitation. She was so slight that China, who was tall and of a healthy weight, felt positively elephantine beside her.

The woman's mouth was not inviting now, not smiling as it had been when she'd taken their order. It was turned down in a stark expression of disapproval — turned toward China.

Jerry's voice rose. "Hey, it *is* Madame Carla."

China tapped her glass. "I'm out of tea."

"Shut up. You get no tea. You can't marry Jerry."

"Why not?"

"Because you're not in love with him."

China shrugged. "I'm of age. Not currently married. I have the weekend off."

Jerry nodded. "Our deal just said 'marry.' There was nothing in it about her being in love with me."

Carla turned on him, the full force of her anger scraping across his face. "You're violating the spirit of the deal."

A man moved up beside her. He was tall, dark-complected, with short hair so immaculately styled that not one strand was out of place. His features suggested they'd been morphed together from photos of an Italian movie star and a Mob contract killer with a sense of humor. His suit was beautifully tailored. And his voice, when he spoke, was death-by-chocolate cake in vocal form: rich, smooth, deep, knee-weakening. "I'm the manager. Is there a problem?"

China tapped her glass again. "She won't get me tea."

The manager smiled. "I'm sorry, I didn't make myself clear. I'm Carla's manager. Please call me Satan. All my friends do."

China blinked at him. "Oh."

Carla jabbed a finger at Jerry. "He's trying to weasel out of our contract terms. She's agreed to marry him, but she doesn't love him."

The manager gave Carla a curious look. "And did the contract say 'love' or 'marry'?"

Carla fumed. "Marry."

He sighed. "One of the classic rookie contract mistakes. You've lost, my dear. And like any gambling establishment, we must accept our losses with the same grace with which we accept our winnings. You've been ungracious. Now apologize."

Carla fidgeted, then, stone-faced, turned between Jerry and China. "I'm very sorry for what I said. I hope you have a lovely two-day marriage."

China smiled at her. "Thank you."

The manager nodded at Carla, and, stiff-backed, she walked to the exit. In a moment she was gone.

The manager gestured, catching the eye of a server at another table, and pointed toward China's glass. He gave China and Jerry a final smile. "I recommend the tiramisu." Then he turned, following Carla, and was gone.

China fanned herself. "Satan's *hot.*"

"Well, he would be."

"I meant... never mind."

After dessert, Jerry walked China to the parking lot half a block away. "Okay, fiancé. Give me some advice so I don't screw up my next relationship. Why did you never think of me 'that way'?"

"Well, it's not going to be the same for every woman. You've got a lot going for you. But everything about you is, well, gentle. You create all the sexual tension of a tame gray cat."

"Ouch."

"I want someone with two sides, a soft side turned toward me and a hard side turned toward the world. If I were lying in a hospital, would you be deadly and ruthless in getting me a kidney? Would you take a bullet for me and then beat the shooter to a pulp? Would you go to war for me?"

"Wow. I *have* a side like that. But it's not attractive."

"It will be when you show it off the right way."

They reached her blue subcompact and she unlocked the driver's door. "Denise in Accounting really likes you, you know."

"She snorts when she laughs."

"So she's not perfect. Neither am I."

"Yes, you are."

"Did I ever mention that I religiously watch *The Bachelor* and *The Bachelorette*? I'm like a crack whore for those shows."

"Okay, maybe not... *completely* perfect."

She smiled at him. "Later, we can talk about how you should show yourself off to other women. We'll have our whole honeymoon for that."

"Great."

She got in, and he leaned in close. "Kiss?"

"No kiss. No getting your hopes up."

"That's okay. It's enough just to be not going to Hell. Thanks for that."

"See you at work tomorrow." She closed the door, started her car, and pulled out.

In his own car, Jerry sat for a moment, pondering his escape. Then he turned the key in the ignition.

The car didn't start. Instead, the dome light came on. Jerry became aware that someone sat in the passenger seat.

He looked over. It was Carla, still in the little black dress, staring soberly at him.

He gave her a blank look. "What?"

"What do you mean, what? She just told you how to make her fall in love with you. You balance Bad Boy Jerry with Good Boy Jerry. Be a hard-edged rogue to the world and a sweetheart to her. That's the magic formula."

"Get out."

"I propose another deal. Twenty-seven more shots at her. Go back in time to when she first joined the firm. Instead of a day, you get a week each time."

He thought about it. Then he leaned in close to her. He glanced down her neckline, to where the pale perfection of her throat disappeared under the black silk V of her dress. "So what are *you* doing tonight?"

"Oh, piss off." She disappeared, leaving behind only a small plume of black smoke. It curled up against the dome light and smelled of egg yolks and fart.

Jerry chuckled to himself and started his car.

Maybe, some time after his heart had recovered from the protracted drubbing it had received on this nearly month-long day, he would indeed ask Denise out on a date.

But not to an amusement park.

About the Author

Best known for his work in the *Star Wars* Expanded Universe, **Aaron Allston** is also a long-time game writer who was inducted into the AAGAD Hall of Fame at Origins 2006. He lives in Central Texas. Please visit his web site at www.aaronallston.com and his weblog at community.aaronallston.com.

Last Man On Earth

Maxwell Alexander Drake

Our Fathers were raised on a simple principle:
grow up, get a job, get married and have children.
And yet, even though we gathered with the family,
to be with them and give them support when the end came,
they died alone—as everyone does.

Now, we have grown up and taken jobs.
We have gotten married, and have children of our own.
Unfortunately, when we die, as we all will,
we will die just as alone as our fathers did before us.

Our children are in the process of growing up.
They will, no doubt, get jobs, find spouses,
and have children of their own someday.
Still, with all the innocent joys of life they now possess,
they will also die, and die alone, as did we and our fathers before.

If the definition of insanity
is doing the same thing time and again,
expecting a different result,
I submit to you that the human race
has been insane for generations.

MAD

My name is Ryan Tillman, and I am the last man on Earth.

I am not sure why I feel compelled to write this, but I do. I am also unsure why I have chosen to survive when no one else has. However, I will let that issue stand for now. Suffice it to say that I have always had an affinity for history. This is funny when you consider the old adage that says, "History is written by the victorious." I do not consider myself to be the victor of anything, but I *can* say that there is no one left on this miserable planet to argue against my points. So, I have chosen to write the history of the final days of the human race; at least, a history from my perspective as I saw the events transpire. Again, there is no one around to disagree.

Who will read this, you ask? Well, that is irony at its finest. I sit here and write, yet for whom, I don't know. I could be cheeky and say that I wrote this for you— whoever or whatever you are. But, I digress.

Since the dawn of time, one of the biggest questions that boggled the imagination of man was how will it all end? How will the great and mighty human empire, which stretches to every corner of our tiny blue world, and even extended its reach into the clouds and beyond to the very heavens, how will it all come crashing down?

Had you asked this question when the great and mighty human empire still existed—and depending on whom you posed the question to—you would have received many different answers. It seems that everyone had a theory as to what would spell doom for mankind.

If you went the religious route, the yielded answer would depend on the faith of the person with whom you spoke.

Buddhism and Hinduism taught that there would be no end to the world, just a new beginning. Humanity would roll on, starting over every so often as the big wheel of creation turned and turned.

If creation was supposed to be a wheel, I think it went flat. Because I have to say from where I'm sitting creation has most defiantly ended.

Jewish and Islamic faiths believed that someday someone would come around and lead them to a golden era, and that only the truly faithful would survive.

I do not think I fit the truly faithful bill. So, either someone made a grievous error in the calculation of how to be right and wrong, or the whole world was full of sinners—not an entirely outrageous idea in and of itself.

As for the Christians, they believed in a more definitive, divine end. They predicted an ending where God himself would clean up everything. That He would fix all that we puny humans had so carelessly ruined. This was, of course, after He sent the evilest of evils to run things into the ground for seven years. Supposedly after all that suffering, by the grace of His loving benevolence, the mighty God would grant man one thousand years of peace.

Sounds like a fair cop. Although if God were so benevolent it always puzzled me why we needed the seven years of pain and agony? But, hey, a few years of suffering for one thousand of prosperity, not a bad trade all things considered.

I will agree that the past few hundred years have indeed been, shall we say, eventful. However, as for a rapture of the church, again I would have to say someone made an error in who was, and who was not, saved. Because if Jesus Christ did come back to collect his flock, he must not have liked what he found and decided it was easier simply to leave the whole lot of us behind.

Going the scientific route is just as gruesome, if not so mystical.

Some scientists believed that a plague or virus would eventually sweep the planet clean of life. It seemed like no matter how advanced medicine became, some persistent microscopic bug rode just a bird-hop, a pig-skip, or a monkey-jump ahead of the curve. Combine that with the ease in which the modern man traveled the globe, and, well, it didn't take a microbiologist to read the writing on that wall.

People did die from plagues, sometimes a few hundred in one country; others by the millions during the pandemics that raged across the planet. Somehow I think an enemy you can't see, feel, or touch is more frightening than one pointing a machinegun at you.

Speaking of machineguns, many surmised that we would one day reach a point where the hatred of our troublesome neighbors would become so great that we would be willing to destroy everything, including ourselves—so long as it meant those bastards over there died with us.

I read somewhere that since the dawn of recorded time there has been a war on this planet in one place or another every day of every year. Ha! Man loves to hate, and boy do we love to hate those guys over there! Ironically, as it turned out in the end, this line of thinking was perhaps the closest hypothesis in the extinction betting pool. But more on that later.

In the early years of the twenty-first century, many scholars had made the claim that economics would be the great equalizer, and that wars would become obsolete.

I think they failed to grasp the nature and depth of our hate.

Oh, don't get me wrong, as the centuries rolled on and what was known as third world countries crawled out of their dark ages and into the modern, informational age, things did equal out across our planet. The former third world people earned an equal amount of money, which allowed them to purchase an equal number of bombs and weaponry with which they could destroy Mother Earth and their fellow humans, well... equally.

And even though people killed people all the way to the bitter end—fighting for their beliefs, against other's beliefs, for more land, more resources, over a political misunderstanding, an old sock—there came a time when it became just too much trouble to go to war. It's hard to travel somewhere and kill someone when you spend the majority of your time simply looking for food.

Personally, I was always a fan of the doomsdayists. The ones that said Mother Nature would take a vindictive hand and punish the human race for being such bad caretakers. That she would smite us with a meteor, or crush us under mounds of ash and lava. Or, maybe, she would slam us with torrential rains and thunderous hurricanes. Others loved to rant about the idea that we would do ourselves in with global warming, over harvesting, or just plain old bad management.

As a species, we humans resemble a virus more than our fellow mammals. We move into an area, stripping it bare, and then move on to another without care or concern for what we leave behind. We were a plague against nature— one could say a pandemic—that is for certain.

Unfortunately for good ole Mother Earth, we humans were industrious creatures with no qualms about finding new ways to desecrate our lands and oceans. Once we had depleted all of the oil and coal the planet had to offer, and evenly distributed their poisons around the globe, we simply found alternate ways to vandalize our world. Sure, nuclear was clean, just not its byproducts and waste. Wind and solar may have once been called 'alternative' energy sources, but the spent batteries, used power cells, dead circuits, fried electronics, and the billions of tons of plastics that were used to hold it all together shouldn't be referred to as an 'alternative' form of garbage. No, had Mother Nature taken a closer look at our résumé, I doubt she would have given us the caretaker job in the first place. Maybe she would have had better luck with the bees.

Overpopulation, now there is a concept I never cared for much when discussing the end of a species. How can anything become extinct by breeding? Isn't that an oxymoron—like military intelligence or jumbo shrimp? Sure enough, overpopulation adds to the wars, plagues, and lack of resources, which ironically leads to even more wars, plagues, and lack of resources.

But aren't those factors then what controls the population?

I mean, if a population is killed off by something like war, you really can't say it went extinct by overpopulation now can you?

In the end, as I sit and write this, I'm not sure if any of it really matters all that much.

So what did happen? Truth be told, it all did.

Several plagues jumped from the animal kingdom and became contagious to humans. A couple even reached pandemic proportions, killing a few million here and there. These deaths didn't really make a dent in the billions of people who were around at the time, but still worthy to be billed as "top vidnews."

The casualties from those, however, paled compared to the religious fanatics who, thanks to economic equality acquired weapons that could level entire metropolitan areas.

Another old adage I love is the one that states, "Anyone can kill the president at any time, so long as they are willing to die in the attempt."

It amazed me that no matter how advanced the human race became, you could always find some schmuck willing to strap a bomb to his chest.

Viva La Revolución!

Even these only took a scant few hundred million innocent lives overall. Again, not all that bad for humankind and its billions.

As I already said, wars rolled right on until the very end —some of them in retaliation for the terrorist acts, others for the usual "we want what you have" greed of man.

Still, the human race marched down the parkways of time.

Over the centuries a plethora of floods, hurricanes, earthquakes, tsunamis, volcanoes, and even one testy rock from space would each claim some here and there. Other than making the vidnews—and having one religious group or another proclaiming that it was a sign of the end of days —it wasn't anything to write home about. Unless, of course, your home was in the path of one of the above.

Food—or lack thereof—was the catalyst of many a war. Larger countries invaded smaller ones; people on both sides would die in the fighting. With fewer mouths to feed, and more resources to produce, everyone was once again happy. Well, except those killed off. But hey, they didn't have a voice anymore anyway.

All of that, however, was just life as usual for the human race. Had nothing changed, I am sure that humanity would still be kicking—and scratching and biting, and possibly even throwing the occasional rock or three. Unfortunately, something did change.

Perhaps I should start from the beginning, or at least, far enough into the past so that you will understand the end that I now face; before everything went to hell in a handbasket.

I, Ryan Tillman, discovered the key to immortality.

Oh, sure, I know what you are thinking. But, it is the truth. And here I am, as testament to that.

What did I do with my wonderful discovery? I could have told people about it, shared my secret with my fellow man. It might have even put an end to all of man's suffering and loss—of starvation, sickness, and pain— everything that leads to death.

But why? What would have been in it for me? To get rich? Have fame and fortune? Status? I agree those are reasons that should have been more than adequate.

Except with my immortality I found that I already had everything there was. All knowledge lay at my feet. Every secret. Every scrap of human intelligence. The total wealth and power and might of the world! All of it here within my grasp. For *me* to use. At *my* whim and for *my* amusement.

At first, I must admit, I was overwhelmed. It took a century with me simply watching to learn what was actually available. But I learned. Hah, I had enough time.

Once I understood that I had been given, along with my longevity, the power and totality in which I could control every aspect of human society—well, I confess, a kind of God complex overtook me. You could say I was a bit drunk with my newfound power.

Looking back now I am sure that at first I meant no harm. It was fun to let slip some carefully guarded government secret, reveal it to the opposition. A secret that people would be upset enough to do something about.

After a few centuries of watching from the sidelines, a man can grow bored. It was entertaining to see smaller nations band together to fight the oppressiveness of the last, great superpower. Like some great Hollywood saga, played out for my pleasure.

It was long overdue, anyway. What was, at the time, the good ole U S of A had outlived its usefulness.

I am not ashamed of the outcome. Yes, millions died. Nevertheless, it paved the way for a much larger, more globally minded government. I saw it as a good thing. I always thought that once the dust settled—and had anyone known of my involvement—I should have received a medal from my fellow man. Perhaps even the Nobel Peace Prize. Well, at least a commendation.

The new world government that emerged was more organized. And, even though I found it harder to manipulate one country, as opposed to many disjointed ones, each with their own agenda. I found that it simply added to the excitement of it all. Oh, at first it was hard to build anything worth watching, certainly nothing that compared to the entertainment of the 'Last Great War' as the history books touted the fall of America. But in time— and with a few pulls on a string here, or a nudge to a particularly corrupt person there—I was able to rebuild some tension and create some separatist factions.

As I said before, humans love to hate.

Yet, I was never able to rekindle that oomph that was so entertaining to watch.

It's like chocolate. Sure, every child loves chocolate. Even adults love it, at least until they eat some Godiva! After that, regular chocolate is just…well…regular. And your taste buds are never again satisfied in quite the same way.

I tried to play nice, I really did! But what are a few sex scandals, political bribes exposed, global blackouts, and the occasional skirmish, when compared to an all-out war? I mean, who wants to live forever if the entertainment gets worse and worse year after year. It would be just like that old show *Saturday Night Live*. The first twenty years were fantastic, but it simply went downhill after that. As if time had sucked the funny out of the world. What? Were the late 1990s and early 2000s really so depressing that no one could write a funny joke?

I, for one, was glad when they finally ripped that show off the air!

Again, I am chasing rabbits, and I don't have much time left. So, to get back to the task at hand, I really did try and play nice. Besides, humans were like cockroaches. No matter what you threw at them, no matter how many died, pockets of them always survived.

So one day in a fit of boredom I thought would kill me, the idea struck. I figured, just as you would do to a grape vine to help it grow better fruit, I could prune things back a bit. Give it some time to grow out again. Let mankind regain some of its former glory. That is all I intended. Besides, I would be there to watch over things. I mean, think about it, how much fun would it be to remake mankind in *my* image? Huh?

So, I unleashed it all. I rained fire down from the heavens with a simple thought. They were the ones who built all the weapons, not me! My only error was underestimating the destructive genius of my fellow man. And that can't be seen as a crime!

I still remember the ecstasy of it—the world glowed and I looked on laughing. It filled me, like an explosive orgasm —No! It was better than sex! Watching it rain down, watching it all burn. It was the most beautiful sight.

Well, perhaps sight is a poor choice of words for me, but again, I digress.

The sheer rapture and elation and power—the knowledge of the brighter future I would build! One that I would create and mold and guide! That is why I did it. How was I supposed to know? How!

Fact of the matter is I don't think it was worth it. I can finally admit that now, even if it is simply to myself. I have subsisted down here so long I have simply lost track. I feel… old, as odd as that is for someone who is immortal to say.

I have searched everywhere and have found not one trace of life. It's just me. I am the last man on earth, and I murdered them all.

> I AM THE LAST MAN ON EARTH, AND I MURDERED THEM ALL. I AM THE LAST MAN ON EARTH, AND I MURDERED THEM ALL. I AM THE LAST MAN ON EARTH, AND I MURDERED THEM ALL. I AM THE LAST MAN ON EARTH, AND I MURDERED THEM ALL. I AM THE LAST MAN ON EARTH, AND I MURDERED THEM ALL. I AM THE LAST MAN ON EARTH, AND I MURDERED THEM ALL. AND I MURDERED THEM ALL. AND I MURDERED THEM ALL. I MURDERED THEM ALL. I MURDERED THEM ALL. I MURDERED THEM ALL. I MURDERED THEM ALL. I MURDERED THEM ALL. I MURDERED THEM ALL. I MURDERED THEM ALL. I MURDERED THEM ALL. I MUR

The endlessly repeated sentence stopped by a glitch rather than design. The words filled the small, green screen —the repetitious rant of some deranged typist. The faint hum of cooling fans hung in the dingy air. A lamp set into one wall, so thickly covered by dust it emitted only the faintest of light, cast deep shadows across the room. The ceiling hung limp from its mountings, and sagged in spots where tiles had come loose. These falling to join the debris that covered the floor.

Eons had passed since anything living had left a footprint in this small room.

The wall opposite the dim light held a bank of computers. A thick black cable, plugged into a central access panel, made its way across the floor and up the side of a tub that sat beside a steel desk that the vidscreen rested upon.

A husk of a body floated in the tub. It may once have been human—possibly even male—but time had pulled from it as much as it could. A few wisps of stringy hair still clung to the scalp surrounding the spot on the forehead in which the black cable had been implanted. At the base of the cable, several smaller wires snaked away and pierced other areas of the skull. Dark cavities sat where eyes once rested, the skin surrounding the sockets pulled into their depths. Bone jutted out from where, at one time, a nose may have been. The mouth gaped open, stretched into a perpetual scream by the dried ligaments that stood out taut on the being's neck just below its paper-thin skin. One emaciated arm, flesh the color of dried leather, dangled over the side of the tub. The ring finger was missing; the digit rested on the floor below. The severed finger had a corroded golden substance edging the spot where it had detached from the hand, giving the only clue as to what may have severed it.

Save for the vidscreen, the desk sat bare except for a raised glass bubble. The bubble, filled with a thin, gray mist, rhythmically pulsed with a red light that played off the shadows of the empty eye sockets of the body in the tub. Suspended in the mist was a message—Warning, Power Failure Eminent.

A loud clack ricocheted off the walls sending a drizzle of fresh dust falling from the ceiling. The whine of a turbine buzzed; the noise of its motor winding down to dissipate into silence as it spun to a stop.

The monitor flashed once and flicked off the moment power was denied to its circuits. In the faint, green afterglow that still resonated from within its CRT, the body shuddered once in the tub, sending a small ripple streaming across the surface of the solution that held it. The ripple lapped against the outer rim, rebounded back toward where it had originated, but lost its momentum in the thick substance, and fell still. Countless centuries had passed since the body in the tub had been connected to the Global Network. Now darkness, and the utter silence of a tomb, enveloped the chamber as Ryan Tillman's body expired.

About the Author

Maxwell **Alexander Drake** is an award-winning SF/ fantasy author and graphic novelist. Among his works: *The Genesis of Oblivion Saga*. Drake teaches creative writing around the country as well as for the library district in Las Vegas, NV. Find out more about him at his website: www.maxwellalexanderdrake.com.

Slug

Janine K. Spendlove

I work at the Pentagon. I could tell you what I do there but then I'd have to kill you.

Heh. Just kidding.

Not about working at the Pentagon, no, that's true. I was kidding about the killing you part. Mostly…

Truth is, if I gave you a detailed rundown of what I do there, day in and day out, you'd probably die of boredom. Basically, I sit in a cubicle in front of a computer screen all day, with the occasional interruption from my office mates coming and going. They're always up to something or other, but not me. Nope, paperwork is the bane of my existence, and yet it's all I do. See? Told ya. Boring. Sadly, the most exciting part of my day is going to pub quiz a couple evenings a week. Oh, and slugging.

Yup, that's right, I'm a slug.

No, not the slimy thing that cruel kids like to pour salt on. A slug is a hitchhiking carpooler. Well, that's not exactly right either. Let me explain. No that would take too long. Let me sum up:

Slugging is a weird type of commuting found in the Washington, DC area. I say weird because when else are people who are driving into the city willing to stop and pick up total strangers? When they're facing Beltway traffic, that's when. You see, to use the HOV lanes you gotta have at least three people in your car. So, you pick up a couple passengers from a slug line, and bam! You just turned a two hour commute into a thirty minute commute. My fellow slugs and I line up in commuter lots—mine's Potomac Mills—waiting for needy drivers to pick us up. And the best part is, it's free!

I'm sure, of course, you've seen the glaring flaw in the system.

You are riding with complete strangers.

In case that didn't sink in, let me repeat. YOU ARE RIDING WITH COMPLETE STRANGERS!

There's a code of conduct (don't touch the music, windows, a/c, NO TALKING, etc.) but that still doesn't prevent all the CRAZIES. Every slugger has a few *interesting* slug line stories, but I don't think any of them compare to what happened to me a couple years back.

I was running behind, so I rushed from my cubicle right around 1645 (that's 4:45pm for those of you who don't run on military time), hustled down to the south parking lot, and got in the slug line for Potomac Mills. I was pretty stressed that I was going to be way late for pub quiz; I had a team depending on me.

Turned out, it was my lucky day! You see, the slug line was pretty long, but a guy from my office, Rich Stevenson, pulled up in his blue Prius and called me out of line. Normally this is a huge no-no; first-come first-served, and no poaching! But it's okay if you know each other. I was kinda surprised to see him since I thought he and Tex, a black cowboy from Oregon (he said he'd punch me if I ever called him "African-American" and I believe him), who also works in my department, were out on a mission or something. They must've wrapped things up early and decided to try to make it to pub quiz too. So I jumped in the back seat. Just as I was leaning forward to say "Hey guys!" a thin, gray arm ripped off the driver's door and yanked Rich right out of his seat. I always told Rich he ought to wear his seatbelt.

Anyways, I only had a second to process that before a bald man, wearing a black suit that was obviously way too short for him, and who looked longer and more stretched out than he ought to have, folded himself into the recently vacated driver's seat. Let me tell you, this guy smelled too – like the cage of your pet lizard that you haven't cleaned out for a couple weeks. He immediately stomped on the gas and swerved around the cars parked in front of us. One tire grazed the curb, and we were all thrown into the air before he sped out of the parking lot, tires squealing.

I lurched around in the back seat and found my face pressed against the left passenger window. In the front seat, Tex was yelling something I couldn't understand while he clung to the dashboard as if that was going to stop the car. The wind from outside whistled loudly through the missing driver's door, but I heard Tex say something that sounded like "Pull over now or this time I won't be so nice!" Guess he and our hijacker knew each other. Meanwhile, Mr. Gray kept right on driving like a maniac.

I decided if I wanted to live that I ought to get a seatbelt on, so I peeled myself off the window and climbed into the right side of the back seat, as far away from Mr. Gray as I could get. Though being that we were in a Prius, that wasn't very far. Tex's threats were beginning to escalate, and as I clicked my seatbelt home, I marveled at his lung capacity; it was making my ears ring!

Of course, that could have been from knocking my head on the window so hard, but trust me, his yelling wasn't helping. Mr. Gray, who clearly had not driven much in his life—if ever—swerved onto I-395S, and as my elbow slammed into the window switch, rolling it down, I breathed a sigh of relief...

We were going in the right direction!

I know it sounds silly how upset I was getting over possibly being late—or worse, missing pub quiz all together—but, you see, I'm pretty good at it, and it's one of those few things in my weekly routine that I really look forward to. I mean, I felt bad that Rich got his car jacked, but he had insurance, and I figured the least Mr. Gray could do was drop me and Tex off at my commuter lot, and we could totally make it to pub quiz in time. On the whole, I'd had worse slug rides up to this point, so I was feeling pretty positive.

That was when Tex finally stopped threatening our abductor and started shouting and gesticulating wildly with one hand while reaching for something in his pocket with the other. I realized why pretty quickly; our abductor had missed the HOV on-ramp!

DUDE! NOT COOL! Now it was going to be at least an hour before we traveled the twenty miles to Potomac Mills!

I was about to say something when Mr. Gray whipped his head to the side, opened his mouth, unfurled a long split tongue, and hissed in Tex's face.

Tex promptly passed out, and I kept my mouth shut. I don't do confrontation, I just process the paperwork.

Mr. Gray looked back at me for a moment, and as I took in his flat, noseless face and thin slit of a mouth, into which his long tongue was retracting, he blinked—sideways.

Yeah, it was as weird as it sounds, and while I'd suspected it, I'd now had it confirmed that he wasn't from around here. I'm pretty sure he was an illegal alien, and not the border-hopping kind. In hindsight, I guess it should have been pretty obvious to me from the get-go what he was—an escapee from the basement of the Pentagon who stole a black suit and made a run for it during rush hour. I probably would have devoted more time to wondering about it if Mr. Gray hadn't slammed on his brakes right then, throwing me into the back of the front seat.

Guess he hit the Beltway traffic backup. It's amazing really, four lanes of traffic—six if you include the HOV lanes—and we were backed completely up. Actually, the HOV lane was moving along just fine, but I wasn't about to tell him that.

We crept along like that for a few minutes; me crouched in the backseat, and the snaky alien guy in the front seat suffering from what one could only describe as a massive case of road rage. He was slamming his hands on the wheel and hissing loudly. I couldn't tell if he was swearing in his language or if it was just plain old hissing. Either way, I figured there was no way I was going to make it to pub quiz on time tonight, so I'd better text another co-worker of mine, Jesse, and have him tell the rest of the gang I was going to be late—if I even made it at all. Traffic was really bad. Probably a wreck or something. So anyways, text sent, and then things got interesting again.

Red and blue lights flared in the shoulder behind us, and when I looked, I saw that a few unmarked, black sedans had crept up, trying to box us in. It was about dang time! I think that's when Mr. Gray figured out we had a tail too, because he slammed on the gas, jerked the wheel to the left, and started zooming up the shoulder at a whopping forty-five miles an hour!

Okay, that may not sound like very much to you right now, but trust me, in this mess it was. We got lots of honks and rude gestures aimed in our direction—I mean, I totally know what the other drivers were thinking "WHAT MAKES YOU SO SPECIAL?"—but we quickly blew by, as did the men in black and police cars chasing us.

Men-in-black you say? Yeah, I mean, who else would be chasing us in their dark, unmarked cars? I was with an alien for goodness sakes!

I was a lot happier now, not gonna lie. There was actually a good chance I'd make it to pub quiz after all! But then, as he sped past the Potomac Mills exit, that hope shattered, and I got pretty pissed off.

I was about to yell at him "WHAT THE HECK, DUDE?" when I remembered what happened when Tex got too lippy. His head still hung limply, but based on the pulse I could see at his neck, he was still alive, so that was good. I guess Mr. Gray took the "no talking on the slug lines" rule pretty seriously. Now, I know you think I was being callous about Tex and his health, but hey, he knew the perils of the job when he signed on.

So, back to my story. I settled myself into my seat to inwardly seethe for however long it took the men-in-black, or the local police, to stop this guy. I mean seriously, of all the selfish… couldn't he have been more considerate and stolen a car that didn't have two slugs inside? I didn't have time for this crap! Unless he was specifically targeting Rich and Tex. I don't know, I just do the paperwork.

We went a few more miles like that, zooming up the shoulder, black cars behind us, Tex's head bobbing around gently, and me glowering at Mr. Gray from the back seat. That's when the helicopter showed up. I'm no pilot, and like I said, I just work in a cubicle, but even I recognized it as not your normal, civilian helicopter.

It was all black, sleek lines, and rocket launchers on the side. Definitely military grade. At least, that's what it looked like to me. I figured it was probably the men in black again, or maybe homeland security—nobody knows what those guys do either.

Mr. Gray realized we were in trouble too, and as I lifted my phone to send another text to Jesse, he swerved left onto the emergency connector to the HOV lane. I didn't bother to tell him that was illegal, because, first of all, I didn't think he'd care, and secondly, the tight turn slammed me into the side of the door, knocking my phone out of my hands and right out the window. Black car number one ran it right over.

Oh well, it was just a work phone anyway. Still, annoying. But I had bigger issues. You see, we were facing oncoming traffic now, and Mr. Gray was playing a very excellent, if not terrifying, game of chicken. At least we were headed back toward Potomac Mills.

Cars dodged and swerved out of our way, causing several pile-ups along the sides of the HOV lane, as our car zoomed down the center, and I prayed that I'd live through the next few minutes. All thoughts of pub quiz were forgotten. At least for the moment.

Tex decided that was a good time to wake up. After getting a quick look at the oncoming traffic, he again reached for whatever he had concealed under his black suit coat. He never reached it, since Mr. Gray took that opportunity to swerve left, slamming Tex's head against the passenger window and knocking him out again. As for me, I had a death grip on the door, and I was developing a permanent wedgie from clenching my cheeks so hard on the seat cushion beneath me.

Just when two massive SUVs were bearing down on us; and it looked like we'd be testing the airbag system on this car real soon, the helicopter landed on the HOV lane, and the SUVs screeched to a halt. So did Mr. Gray. And so did the men in black behind us.

Mr. Gray leapt from the car and took off running before we were even fully stopped, and a bunch of men in black ran after him. I finally felt my cheeks unclench. Jesse's face popped into my open window—figures he'd been on that helicopter. He tipped up his black sunglasses and asked if I was okay. I waved him to Tex and shakily got out. I saw another office mate, Aimee, climbing out of one of the black cars behind me, and after she waved me over to give me a ride out of there, I hollered at Jesse that I'd tell the team he'd be late for pub quiz tonight. He nodded and then went back to taking care of Tex. As for me, I loosened my black tie, took off my black coat (office dress code, even for paper pushers), and jumped into the office sedan with Aimee.

And yeah, I made it to pub quiz that night, and our team didn't do too badly. Oh, and to this day I still ride the slug lines into work—I mean really, after an episode like that, how could any ride possibly be worse?

About the Author

Janine K. Spendlove is a KC-130 pilot in the United States Marine Corps. In the Science Fiction and Fantasy World she is primarily known for her best-selling trilogy, War of the Seasons. She has several short stories published in various anthologies alongside such authors as Aaron Allston, Jean Rabe, Michael A. Stackpole, Bryan Young, and Timothy Zahn. She is also the co-founder of GeekGirlsRun, a community for geek girls (and guys) who just want to run, share, have fun, and encourage each other. A graduate of Brigham Young University, Janine loves pugs, enjoys knitting, making costumes, playing Beatles tunes on her guitar, and spending time with her family. She resides with her husband and daughter in Washington, DC. She is currently at work on her next novel. Find out more at JanineSpendlove.com.

Adventure of the Ghost Watch

Michael A. Stackpole

Jack Card put his book down and answered the door.

A smiling man in a red uniform held up an envelope. "I have a message here for Master John Card. Is that you?"

"Yes, sir." Jack opened the door and signed for the ivory color envelope. He took it, and then looked up. "I'm sorry, I don't have any money. I can ask my mom…"

The messenger held a hand up. "It's been taken care of, son. Enjoy your afternoon."

Jack smiled and closed the door. The envelope had no postmark and no address. His name had been written in a flowing, elegant hand. Each letter stood out clearly.

He carried it into the kitchen. "Mom, Aunt Flora sent me an invitation."

Jack's mom glanced up. She was elbow deep in making lasagna. "Have you opened it?"

"Nope." He smiled. "Aunt Flora wouldn't have sent it if she'd not already asked you if I could go. Is it another one of her escapades?"

His mother blew a lock of brown hair back out of her face. "You'll go, and you'll be respectful. She depends on you, you know."

The brown-eyed boy slid a thumb under the flap and gently tore the envelope open. The notecard within matched the envelope's color. The initials FW stood out at the top, embossed as they were in gold. He scanned the note, and then read it aloud to his mother.

Dear Master John,

I request the pleasure of your company this evening, for a midnight tour of the Shippington Mansion. Doctor E. Everett Everson of the Everson Institute of Ectoplasmic Investigation is going to show us a ghost.

Yours sincerely,
Miss Flora Williams

A ghost! Jack's heart skipped a beat. He knew there was no such thing as ghosts, but everyone in town knew the Shippington Mansion was haunted. Jack had shivered whenever biking past it after dark. Even on a dare, he wouldn't go near the place on Halloween.

The fear passed. The idea of seeing a ghost thrilled him. Jack loved reading about history and science and archeology, but being only twelve, he'd not gotten to do anything he could call field research. Well, maybe a few of the other outings with Aunt Flora would count, but this would be the first real expedition into the unknown.

"Is this for real, mom?"

Mina Card smiled indulgently. "Aunt Flora was determined to go. Doctor Everson is hoping she'll help fund more research. I tried to talk her out of it, but she just said I was too set in my ways to see the possibilities in the world. She suggested you would be suitable company."

Jack nodded. He loved Aunt Flora—really his Great Grand-aunt Flora. She drifted through life, being very lucky—though his father thought she was very shrewd and just pretended to be daffy. She'd made a lot of money down through the years investing with people she trusted —like that "awkward Gates boy" as she described Microsoft's founder.

"You want me to look out for her, right?"

His mother nodded. "You're a big boy now, Jack, and a pretty smart one."

"I'm not smart, mom, I just remember things."

"Well, remember this: your aunt is generous to a fault. People will take advantage of her. She'll listen to you. Don't let this Doctor Everson talk her into writing a check."

"Got it, Mom."

"Your father and I will be waiting up for you."

"Thanks, Mom." Jack slipped the note back into the envelope. "I better go get ready."

"Sounds like you'll be packing for an expedition to the Amazon."

"Not quite." He headed for his room. "But if I'm going to meet a ghost, I don't want to go unprepared."

As it turned out, Jack didn't have any ghost-hunting gear. He ransacked his desk. Nothing. He went through the shoe boxes tucked under his bed. He came up empty there, too. His best effort produced a compass, a pocket knife, and a wind-up flashlight.

He sat on his bed. The compass, pocket knife, and flashlight weren't bad adventuring equipment, but he wasn't sure they'd help him in catching ghost. All the TV shows had guys with fancy detectors and expensive cameras. They had the sort of equipment Doctor Everson would have.

Then it dawned on Jack. Even with all that fancy gear, none of them had ever caught a ghost.

Another thought came to him. He wasn't really going along to catch a ghost. He was going along to see if Doctor Everson was telling the truth. Given that Doctor Everson was a doctor, he had to be pretty smart. And because he did research, he had to know his stuff on ghosts. Or on tricking people into believing there were ghosts.

If he was lying, it wouldn't be easy to catch him. Jack filled his pockets with his tools as his mom called him for dinner. Still, if that's what it took to protect Aunt Flora, Jack would find a way to do it.

Even though the summer's heat kept the night warm, Aunt Flora wore a coat and dark slacks. She'd always said Jack got his skinniness from her side of the family, and teased him that someday his brown hair would be as white as hers. Slender though she was, the hand gripping his shoulder had strength, and her blue eyes still flashed with mischief.

Several other families gathered on the sidewalk in front of the Shippington Mansion. Jack recognized an Asian kid from the swimming pool at the YMCA. Harry Lee was his name. He was there with his parents. Harry had just moved to town, so Jack didn't know him more than to nod at him. Harry had earphones in and was looking at an iPod Touch, concentrating seriously on something.

The Shippington Mansion was one of the oldest buildings in town. It brooded, all dark, at the top of the hill. A wrought-iron fence surrounded it. Six gables rose from the roof and a porch ran three-quarters of the way around the building. Jack had seen old pictures, back when the house had been kept up. He felt sad seeing it having been neglected. Still the mansion had fared far better than the decrepit outbuildings in the overgrown back yard.

Doctor E. Everett Everson emerged from the dark building and strode boldly down to the gate. A plump man, he wore a dark wool suit with a bright red vest beneath and a monocle over his right eye. It popped out when he saw Aunt Flora. He greeted her happily and kissed her hand. She giggled.

"And this must be your nephew, John." The man ruffled Jack's hair, which he hated. "Welcome to the Mansion, son."

"Thank you."

Doctor Everson greeted the others just as profusely. At least Harry didn't get his hair messed up. The doctor waved everyone through the gate and stopped them on the porch.

"Before we go in, it's important to sort fact from fiction. Many of you have grown up here, others of you are new, yet you've all heard the stories. Let me tell you what we truly know about the tragedy that unfolded here, this very night, July 15th, in 1882." As Everson spoke he hooked his thumbs in his vest's pockets. "Hugh Shippington was a very wealthy man, with homes from New York to California. This building was his newest and best loved. Workmen had finished it a month before, and he stopped in it for the first time this very day in 1882. He so loved it that he immediately sent a telegram to his family in New York, telling them to come at once. He sent that telegram at noon.

"Ten that evening he got a telegram from New York. His house in the city had burned down and his family had all been killed. He tried to get a train back east immediately, but the next locomotive would not be coming through until the following morning. So he spent his first night in his new home in mourning and, at midnight, he died of a broken heart."

Aunt Flora clutched Jack's shoulder. "That is so sad."

"True, Miss Williams, but here is the odd part. His family, upon receipt of his telegram, had not even bothered to pack. They headed here immediately. They arrived the following afternoon to learn the bad news—double bad news, since they'd not known their home had burned. The family moved in and remained a year before the anniversary of Hugh's death." Everson looked straight at Jack. "Can you imagine what happened then?"

Jack didn't need to imagine. He knew the stories. "The ghost of Hugh Shippington chased them all out since he was waiting for his family to join him."

"Exactly."

The other guests gasped, save for Harry. He gave Jack a disgusted look.

Jack shrugged. "It's not like I believe."

"Good lad," shouted the doctor, believing Jack had been speaking to him. "In science we don't go by belief, we only accept *proof*. In my researches I've used the finest equipment and most sensitive devices to amass evidence. That evidence is overwhelming. Ghosts exist, ladies and gentlemen. Tonight you'll see a ghost with your own eyes."

Doctor Everson pulled an antique pocket watch from his vest pocket. He showed both sides, including the ornate scrollwork and monogram HS. "This was Hugh Shippington's own watch. It lay on his nightside table as he died. Hugh Shippington will appear to us when his own watch strikes midnight."

Again more gasps.

The doctor held a hand up. "We have, my associates and I, thoroughly gone through the house. All power is off—a safety precaution since electricity was installed in the 1920s and last maintained in the 1940s. I'd ask you all to turn off any cell phones and you, young man, that music thing. No recording devices, please. We don't need electromagnetic pulses interfering with ectoplasmic transference."

The adults all nodded, but Jack and Harry exchanged glances. Jack wasn't one hundred percent sure what "ectoplasmic transference" was. It sounded like hokum and nonsense.

As they filtered into the mansion, Harry fell in line behind him. "Techno-babble."

Jack smiled, keeping his voice low. "Worse than Star Trek."

Harry snorted. Then they separated as the group entered the living room. Two rows of folding chairs had been set up in a semicircle facing the fireplace. Jack sat next to Aunt Flora in the front row, all the way over on the left side, and Harry opposite him on the right. The others filled in toward the middle. Most folks tried to look unimpressed. Little shivers here and there revealed their true feelings.

Doctor Everson wound the Shippington watch, and then placed it in a bell jar on the center of the mantle. Candles burned in rows on either side of it, providing all of the room's illumination. The flickering flames made shadows dance. Combined with the musty scent, faded wallpaper and dirty tin ceiling, the wavering candlelight made things spookier than a Halloween haunted house.

Everson returned his monocle to his eye. "Ladies and gentlemen, we are all rational beings, but what you shall witness tonight will carry you beyond reason. To create a more perfect environment for Hugh Shippington, we will douse all of the candles just prior to midnight. This should keep him calm. I will attempt contact with him, but whatever you do, you must not speak, or leave your chairs. This is for your own safety."

Everson's emphasis on *safety* sent a shiver down Jack's spine. He blushed. He was pretty sure Doctor Everson was a better actor than he was a scientist.

The bulbous man went on, pacing before the fireplace. "You may hear things. You may feel things. Many people report feeling a chill. My apologies for not telling you to bring a sweater." He looked straight at Aunt Flora. "If you require my jacket, Miss Williams, I shall be happy to oblige you."

"You're very kind, Doctor Everson, but I shall be fine."

"Very well." He glanced at the watch, then took out a dark handkerchief and blotted sweat from his forehead. "Hugh shall be with us very shortly. Please, if you all could join hands. And you, the young gentlemen on the end, if you could reach back to take a hand in the second row. We'll have a nice little circle. I shall take up my position in the back of the room, to be ready for him."

Everson worked his way down the line of candles. With each one blown out, darkness seeped into the room. Jack held Aunt Flora's slender hand in his left, and extended his right back to a woman in the second row. Both women shivered and Jack almost yelped as something brushed by him in the darkness.

It was Doctor Everson, slipping past. The heavy man's steps made the floorboards creak. "Very soon now. When the watch chimes we should have our manifestation."

Jack sat there, the only sounds he could hear being his heart pounding and the squeaks of people shifting in their chairs. He looked for anything, but in the utter darkness he couldn't even see his aunt.

Then, before he saw anything or heard anything, he felt something. The air stirred. Not much, but just enough. And it became colder. A chill blanketed the room and Aunt Flora began to shiver for real.

Then the watch rang. It sounded with a tiny *ding* for each hour. Jack thought it was a pretty sound, but somehow it echoed far louder in the room than it should have. The sound grew and lingered. The echoes remained long after the watched stopped pealing.

In their wake came a scraping sound. Definitely shoe leather on wood. It became louder, as if a man was approaching from a great distance. And a voice began. A whisper, nothing more.

"Who is here in my house?"

Jack wasn't sure he'd heard it the first time. Even the second he didn't catch all the words, but the third, well. The third time the ghost spoke more clearly and loudly. "Who is in my house?"

Everson's voice boomed confidently from the back of the room. "Mr. Shippington, I am Doctor E. Everett Everson."

"Doctor Everson? Do I know you, sir?"

"No, sir, you do not, yet."

The ghost's voice came from the center of the room, right inside their midst. "Do you know how to cure a broken heart, Doctor Everson? Do you know my family lies dead in New York? Have you any idea the pain of separation, sir?"

Everson kept his voice calm. "I have some understanding of the matter, sir. I hope, through my work, to be able to assist you."

"Assist me?" The ghost laughed and fear trickled down Jack's spine. "My family is dead. I shall never rest until I rend the veil between life and death and look up on them again. This I shall do, mark my words. Nothing you can do will ease my pain! Be gone from my house."

Aunt Flora clutched Jack's hand with all her strength.

The ghost shrieked. "Be gone, all of you, and damn you to Hell!"

Hugh Shippington's curse rang in their ears, then silence fell. Jack strained to hear anything, but short of old-house creaks and pops, he got nothing until Everson returned to the front of the room. The man struck a wooden match.

The doctor's expression betrayed nervousness in the light of that match. "Ladies and gentlemen, never, in all my years, have I faced so strong a presence."

He turned and lit the candles again, then tossed the match into the fireplace to die. "As you can see, as you doubtless felt, Hugh Shippington answered the call of midnight on his watch. The Shippington Mansion is a deep well of ectoplasmic activity. I dare say—mere speculation, of course—that this location may mark a thinning of the barrier between life and death. It is the perfect place for my researches to continue. However, in the Mansion's current state…"

The woman behind Aunt Flora raised a hand. "How much money do you need to continue, Doctor Everson?"

The large man blinked. "You anticipate me. I had more words to say, but if you wish to cut to the point."

"Your work is very important, Doctor. I see no reason any of us would wish to waste your valuable time." The woman looked around. Others, including Aunt Flora, nodded. "I can write you a check for twenty thousand right now, Doctor. Will that help?"

"Oh my, yes, very generous. That would keep us going for several months." Everson wiped his monocle on his jacket's lapel. "If any of the rest of you were to see it within your powers to contribute."

Aunt Flora smiled. "How much to endow the project in its entirety?"

"Miss Williams, it would be a million dollars, but I fear I could not impose on your generosity so mightily."

Jack's aunt laughed, her hand rising to her throat. "Doctor Everson, it is merely money. I should be glad to write the check this instant, with one tiny provision."

Everson nodded. "Yes?"

"Provided my nephew, John, thinks I should write it."

Everson smiled. "Well, John. You look to be a smart lad. What say you? Shall we let your aunt fund the work that will bring peace to tormented souls like Hugh Shippington?"

Everyone turned to look at Jack.

He swallowed hard. "I guess that sort of work would be very important. It would probably be worth every penny spent on it."

"Quite so, lad, thank you."

Jack held a hand up. "The problem is, you're lying about the ghost."

Everson's eyes grew large. "How dare you?"

Aunt Flora turned to Jack. "That's a serious charge, John."

"I know." Jack drew confidence from the pride on his Aunt's face. "You said the ghost would come at midnight on the day he died. You set his watch to chime at midnight."

Everson turned and waved a hand at the watch. "You all saw. It's fifteen past, now."

"Yes, fifteen past midnight, Daylight Savings Time." Jack shrugged. "The United States didn't start observing Daylight Savings Time until 1918. If Hugh Shippington was going to show up, he would have done it at eleven in the evening, because that was his midnight!"

The woman who had offered the first pledge sputtered. "But the ghost came to the watch. We felt the chill, we heard him speak. You're too young to understand."

"You're changing things. That's not what Doctor Everson told us." Jack gasped. She wouldn't let herself see the lie. Others nodded in agreement with her.

Then Harry stood up, brandishing his iPod. "He lied about no electricity, too. He has a wifi network set up in the house."

"But the chill..." Aunt Flora looked at Harry. "Why did we feel cold?"

"I don't know for sure, but I bet he has an air conditioner in one of the shacks out back. He ran conduit in and it came down through the holes in the tin ceiling. He could control that, and the sounds, from an iPhone or iPod."

Jack nodded. "Which is why he stood in the back, so we couldn't see the light. And he covered it with his handkerchief to hide it."

Everson puffed himself up. "This is preposterous. I have never been so insulted. To have two brats interrupt serious work..."

Harry's mother got up and a pair of handcuff appeared from her purse. "One of these brats happens to be my son, Doctor Everson, and I happen to be a detective with the fraud squad. I hope you have good answers for all the questions we're going to be asking you.

Harry's mother called for back-up. Forensic experts arrived with uniformed policemen. They swept the mansion and found not only the wifi network Harry had discovered, but wireless speakers for making the noise, and a heavy-duty air conditioner with generator out in the old smokehouse.

Pretty much everyone else cleared out, save for the woman who had been the first to pledge. Harry's mom brought her in for questioning, too. It turned out that she was in cahoots with Everson, encouraging others to invest.

Aunt Flora allowed Jack to stick around and watch the police work for awhile, then thanked Harry. "You saved me a great deal of money, the both of you. You make quite a team."

Jack smiled and offered Harry his hand. "I guess I'll see you at the Y. We can eat lunch together, if you want."

"That's cool. Thank you." Harry watched as the squad car carrying Everson headed off. "He'll be convicted, right? He's not going to get off."

"Him, being found innocent?" Jack shook his head. "Not a ghost of a chance."

About the Author

Michael A. Stackpole is an award-winning author, editor, screenwriter, graphic novelist, game designer, computer game designer and podcaster. He has an asteroid named after him. You can learn more about him and his work at stormwolf.com.

Adventure of the Ghost Watch is his first story about Jack Card, Boy Skeptic.

The Old Gods

C.S. Marks

He tried to warn her.

It had been a bad year—a drought year—and the pickings were lean. Though they had known it was forbidden, the Clan had moved into the Gods' sanctuary out of requirement. At first it was like heaven, with abundant food and warmth and soft beds for the taking. Their bellies were filled and the Gods left them alone—it made them careless after awhile. Whisperings started that the Gods were content—that they were even kind. Perhaps they would not demand a sacrifice, as the Elders had said. The Elders were long gone...dead the past winter. It had been a bad one. Perhaps this winter the Gods would keep them safe.

The words of the Elders would not leave him: the Gods may appear to be kind, but they will exact their tributes. One day, the first of you will not return...then others will fall until your numbers diminish to their satisfaction. They guard their abundance with a jealous hand!

He heard more whisperings. (Perhaps our prayers have been answered. Perhaps if we praise the Gods they will favor us and we will be safe here. If we only worship them, they will love us.) Only his voice (and hers) stood in dissent. What of the Old Gods? Would they not be angry?

His people had feared them since the Beginning. They did not grant abundance—only swift death. They did not come often, but when they were angry they struck without warning, in daylight or in darkness. They came on enormous, stinking black wings, or thrust from the shadows in a mass of armor and muscle and teeth. No one escaped them.

The first who failed to return set off more whisperings. (Brodda has always been the adventurous type. Perhaps he has gone off to start a clan of his own—after all, he has been quarreling with the Chief. He had no family, and he has always wanted to be Chief.) They continued to grow fat at the Gods' expense. Could they not see the danger? When another of their best hunters disappeared, they wondered. This one had a family—a big one, with many sons and daughters.

We must try harder! they said. (The Gods have taken their tribute, and now we must praise them or they will be angry. It is our fault that our hunters have been lost.) Some of them turned on him then, for he had spoken of the Old Gods, and his devotion to them was well known.

Out of fear and anger, the Clan had driven him into the farthest corner of the Sanctuary, threatening him with death should he return. Of course, she had come with him, shivering beside him in the dark. No member with any sense would wish to be isolated—easy pickings for the Old Gods. There was little food here, and hunger gnawed at them both.

She was the first to find it—the offering. Shiny and black, smooth as still water on a moonless night, it was like nothing they had ever seen before. It was beautiful, yet terrible in its strangeness. The most wondrous, irresistible smell wafted forth from it, turning stomachs into raging demons that would not be denied. She smelled it, too. She had always been the braver and more foolhardy one. Did she not detect the other smell? He did. There was a darker odor beneath the beautiful one.

He tried to warn her, but she didn't hear him. She stretched forward, trying to reach the source of the heavenly smell—rich food that would keep her from hunger for a long time—straining on her feet, reaching...reaching...

The flurry of motion and noise that was her death startled him so badly that he did not see exactly what happened. The black thing had clamped down on her with terrible jaws as she tried, too late, to avoid it. Her body, writhing against the polished blackness, fell off the edge of a nearby ledge to the floor of the Sanctuary. He peered over into the dark—just enough light to see her final, feeble twitching— and he knew she was gone. A single drop of her blood, rapidly congealing, was the only evidence that she had ever been alive. He turned, stunned by what he had seen, trying to breathe and slow the hammering of his heart.

He crouched in a corner, grieving for her. How had she not smelled the reek of old death upon it? What would he do without her? She was the one who calmed his fears. She was the one who had promised to bear his children. At least her death had been quick. He had felt her light go out...she never knew what had happened to her. Against all his nature, he wanted to die with her.

Something made him turn and peer into the blackness. (I can help you. I can take your grief away...)

Two pinpoints of light. That was all he could see of it at first. He heard a soft rustling sound...barely. The points drew nearer. He knew then that this was one of the Old Gods.

He had worshipped it, and it had come to take away his pain. He had not known they could be kind...

(Do not flee...do not struggle. Here there is warmth and release. I will take your body into Mine.)

He did not flee—he could not make his feet move. He was mesmerized. (Take me, then.) The black orbs, with their pinpoints of reflected light, drew back in preparation.

He saw a flash of movement, a gaping pink maw, and felt the pain as the fangs of the Old God struck him. He was nearly knocked senseless, but not quite.

Not quite.

Black scales enveloped him, breaking bones and taking his breath from his body, mangling him into a grotesque form with no power even to scream. He had certainly been wrong about one thing: his death would not be quick. His terrified heart burst as the pressure in his veins reached the critical point and his eyes glazed over. Still, he was aware. The creature relaxed its grip on him as his body twitched with agonal breaths and darkness overcame his thoughts at last...all but one.

Now it will feed.

(Well, that's three of them gone now. These new traps are so much more effective than the old ones! I wish they wouldn't fall all the way to the floor, though...makes me wonder if they suffer a little.) She bent down to pick up the black plastic trap, noting with satisfaction the stiffening corpse of the white-footed mouse—a female. (I doubt this one suffered. Wham! Right in the neck.)

She closed the pantry door and, with a gentle squeeze of the 'Tom Cat' trap, released its victim, tossing it into the yard.

"Here Kitty, Kitty!"

She turned to stand by the laundry tub, giving her hands a quick wash, when something made her glance down at the floor beside her left foot.

A medium-sized blacksnake had shot out from under the pantry door, its black eyes constricting to golden in the full daylight. It froze—it had not expected to see anyone there, let alone this giantess. It had thought to take a drink from the open drain of the laundry tub, but now thought better of it, recoiling back into hiding before she could react.

She stood for a moment, fighting the urge to let out a yell. She was somewhat disgusted with herself—she knew the creature was harmless—but it had come within inches of her left foot. (Calm down. It's only a blacksnake. You're not the only one trapping mice today!) She recalled the shed skins she had been noticing around the front porch lately. She knew a snake of that size could easily gain access anywhere the mice could. This made complete sense. Yet even after her heart had slowed to its normal rhythm, the dread would remain. It would be awhile before she opened the pantry door again.

Despite their understanding, even the New Gods feared the Old.

About the Author

C.S. **Marks** is often described as a "Renaissance Woman." She holds a Ph.D. in biology and is a full professor at Saint Mary-of-the-Woods College in Indiana, where she teaches biology and equine science. She's also an artist and has rendered the covers of her novels. When she's not writing or teaching, she enjoys archery, singing Celtic music, crafting longbows with primitive tools, and riding. An accomplished horsewoman, she is among the few Americans to have completed the prestigious "Tom Quilty" Australian national championship hundred-mile ride. She shares her forest home with her husband, Jeff, ten dogs (predominantly Welsh Corgis), and five horses. Visit her website at www.elfhunter.net.

For Every Time, A Season

Donald J. Bingle

The first sign was the tall grass receding into the soil.

A few weeks later, the grass was entirely gone and a rich layer of loose loam lay upon the earth. But then the water welled up from the forest floor and froze, gray and dirty, covering the birthing ground all Winter.

As the season progressed, the snow grew incrementally cleaner and fluffier, until one day—unencumbered by dirt —it floated heavenward to form gray clouds. The dark clouds, in turn, warmed in the sky above their charcoal shadows and became puffy and white and fled to the western skies, leaving only blue heavens and bright light streaming from the earth to the sun above.

As the snows departed and the season of Float arrived, he saw a telltale greasy residue had burgeoned forth from the ground beneath the protective cap of slush and snow, making clear that the process of creation was underway. As always, the myriad creatures that combined and conspired to cause creation waddled and slithered and whispered in, fat and bloated, regurgitating up their individual contributions to the collective cause, each adding just a tiny bit. And the greasy spot of earth grew damper and darker and larger, and the worms and the blowflies and the maggots intertwined in the muck of life to give it form and substance and structure, building the basic components bit by bit.

They called it the miracle of life, but he knew better. He was no mystic, no fanatic, no believer in unproven religions. He was a man of intelligence and science and understanding and logic. And being all of those things, he knew the truth. He understood the process. Chemical, of course. The creatures each picking up from the earth nuggets of the nutrients and chemicals and components best suited to their task, then their bodily systems combined those nutrients into higher and higher molecular forms: proteins and sugars and amino acids—even crystallizing bits of salt and calcium structure.

Scientists did not yet understand completely how the various creatures knew how and when and where to combine their contributions toward creation—a gap of understanding that gave the religious and the irrational grounds for their outlandish convictions—but cooperate they did. The harder components comprising the infrastructure were the first completed for the most part. Then layer after layer of softer tissue was added until the form began to take shape, began to change from a festering pile of ooze and squishy bits into a cohesive mass of muscle and organ, eventually covered by skin and infused with blood.

The progress was slow, but sure. He saw the body—it was well enough along now to call it that—each day as he walked past, toe and heel. At first he barely glimpsed it with his peripheral vision as he looked straight back upon his path. As he passed, though, he turned to gaze upon it with attention, until far enough away that he could straighten his view and look upon it from a distance, in its setting.

As time passed, he became more and more obsessed with this particular construct—a female of about his age. And over time, he became emotionally attached to the composing body, visiting the birthing ground each day, watching the progress, watching the hideous spot of grease turn to bone and flesh, then into a fully-formed woman, naked and pale. His feelings for her formed and firmed, even as she did, growing from interest to fondness to love. He obsessed about her, became possessive of her, even before she was born.

No one else came this way. No one else took this path through the dark woods, which each Float season captured million upon million of the simple leaves the ground gave forth each Winter beneath the snow. As Float progressed to Summer, the trees would string up the ensnared leaves and infuse them with moisture and color, plumping them as they moved from scraggly brown to vibrant red, then orange, then yellow and green. Then, when the cooling of Wet arrived and water abandoned its salts and fled from the seas to the rivers and streams and creeks to fly up from the land into the sky, the trees would swallow up the leaves, a last nourishment before the bleak, harsh Winter.

But now, in Summer, the forest was thick and tangled and nigh impassable to the casual wanderer. Only he knew the easy way through the concealing foliage. No one else knew, he was certain, that she was birthing. She was for him alone.

And finally one bright day as the sun sauntered toward the distant hills in the east, he saw that she was almost complete. The blood of the earth flowed forth into a long gash across her neck and into a dozen other smaller, deeper gashes across her midsection in a rush of creation. Her color warmed from white to pink as the heat of birth gathered in her bosom. He knelt over her and felt her chest and was fortunate enough to feel the first beat of her heart and the gentle sway of the first breath of life flowing past his cheek as it entered her pinking lips.

He hugged her as she came to life, cradling her in his arms, trembling in excitement and exhilaration. She was meant to be his; he knew it. Only the morning before, he had found in the woods the glinting silver sealing tool that would be perfect to close up the gashes in her neck and abdomen, once the earth's lifeblood had finished infusing her with life. It was a near thing, though, and he had to thrust and thrust from her in a heated frenzy of life-giving passion to seal them all up in quick succession and ecstatic sensation—the flush of activity giving him a rush of excitement.

She struggled with him as he completed his task. That often happened with the newly birthed—their faculties were scrambled in the first few moments. But he grasped her tightly; he had to maintain his grip on her all the way back to his house, clamping his hand hard upon her mouth during the walk through the now deeply dark woods.

He took her straight-away to the basement, beneath his remote homestead, binding her with restraints to prevent her from fleeing recklessly into the cruel world, away from his love and protection. No one must know of her birth, of her life, until she was ready ... until he was ready. He savored what was to come. The days and nights of bringing her fully to life and health, the looking back at their moments together as the future spread out behind them, always out-of-sight, always unknown and unseen until it happened. At first she might fear him, might struggle against him, might seek out others to undo her complicated thoughts and gruesome fears and bring her to the simple understanding of life. But the day would come when she would no longer cringe during his touch.

One day she would come to trust and love him. And when that happened, he would release her to the big, wide world. If you love someone, they said, you must set them free. And he would, because he loved as no other. Oh, he would watch her from afar, constantly, almost compulsively at first, but over time the compulsion would fade ... it always did. As he cared less, he would watch her less and less. He would take his journals of their life together, listings of her habits and likes, and subject them to the nib on his eraser, sucking the ink from the willing paper, until they vanished from the record. Eventually, he would begin to forget her, recognizing her only sporadically, until that fateful day when he would see her and feel her memory flee in a spark of forgetting from his mind.

And, when that happened, he would go once again deep into the woods, and find another set of journals buried near the swamp, by the big, shrinking willow. The journals would tell him the next place to look for a greasy spot and another bit of ecstasy in his life. That's what he did each time he forgot his last birthed love, and he longed to repeat the process again and again.

He loved to birth. He longed to birth. He lived to birth. And no one would stop him from birthing again.

He never understood institutional birthing—digging up a box from a labeled spot in the ground with a crowd of others, then bundling it into a hearse to a parlor where the chemicals in it were replaced with blood, then sending it to a hospital for sparking to life, most often followed by days, if not months, of tubes and machines until the body was fully functional.

What kind of birth was that?

Tragic and depressing, at least until the process was complete.

He preferred a quick birth. That's what he'd had. A burst of electricity spreading out from his body into a metal chair, with a blissfully short confinement afterward. But, of course, he was no fool. He was a scientist, a man of intelligence and understanding. He understood the way of the world. He couldn't birth indefinitely.

Time only flows in one direction.

Already he felt the change beginning. His passion was slipping away as his body shrunk in size. He only probably had time for two, maybe three, more births. In but a few short years, he would be too small to birth anything but dogs and cats. By then, the state, in its beneficence, would force him into a retirement facility, where his lifetime of knowledge would be extracted, his mind would grow feeble and dim, and he would grow tiny and stupid and completely dependent.

It frightened him, the loss of the power of birthing. He would not give it up, not until he had to—even if he was reduced to using a transmogrifying glass to soak up a pin point of the light of the earth to birth small ants in a burst of flame and a flurry of smoke. He knew the statistics. Many serial birthers ended up that way. Some saw it as sad, even pathetic. But they didn't understand the rush of birthing with your own hand.

Besides, the ants and bugs and worms of the world, they had the real power of birthing. To bring more of such miraculous, noble creatures into the world with a flash of light—that was sublime. That was birthing a true birther. That was the power of creation.

He wasn't a religious man, but he had to admit, that flash of light made him feel like a god.

There. There was the next spot. The tall grass was shorter there today, shrinking faster than the blades nearby. In a few months there would be another greasy spot in the dirt. He felt his excitement grow with the realization that once again the power of life flowed in his hands alone. It was a simple matter of effect and cause.

He would commit birth here in just a few months, at the change of seasons. He knew it as sure as the sun set in the east.

It was only a matter of time.

About the Author

Donald J. Bingle is an oft-published author in the science fiction, fantasy, horror, thriller, romance, steampunk, and comedy genres. His novels include: *Net Impact* (spy thriller), *GREENSWORD* (darkly comedic eco-thriller), and *Forced Conversion* (near-future military scifi). Many of his three dozen short stories are available in hard copy and for Kindle and Nook, including his Writer on Demand short story collections: *Tales of Gamers and Gaming*; *Tales of Humorous Horror*; *Tales out of Time*; and *Grim, Fair e-Tales*. Find out more at www.donaldjbingle.com or look for me on Twitter, Facebook, Goodreads, Peroozal, or Shelfari.

Know Your Nemesis

Kelly Swails

I had gotten a bad start to the day—a faulty alarm clock and a roommate with a vendetta will do that—but by the time third period rolled around my mood had improved. A student at the Preparatory High School for Challenged Youth for a few weeks, I had finally started to get the hang of things. People think our school is an institution for wanna-be drug addicts, thieves, and general miscreants whose students are one step away from juvie or jail, and they're not far off.

We're not here to get on the straight and narrow path, though.

This school grooms tomorrow's world leaders. Dictators, anarchists, that sort of thing. It's a lot more work than it sounds.

Third period is Know Your Nemesis, a required class for all freshmen. Like I said, I had finally recovered from my cruddy morning and pulled up the textbook on my tablet as the bell rang. Everyone settled in as Mr. Kline stood at the lectern.

"Today we're starting a new project," he said. A few kids groaned as he continued. "You will learn how to take out an enemy. I will draw names to pair you up, and you'll have one week to kill each other."

That got everyone's attention. I raised my hand. "Sir? Did you just say 'kill?' Because that seems a bit extreme."

That got a nervous titter from the class as Kline gave me a patient smile. "Your objective will be to get close enough to your enemy to attach a red 'X'—which I will provide you—on their back. The assignment is worth two hundred points. For every day your opponent is still 'alive' you lose twenty points. Questions?"

A pretty blond girl in the front row raised her hand. "So if we do the deed on the first day we get full credit, and if we do it on the last day we get . . . what?" she said.

Kline answered: "If it happens on Friday, day seven, you'd get eighty. Six days of misses at twenty points lost each . . . is one hundred and twenty from two hundred. Eighty."

"Got it. Thanks." She smiled sweetly before her eyes turned shrewd.

"Let's draw the names," Kline said. He started the tablet on his podium and a screen lit up behind him. He opened a random-name generator and pressed start. Pairs of names tumbled onto the screen and he dragged them over to the side, making a list of pairs. Every time my name didn't come up my stomach clenched a little harder. Finally, when there were six names left, mine came up.

"Sally Clark," Kline said. "You'll go toe-to-toe with... Mallory Harper." He flicked the screen. "Scott Wu, you'll be paired with ..."

I picked at my thumbnail as I watched Mallory Harper. She was easily the top girl in our class. She lived two floors above me, but I had never spoken to her. Her parents and grandparents on both sides are alumni and everyone says one of her aunts has a stronghold over the Italian prime minister. She aced the Fun with Nanotech test last week, and I had heard she hadn't studied for it. I don't know how much of that is true. She was the last person I wanted gunning for me.

My body went cold and I'm pretty sure I stopped breathing. Mallory Harper. I glanced at her and she smiled and gave me a little wave. She looked genuinely excited, not in an "I'm going to kill you" way, but in a "this is going to be so cool" way. Her enthusiasm made it worse. I returned a feeble wave of my own as my breakfast rumbled in my stomach. So much for my day getting better.

A few hours later I found a quiet corner table in the cafeteria and poked at my macaroni salad. I tuned out the noise of five hundred rowdy students as I tried to work out a plan. I scanned the crowd. Mallory was nowhere to be seen. So much for being the first to make a Kill.

"Tough break, Sally," someone said as a tray full of food thumped onto the table.

I jumped. "Hey, Cody," I said.

"Did I scare you?"

"No," I lied.

"If I was able to sneak up on ya, Mallory's going to get you in no time."

"Thanks for your confidence," I said. I moved noodles around my plate a little more before sliding my tray away. "How'd you find out about it so quick, anyway?"

"Adam told me in Monologues for the Masses," he said. He pushed his bangs out of his eyes. They were always in the way, and he had a certain move he did to push them to the side, sort of a swoosh-duck-tuck, but they never stayed long. He looked like a shaggy stray dog, one of the cute ones that was, however, smelly enough to keep you from taking it home. He was the first kid I met at the school and probably my best friend.

"Good news travels fast," I said. "Got any ideas for me?"

"You could sneak into her room and wait for her. Stealth attack."

I nibbled my lip. "That could work. Or I can pay someone on her floor to let me know when she's in her room."

"Bribery! An excellent way to go." He took a huge bite of his ham sandwich. "You know what else would work?" he said around a mouthful of food.

"Manners?"

He shook his head and swallowed. "Just get her before your Nemesis class tomorrow. You know she's going to be there."

"Already thought of that," I said. "Kline's called a truce for the duration of the class period, as well as fifteen minutes before and fifteen minutes after."

"Hmmmmm. Smart move on his part," Cody said.

"I think he's probably given this assignment before," I said.

Cody did a double take before gesturing wildly. "Oh, crap. Move it!" he said a half second before I felt pressure on my back.

"Hi, Sally." A familiar voice said.

My heart sank as I turned around. Mallory had tagged me, but she didn't look too happy about it. I pulled my shirt and looked at the big red "X" on my back. "How did you—" I said as I spotted her move. I had put my back to the wall at the corner-most table in the room thinking it would give me some protection, but I hadn't accounted for a broom closet. A door stood open in the corner, its shelves of spray bottles mocking me.

"Sign the form?" she said as she pulled a folded paper from her pocket.

"Sure." I accepted her pen and scribbled my name on the "deceased" line and noted the date and time.

"Witness?" she pushed the sheet to Cody.

"Is it too late to say that I was her bodyguard and would have stopped you?" he said to Mallory.

"Just sign it," I said.

Cody grimaced and signed his part. "I was just trying to help," he mumbled.

Mallory examined the paper for a moment before folding it and putting it in her pocket. "Good luck," she said as walked away.

"At least she was nice about it," Cody said.

"Yeah," I folded my arms on the table and rested my head. Somehow her congeniality made it worse.

"Look on the bright side," Cody said.

"And that is?"

"It's already over."

I lifted my head. "You're right." I sat up and watched him eat a brownie in two bites. "Maybe I'm looking at this all wrong."

"Don't go too far," he said. "You still bit the dust within two hours of getting the assignment."

I waved him off. "Yeah. Whatever." As bad as it sucked probably being the first kid in the class to get killed, it was a relief, too. I didn't have to constantly look over my shoulder or be on the defensive. I could concentrate all my efforts on offensive maneuvers. If I understood the assignment correctly, I still had to tag her.

I grabbed my tray. "I gotta go."

"Where're you going?"

"The library. I can sneak in twenty minutes of research before class."

"That's the spirit." He eyed my tray. "Are you going to eat that apple?"

I rolled my eyes and handed it to him. Leave it to Cody to think about food at a time like this.

By the time evening study hours were over, I had my plan ready. First, I'd try a direct attack. If that didn't work, I'd go from behind. If that failed, I'd try the flank. If all that didn't work, well, I'd have to check another military strategy book out of the library.

After lights out, I waited until my roommate fell into a deep sleep—Skye has a peculiar way of snoring when she's all the way out—before flipping the blankets aside, grabbing my tools, and sneaking from my room. The hallway was dark and the stairwell was even darker. I climbed two flights of stairs. Mallory's hallway was as dark as mine. It felt weird being on another floor. The rooms were all in the same place and the carpeting was the same, but it was just *different*. I pushed the disorientation from my mind and padded down the hall. I froze when someone sneezed in their room and continued once I couldn't hear the blood pulse in my ears. A few moments later I stood in front of room 405. Mallory's room. I knelt and used my lock picks on the door. The quiet scrap of metal on metal sounded loud as I worked the tumblers. They finally clicked and I smiled. I put away my tools, stood, and slowly opened the door.

I had a moment to enjoy my imminent success before something hard and round hit my face. I jerked and flailed, but my arm caught a wire and something else hit my thighs. I tried to walk, but whatever had caught my arms had wrapped around my ankles and I fell. Pain exploded behind my eyes as I saw stars. A bell jangled—it sounded like an old-school metal alarm clock—and the lights flicked on.

"You were right," a girl said.

"Hey, Sally." Mallory stood over me. "You okay?"

I blinked against the sudden brightness. "Yes." I touched my head and felt something wet. My fingers came away red. "Maybe not. I'm bleeding."

"I told you not to use wine bottles," the girl who must have been Mallory's roommate said. She wore pink pajamas covered in cute little bunnies. "Where'd you even get them?"

"Garbage in the teacher's lounge," she said. "They're a bunch of alcoholics after hours."

"What the hell is going on? It's after lights out." A girl who looked old enough to be a senior stood over me. She must be their floor monitor.

"Sorry, Gina," Mallory said. "Sally's my nemesis."

"Oh." She gave me a once over. "The one you nailed in the cafeteria?"

"Yeah."

"Right. Well, hurry up. You've managed to wake the entire floor." She closed the door behind her.

Mallory's roommate crossed her arms and shook her head. "You're a genius," she said. "Look at this. You've completely disabled her. If the bottle had been heavier, I bet she would have lost consciousness—"

"Would you guys mind deconstructing the scene after you help me up?" I said. "And I need a towel."

"Oh! Right." Mallory untangled the lines as her roommate gave me a washcloth. Even I had to admit the trap had been good. Once she got me free they both helped me to my feet.

"Do you need the nurse?"

"I'm fine." Other than my throbbing head and my wounded pride, it was the truth. I shifted my weight and made a mental note: things get awkward after a thwarted assassination attempt. "Well, see you tomorrow," I said.

"See ya."

I stepped over the mess of wires and bottles and headed downstairs.

It turned out I needed five stitches. They were still tender the next day at lunch when I outlined my plan for Cody.

"Are you sure this is going to work?" He peered into the cafeteria as other students streamed in for lunch. "Aren't you just begging for ridicule?"

I tucked my hair behind my ears before I dug into my backpack for the red "X." I found it jammed between two books and pulled it out. "What do you mean?"

"I mean this is where she got you—"

"That's what makes it perfect," I said. "She won't be expecting it."

"She's good enough to expect the unexpected," he said.

I slung the pack over my shoulder and scowled at Cody. "Whose side are you on?"

"You know I'm on yours. That's why I don't want you to make a fool of yourself. You walk in there and fail everyone's gonna see it."

"It's a bold move," I said.

"Sure. But it's maybe not the most thought-out plan ever."

I glanced into the cafeteria. Mallory sat at a table with some of the kids from the debate team. I gave myself a mental push forward and weaved through the tables. My heart pounded and my back started to sweat. Apparently I was more worried about screwing this up than I had let on to Cody. I got about two tables away when a beefy guy stepped in front of me.

"Sorry, Sally," he said. "No farther."

I stepped back and took him in. He wore fatigues, combat boots, and a shaved head. One of the military specialists. My stomach tightened.

"What's your name?" I thought he was a junior named Steven, but I didn't want to let on that I knew that. Always better to let your enemy think you know less than you do.

He ignored me. "You aren't getting any closer to Mallory."

I patted him on the arm as though we were old friends. His muscles tensed beneath my hand and I pretended he couldn't break me in half without breathing hard. "It's been nice chatting with you." I moved to walk past him.

He grabbed my arm, not hard enough to hurt but firm enough to show he meant business. "I said you're not getting any closer."

A few kids at some of the nearby tables noticed our little dance. I ignored their glances and turned to Steven. "Tell me, how much is Mallory paying you to guard her?"

His eyes clouded over. "I can't answer that."

"Oh, I see. You vowed to protect her and telling me would go against your honor code. Or something." The military people were so easy to read. I peeled his fingers off my arm and gripped the red "X" in my hand so hard the cardboard cut into my flesh. "Tell you what. I won't press you to break your honor if you don't give me any more trouble. Got it?" I walked away.

Or I tried to. He wrapped his arms around my waist and lifted. That got everyone's attention. Kids pointed and some guy at a table filled with seniors whooped as I uselessly kicked my feet. Mallory turned in her chair and gave me a sheepish grin.

My face felt hot and sweat made my back sticky. This was the most humiliated I had been since the Great Onslaught Debacle on the very first day of school.

Steven walked me to the door of the cafeteria and deposited me outside. "If you try getting close to her again I won't be so gentle," he said kindly.

"Thanks for the warning."

He walked away and I tried to look casual as I smoothed my hair.

Cody leaned against the wall as he ate from a bag of pretzels. "So how'd it go?" He obviously knew the answer.

"She hired a bodyguard." Why hadn't I thought of that?

"Told ya it wouldn't work." He tossed me a wrapped sandwich that he must have bought while I was trying to accost Mallory.

I snatched it from the air. I might be the joke of the school, but at least I wouldn't be hungry. "Shut up."

By Thursday I decided it was time to go for the flank. After my last class got out I raced to the dorms and knocked on Mallory's door. Her roommate answered and smirked when she saw it was me.

"Mallory's not here."

"I know. She's at debate practice until five," I said before I could stop myself. I had to work on this "never let people know how much information you have" thing. "Anyway, I'm not here for her. I came to talk to you. Can I come in?"

This managed to surprise her. "Sure."

"We've never been introduced. I'm Sally." I felt dumb but I stuck out hand. Diplomacy sometimes worked, right?

"Erin," she said as she shook. Her hair was glossy black, heavy eyeliner rimmed her eyes, and she'd painted her nails a deep purple. She was either going to a meeting of Goths or she was one of the few anarchy girls at the school. It contradicted the bunny pajamas so much I paused to get my bearings.

"Listen, Erin, I'm going to be straight with you. I am down to the last twenty-four hours of this assignment and I need some help. You're her roommate. You must know something that I can use against her."

Erin crossed her arms. "Even if there were, I wouldn't tell you."

"She pay you off, too?" I said. Mallory really was a genius.

"No," Erin said. "No. She's just a cool girl."

"There's got to be something about her that makes you mad."

Erin shrugged. "She snores. That's about it. But I have earplugs. It's not a thing."

"I don't suppose you'll accept a bribe? I could do all your homework for a week in exchange for letting me at her?"

Erin shook her head. "Good effort, though."

"Can I pay you to 'kill' her for me?"

"Not a chance."

"Do you know anyone who would?"

Erin thought for a second before shaking her head. "Nope. No one comes to mind."

I threw up my hands. "Great. I have the only 'nemesis' that doesn't have enemies."

"Sorry," Erin said, sounding anything but.

"Whatever," I mumbled as I headed for the door.

"I'm rooting for you to get her," Erin said. "For what it's worth. Not that I want to see her go down, but you're an underdog. I'm a sucker for the lovable loser."

"That's really heartwarming," I said as I left. So much for my flanking maneuver.

Friday morning Cody walked to class with me as I told him about my meeting with Erin.

"And then—get this—she called me a lovable loser," I said.

"You are a lovable loser," Cody said. "You're like the class mascot."

"Perfect. Mallory's a legend and I'm a mascot. You're supposed to be making me feel better."

"I'm also your friend, and that means I don't lie to you," he said.

"Try making an exception this one time," I said.

"Hey, would you wait for me a second?" Cody walked in front of the building that housed the library. "I have to check out *The Prince* for a paper."

"I can't believe you don't own it already." I said.

"Machiavelli isn't really my kind of guy," he said.

I sighed. "I'll wait as long as you return this for me." I dropped my pack to the ground and rummaged around inside. I pulled out the military strategy book and handed it to him. "So much for research."

"You haven't lost yet," he said.

"I have less than two hours," I said.

He answered by walking into the library. I zipped my pack closed and looked out over the campus. The library sat on top of a hill and so had a wide set of steep stairs leading to the school grounds. The building looked pretty majestic at night. As I watched students walk to class I thought about how I was going to make up the points for completely failing to 'kill' Mallory. Maybe Mr. Kline would accept a bribe, but I doubted it. The teachers had to be impervious to the methods they taught, right?

I was so deep in thought I didn't hear anyone approach until Mallory spoke in my ear. "Good job," she said.

I jumped. I really had to learn to be more aware of my surroundings. "For what?" I said. "Improving your reputation?" I tried to put bite into the words but failed. Mallory was a crappy nemesis because it was hard to hate her. Or maybe that made her a really great nemesis.

"No," she said. "For killing me. You snuck up behind me and 'pushed' me down the stairs," she said.

I looked at her for a long moment before I got it. Could she really be helping me? What was her motive?

"Okay," I said slowly. I looked behind her. "Where's your bodyguard?"

"I only hired him through Thursday," she said. "A grievous error on my part, as it turned out. Stop looking at me like that."

"I can't help it. I'm trying to figure out why you're helping me."

"You worked really hard to get at me," she said. "Erin told me you tried to bribe her—"

"I prefer the term *persuade*," I said.

"Plus that fiasco in the cafeteria was pretty bold," she said. "And trying to get at me in my own room! I actually didn't think you'd try that even though I set a trap."

I stared at her honest face. "Are you patronizing me?"

"No! I just don't want to see you fail." She paused. "Maybe I do have one motive."

"I knew it. What do you want? Don't get me wrong, I'll totally go along with this, but—"

"I want to be your friend," she said.

I blinked. One of the best students in our class wanted to be my friend? "That's it?"

"Yeah." She smiled, and this time it looked a little sad. "I really don't have that all that many friends. Not good ones."

I nodded as I pretended to think it over. "You got yourself a deal." We shook hands before I dug the red "X" out of my backpack. It had gotten buried on the bottom and looked a little worse for wear. I stuck it to her back and pressed down. "There. You're dead." I smiled back at her.

"What's going on?" Cody said as he walked out of the library. "I leave you for two minutes and you manage to kill Mallory?"

"Yeah," I said. "I'm stealthy like that."

Cody squinted at me. "You're not stealthy."

"She pushed me down the stairs," Mallory said. "It was pretty slick."

Cody put his hands on his hips and looked from Mallory to me and back again. I kept my face as open as possible, but Cody knew me well enough to know when I'm full of it. Apparently he decided to let it go. "I assume you need a witness?"

"Oh. Right," I pulled the sheet from my pack and got the necessary signatures. Once everything was official I put it in my jeans pocket for safe keeping. It would be like me to get the 'kill' then lose the proof.

Mallory weaved her arms into mine and Cody's. "Shall we?" she said.

"Let's," I said.

"This is all very weird," Cody said.

"Just go with it," I said before walking to the first class of the morning with the best friend and the best nemesis a girl could ask for.

About the Author

According to family legend, **Kelly Swails** learned to read by perusing Archie comics at the age of three. (She loved Jughead the most.) As a child she would read anything with words—magazines, books, comics, cereal boxes. She wrote her first bona-fide short story in sixth grade, about a feminist and a misogynist watching the destruction of Earth from their spaceship. After that foray into SF, she tried her hand at mystery, horror, and teen romance. Her medical mind pulled her into clinical laboratory science, but she continues to write short stories and YA novels. She has been published in numerous anthologies. Visit her website at www.kellyswails.com.

My Faire Lady

Jean Rabe

I started obsessing about the green babe four years ago
when my girlfriend waggled discount coupons in my face
and talked me into going to the local Renaissance Faire.
She'd been a medieval history major in college, and she
ooohed and aaaahed at all the lavish costumes and was in
the front row when the queen and her court rode by. I had
to admit it was fun, like walking onto the set of some low-
budget sword and sorcery flick. More than a few female
faire patrons had their boobs pushed up to their chins by
corsets, cinched so tight they were straining the brocade.
You couldn't help but stare.

I didn't care much for the music, and you couldn't escape
it. There were strolling minstrels everywhere . . . harps,
lutes, flutes, odd-looking instruments I couldn't put a name
to, all playing fancy old tunes that didn't have any lyrics.

The food was pretty good, and the beer went down quick
because the temp was pushing ninety. We found a patch of
shade and watched two middle-aged men in leotards
swatting each other with stage swords. Then my girlfriend
had her face painted, a purple and blue butterfly spread
across her nose and cheeks, and had some flowers braided
in her hair. She skipped away to watch the "courtly
dances," and I took in the joust.

I was on my way to meet back up with her when the green babe caught my eye.

She was clearly part of the faire, a paid employee like the kissing bandit and the beggars, the fortune teller and the dude who did some glass blowing. But she was a little out of place. This park was supposed to be a re-creation of Bristol, England, during the renaissance. And here she was, a piece of a fairy tale or some such, a dryad or forest sprite or pixie. I'd played D&D in high school, and she looked just like one of them fey temptresses out of the Monster Manual. She'd been airbrushed green . . . legs, arms, face, all of it, and she had on this little green leather tunic that covered only my imagination. She was barefoot, and her hair was short and . . . wait for it . . . green. Her eyes were green, too, and the skin at the corners of them crinkled like the veins of leaves when she smiled.

Basically, she was every shade of green you could think of, all blended together like a sidewalk chalk painting of a forest that had been caught in the rain. I knew at that moment I had to . . . what is that cliché? . . . make her mine.

She slipped from tree to tree just this side of the line of port-a-potties, stopping to pose for pictures with some of the passersby. She did these little pirouettes and leaps and ran her fingers across flower petals like she was playing a piano. I took out my cell phone and snapped a couple of pictures. She crooked her finger, and so I obliged and came closer.

"What's your name?" I asked.

She didn't answer. I hadn't seen her talk to anybody; part of her shtick, I guess.

Up close, I could see that the green paint hadn't quite covered everything, as there was a faint line of pink skin showing at her hairline by her pointed ears. She smelled of summer, of wildflowers and the filigree of dew that clung to the ferns at her feet. I took a deep whiff and was intoxicated.

"C'mon, what's your name?"

She darted away, posing for another guy with a camera.

I would've watched her longer, but my girlfriend found me and tugged me toward a row of shops that looked weathered and authentic and were dabbed with pastel colors on their shutters and window boxes. I had another beer . . . two . . . while she perused the jewelry and bought a pair of earrings that set me back forty bucks. I emptied the rest of my wallet on hand-made soap and bath salts she insisted she needed, and then I reached for the credit card when she picked up a T-shirt and a refrigerator magnet at the gift shop on the way out the gate.

I came back the next dozen weekends without her.

I had to see more of the green babe.

The faire ran every summer weekend, ending on Labor Day. I'd hoped to get the green babe's phone number during one of my visits, but that didn't happen. We were, however, spending more time together—all her breaks and her lunch hours. Halfway through the summer she told me her name was Aisling. She didn't say anything else, but it was a start. On the last weekend of the season, we shared a bottle of sweet strawberry wine and a very long kiss.

The next year I went to work at the faire. It didn't interfere with my day job; an eighth-grade English teacher, I had the summers off anyway. And my girlfriend . . . my ex . . . and I had parted ways and so I didn't have any other demands on my time. I'd applied on-line in the spring and got a spot in a leatherworker's shop. He made boots and belts, handled special orders, and all I had to do was sell his wares and take a few folks' measurements for custom work. I had to dress authentic, part of the employment requirements, and the two outfits—one for Saturdays and one for Sundays—set me back about five hundred bucks. The boots were half again that much, as I had to buy them from the guy I was working for. I wasn't sure I'd earn enough to cover my expenses. But the upshot was that the leatherworker was the closest vendor to where Aisling pranced.

I guess you could say I was obsessed with her.

I could watch her from the front of the shop, and on my breaks I'd wander closer. She was practically all I could think about, always smelling of summer and moving among the ferns like she was the most graceful creature God had put on this Earth.

And he'd put her there just for me.

There was a little one-room apartment above the leatherworker's, and I stayed there on weekends. It was for security, to make sure no one broke in and swiped any boots or raided the cashbox. The bed wasn't comfortable, there was no indoor plumbing, and there were no screens on the windows. The faire insisted the buildings be just like they were centuries past . . . and that meant the mosquitoes were free to come in and feast. Aisling stashed her airbrush equipment in the storage closet and stayed with me.

It didn't take me long to find out she was also green under her skimpy leather outfit . . . easier, she said, to airbrush herself and then put on the bits of leather. Speaking of leather, I made her a few new outfits, none of which required much material, and it gave me practice working with dyes. I made her some sandals, too, so her toes could breathe, along with a belt that I tooled to look like an emerald snake had wrapped around her tiny waist.

I'd never seen her without the green paint. She showered at this little stall for employees and shop owners when I wasn't looking. Maybe she had some splotchy skin condition like Michael Jackson supposedly had. I never asked her about it; I didn't want to pry or say anything that might upset her. I wasn't sure I really had her, but I was sure I didn't want to risk losing her.

She told me Aisling was an Irish name that meant "wished for." She was certainly everything I'd wished for . . . beautiful, charming, intelligent, beautiful, green, beautiful, and she never talked too much, which I'd come to consider delightful. If she was Irish, I couldn't tell from her accent; she really didn't have one. But her voice was incredible, brittle and musical at the same time.

We'd watch the sunrise from the apartment's front window, a syrupy orange haze that swept through the trees across the horizon. Some mornings the color hung so low I worried it would smother the faire grounds. But as we stared, it would always lighten and brighten, turning so blue that it seemed to pulse with an otherworldly sheen. Everything was more intense and amazing with Aisling at my side. Magical.

She'd slip outside to use the shower, come back, and then I'd hear the gentle hiss of her airbrush while I dressed in one of my outfits and struggled into my boots. It was a comfortable morning routine that ended when she was out the backdoor to pirouette for the faire patrons, and I was opening the shop and hoping for good sales . . . all the while keeping an eye on her.

"I love you," she said, as our second summer drew to an end. She said something else, but the breeze sweeping through the apartment stole the rest of her words.

"I love you, too," I answered. I meant it. "I want to spend the rest of my life with you."

I'd never seen her smile so bright.

She still wouldn't give me a phone number, nor agree to come to my place when the faire closed for the season. I didn't know where she lived come fall, other than "with friends." She didn't have a Facebook account, didn't twitter, didn't own an iPad or an iPhone, didn't even have a laptop.

"Stay with me when school starts," I tried again.

"Not this year," she said. I felt more than heard those three heavy words.

"Next?" I asked. "Next year?"

She kissed me a long while.

The following summer I offered to buy the place from my boss. He was getting up there in age, his skin as wrinkled and cracked as an old piece of leather that had been left untreated. After I'd spotted one of his brochures about retirement homes, and pointed out how lovely one of the places looked, it didn't take much convincing to get him to hand over the deed to the shop. I'd paid enough attention that I could make even the most elaborate boots and slippers and pouches on my own, and I had saved enough from my teaching gig so I could manage a down payment on the shop. I'd been spending all my evenings after school practicing tooling and embossing, and I'd ordered a few more outfits from a place online so I could expand my faire wardrobe . . . the most expensive a tunic dyed green to match Aisling's airbrushed skin.

Aisling was happy that I'd decided to become a permanent fixture in Bristol. After hours she helped me tidy up the place, and she had an eye for how to best display the boots and belts. She couldn't help me with the accounting part of it, though, and so I hired one of my old D&D buddies to work the shop a few hours on Saturdays and keep the books. His day job was in an accounting firm, so we were pretty much set.

On opening weekend of that fourth summer my ex-girlfriend strolled by. I waved to her and she came over, in the company of two mutual friends from college. They looked over my goods, and my ex bought a pair of suede moccasins. Not once did she act like she even recognized me. I suppose I had that coming, dumping her and all for Aisling. At least I had the satisfaction of overcharging her a few bucks. Good thing, I needed the money.

It turned out to be a brutal summer. The economy in the crapper, people weren't spending as much as the year before, and my sales were awful. To add to the misery, it was hot. I don't think it rained an hour in all of July.

From the front of the shop I watched the wind tease dust devils into playing across the paths, little swirls of earth twisting their way to the patch of wilting ferns that Aisling pranced through. The heat didn't seem to bother her. I'd never seen her sweat.

Not even in the evenings when we desperately enjoyed each other's company.

On the last weekend of the season my ex came back, demanding I re-stitch the soles of the moccasins she'd bought from me. Again, she didn't let on that she knew me. But by now I knew why. I looked cracked and weathered like a piece of old leather that hadn't been cared for. She couldn't have recognized me. I was thirty, but I appeared more than twice that, the mirror image of the man I'd bought the shop from.

"Wait, please," I told her. "This will only take a few minutes." I reached for a needle.

That morning I had watched Aisling use her airbrush. She painted a thin line of peach-colored paint along her hairline by her pointed ear. That one little streak made her look human, like she'd missed covering up a spot of flesh. Everyone else thought it was the green that she spray-painted on.

I'd known the previous summer I was getting old, and in the off season the other teachers had stared at me and murmured behind my stooped back. It was Aisling's doing, draining me of life like a vampire might have . . . if such existed. If I could have broken free of her charms, I could have saved myself.

Or could I?

These brief summers with her were certainly worth losing decades.

She'd stolen my heart and soul that first Saturday I'd spotted her, sealed the deal with strawberry wine and that first long kiss.

She'd confessed to me one ardent night weeks ago that she was, indeed, Irish—a Leanhaun Shee, who was out of sync with time, centuries old and centuries left to live, feeding off the life force of others. Feeding off me. The Leanhaun Shee, or Faerie Queen—I learned from reading a Celtic mythology book a seller four shops down had on display—gives a man inspiration while he gives up his essence. She inspired me to become a leatherworker and to see the world with a poet's eyes. To see the sunrise as syrup and to adore the music of the faire's strolling minstrels.

Mostly, she inspired me to love with all of my being.

"There, finished. Better than new." I reached over the counter and handed my ex her repaired moccasins, then I looked down at my desk. There was an assortment of retirement home brochures splayed across it. I pointed to one. It had the most perfect green roof.

Amid the ferns in front of the port-a-potties, Aisling did a graceful pirouette. She crooked her finger at a young man who snapped her picture with his cell phone.

About the Author

Jean **Rabe** is the author of 30 fantasy and adventure novels and more short stories than she cares to admit. She's edited two dozen anthologies. When she isn't writing or editing she tosses tennis balls to her moose-sized dog and dabbles in fantasy football leagues. Visit her website at www.jeanrabe.com.

The Tinker's Music Box

Jennifer Brozek

"It's my wife. She means everything to me. You've got to protect her when I'm gone," Patrick Smithson said as he caressed the music box sitting on the table between them. The table sat beneath the second story window of the inn room that belonged to the man Patrick was speaking so earnestly too: bounty hunter Eric Hamblin. The rest of the room was taken up by the single bed, a cedar chest, and a smaller table that held a wash basin and a pitcher of water. It was as private as a stranger could get in town.

Eric looked at the music box. It was a thing of beauty with an inlaid ivory and rosewood case. About the size of a small breadbox, its interior showed two brass cylinders—one smooth and one picked with a song. There were several switches on the inside and a ratchet winding handle. All of the hardware was substantially gilded, and told a tale of care, craftsmanship, and love. But to call it his wife, was a bit unusual.

"Mr. Smithson…"

"Patrick, my boy," the old man interrupted with a smile. "I insist."

Eric nodded and started again, "Patrick… she is a beautiful music box, but I'm not a bank or a safe. Don't you think those would be better places for your treasure?"

"And lock my Clara up in the dark? No sir!" He shook his head with the air of a man who does not understand the stupidity in front of him.

"The music box, Clara, is a masterful…"

"Are you daft? Clara isn't the music box."

I think the old man is addle-brained, Joseph said in Eric's head. *I can't follow his words.*

Eric nodded to himself and to the spirit riding his body. The spirit in question was Joseph Lamb, Sheriff cum preacher, murdered by his own pistol, and now the Lion of God—protector of the innocent and exactor of God's vengeance—in one incorporeal package. He had chosen to sit this one out and let Eric make the decision.

Eric sat back and sighed. "You have the better of me. I don't understand."

Patrick gave Eric an earnest look. "I'm not just a tinker. I was a watchmaker. One of the best. But I discovered something… *invented* something marvelous. It's very complex and involves things you wouldn't understand." He patted the music box. "That was back East. I knew I had to come west to get away from people who knew I was working on something special. But, there's little call for watchmakers out here in Arizona. Now tinkers, that was a different story."

"Yes, but what does all this have to do with your wife?" Eric shook his head. "For that matter, where is your wife? Don't you think she should have a say in this?"

The look of pride on Patrick's face scared Eric.

"Mr. Hamblin, Clara is *in* the music box."

Joseph's wordless surprise mirrored Eric's quiet question of, "Pardon?"

Patrick gently ran his fingertip over the non-smooth music cylinder. "Clara, my love, this is her soul here. As she died of consumption, I drew her last breathe into the music box with this." He touched a switch on the side of the cylinder.

Eric saw that the other cylinder had an identical switch and did not know whether he should be impressed or horrified.

Joseph had no such qualms. *Blasphemy!* his voice rumbled in Eric's head.

Patrick, unaware of the silent criticism continued. "Clara and I have been together like this for forty-two years. Forty-two happy years." The smile disappeared. "But now I'm dying and we have no children. I must find a way to protect her. I must."

Eric swallowed, his mouth dry. "What does Clara think of this?"

"Finding and hiring you was her idea," Patrick said.

"**I** can't believe you agreed to this," Joseph said as he paced the room. "The very notion that a soul could be captured, imprisoned, in any clockwork is beyond the pale."

Eric, still sitting at the table, looking at the music box, smiled. "Beyond the pale? 17th century poetry? You are upset." If Joseph had a body, he knew that the man's well worn boots would be stomping out a temper tantrum on the hardwood floor. Instead, he paced in silent fury.

"Yes," Joseph nodded. "I am. That thing should be destroyed. If her soul is in it, it needs to continue on to its final place. Man was not meant to capture souls."

"How do you know destroying it won't destroy the soul?" Eric's voice was mild and curious. He had not seen Joseph this upset before. Not even when the gun that was his body on this mortal plane was shot, actually damaging the spirit.

"It won't." His voice was short and final. "That woman's soul has been denied its final judging. She could have been tortured all these years. How are we to know?"

"That woman's soul could be just fine and she could be happy," Eric countered. "You're right... we can't know. And I'm not willing to possibly destroy a soul without knowing for sure."

"Perhaps someone would like to ask 'the woman'?" a woman's voice said. With neither fuss nor fanfare, there she was, sitting in the chair formerly occupied by her husband; a brunette with her long hair in a bun, wearing a cornflower blue walking outfit. "Perhaps 'the woman' would know a thing or two about the state of her soul or the home in which it resides."

Eric and Joseph turned in surprise. Eric stood with his hand on the gun and frowned at her, "Clara Smithson?"

She nodded. "I am."

"You've been listening all this time?"

"Yes."

"Why haven't you made yourself known before now?" Joseph asked.

Clara gave an elegant shrug of her shoulders, "I had not been invited." Turning to Eric, she tilted her head, "I thought you would have asked to see me, meet me, at least. I am surprised you took him at his word. In truth, his words were addle-brained to the unknowing ear."

Eric looked between Clara and Joseph, his hand still on the gun. "You heard him."

Clara stood and walked to Eric, reaching out her hand to his armed one. "I did. And I can see him. There is no need for this." She pressed her hand down through his and trailed her fingers over the butt of the gun. "I am one woman with no weapons."

Eric felt a wisp of cold on and in his hand as her ghostly fingers slipped through his flesh.

"You are nothing," Joseph said abruptly. "You are the shadow of a soul and must be destroyed."

Eric and Clara looked at Joseph.

"She looks like a spirit to me," Eric said. "And she can see you."

"That doesn't matter. She has passed by her time in this mortal realm."

"As have you." Clara tilted her head, "Why do you fear me so?"

Eric realized that Clara was right. Joseph was afraid and reacting in anger. That was an unaccustomed emotion. He watched as Clara approached Joseph. For the first time, Eric watched the Lion of God retreat. Then he watched Joseph's face harden as the spirit stood his ground. Clara and he stood an arm's width from each other.

"You don't belong here," Joseph said.

"And you do?" Clara asked.

"I do. I have a purpose."

"Do you know for certain that I do not have a purpose as well?"

"I was given my purpose by God. I chose to become his avenging angel."

"I was given a choice of dying or remaining with my husband. I chose to stay by his side as a good wife would."

"It's not the same," Joseph said, dismissing her. He walked forward, intending to walk through her but was shocked when their shoulders collided.

Eric noted that Clara looked as shocked as Joseph did. "You can touch each other," he observed.

"That much is obvious," Clara said returning to the table to stand by her husband's music box.

"You didn't expect it. You both thought that you would slide through each other. But you can touch each other," he repeated thoughtfully. "You knew." He turned to Joseph. "You knew that you could feel her."

Joseph shook his head. "No." He looked at his feet for a moment and then looked up again. "No, I didn't know, but I suspected. I wasn't sure until then."

"That's what you were afraid of. Why?" Eric asked.

Clara looked at Eric with hungry doe eyes."I haven't felt anything for forty-two years. Not since I died. The sensation was… was…"

"Welcome…" Joseph murmured more to himself than anyone else.

Eric looked between them. "He felt something a few months back. Pain. He was hurt. But now he has the chance to feel something more."

Joseph gave him a sharp look. "No. I will not. That is not my duty."

"Ah, but a man is not all duty. Perhaps Clara is here for another duty. To reward your service." Eric's voice was soft and tempting. Joseph stared at him and for a moment Eric frowned at himself for having such a thought. But he felt compelled to continue despite the thought's unsavory nature. "Think of it. Why else would this music box be put in our path?"

Joseph's face was a thundercloud of conflicting emotions, "Blasphemy!"

"She could be your reward for good service. To ease your loneliness," Eric continued. "You don't think I can't feel it when you spiritride me? I can."

So intent on Joseph, Eric did not notice Clara shifting towards him until she reached out and yanked the 1851 Colt revolver from his gun belt. The engraved flames on its barrel seemed to flicker as she pointed it at Eric. "I will kill you both before I allow anyone to touch me without my permission."

Eric stepped away from Clara. "Why didn't you warn me she'd be able to take your gun?"

"I didn't know and I wasn't the one offering her up as a prize," Joseph said.

"Maybe I don't want to die," Clara continued over their surprise. "And maybe I don't want to be offered like a Calico Queen to the first man who comes by. I am a respectable married woman."

"Can she shoot the gun? How is she even holding it?" Eric asked, his hands raised.

"I don't know," Joseph admitted. "It is God's Will that fires the pistol." Then he looked at Eric. "I suppose we'll find out when she shoots you."

"Me?"

"You were the one offering her up to me like a whoremonger."

"Not seriously," Eric said. His face flushed with embarrassment as he looked at Clara. "I apologize if I upset you. I was only testing him. He's constantly testing me; my beliefs and morals. When I discovered how unsettled he was at his ability to feel you, your presence, I thought only to test him in the same way."

"You, Mr. Hamblin, are a cad and I will not be used like this. I will not be offered up as a whore for some other spirit because we can sense each other. I do not care if it was a test. What if he had decided you were right? Dead or not, I am a respectable married woman and I will not have it!" Her voice rose with her anger.

Neither Eric nor Joseph had time to protest Clara's words before the door to their inn room broke in with a loud breaking of wood followed by an even louder crash of the Colt revolver going off in Clara's hand. Standing in the middle of the broken doorway was Patrick. He had one hand raised with a large iron hammer and the other hand clutched his chest where crimson blood spilled between his fingers. "Clara?" he asked, confused, before he dropped the hammer to the floor and sank to his knees.

Clara, also shocked and confused, dropped the Colt and rushed to her husband's side. "Patrick, oh, Patrick!" She reached for him but her arms slid through his flesh as he shifted, falling on his back.

"Heard you yelling. Came to rescue you," Patrick wheezed.

She looked up at them, "Help him!"

"Your aim was true," Joseph said. He did not move from his spot. Though, he glanced out the broken door and saw that the entirety of the inn was showing a remarkable sense of self preservation and not coming to look at the ruckus.

"Just wanted to take care of you." Patrick's voice was fading and he lost his struggle to lift his hand up to his wife's face.

Eric hesitated a moment before reaching a decision and then crossed the room to the music box. He flipped the switch next to the smooth music cylinder and watched it turn. Then, he watched Patrick's face, watched him take his last few breaths as Clara sobbed in keening wails above her husband's body. When Eric looked back at the music cylinder, it was no longer smooth. He turned off the switch and contemplated the music box.

"What did you do?" Joseph asked.

"I did what I thought ought to be done. And maybe, if you weren't trying to be so high and mighty, you'd be trying to help that poor woman." Eric gestured at the sobbing spirit with his chin. "I can't touch her but you can."

Eric took the blanket from the bed and covered Patrick's body. Joseph made no move towards Clara or Eric. He watched them with conflicted eyes.

"Shhh, Miss Clara. Shhh." Eric hunkered down and tried to look her in the face, trying to comfort her. "How long after your death did you know you were a spirit?"

She looked up at him, confused. "What do you mean?"

Speaking in tones reserved for frightened animals and hysterical children, Eric smiled at her and repeated, "How long after your death did you know you were a spirit?"

"Almost immediately. I no longer felt pain."

"I'm no longer in pain, my love." Patrick, looking younger and healthier, stood next to the music box. "I don't know why I didn't think to hire someone to draw my soul into the music box to be with you. It seems so obvious now." He nodded to Eric, "Young man, I owe you a debt."

Clara looked over her shoulder and saw Patrick. He opened his arms to her. With a whirl of skirts, she rose and ran to him. For the first time in decades, the two embraced and this time her tears were of joy. Eric stepped over to Joseph's side and watched the Smithsons. "Is it still blasphemy?" he asked.

As the ghosts disappeared, Joseph shook his head. "I don't know." They stood in silence for a moment longer before Joseph added, "I don't appreciate your idea of a test."

"Now you know how I feel when you do it to me." Eric said, "But you were tempted."

"Yes," Joseph agreed. "In life, as much as I tried to be a good man, I wasn't. I enjoyed life as much as any other man did. Without the temptations of the flesh, I can be the Lord's instrument. With her here, it would be much more difficult."

"What do we do now?"

Patrick answered the question before Joseph could. Once more, the spirits of the music box appeared without warning. Patrick and Clara stood side by side, her arm linked in his. "You must destroy the music box," Patrick said. "It is much too dangerous to have around. My invention is extraordinary and not something I want in the hands of evil men."

Clara glanced at Eric.

Patrick saw the disbelieving looks on Eric and Joseph's faces. "Clara and I have had a long talk. Time within the music box is different than here. It is possible that dangerous people will come looking once news of my death reaches them."

"We could neglect to mention that you died," Eric said.

Clara shook her head and Patrick said, "We have decided. Now that we are reunited, it is time for both of us to continue on. We are ready."

"But, what if destroying the music box destroys the two of you?"

"Then that is what God wills," Clara said. "Man was never meant to live beyond this life."

Eric nodded, "How do I do it?"

"I'll tell you," Patrick said. "My tools are at my belt." He pointed to the blanket covered body. "But, I think you should destroy it away from other people. Just to be certain no one else is hurt. The clockwork is special."

Joseph and Eric sat around the campfire with a thick smelting pot hung over hot glowing coals. They were hunkered down at the base of a butte out of the wind; the Arizona desert was gusty around them with dust devils whirling in and out of existence. As Eric took apart the music box piece by piece, he slowly added each wooden part to the fire to burn and each metal part to the pot to melt. He paused when he got to the cylinders containing Patrick and Clara's souls. "Why do you think He allowed it? Her shooting her husband?"

Joseph was slow in answering. Finally he said, "I think he was giving them what they wanted; to be reunited. We both know that revolver will not fire unless it's doing God's will."

Eric raised an eyebrow. "You don't think it was to punish him for the music box?"

Joseph shook his head. "No."

He nodded. "I don't know why I started testing you. I'd never thought about testing you before. And you know me, I would never offer a woman up to another man as a prize. Not after what happened to my sister. The more I think about what I said, the angrier I get at myself."

"Maybe it wasn't you talking."

Eric put the cylinders to the side, unable to make himself put them into the pot for melting. He unscrewed the bottom of the music box to look at the clockwork mechanism below and was startled at its complexity. The entire thing was a work of art in and of itself. He really had no idea where to begin taking it apart. Then he remembered he was destroying the machine and used a small chisel to start prying gears and springs out, adding each to the pot of melting metal. "You think the Lord was using me to test you."

"I do."

"Why?"

Joseph shrugged. "I told you. I was once human with a man's desires. Maybe He thought to tempt me with the pleasures of the flesh again."

Eric took the sideboard rosewood pieces of the case and added them to the fire. Using the chisel, he pried up more of the complex clockwork. "Or maybe He wanted to remind you what it was like to be human with human emotions and needs."

Joseph frowned but said nothing.

"You're all fire and brimstone and that's fine for those who deserve God's vengeance. But the Smithsons, they didn't deserve that. It was an old man trying to protect his wife's spirit when he was gone. Instead of offering that protection, you judged them." Eric, impatient with prying the last of the gears off the baseboard of the music box's remains, tossed the entire thing into the fire, sending a shower of sparks dancing into the noon sun.

"You're more than just the Lion of God, Joseph Lamb. You're a protector of the innocent as well. I think it's something you needed reminding of." Eric picked up the two cylinders and stared at them. "Maybe that's why all this happened."

Eric did not look at his mentor as he put the two cylinders into the smelting pot. After a moment, the wind whipped up around the campsite, blowing sand into their faces. Eric covered his eyes with an arm until the unnatural wind died down and left with the sound of a sigh. Inside the pot of partially melted metal, the cylinders were gone.

Joseph's voice was soft. "I reckon you might be right. It's something I'm going to have to think about."

About the Author

Jennifer **Brozek** of Bothell, WA, is an award winning author and editor. She has been writing roleplaying games and professionally publishing fiction since 2004. She has won awards for both game design and editing. With the number of edited anthologies, fiction sales, RPG books and the non-fiction articles and book under her belt, Jennifer is often considered a Renaissance Woman, but she prefers to be known as a wordslinger and optimist. Read more about her at her blog: http://jennifer-brozek.livejournal.com/.

Under a Thin Veneer

Daniel Myers

The conversation around Lord Charles Crampton's dinner table was unusually subdued that day. From the moment the guests picked up their oyster forks, the only conversation was that prompted by Lady Eugenia Crampton in her role as hostess. As the soup course was served, she was starting to feel concerned, and by the time the fish course was brought out she was convinced that the whole evening was going to be a disaster.

Her question to Jonathan Bedford about the Countess Moncreiffe's latest art acquisition from the east got a disinterested response. One would think he would have at least a vague idea what his aunt was up to.

Her inquiry into when William Densmore's brother would be returning from Africa was answered only with "Quite soon, I hope."

She even asked Lady Elizabeth Primrose how she was settling into the old Wilkinson house, but apparently Lady Elizabeth had not yet stayed there overnight.

Meanwhile, the servants busied themselves, removing each dish and replacing it with the next. It was only as the remains of the fish course were being cleared away that William finally broached the subject that she'd hoped for.

She would have brought it up herself, but that would be too much like bragging.

"Charles, I've heard that you were at Madame Krusslov's seance this past Thursday."

"I'm embarrassed to say I was." Charles paused as he was served some cucumber salad. "It was a mistake to get involved in that nonsense, and I knew it at the time."

That was not the response Eugenia wanted to hear. She saw Charles' sister, Millicent Densmore, turn to him with a look of surprise. Like herself, Millicent had obviously been expecting Charles to happily dive into a long detailed story, as he usually did at the slightest provocation, but his tone of his voice was uncharacteristically dismissive. Perhaps, with a bit of encouragement, he would go on. She caught Millicent's eye and gave her just the hint of a nod.

"They're saying that Madame Krusslov was attacked by some kind of wild animal, and that you fought the beast off," Millicent said.

Charles poked at his salad and scowled, and for a moment Eugenia thought he was going to ignore the remark. Fortunately the desire to tell a tale of his own heroics overcame his distaste for the occult.

"Do you want to know what really happened?" he asked.

"Yes, please. The stories going about are quite ridiculous," she said.

Charles looked around the table to see his guests all looking to him intently. Eugenia quickly feigned disinterest. If he saw that she wanted him to talk about it, he would certainly stop. "Fine then," he said, "but I'll have no interruptions." He drank a little wine to clear his throat. "First, it wasn't an animal of any sort. It was a demon."

"It was in the middle of breakfast when the butler brought the invitation for Eugenia. She's been rather keen on these spiritualists for a while now, and I'm sure they've all got her marked as an easy target. Of course I didn't want anything to do with all that twaddle and refused, but then she found out that Countess Moncreiffe was going to be there, and all hope was lost. Once Eugenia has her mind set on something, she can make things insufferably difficult until she gets her way. I could only hope that that fraud, Krusslov, would put on an entertaining show.

"We arrived a bit early at that place she's rented in town. I'd read up a bit on how these charlatans operate, and of course I saw that Houdini fellow when he lectured in London, so I had a good idea of what to look for. To my surprise though, when we were ushered into the drawing room we found it nearly empty. Almost all of the furniture had been taken out, and there was none of the trappings that these table-rappers usually keep around them. Why, even the carpet had been rolled up and moved to the side. All that remained was a small, low table with an old brass-bound chest sitting on top.

"As you can imagine, I wasn't going to be kept standing while we waited, so I called for chairs to be brought for me and Eugenia. The help started to make some kind of silly excuse but relented when I made it clear that we would leave if we weren't properly accommodated. Several folding chairs were quickly brought in, for us as well as some of the other guests who were arriving by then. We sat there for a bit, waiting with nothing to do but make idyll chit chat or stare at the horrible old wallpaper.

"Madame Krusslov came in precisely at eight wearing these garish robes. Really she looked quite like a peacock. I must say though that she was at least punctual; it was eight o'clock on the dot. She then started nattering on about the spirit world and ancient secrets. You know the kind of thing. It's the same nonsense that all of those spritualists say. She opened the chest and took out a piece of chalk, some white candles, and a worn black book. What followed was a long, awkward time where she drew lines upon the floor, making us get up and move our chairs when we were in her way. By the time she was finished, a large part of the room was taken up by a curious thirteen-pointed figure inscribed within a circle. She walked around the figure, and at each point on the design she placed and lit a candle, and then she carefully stepped near the center and began to chant."

Charles paused while the servants took away the empty plates from the mushroom croquettes and replaced them with the fowl course, roast turkey. The guests all still seemed interested, so he continued.

"Up until this point, things had been fairly novel. None of the spiritualists I'd seen or read about had included this sort of set up in their shows, but then she disappointed me by falling back on the typical routine of standing with closed eyes, moaning and croaking. To make it worse, none of what she said was at all intelligible. I was about to walk out of the proceedings when, much to my astonishment, a strange form began to appear in the middle of the room.

"It was dark and hazy, almost as if it were made of smoke. I wondered at first if Krusslov had some kind of smudge pot hidden away beneath the floorboards, but instead of dissipating like it should, it was becoming solid right before my eyes. It took the shape of a proper demon, with horns and talons and fangs. The bottom half was still vague with shadows, but the top was as clear as day. I thought the illusion was very impressive. Krusslov had repaired her reputation as an entertainer in my eyes. I've seen tricks by the best of magicians that were nowhere near as well done, and here she'd managed such a realistic thing with an audience all around her. I assumed it must have been done with mirrors or perhaps a projector, and there was even a hint of sulfur in the air. I must admit I chuckled out loud as I made to move in for a closer look at its face. That's when Eugenia grabbed my arm, and a good thing too.

"We were at the side of the circle, and had a perfect view of both the demon and Krusslov. She'd continued her babble as the thing appeared, but she must have had her eyes closed the whole time, for when she opened them she stopped chanting and gasped in surprise. I was just about to applaud her theatrics when the thing reached out with one horribly talon-edged hand and slashed her viciously across the face. Krusslov collapsed to the floor, with blood pouring from her and pooling on the hardwood floor."

Eugenia looked from Charles to her dinner guests and saw how most of them had set down their forks. She nodded to one of the servants and they began to clear away the main course and serve the fruit in jelly.

Charles continued, oblivious. "It was at that point that the whole thing changed for me. This was no illusion, no show to reel in the gullible. The sound of Krusslov's body as it struck the ground, the smell of her blood filling the room, these I knew all to well from my experiences in the Great War. The thing before me was indeed some hell-spawned monstrosity, somehow brought into the world of light. There were people in grave peril - most importantly, my Eugenia.

"So I did what any good soldier would do; I found a weapon and attacked. The only thing readily available was the folding chair I'd been using earlier. I picked it up, stepped into the circle, and brought it down with all my might upon its head. Then the beast gave a roar that shook the room and turned its gaze upon me. I looked into its eyes and saw only cold, malevolence and murder. I was frozen on the spot, but I'm not ashamed to say it. I've held my ground in battle when others ran, so I know it wasn't fear but something more akin to hypnosis. I simply couldn't move. My limbs would not obey me. The thing lifted its arms as if preparing to strike, but as it did so it suddenly turned transparent, insubstantial. In a trice it had vanished, presumably back to wherever such things belong."

"After that it was a matter of first aid for Krusslov until a doctor could be found," Charles said.

Eugenia looked about the table and saw a wide range of reactions. Lady Elizabeth was staring, slackjawed. Millicent's face held an expression of stark disbelief. Jonathan's smile showed he thought the whole thing was some kind of strange joke. To his right, Lady Constance Mayfield, who had been silent through most of dinner, wore an impassive, almost thoughtful look.

"But surely you don't think it truly was a demon," William spoke up. "Perhaps it was a bear. I've heard some circus men dress bears up as monsters to make their shows more exciting. Madame Krusslov might have had one for her act that somehow got loose."

"Maybe so. But I've hunted bears before, and I've even had one charging me as close as we are now. That thing did not look or act anything like a bear."

Charles turned his attention to the coffee being served, and Eugenia favored him with the look she usually saved for when she thought he was being daft.

"Well, that's enough of such things," Charles said. "Gentlemen, there's a nice bottle of port in the library that I've been saving. If you'd care to join me, we'll meet with the ladies after."

The men stood, waiting for the women to leave the room before heading off themselves.

Once settled in the drawing room, Millicent turned to Lady Crampton and asked with a smile, "Eugenia, did he really fight off a demon with a chair?"

"Oh, heavens no," she replied, "although I'm sure that's how he sees it."

The others in the room relaxed visibly, and Lady Primrose let out a nervous giggle.

"So it was a bear after all," Millicent said.

"No, it truly was a demon."

"But how? Do you mean to tell me you believe such a thing is possible?"

"Not only do I believe it, but I was the one who helped Ludmilla Krusslov work out the summoning." Eugenia glanced around quickly at the others. Their expressions were a perfect mix of disbelief and rapt attention.

"I've been corresponding with Ludmilla for the past year, ever since she purchased the book from a horrid little American. You see, Arthur Spurlock was a cousin of mine.

He was a bit of an expert on the Egyptian occult, and I learned quite a lot from him before his death."

She paused for a moment to look for any strong reaction, but none came. "I am rather surprised that she tried that particular incantation though," she continued. "If the beast had gone free, it would have been positively terrible. It could have killed thousands."

Another pause and still no response, though Constance was looking thoughtful. "Well, Ludmilla never did seem particularly bright. Fortunately I knew how to deal with the thing. While Charles was making a fool of himself shouting and waving his arms about, I kicked one of the candles over to put it out, and then scuffed away a point from the ward. That broke the spell, and sent the wretched thing back home."

Still no response. Eugenia wondered if she'd ever again find someone worth talking to. She turned and gestured to the butler for a glass of sherry.

The butler turned to Lady Constance, who also accepted some sherry. She took a small sip and then said quietly, "I didn't know you were related to Spurlock. Have you read his 'De Rege Daemonum'?"

Eugenia could hardly repress her look of glee. "Oh yes," she said.

About the Author

Daniel "Doc" **Myers** writes cookbooks and short stories, a combination that has his characters well-fed. He started cooking at a young age and has spent the past dozen years seriously studying medieval cooking. He is a member of the SCA (Middle Kingdom, Barony of the Flaming Gryphon), a medieval re-creation organization, and practices his craft by cooking feasts, researching, and giving occasional lectures to those who don't run away fast enough. Daniel lives in Loveland, Ohio, with his wife and two children. He is currently employed as a database programmer, and would be happy to accept large grants of cash to start a medieval themed restaurant. His co-workers in the IT department are still quite baffled by the whole thing.

Deep Salvage

Bryan Young

"Hey, Felix. Get up here. We're picking up a faint distress call."

"From where?"

"There's a mass of asteroid debris not far from here, it's at about seven-by-six-fourteen."

Felix came up into the cockpit, sitting in the navigator's chair, right next to Elliot, his comrade and business partner. "That's not too far. Can you get a readout on the ship?"

"The signal's faint, like I told you. I'm not picking up any ID in the comm-packet."

Felix stroked his chin, taking in the star chart on his display. It wasn't too much of a detour, and deep salvage had always been the most profitable. If there were survivors aboard, it might not be worth the time. Tow jobs didn't pay much.

Elliot knew exactly what Felix was thinking, and pulled up some more information. "That beacon's been going for months. There's a pretty good chance there's no one left on board after all that time."

"Hmmm..."

"Listen, Felix, I say we head out there anyway. Even if by chance there is someone alive, we can at least pay back expenses for the sidetrack. Get something out of it. If it were me out there, I wouldn't care who showed up if my boat was lost in space. I'd pay for the rescue. And if—more likely—everyone's dead, that works out even better and we can salvage the whole damn thing."

"Fine. Get us over there. I'll gear up. What's our ETA if we leave now?"

"Not long. She's real close. Ten minutes maybe. Twenty?"

"Let me know if we pick up the ID on the ship."

"Aye, aye."

While Elliot and Felix were technically business partners and equals, there was something that went unsaid that Felix was the captain. Perhaps it was his dominant personality that seemed to work overtime to overcome his diminutive stature. He wasn't higher than a hundred and sixty centimeters and had little meat on him to speak of. His thick, black hair dangling down to his chin might have added the most weight of any feature on his body.

Elliot was taller, but no less lanky, and his hair was cropped short in a tight military cut, though he'd never served a day in his life. Together they made quite a team, balancing out each others' weaknesses. Elliot was better with the ship and the technical challenges of a two-man salvage team, Felix was better at business and making the hard decisions.

Their uniforms were identical, blue work coveralls with thick metal seals around the necks in case they had to put on their pressure helmets.

The Emerald Anvil, their ship, was a nimble vessel in her day, but had started falling apart long before her current owners came into possession of her. Her once brilliant green coat had faded to a dingy greenish-black.

In his quarters, Felix strapped his laser pistol to his hip and slung his rebreather tanks over his shoulder. He collected his gloves and fishbowl helmet and left for the airlock, where they'd be docking with the derelict craft.

The docking airlock was down a long, narrow, coffin-shaped corridor at the bottom of the ship. Felix walked down the hallways slowly, psyching himself up in nervous anticipation. He never knew exactly what he'd find on the other side of the airlock on a salvage operation.

Felix and Elliot had to be ready for anything. Perhaps the distress call was a ruse by pirates and the entire thing was an ambush. Even a ship as old and abused as *The Emerald Anvil* was worth a pretty penny on the black market.

Or what if there was a plague aboard? Or an infestation of the undead?

Once, they'd opened the airlock and were facing nothing but hard vacuum. A meteor had shot straight through their docking tunnel and sucked all the air out of their target ship.

Space was a dangerous place. Especially out here on the edge of it, away from standard routes.

The ship shuddered, almost as if it were coming in contact with something else.

"Felix," Elliot's voice came down through the comm-system. "We're here. I've started the docking procedure and set us on auto-pilot."

"Any luck with the ID?"

"No, but I did get a make and model on it. She's big, a pleasure yacht."

"A Paradise model?"

"Yeah."

"That's good. Big cargo holds. Lots of room for booty."

"My thoughts exactly. I'm not getting a reading on atmo, though."

"No air?"

"There could be. I'm not getting a reading one way or the other from here."

"All right. Suit up and come on down. Then we'll head in."

"Aye, aye."

Felix could hear the mechanical parts whirring into place all around him. Though the artificial gravity field prevented him from feeling the majority of movement, he knew that he'd been lowered into place, hooking up with the docking tube on the pleasure yacht.

Elliot had arrived behind Felix in full gear. His fishbowl and gloves already sealed to his pressure suit. His voice was a muted echo beneath the glass. "You ready?"

Felix snapped the last clasp in place on his helmet and turned dial on the side of the helmet, pressurizing his entire suit. "Ready as I'll ever be."

Opening up the control panel for the airlock, Elliot pushed three buttons and turned a dial, engaging the computer. The computer spoke over the comm system in a robotic, female tone. "Airlock depressurization in ten seconds."

Even through their helmets they could hear the machinery around them.

Felix felt anticipation welling in his chest, adrenaline coursing throughout his body. He was ready for a fight and his fingers twitched toward the laser pistol on his belt, just in case.

"Five seconds."

Felix knew that Elliot just loved the rush.

"Airlock opening."

The metal, coffin-shaped door separated at its center, sending half of the door into the ceiling and the other half into the floor. Gravity wobbled as the ship took into account the competing atmosphere in the other ship and compensated accordingly.

On the other side was blackness.

Felix shouted into the corridor. "Computer, lights."

But there was no response. If the computer on the yacht was on and recognized his command, it made no effort to comply.

Looking at the computer readout on the *Anvil*, Elliot pulled back the dial on his fishbowl. "We've got oxygen over there, no problem. Life support isn't out. No airborne pathogens detected, either. I think we're good to go."

"Gotcha."

Elliot took off the top of his helmet and his gloves, Felix did the same. If the air was good, there was no reason to be encumbered by the thick gloves and helmet.

Felix drew his pistol, taking a few cautious steps into the dark entry corridor of the foreign ship. "Hello! Anybody home?"

There was no response, expect from Elliot. "You think they're dead?"

"Let's make our way to the bridge."

"That's what I was thinkin'. If nothing else, we can check the log and the manifest. See what happened to 'em and see what's worth taking."

Opening a storage panel in the wall, Elliot pulled out two light sticks and handed one to Felix. "Let's get a move on."

With his laser pistol raised and set for stun, Felix took the lead. They took slow, cautious steps through the docking corridor on the yacht. Beams of light from their sticks illuminated their way. "It's clean here. No signs of anything out of the ordinary."

"Then why aren't the lights working?"

"We'll find out soon enough, won't we?"

Pleasure yachts were the most luxurious crafts in the galaxy, and none were more decadent than the Paradise line. They had every convenience you could ask for. It even had a food re-sequencer on board that could turn the normal protein rations found so commonly in space into just about any delicacy imaginable. The cargo bays were more often than not turned into recreation areas with holo-simulators that could make passengers feel like they were playing games out in the sun of the world of their choosing.

They were the most expensive ships in this size-class for a reason.

The docking corridor opened into the main common area on the pleasure yacht. In the dark it didn't seem as inviting and comfortable as it should. It felt eerie.

Felix swept his light across the room, revealing its details one by one. There were couches all along the back walls, and all sorts of monitors and gaming devices set up on the side wall. There were two holographic paintings above the couch and below that was a pool of violet blood . . .

"Elliot. You need to see this."

Turning, Elliot aimed his light at the trail of blood. It led around the corner toward the cargo bay.

Elliot's voice was a harsh whisper. "You think one of them went crazy and offed the others?"

"Space madness? On a Pleasure yacht? I doubt it."

Before Elliot could protest, Felix was across the common room, following the trail of blood. "Hey, wait."

They found the owner of the blood just around the corner. He was tall, broad, and of bluish skin. His head was bald and he had a face that looked more serpentine than human. Felix knew at once the species. "This is a Dracadian ship."

Elliot caught up, startled at the sight of the mangled corpse. The blood led to a deep chunk missing from his torso. "What would Dracadians be doing all the way out here? And what could do that?"

"There are a thousand things in this galaxy that could do something like that."

"But isolated out in the middle of nowhere on a Paradise class ship?"

Felix knelt over the Dracadian, looking for any clues to the possible culprit. The closer he got, the more obvious the answer became.

It was a bite mark.

The resolve in Felix grew, not letting this unnerve him. Elliot on the other hand looked shaken. Dracadians were renowned for their strength and courage in the fight. Rich Dracadians had almost always won their riches in battle. "I do not feel good about this at all, Felix."

"You said yourself the beacon's been going for months. If there was still something around here that could hurt us, it probably would have chewed the rest of this poor bastard to bits."

"Let's get to the bridge."

"Agreed." Felix used his flashlight to point back the way they came. "The bridge should be back through there."

"Lead the way."

The common room was the center of the ship and all roads led to and from there. They'd have to cross through it. There were five corridors, leading out like spokes to various destinations. "Which one?"

"Straight ahead," Felix said, pointing his laser pistol in the right direction.

"I was afraid you were gonna say that."

The corridor straight ahead had a light flickering on and off like a strobe.

"Don't be scared, Elliot. We're gonna be just fine." Felix was thinking about how much this ship could go for if they made the necessary repairs, fixed the lights, and sold it off to the highest bidder. They probably wouldn't get current market value for it, but damn near close enough, and that would be more money than they'd seen in a decade of deep salvage operations. Most clunkers they pulled in weren't good for much else but scrap. And aside from the lights and the computer, Felix hoped there was much else wrong with the thing.

Well, aside from whatever it was that ate the passenger . . .

Step after careful step, they got closer to the bridge. The strobe effect hadn't lessened, though Felix thought he could make out what was causing it. A chewed power cable dangled from the ceiling, arcing and sparking, causing the frightening white flicker. He heard the sparking like a heavy rumble in the bottom of his chest and he could smell the pungent ozone in the air.

The door to the bridge was wide open, and there didn't seem to be a sign of survivors. Each of them swept the room with their lights, looking, but nothing seemed out of the ordinary but the flickering power cable.

Comfort and automation were the two primary functions of the bridge on a pleasure yacht, so the captain's chair was obviously plush and cushy, and the monitor in front it was massive. The control interface was entirely holographic, though, a technology much more advanced than the touchscreens and keyboards found on *The Emerald Anvil*.

"There's the computer, Elliot. Tell me what happened here. I'll cover the door."

Felix turned, facing out, training his pistol down the rounded corridor. Elliot stepped cautiously toward the captain's chair, training his light on it as though some ghastly thing might materialize between him and his quarry.

Elliot reached out, spinning the chair around so he could sit in it, but it was occupied by the bottom half of the Dracation pilot. His entire top half had been chewed off. "Sweet Son of Maulnar!"

Felix snapped around. "What? What is it?"

Elliot put his hand on his heart. "I found the captain."

"Oh." Felix walked over to the chair, kicking the legs to the floor, offering Elliot a seat. "Don't be shy. He's not going to bite anybody. Find out what we're dealing with here."

Felix returned to staring out into the empty, blackened corridor. He crossed his wrists, keeping the beam of light in front of him and the pistol aimed forward against any potential harm. He tried picking up sounds not common to a ship renowned for silent running, but all he could hear was his own, even breathing and the sounds of Elliot at his back, struggling with the computer interface.

"Oh."

"What?"

"Oh, this is bad."

"Bad?"

"Yeah, Felix."

"How bad?"

"These guys have been out here drifting for just over two months, Earth standard."

"That doesn't sound bad."

"They were transporting a Dracadian brevel."

"What's a Dracadian brevel?"

"When I say Dracadian brevel, Felix, you think Earth tiger. But twice as big, twice as mean, and twice as rare. They're man eaters."

"Clearly." Felix's mind began processing the angles. "Any profit in capturing it?"

"We don't even know if it's still alive."

"Anything else on the manifest?"

"They had an entire exotic zoo in the cargo hold. My guess is the brevel got loose and ate most of the inventory, then turned to the crew."

Felix was about to say something, but the sound of a low, guttural rumble wafted into the room. He dragged his beam of light up and down the corridor, looking for any sign of pending doom. "I think it came from the ventilation system."

"It could be anywhere."

"Elliot, I think we should get out of here."

"Yeah." Bringing his own laser pistol to bear, Elliot stepped over the pilot's legs and squared up behind his partner. "What are you thinking?"

His voice grew quiet. "I'm thinking we take it slow and by the numbers. I'll go first. We head right back the way we came. No sense in dying on the job. We'll seal the hatch and be on our way. There are other derelicts out there."

"What if it gets on our ship? That thing? Think it might go through the airlock?"

Felix hadn't thought of that. If it had spent the last two months in the dark, it might be attracted to the light of their ship. "Let's not think about that." Felix was hit with dread. He wanted to stay strong as a show of courage for his partner. "Any way you can get the lights up on this yacht, Elliot? Better to see our way back."

"I tried. There aren't any lights left. I don't think our friend out there likes the light very much. Maybe it turned 'em off."

Felix took a few tepid steps into the corridor, gun raised, his thick beam of light cutting through the dark. The only movement he could see was snippets of his own shadow created by Elliot's torch.

Sweat beaded on his brow. A voice inside him, one that was usually quiet, screamed that he needed to run. But run to where?

"Did you hear that?" Elliot's eyes were wide.

"Yeah, I heard it." Felix put a finger to his lips and reached the end of the hallway. Their most difficult task would be crossing the large, open common room, with paths leading everywhere. He smirked, thinking about how easy it was to cross when they weren't worrying about a loose shoulder-high zoo creature that could bite people in half.

Felix took a deep breath and strode into the middle of the room. He took a long hard look down each corridor, as far as his light would reach, hoping to catch a glimpse of the monster so he could tag it with his laser pistol. Slowly reaching out with his index finger, he adjusted the safety on the gun, altering its power from stun to kill. He thought it was too bad it didn't have a setting for "vaporize wild beast." Kill would have to do.

Elliot had matched his pace to the center of the room, staying back to back. He shined his light into each of the corridors.

The growling returned. It didn't seem to come from any direction in particular.

Felix whispered: "Toss your light stick. The thing doesn't like light, right?"

Elliot pitched it down the flickering corridor, the brilliant shaft of light swirling end over end until it clattered at the back of the hallway.

Felix oriented himself in the direction they needed to run, then tossed his torch down the corridor where'd they'd found the first body. "Run!" Felix sprinted straight ahead, Elliot obeying orders and following closely behind him.

A deafening roar cut through the recycled air. It curdled the blood in Felix's veins. He was certain his skin had blanched white in fear. But he had reason to hope. He could see, vaguely, the light of his own ship at the end of the tunnel. The creature that clearly was pursuing them hadn't boarded their ship. But how far behind them was it.

"Agh!"

"Elliot?"

The growl grew louder.

"Elliot?" Felix ran faster as he called.

"Felix!"

Against his better judgment, Felix turned, knowing full well the creature had his partner. "Elliot?" He saw the glinting eyes of the brevel and heard a gurgling sound and something he imagined was flesh rending. The monster was eating Elliot alive.

Felix could actually feel the brevel growling, the sound coming through the floor of the corridor and up through his feet. The beast gnawed viciously on the remains of Elliot, and Felix was rooted to the spot. The monster took huge hunks of fresh meat and whipped them back and forth like a dog with a chew toy.

Hit with a spray of fluid, Felix regained his senses, snapped up the laser pistol from his hip and fired madly. It didn't matter if he hit Elliot, Elliot was dead already.

Each individual laser blast illuminated the room in a stunning azure light, giving Felix the briefest of glimpses of the brevel. In the gleaming blue flashes, the thing looked more monstrous and terrifying than he'd imagined. It stood shoulder high on all fours and seemed to be covered in a thick hide of black and gray fur. Its teeth were black and dripping mucous.

No. Felix caught himself. That wasn't mucous. That was Elliot's blood. Everything Elliot was or ever would be dripped down to the floor, off the fangs of the Dracadian predator.

Firing two more ineffective shots into the thing, Felix turned his back on the creature and he ran toward the light of his own ship.

Could Felix even hope to outrun it?

Pumping his legs, harder, faster than he had in years, he willed himself to make it to the threshold. Once he got across, he'd be able to slam the emergency hatch and leave the nightmare behind him.

But he could almost feel the hot, sour breath of the monster on his neck. It reeked with the tangy smell of Elliot's blood. The beast was too close.

Hoping to buy himself precious seconds, Felix glanced over his shoulder, pistol raised.

Time stood still.

In the dim light from *The Emerald Anvil's* corridor, Felix saw burn marks on the monster where he'd been blasted with lasers. Felix aimed for the face. Once, twice, three times, he squeezed the trigger.

It let out a sharp, wounded squeal and rocked back. But it shook off the sting and howled.

Felix had succeeded in little more than angering it. The thing came forward, just as Felix turned tail and ran across the threshold. With a clenched fist, he hit the button that would shut the airlock and guarantee him his safety...

...but the door moved at a glacial pace.

"Close! Damn it, close!

Felix continued to fire, the lasers growing weaker with each shot, his battery draining. Then the beast's maw was there, open and dark as a cave. The roar could hace shattered an ear drum.

"Close!"

The door snapped shut with a hiss as the *Anvil* re-pressurized.

It was over. The beast was shut out.

The whole ordeal was over.

Felix collapsed, tears flowing. He spent a few long moments there on the floor of the ship, sobbing gently.

He picked himself up, took in a deep breath, and made it to the bridge of his ship.

Sitting in the pilot's chair, Felix wiped the tears from his face. He'd have time to mourn Elliot later. A thought played in his head. He could certainly make a tidy profit on this little excursion.

Felix moved is hands over the controls, plotting in a course to tow the pleasure yacht into the nearest shipyard. He grimaced. Navigation had been Elliot's job.

He activated the long distance comm unit. "Outland Shipyard, this is *The Emerald Anvil*, towing a Paradise class salvage vessel inbound. I'm reading my ETA at your station as two days. Copy?"

"We read you. Paradise class, eh? I can get rid of those fast. We'll be waitin' for ya. See ya in a couple of days. Over."

Felix closed his eyes, overwhelmed. Then, quietly, "Over and out."

About the Author

Bryan Young is the author of *Lost at the Con* and is an award winning documentary film producer. He's also the editor-in-chief of the geek news and review site Big Shiny Robot! He calls Salt Lake City his home, and you can read more about his work at www.bryanyoungfiction.com.

Impression

Tracy Chowdhury

Sirion was excited. Finally his father had acquiesced to his wishes . . . he could scarcely believe they were so close. Alongside the rangers that escorted them, they walked through the Galdean Forest, a place where Sirion would find what he dreamed of—a corubis companion, a creature that would love him unconditionally.

Just barely into adolescence, Servial had taken Sirion from his home in Elvanadahar. Sirion missed his mother and sister, but he loved life with his father, where he was expected to excel at the tasks set before him. They had recently left the city of Grondor, where he had been in the midst of weapons training. However, after several mooncycles of performing so well, Sirion was being rewarded with this opportunity to pursue a companion.

One of the rangers, Donal, spoke as they walked. "There are two litters of juven ready for *impression*," he said. "Quite a few individuals have been deemed suitable, at least six. That is uncommon. Inasmuch, Samsin felt it would be acceptable for there to be an outsider or two participating in the *impression*. Your son will only have to pass the preliminary tests necessary to participate."

Servial frowned. "What tests? I wasn't made aware of any tests."

Donal shrugged. "If your son is worthy, he will easily pass them. By the looks of the boy, and the information you passed to Samsin a couple days ago, I doubt there will be any problem."

Sirion regarded both men solemnly as they turned back to glance at him. Tests. What kind of tests? Did he not have enough of those already without having to endure more to meet the corubis who would be his companion?

Sirion continued to follow behind as they journeyed deeper into the forest. It was much different than Elvandahar, the leaves on the trees shades of green instead of silver. And the trees weren't nearly as large as the massive silver oaks that dominated the forests of his home. However, it didn't bother Sirion overly much, for he still felt comfortable beneath the canopy.

It was just past midday before Donal and his accompanying rangers slowed. "The den is close, but I still need to make Samsin aware of your arrival."

Servial nodded. "Please, go ahead and do what you must."

Donal gestured one of his men forward. After speaking to the other ranger in a low voice, the man sprinted into the forest ahead of them. They waited only a short time before the ranger returned. Given a nod of acceptance, they continued. Sirion realized when they had reached the den; the opening was obscured in the mildly hilled landscape. When they approached, a hinterlean man stepped out.

"I am Samsin. It is good to have you. We don't have Elvandaharians visit very often."

Servial returned the smile. "It is good to be here. However, I wasn't aware of any tests my son would be made to undertake before he would be considered for the ceremony."

Samsin held out his hand in greeting. "'Tis really not much more than a formality. All we need is to be certain of a candidate's potential battle prowess prior to acceptance. Of course, we want to produce the best pairs."

Servial accepted the proffered arm, gripping it tightly. "But we don't belong here. Why would you even bother with such a formality with us? Truthfully, why bother having us here at all?"

"It's because we have quite a few juven this time, and not as many young hinterleans from whom they may choose. And since all of them undergo the tests, so must your son...if even just for the simple sake of 'fairness'." He shook his head and gave a humorless chuckle. "I would hate for Sirion to suffer being ostracized because he wasn't required to go through the same trials as everyone else."

Servial nodded. "All right. It's agreed. When does Sirion begin?"

Samsin nodded. "Right away." He gestured toward another man who had stepped forth from the den opening. "This is Randik. He will be by Sirion's side for much of the duration of the testing and rituals."

Servial frowned. "Are you saying that I won't have any contact with Sirion?"

Samsin nodded. "Sirion will remain apart from any outside influence until the rituals and concluding ceremony are complete. The first ritual commences when the candidates meet the corubis dams. They will reject any candidates they feel are unacceptable. A couple days later will be the *searching*. If an initial connection is made, there will be a concluding ceremony where the *impression* is made complete. During all of this you are free to reside in any of the daladins we have made available for your use. In five days we will either bring Sirion to you without a companion, or in six you will have the opportunity to watch the *impression* ceremony."

Servial put a hand on Sirion's shoulder and gave a small squeeze. "Good luck, son."

Sirion remained solemn. "When next you see me I will have a companion by my side."

It was early morning as Sirion silently stood with the other candidates. Most of them were much like him, boys in the middle of their transition into manhood. One of them was a bit older, already a man, but still young. Yet another was a girl, one who had shown proficiency for the requirements to be a good ranger. There were several female rangers with corubis companions in the Galdean Forest. Sirion had seen a few of them himself while he still lived in Elvandahar.

Sirion studied the rangers who had arrived. They were the mentors who had been working with them for the past few days as they underwent the tests and the ritual of meeting of the dams. They also aided them in becoming acclimated to the general vicinity. As Sirion soon discovered, most of the candidates had come from other regions of the forest and were unfamiliar with the surrounding territory. And as for the tests, Sirion had found them all to be quite basic.

"The *searching* will be unlike any rite you have taken part in before," said Samsin. "It will not involve sitting before a fire, drinking a special drink, or receiving a mark. Instead, you will be wandering the forest. The corubis will be set loose. You will search for them, just as they will search for each of you. When you encounter a corubis, you will exercise the training we gave you. If it is meant to be, you will walk out of these woods with a new friend at your side. If not...there is always next time."

Another of the rangers began to speak, the one known as Gondolin. "Until now, we have been by your side. We have acted as guides through the forest, mentors for the tests, and instructors who have taught you the basics of animal handling. Now you are on your own."

Sirion turned his attention to his own mentor as Randik took a turn to speak. "Of course, we can't tell you everything about the *impression* process. To do so would ruin it for you. But one thing I will say is . . . don't be afraid to reach out. These corubis are young. Right now, you all are a bit more developed than they. The juven might need some time to acclimate. You might encounter an individual only to see him or her again at a later time. Sometimes it is deliberate, that animal somehow knowing that you are the one for whom they are searching."

Samsin clapped his hands together. "Enough talk. Now is the time to begin the *searching*. You will have all day, but when the sun begins to set, you all should meet back here. Understood?"

Sirion nodded.

"Then go," said Randik.

Sirion broke away and jogged into the forest. Within moments, Sirion was far away from the others. He slowed his stride and thought of the past few days spent in

Galdea. After passing his tests and initial ritual, he had been allowed to see the young corubis for whom he would be *searching*. The underground den was vast, the walls held in place by sturdy oak beams. Every so often he could see where the packed soil crumbled away, and he imagined that it was maintained periodically by someone dedicated to the task.

The corubis lay all about the place, resting after a morning spent in vigorous activity. The afternoons would be dedicated to instruction, consisting mostly of hunting. In spite of the color and markings one would see in just about any corubis individual, Sirion could discern between the juven of the two litters. Brinda's juven all had a more reddish shade than those belonging to Galasha. They were also a bit feistier. When Sirion had voiced these observations to Randik, he noted the surprise on the ranger's face. Mayhap not many cared enough to perceive such details. After answering a few of Sirion's questions, Randik had explained that there were other young corubis around the forest, but their temperament would not make them appropriate choices for *impression*. "Not every corubis can be a companion, Sirion, just like every ranger should not share a companionship."

Sirion took himself out of his reverie and focused on the path before him. It was only then he realized he was walking in a deeper part of the wood. The trees were more abundant, and the foliage thicker, in spite of the increased competition for light, space, and water. He couldn't help feeling nervous, for he had never been lost before, at least not by himself. He and his father had gotten lost many times, but Servial had always been able to back track them to a familiar place.

Sirion cursed under his breath just as he saw something moving in the trees ahead. He stopped, waiting for whatever it was to materialize. He considered calling out, just to find out if it was another candidate, but decided to remain silent. He would find out one way or the other if he just practiced a bit of patience.

A moment later a corubis walked into view. The animal watched Sirion intently. In spite of the decreased light, he could tell it was a juven from Brinda's litter. Sirion slowly approached. Just entering adolescence, the juven was a bit gangly, the legs appearing much longer than they would on an adult. The body had yet to catch up. The head was a bit bigger too, and the feet. The tail curved over the hindquarters; it would grow larger with the thick fur that would develop over the next few years.

It was a female, the only female from Brinda's litter. Sirion smiled as he reached his hand toward the corubis. He remembered liking her right away, for she was a bit different from the others. She placed the side of her face along his palm and allowed him to run his hand along until it reached the soft fur at her neck. He scratched her there for a few moments before she turned to look him in the eyes. Then, with an expression he thought bordered on regret, she turned and melted back into the trees. She was not the one for him.

Sirion made his way for what seemed like another hour. He was definitely lost. Damnation, how could he have been so stupid? To leave the others the way he did, with no concerted effort to get his bearings? Servial would be profoundly upset when he found out.

Sirion suddenly stopped to find another corubis. The animal seemed to sense his unease but approached anyway. It was a male, the largest from Galasha's litter.

Once the beast was close enough, Sirion stretched out his hand. The corubis placed his face in Sirion's palm to take advantage of the scratching he imagined he might receive. Sirion obliged, thrusting his fingers deep into the thick fur surrounding the juven's neck. Several moments later, the corubis turned to look at him with an intense gaze and then moved away. Just like before, the connection simply wasn't there.

Sirion continued through the forest. He saw a couple more corubis moving like dappled shadows through the trees. However, they didn't stop to greet Sirion. He took a deep breath and considered his options. Either he could stay put and hope the others found him, or continue moving and hope that he found a recognizable landmark.

It was then he got the sensation he was being watched.

Sirion waited. Finally it materialized from out of the trees. It was a corubis, a juven at least several moon cycles older than the ones he'd seen previously. It was big, with an aura of wildness. He didn't recollect it as belonging to either of the litters that had been loosed.

He remembered Randik's words: "Not every corubis can be a companion..."

He held his ground as the corubis slowly emerged from the trees. The juven had been well hidden there, mayhap because of the higher contrast between his dapples and undercoat. Sirion struggled to maintain his calm as he felt his heart increase in tempo. He had no idea what the corubis might do, and the beast didn't seem to have a very friendly demeanor. Randik had told him that a wild corubis could be dangerous. Deadly. The corubis stopped in front of him, and Sirion tentatively held out his hand, palm facing to the side in a gesture of greeting from one equal to another. To have ones' palm facing up was a sign of submission, and to have the palm down was construed as dominating. When searching for a companion, neither of the latter would suffice, for the relationship between the faelin and his companion was one borne of equality.

The corubis looked at the hand and then cocked his head to the side, regarding Sirion intently. Then, satisfied that Sirion was sincere in his greeting, the corubis placed his face against his hand. Sirion felt his heart skip a beat. He sensed a kinship about the juven and sank his fingers into the pale tawny ruff. The juven leaned into the touch and after a few moments, Sirion felt himself toppling backwards.

Sirion looked up at the corubis standing over him. He saw the merriment reflected in the juven's eyes, obviously having found humor in Sirion's loss of balance. Sirion smiled when the juven came to snuffle; he wrapped his arms around the animal's neck.

Sirion had found his best friend.

Darkness fell. The flames of the central fire rose high. Across the fire sat the family and friends of the candidates. On both sides of Sirion were the six others who had found kinship with each one of the corubis juven from the litters. Every once in a while they would cast a questioning glance.

Sirion kept his eyes averted. Considering the circumstances of his return, he felt ill at ease. A patrolling ranger had noted their approach, and when he voiced an alarm, the place was suddenly a flurry of activity. It wasn't long before Samsin had come upon the scene. "You know that juven was not meant to be part of the ritual. That one is wild. Why is he now standing there beside you?" Samsin had asked.

Sirion had frowned and cocked his head at the absurdity of the question. "Would you have resisted the approach of the corubis who was intended to be *your* companion? And once the connection was made, would you have walked away? Would you have wanted to?"

Sirion had seen that the man was taken aback. Samsin was speculative for a moment before making a response. "I am not an unreasonable man. I cannot agree with this companionship, but I will allow the completion of the rite that will bind the two of you together. Beyond that, you are both free to leave and never return."

Sirion had given a curt nod. "Fine, then. I accept your terms."

Now, as he sat before the bonfire, Sirion couldn't wait to leave. He had decided that he didn't like Galdea, and the only good thing about his visit was finding his companion. Sirion would have no problem staying away, and the way he imagined it, his companion probably shared the sentiment.

The corubis were brought out to sit at the periphery, his own companion among them. Samsin, Randik, and Gondolin moved to stand before the fire. They were the epitome of solemnity. By now his father had surely heard of what had happened and he couldn't help wondering what Servial's reaction would be when they were back in one another's company.

But for now, all he needed was to get through the remainder of the ritual.

"...Sirion Timberlyn. He and the wild juven happened to meet in the forest and an unexpected connection was made. He will be the first to complete the rite," said Samsin.

Sirion stood and stepped forward. The juven did the same, and they met in front of the rangers. Randik silently took Sirion's hand and placed it alongside the face of the corubis, just as Sirion had done when they first met. "As individuals you *searched* and found one another. From this night onward, you will become one, brothers bound by love and blood," Samsin intoned.

At that moment, the juven opened his mouth, and before Sirion could react, had bitten into the flesh of his hand. It was an unexpected move, and Sirion restrained the cry that threatened to emerge. He looked at the juven accusingly... *why would he do this now? Why would he turn on me when I had thought we would be such good friends, when I thought...*

All of a sudden, Sirion felt an explosion of senses in his mind. He could feel the ground beneath padded feet, the finer nuances in the sound of the crackling fire behind the rangers, the smell of roasting ptarmigan in the air he hadn't noticed until now. Feelings of love and devotion welled up inside of Sirion and he looked into the eyes of the juven.

The emotions he felt in his mind were not his own. They were from the corubis, and it touched him to the core of his being. Tears streamed down his face and he fell to his knees before the creature. He spoke with a tremulous voice. "I am honored you have chosen me, and I will stand by your side forever."

Sirion felt the soft fur of the juven's face alongside his, and he felt complete.

About the Author

Tracy **Chowdhury** spent much of her childhood in imaginary play, fascinated by the possibility of magic and intrigued by dragons, fairies, unicorns, and other mystical beings. She holds a degree in zoology from Miami University and is co-author of two fantasy/adventure series: *Shadow Over Shandahar* and *Dark Mists of Ansalar*. She also has two short stories published in the Missing Pieces anthologies. Tracy lives in Cincinnati, Ohio with her husband, four children, and sphynx cat. Visit her website at worldofshandahar.com.

Sanction

Gregory A. Wilson

"I have an army," Shessen Zu said.

He stood in the center of the Room of Silence, arms folded rigidly against his chest, clad in the outfit of the Seven Generals: full armor of interlocking plates of darkmetal, ceremonial dagger in a leather sheath at his waist, agonizingly sharp shanto in a worked leather scabbard on the opposite side, dark crimson cloak flowing behind him. He was tall, much taller than anyone else at the Placid Temple, and his dark eyebrows stuck out over a pair of smoldering brown eyes which were fixed—as they had been for the past ten minutes—on the back of a small figure, dressed in a robe of simple brown cloth, kneeling in front of the equally small and simple Altar of Remembrance.

Jheng Yao, standing next to Shessen Zu, ran a hand through his dark hair and cleared his throat uneasily. He had expected this eventuality—as indeed he expected everything which ultimately came to pass—for two weeks now, ever since the young messenger had come stumbling into the front hall of the Placid Temple, drunk with exhaustion, staying conscious just long enough to pay his respects to the Blessed Channel Jhu before collapsing. But the message he carried, on a piece of rolled up parchment in an inside pocket of his cloak, was clear enough.

Shessen Zu demands sanction from the Blessed Channel Jhu. He is less than two days away.

Sanction, as Jheng Yao thought about it sourly, was perhaps the most irritating of words. Its literal meaning never fit with the actual situations in which it was applied. To sanction meant to approve of, to support, even to encourage, and there was very little in Shessen Zu's background which would have given the Placid Temple good reason to approve, support, or encourage him to do anything other than retire and return to a life of quiet contemplation. But Shessen Zu had left that life behind many years ago. He was all honed sharpness now, all edges and angles and points, and there was nothing for him here anymore.

Except, of course, sanction. There was that.

"I have an army," Shessen Zu repeated, his voice louder. To speak in the Room of Silence was a violation of centuries-old tradition, but then the First General had showed little interest in respecting any of the Placid Temple's other traditions to this point. He opened his mouth as if to speak again, but stopped as the small figure finally stood, with slow and great effort, and turned to face him. The small man's face was old, lined and creased like parchment upon which words had been written and rewritten countless times, until it had grown so thin that a simple breeze might break it into a thousand constituent parts, floating away on the wind. A thin white beard outlined the mouth and ran along the jaw line to the ear, while equally thin white eyebrows rounded over the eyes, their color as deep blue as the Sparkling Sea.

The figure's steady, fathomless gaze caught and held Shessen Zu's fierce one for a long moment, and Jheng Yao sensed a slight shift in the First General's posture. But before he had time to process it, the figure lowered his gaze, turned and shuffled for the exit of the Room of Silence. Shessen Zu blinked, then turned and marched after him, slow but steady, with Jheng Yao close behind.

Ever since he was a little boy, Jheng Yao had felt a sense of relief when leaving the Room of Silence. Though there was comfort to be had in the peaceful quiet of the chamber, his thoughts often ran too quickly without tasks to keep them busy. And for all his love for the Placid Temple and the edicts of the Blessed Channel Jhu, there was terror in the introspection it demanded of its adherents. There was no way to hide from oneself, after all. So Jheng Yao had been fortunate that he had found something which fit both his talents and his terrors: Scribe of the Placid Temple, the one person—besides the Blessed Channel, when he so wished it—permitted to speak within and without the temple walls. But even for him, speech was forbidden within the Room of Silence—and so he was glad to leave it, hearing the sounds of spring morning wash over him as they crossed into the courtyard: birds twittering, the reeds near the pond at the center of the courtyard rustling in the soft breeze.

The First General, of course, seemed singularly unmoved by any such considerations. Jheng Yao could practically hear his teeth grinding, the impact of his metal boots on the flat stone echoing through the courtyard as they walked along. "I will have an answer," he finally said, voice strained, as they came alongside the pond and stopped. The old man was gazing into the depths of the pond, watching with what looked like a small smile as the orange and purple carvoy fish swam to and fro below the gently rippling surface of the water, and showed no sign of having heard Shessen Zu.

"I have been—out of respect for the Placid Temple's traditions and, of course, yourself—more than patient so far," Shessen Zu said. Jheng Yao winced—using any but the old man's full ceremonial title when addressing him was a horrific breach of decorum, though he doubted very much the First General would care—but the old man still had no reaction, staring down into the water. "But that patience cannot continue. I must march in the morning, and I must have sanction by then."

Jheng Yao cleared his throat again. "Such sanction is unprecedented with so little time to consider the request, most revered First General. The Blessed Channel must meditate and pray about the possibilities, and—"

"I am not addressing you," Shessen Zu snapped, not even looking in Jheng Yao's direction. "If I desire conversation from servants I'll ask for it. The only one who can answer my request is him. And I will have that answer now, Blessed Channel." His relentless gaze bore into the old man tranquilly observing the fish. "I have an army," he said for the third time after a long moment. "You need only tell me whether you grant sanction for the army to operate as it must."

"You have an army," the Blessed Channel Jhu said, somewhat feebly, after a long pause. He looked up and smiled at Shessen Zu, who for a moment was startled into silence. "They say it is a strong army. Far stronger than any in the province, or indeed the nation. It is well trained, and highly loyal." He walked slowly to the edge of the courtyard and looked out. "And as I might have expected, it is legion."

Jheng Yao, coming alongside the First General and the Blessed Channel, gasped. In ancient times the Placid Temple had been built on a flat-topped hill with a commanding view of the surrounding countryside, and Jheng Yao had spent much of his childhood gazing out at the land beyond. To the north and south lay miles and miles of grassland, rocks and gently rolling hills, spotted here and there with a few low trees and bushes. Close by to the east stretched the border separating the nation of Yinshan from its neighbor Beisheng, so close he could see the guard towers of Beisheng standing watch over its side of the divide. And to the west the land gradually sloped upwards to the foothills and mountains which separated the narrow eastern portion of Yinshan from the rest of the country, where most of its people lived, worked and governed.

But there was more than that today. For as Jheng Yao looked to the west, he saw flags fluttering in the breeze: hundreds, thousands of them, a rainbow of colors reflecting the different provinces, principalities and villages of Yinshan—but also the dominant color of dark crimson, the chosen color of the First General. The spearheads and tall shields held by each soldier glinted in the sun, and the spear shafts waved gently to and fro like the grass on which the soldiers stood. As he stared, Jheng Yao thought he heard Shessen Zu give a small, satisfied grunt of approval.

"Legion, yes," Shessen Zu said. "The largest army ever assembled, and the most disciplined. I have personally seen to the training of the division commanders, and they in turn have drilled the soldiers until one of my divisions could wipe out any other nation's entire force." He turned to the Blessed Channel, still looking out at the army tranquilly. "And now they will have the chance to do so.

They await only your sanction; the same sanction you gave many years ago. I ask nothing I have not asked before."

The Blessed Channel Jhu's expression did not change. "Your reasons for asking have changed, Shessen Zu."

The First General stiffened at the use of his familiar name, his dark eyebrows gathered into disapproving angles. "That is not true. You of all people should know it is not true." He turned away again and gazed out on his army. "When I came here ten years ago, I was young and foolish. I knew nothing of the world or its workings—only that I needed to do something, anything, to keep Yinshan from tearing itself apart." He sighed, his eyes suddenly losing focus. "My father was old then...weak and feeble. His strength had gone, but he had the sense to send me here for counsel and learning—to become more than the young fool I was. To shape me into the leader I needed to be to restore the faith of my people." He looked back at the Blessed Channel. "And I was shaped into that leader. What I learned here made me strong enough to unify our people, to resist invasion. To become First General. I ask nothing more than the same support now."

"Ten years ago," the Blessed Channel said after a long moment, still staring at the First General's army, "you asked for sanction to protect Yinshan from invasion. You asked for sanction to repel invaders and restore the peace. And the Placid Temple gave you sanction to do those things."

"And I did them," Shessen Zu said, a slightly petulant edge to his voice. "I did what I was tasked with doing. I drove back the invaders from Beisheng. I annihilated their army. I unified our people." Jheng Yao watched as the First General lifted his angular chin into a defiant line. "I saved Yinshan, and I became First General because of it."

"That is true," the Blessed Channel said, nodding his head once in acknowledgement. "It is why we gave you sanction."

"The time is no different now," Shessen Zu said insistently. "Yinshan must grow, expand, if it is to stay unified and remain as one people. Beisheng attacked us ten years ago. They must pay the price for that attack now."

"Did they not pay the price for it then?" the Blessed Channel Jhu asked quietly.

"No," Shessen Zu replied immediately, biting off the word as he spoke it. "Too many of us paid our lives to protect Yinshan. There was no reckoning for Beisheng. The destruction of their army served only to stop their invasion. It did not render judgment on their actions."

"Such judgment," the Blessed Channel Jhu said, watching as a hawk soared overheard, making several wide circles over the numberless soldiers before flying off into the distance, "is neither yours, nor ours, nor any mortal's in the world to render. We taught you many things when you were with us, Shessen Zu. Strength, yes; will, yes." Suddenly he turned his gaze to the First General's. "But also wisdom. Humility. Most of all, mercy. The knowledge that vengeance is as fleeting as the wind which sweeps over these plains, as transient and shallow as a child's sand structure swept away by the sea. Those last lessons were far more important than the first ones, yet you seem to have forgotten them."

Shessen Zu's face worked, his features contorted to a scowl, and Jheng Yao waited for the reaction he knew was coming. "When I came here," the First General finally said, his voice a low, menacing rumble. "You taught me how to find my strength from the earth. My passion from the wind. My fury from the storm. I took those lessons and saved Yinshan. But now you have become weak, feeble...

155

like my father was." His fists clenched at his sides. "You no longer have the strength to advise the Seven Generals, nor the wisdom to keep our country safe. So I will no longer ask. I will no longer beg. Now I demand. I have an army. You will give me sanction. You will give it to me now, and I will march into Beisheng and show the world how strong Yinshan has truly become."

Jheng Yao gasped again. "You would threaten—" But the First General turned to him with such a look of murderous fury that the Scribe of the Placid Temple fell silent.

Shessen Zu stared at Jheng Yao for another moment before turning to the Blessed Channel. "I will have your answer," he said, his voice now ragged with passion.

The Blessed Channel Jhu regarded him for a long moment.

"No," he finally said.

Shessen Zu's face contorted in rage again, and his hand drew back from his hip; for a moment Jheng Yao feared he would strike the Blessed Channel where he stood. But then the hand dropped again, and the First General turned on his heel and strode away. He stopped after a few steps. "You have until morning," he said over his shoulder. "When the sun rises, I will ask again. And if you do not grant me sanction then, I will invade Beisheng anyway. Once I have brought them to heel, I will return. He looked back. "I will return, and I will level the Placid Temple when I come." Then he turned away again, and with a swirl of his dark crimson cloak he was gone.

Jheng Yao swallowed. "Blessed Channel Jhu—what can be done?"

The Blessed Channel was now looking down at the ground. With an effort he lowered himself to a sitting position, still gazing downward, and placed his hand, palm up, on the ground. A small black ant crawled onto his palm.

"Blessed Channel?" Jheng Yao said. But the Blessed Channel Jhu did not seem to notice, smiling at the black ant crawling over the mountains and valleys of his wrinkled palm. "Blessed Channel?" Jheng Yao said again, a little more insistently than was strictly polite.

"Yes, Scribe," the Blessed Channel responded at last, still looking at the ant.

"What can we do?" Jheng Yao repeated. He looked out at the First General's army, a menacing sea waiting to sweep over the Placid Temple. "Even if word could reach the armies of the other generals, and even if they could all come to defend us by tomorrow morning, the First General's army is far greater than all of theirs combined. How can we refuse him sanction?"

The Blessed Channel Jhu frowned ever so slightly as he looked up at Jheng Yao. "Because we must not grant it."

Jheng Yao shrugged his shoulders, feeling helpless. "But we will be destroyed, and Beisheng too. We cannot stop Shessen Zu."

The Blessed Channel nodded thoughtfully. "You expect that he will succeed?"

Jheng Yao nodded, somewhat surprised. "Yes, Blessed Channel. I can see no other outcome."

The old man nodded again. "Then we must be prepared for that outcome, Scribe. We will each consider it this evening. And then we will see what the morning brings." And he looked back at the ant which had made its way to his thumb and was now beginning to climb it, slowly and patiently.

That night passed poorly for Jheng Yao, tossing and turning on his simple cloth mat on the floor of the Scribe's room. His love for the Placid Temple and the Blessed Channel Jhu was fighting with his knowledge of the world, and no matter how many times he ran over the possibilities in his head, he could see no way to avoid war and absolute destruction. The First General would never relent…and the Blessed Channel would never turn from a path he had set for himself and the Placid Temple. And all for sanction, a ceremonial mark of approval which, as important as it might be to the people of Yinshan, would have no effect one way or the other on the ability of Shessen Zu's army to overwhelm his foes. Jheng Yao knew more of the ways of the world than the other residents of the Placid Temple—and he knew that no respect for wisdom or age would hold back the First General.

"There must be something words can do," he said to the heavy darkness. "There must be something I can say." But the darkness did not reply, and Jheng Yao, tears in his eyes, rolled to and fro on his mat until he finally dropped into a restless sleep filled with dark dreams and darker outcomes.

He was woken by the rays of the early morning sun hitting his face, blinding him as he opened his eyes and rolled into a sitting position. Suddenly he heard shouts and the sound of clashing metal outside, and he quickly put on his sandals before clambering to his feet and running from the room. As he descended the stairs the noise got louder until he emerged from the temple, blinking in the brilliant sunshine.

The Blessed Channel Jhu was at the edge of the temple courtyard again, staring out onto the land beyond as several monks from the Placid Temple stood behind him at a respectful distance. As Jheng Yao stopped next to the Blessed Channel, his heart sank. The First General's army was still there, but now it was positioned away from the Placid Temple, looking like the vast head of a spear pointed directly at the border of Beisheng. Sitting on a magnificent horse, armor and helmet shining in the sun, was Shessen Zu, his hand in the air; the shouts coming from his soldiers had stopped, presumably at his command. On another horse next to him was the flagmaster, holding black and white triangular flags on two long poles. After a moment, the flagmaster hoisted both flags into the air.

Jheng Yao was no warrior, but he knew well enough what this communication meant. The white flag meant yes; the black flag no.

Sanction, or no sanction.

There was a pause. Then the Blessed Channel nodded to one of the monks behind him, and as Jheng Yao looked he saw the young monk lift a tall pole resting in the grass into the air. Fluttering from the top was a black flag.

No.

A long time passed. Then Shessen Zu turned his horse away, and a horn blast echoed from his vicinity, immediately echoed by other horns in the distance. Slowly, inexorably, the army of the First General began to move away, towards the border of Beisheng. Jheng Yao felt a lump in his throat as he watched.

He heard a voice. It was quiet, but familiar. And as he looked over, he saw that the Blessed Channel Jhu had his eyes closed, his arms outstretched toward the army. At first the words were strange, foreign, but as Jheng Yao listened he began to notice a familiar pattern, reminding him of something in his studies from long ago. Something very old, something…

Then it hit him. They were familiar words after all, but in the wrong order, the wrong cadence, the wrong inflection. It was—

"Sanction," he breathed. "The words of sanction. In reverse."

As he watched, the army of the First General grew smaller in the distance…but much smaller, and much too quickly. After a few moments he saw the disciplined formations beginning to break apart, the inexorable forward push becoming confused, disjointed. The army grew smaller, its advance more disrupted, until Jheng Yao could no longer see anything but Shessen Zu on his horse. Within a minute the army was gone, replaced by the usual grassland waving softly in the gentle breeze. Only the First General remained, his horse now motionless beneath him.

Jheng Yao stared, mouth agape. After a few moments he turned to the Blessed Channel Jhu, whose eyes were open, his face looking more wizened and lined than ever. His expression was serious…even sad.

"Blessed Channel Jhu," Jheng Yao finally managed. "What did you do?"

At first the old man did not answer. But finally, as if he was only now hearing the question, he glanced at Jheng Yao. "We revoked sanction," he replied simply. "Did you not expect it?"

Jheng Yao shook his head mutely.

The Blessed Channel nodded and looked back at the empty fields below, where thousands of soldiers had stood just a minute before. "Sanction, Jheng Yao, is not permanent. It must first be earned, and then it must be kept. When Shessen Zu came to us, we taught him as best we could. Some taught him of strength, others of skill. But I taught him in the ways of mercy and humility…and I failed. I failed twice, for he did not learn my lessons, and I did not know that he had not learned them. And so when he requested sanction, we granted it to him. We gave him an army."

"From where?" Jheng Yao asked, his voice strained.

The Blessed Channel smiled. "Why, from everywhere." He motioned above, below, the sweep of his arm taking in the world around the Placid Temple. "The birds who fly, the animals who run, the insects who scurry. At the time Shessen Zu's need was great, and his motives true. So we gave him sanction, and gave him his army. We did what had to be done."

"He did not know?" Jheng Yao said, thinking suddenly of the ant on the palm of the Blessed Channel Jhu's hand.

"No," the Blessed Channel replied. "He knew only that he had sent out a call for soldiers to come to the defense of Yinshan, and day after day those soldiers came until his army was formed. So he drew strength and courage from the rightness of his cause, and he defended Yinshan and drove the forces of Beisheng back. Then he went away, and I was troubled, for though Yinshan needed to be united, I did not know if the power of the army he commanded would stir other thoughts in him." He paused for a moment, looking out at the motionless figure of Shessen Zu. "And there I failed a third time, for I thought he would eventually learn the traits of mercy and humility if he did not already have them But he became First General, and his thoughts turned to power and domination…and vengeance. When he came to us this time, he wished for our sanction to give him the moral right to wage war."

"Yet he did not know that sanction had made it possible for him to wage war at all." Jheng Yao ran a hand through his black hair. "Where did the army go?"

"Back to where it came," the Blessed Channel said, looking down at the ground.

Jheng Yao saw a black ant scurry past his sandaled feet, and nodded slowly.

"Then I understand what has happened, though for the first time I did not expect it," the Scribe of the Placid Temple said with a small smile. "But what—" He was interrupted by a horn blast, and looking up he saw the First General galloping wildly away from the Placid Temple, towards the border of Beisheng, his horn echoing over the fields again and again.

Jheng Yao looked at the Blessed Channel Jhu, and was surprised to see a single tear roll down the old man's cheek as he watched the ant. As he turned back, he saw what looked like dark rain whistling from the guard towers on Beisheng's side of the border, and a few seconds later he saw Shessen Zu's horse jerk as if it had hit an invisible wall. In an instant the First General disappeared from view. His last horn blast was cut off, replaced by a heavy, brooding silence.

For several minutes all was quiet. Finally Jheng Yao spoke. "A fool," he said angrily. "A child, and a fool. A bad student, and an arrogant—"

"Shhh," the Blessed Channel Jhu said, kneeling on the ground, watching his hand as a small black ant made its way around its lined, undulating contours. "He was the

First General. He had an army." He smiled as the ant paused at the base of his thumb before beginning its upward journey. "For a short time, he had sanction."

About the Author

Gregory **A. Wilson** is currently an Associate Professor of English at St. John's University in New York City, where he teaches creative writing, science fiction and fantasy fiction along with various other courses in literature. He has published numerous articles and book chapters on a variety of academic subjects; his first academic book, *The Problem in the Middle: Liminal Space and the Court Masque* (Clemson University Press), was published in 2007, and his first novel, a work of epic fantasy entitled *The Third Sign*, was published by Gale Cengage in 2009. He regularly reads from his work and serves as a panelist at conferences across the country and is a member of Codex, the Writers' Symposium, and several other author groups on and offline. He is currently submitting his second and third novels, *Icarus* and *Grayshade* respectively, to publishers, and has two recent short stories out: one in the ForeWord 2012 Book of the Year nominated *When the Villain Comes Home* anthology, edited by Ed Greenwood and Gabrielle Harbowy, and one in the *Triumph Over Tragedy* anthology, alongside the work of authors like Robert Silverberg and Marion Zimmer Bradley. He has three articles published in the *SFWA Bulletin* and is in the planning stages for a proposed anthology of stories considering speculative fiction and politics, co-edited by two time Hugo nominee John Helfers and with a number of well-known authors already on board. He is also the co-host (with fellow speculative fiction author Brad Beaulieu) of **Speculate! The Podcast for Writers, Readers and Fans**, a critically acclaimed show which discusses and interviews the creators of speculative fiction of all sorts and types. See and hear the details at www.speculatesf.com. He lives with his wife Clea, daughter Senavene — named at his wife's urging for a character in *The Third Sign*, for which he hopes his daughter will forgive him — and dog Lilo in Riverdale, NY. His virtual home is www.gregoryawilson.com.

Fair Game

Dylan Birtolo

Evan dropped low as a fist flew at his head. He barely managed to get out of the way as it slammed into the fence behind him with a rattle. Evan slapped his palms against the mat and pushed, springing to the side like a cat. His opponent slammed his other fist into the ground where Evan had been moments before, causing vibrations to course through Evan's legs as he rose to a standing position. The fighter narrowed his eyes and shook his fist out to the side, spraying drops of blood on the already-stained mat. He brought his hands up in front of his chest and cracked his knuckles, a sound heard above the roar of the spectators just outside the cage.

"I just have to hit you once, little man." Ty "the Hammer" Jacobs had arms that were as big around as most men's legs, and his hands resembled paws. Over half of his victories in the cage were the result of a single punch.

As Ty charged in again, Evan bent his knees and lowered his center getting ready to react. Ty led his charge with his right hand. Evan ducked under it, bringing his elbow hard into Ty's ribs. The larger man grunted and swung his left hand around at waist height. Evan sprang off his toes away from the blow. It was too close to dodge, but he absorbed most of the impact with his movement. Ty tried to press his advantage, coming in hard and fast.

The crowd cheered louder as their blood rage increased. Rather than trying to retreat, Evan pushed forward and stayed low under Ty's reach. Evan drove his fist into Ty's stomach as he passed. Ty twisted to face the smaller fighter, but Evan followed around him, keeping to Ty's back. As they turned, Evan took a few extra steps and jumped, turning to push his feet off of the cage wall. He used the momentum to push himself higher, getting his waist as high as Ty's head. He dropped down, slamming his right elbow into Ty where the neck met the shoulder.

There was a solid thud as Ty dropped to one knee. Evan rushed in and wrapped his arm around Ty's neck, trying to choke him. Ty reached back over his head, making a wild grab for Evan's face. Evan let go of his choke hold to fade out of range. Ty twisted towards him, still on one knee and rubbing his neck with his left hand. Evan jumped forward on one leg and snapped his other one around, connecting his shin with Ty's jaw. The larger man's head snapped to the side, forcing him to put his hand down on the mat to stay upright. Evan landed several blows in quick succession until Ty dropped to the mat.

The roar was deafening as Evan stood over his vanquished opponent and lifted both hands toward the ceiling. He turned in a slow circle, basking in the attention of the crowd. The announcer could barely be heard through the speakers as he announced the victor. After a full revolution, Evan dropped his hands to his side and took several deep breaths.

At his feet, Ty rolled onto his back and looked up at Evan with glassy eyes. Evan smiled and offered his hand. Ty took the offering, and Evan helped pull the other warrior to his feet. Evan clapped his opponent on the upper arm before giving the crowd a final wave and walking out of the cage.

Evan walked into the locker room, picking up one of the small towels sitting on the table in the corner. He grabbed his bag from his locker and slid it under the bench in the middle of the room. As he sat, he began wiping off his sweat. After mopping his face, he noticed red trails left behind on the dingy fabric. With a deep breath, he leaned forward and hung his head between his knees. Blood pooled at the tip of his nose and dropped to the floor leaving a small splash. He didn't look up as Cal walked into the room. Cal had a large grin on his face as he walked over and clapped Evan on the back.

"You were amazing in there, Evan! The other guy couldn't even touch you!"

Evan wiped his face again with his towel and looked up, "What can I say? All that fighting in the backyard with you must finally be paying off."

"Just trying to keep you alive, buddy."

"You must be doing something right then. I'm still here." Evan had a smile on his face as he stood. "I'm going to hit the showers. I can't wait to get home and crash."

Cal's face changed to an expression of concern. "You alright, Evan?" He brushed his nose with the back of his fingers and nodded at Evan. "You've got some blood there."

Evan reached up and wiped his face again. "Yeah, he must have got me."

"I thought he never touched you."

Evan shrugged.

"You've got some here too," Cal reached up and pointed his face on either side of his nose. "You're bleeding from your eyes, man."

Evan turned away as he brought the towel up to clean himself. "It's nothing."

Cal reached out and caught his friend's shoulder, turning Evan to face him. "It's not nothing. What the hell is going on?"

Evan sat on the bench with a sigh. "It just happens sometimes."

"How long has this been happening? Is it a concussion?" Cal sat as well. "You've been fighting for a while. It could have been any one of the hits to the head."

There was a pause as Evan stared into the distance and Cal stared at his friend.

"Come to think of it," Cal said slowly, taking his time with each word. "You've never taken a hit to the head, have you?"

"Not really, no."

"How the hell is that possible? You're good, but no one's that good."

There was another lengthy pause.

"If I tell you, it's just between us."

"Hey, you know you can call me to help you bury the bodies."

"Well, for as long as I can remember, I've had this ..." he trailed off, searching for the right word. He reached up and checked his face again, but it seemed as if the bleeding had stopped. "I guess you'd call it a trick. When something happens, I can see it happen and then go back to right before it."

Cal glowered. "Seriously, man. What's wrong?"

Evan tossed the towel into a corner of the room and shrugged. "You asked, and that's the truth."

"So you're saying you can go back in time."

"Yeah, whatever, I'm going to hit the showers." Evan stood up and tried to walk past Cal. Cal jumped up and stopped him with his hand on Evan's chest.

"Look, you can't expect me to believe that. Why don't you tell me what's really going on? And what does that have to do with the blood?"

Evan went over to his bag. He opened the small pouch on the end and pulled out three dice. He handed them to Cal who raised a single eyebrow in response.

"Roll them, right here on the floor."

With a shrug, Cal bent low and casually tossed the dice in front of him.

"Six, two, three." Evan said as the dice tumbled, pointing to each one in turn.

When they came to a rest on the cement floor, they showed the predicted numbers. Cal looked at the dice and then looked up at his friend. "Weighted dice?"

"Try again."

Cal picked up the dice and shook them for several seconds in his hand. He stared at his friend as he tossed them to the ground. Evan never looked away from his friend's gaze.

"Four, five, two."

Cal looked down and watched the dice. When they stopped, Evan was right with his predictions. Cal snapped his head up, eyes wide.

"Holy…" was the only word to escape his lips.

Evan placed the tips of his fingers against his head and winced. A new drop of blood formed in his left eye and started to leave a trail down his face.

"You okay?" Cal asked.

"Yeah, I'll be fine. It just hurts when I do it sometimes."

"How does it work?"

"Well, it just happens. Like when Ty was about to hit me, I went back and changed what I was doing so he'd miss."

"Holy crap, you've got to be kidding. You mean you could go back to the start of the fight and do it all over again?"

Evan shook his head and snorted. "Not even close. I think the most I've ever tried to go back was about ten seconds. I blacked out and woke up in a pool of my own blood. Not to mention feeling hung over worse than you were that time in Reno."

Cal winced at the memory.

"Anyways, I used to be able to do it for a second or two. But after that experiment, I can barely get any time at all; just enough to change some small stuff."

"Why are you wasting this gift in the ring?"

"What else could I possibly do with it? We're talking such little time."

Cal shrugged. "What about craps tables?"

Evan grinned. "I did think about it, but there's not enough time to go back and set bets. Not to mention, I don't think they'd like me bleeding all over their fancy tables."

"And they'd kick you out when they caught on to you."

"Exactly. So, can I go shower now?"

Evan leaned against the bus shelter, his arms crossed. He rested his chin against his chest to keep the wind from biting his exposed neck. The sound of crunching snow came from all around him as people walked down the sidewalk. He saw his bus coming down the street and gradually slow to a stop. As the door opened, Evan stood beside it and held out his hand to help a woman get onto the bus. She thanked him as she made her way to a seat. Evan climbed up after her and scanned his bus pass. He sat down a few rows behind the driver and stared out the window.

The bus was fairly empty this late in the evening. The streets were also largely deserted, most people opting not to brave the winter storm and treacherous roads. The bus made good time as it sped past several stops without slowing to pick up or drop off passengers. Evan idly traced some designs on the window in the condensation.

A sudden lurch threw him against the seat in front of him with a solid impact as the bus driver slammed on the brakes. Evan heard the tires lock and grind across the snow and ice on the roads. The bus hit something and Evan heard a sickening crunch over the sounds of the sliding vehicle. He pushed himself off the seat and looked through the windshield. Two limp bodies slid through the snow, illuminated by the headlights.

Evan clenched his jaw and moved backwards. His head felt like it would explode as he lurched through recent events in reverse. His body moved of its own accord, backing through the motions it had just taken. His teeth ground together so hard he thought they would shatter, but he forced himself to go back further. The street lights passed the window as the bus drove in reverse, until it was a block away from the impending accident.

With a gasp, Evan released his grip on the flow of time. Blackness crowded in around the corners of his vision with alarming speed. Closing his eyes, he forced himself to reach up to the cord hanging on the wall above the seats. It felt like he was trying to summit a mountain. With a grunt, he lurched, getting close enough to curl the tips of his fingers over the cord. As his body dropped to the floor of the bus, he heard the telltale bell indicating a request for a stop. From somewhere in the back of his consciousness, he heard a scream.

Evan sat on the bench of the locker room wrapping tape around his hands. Even this far removed from the ring, he heard the crowd making noise. Cal sat next to him, his hands laced together under his chin and his elbows resting on his knees. Evan went through his routine with very deliberate motions as he got ready for his upcoming bout.

"You sure you want to do this?" Cal asked.

Evan forced a grim smile, curling up one corner of his mouth. "Not really. But it's not like I have much of a choice, now do I?"

"You could always forfeit."

Evan put his arms down on the bench and turned to look at his friend. "I do that, and I'll lose everything 'cause of breaking my contract. That's if I'm lucky. If I'm unlucky, some guy with no neck shows up to break my legs." Evan took a deep breath. "Besides, even if I lose, it's a championship. The take might be good enough to retire."

"And you're too damn proud to step down."

Evan chuckled. "I suppose that's true too." He finished wrapping his hands and wrists. He flexed them several times, and then clapped his hands together.

"Are you sure it's gone?"

Evan shrugged.

"Have you even tried? That guy out there could pound you to a pulp."

"No, I haven't. Ever since I woke up in the hospital, just thinking about it gives me a headache and my nose bleeds. Looks like we get to see how much those sparring rounds paid off."

Looking up at the clock, Evan took one final deep breath before pushing off the bench and bounding to his feet. He turned and offered a hand to Cal. Cal took it and stood next to his friend. He clapped him once on the shoulder, and the two of them walked to the door leading to the ring. The crowd was deafening as they opened the doors. Evan kept his chin high and lifted his arms as he strode toward the arena.

About the Author

Dylan Birtolo has always been a storyteller. No matter how much other things have changed, that aspect has not. He currently resides in the Pacific Northwest where he spends his time as a writer, a gamer, and a professional sword-swinger. He has published a couple of fantasy novels and several short stories in multiple anthologies. He has also written pieces for game companies set in their worlds and co-authored a gaming manual. He trains with the Seattle Knights, an acting troop that focuses on stage combat. Endeavoring to be a true jack of all trades, he has worked as a software engineer, a veterinary technician in an emergency hospital, a martial arts instructor, a rock climbing guide, and a lab tech. He's had the honor of jousting, and yes, the armor is real—it weighs more than a hundred and twenty pounds. You can read more about him and his works at www.dylanbirtolo.com.

Merchant: Market

Story One of Bundle One of the Terrene Chronicles

R.T. Kaelin

7th day of the Turn of Sutri, 4973

The marketplace buzzed with a chaotic, urgent energy.

On the first Seventhday of each turn, the great bazaar at Deepwell in Thimbletoe Province drew patrons from all over, making it one of the better-attended trading posts in the Five Boroughs. Today's crowd was no exception. In fact, by Nundle's estimation, the crowd this day was a bit larger than normal as the first selections of summer produce were now available.

Close to a thousand figures scurried in the sun-soaked market, hurrying from stall to booth, pausing to inspect the goods on display, and—if the merchant was lucky— haggling over merchandise and price. The bulk of those moving through the rows of booths were tombles, of course, but a number of tall longlegs from Cartu wandered the market as well. A singular saeljul had wandered through earlier, causing a bit of excitement in Merchant's Row.

It had been early in the morning—the hazy fog had yet to burn off—when the ijul had wandered down the way, past Nundle's stall. Nundle had done his best to interest the visitor from Jularrn in a long-term contract for shipments of red apples from Alewold. The pale, blond ijul had ignored his pleas, wearing a scornful expression while moving past Nundle's stand. Unfortunately, the exchange had been a harbinger of what Nundle's day would be like.

Midday was nigh and a thoroughly dejected Nundle sat on his three-legged stool, staring at the passersby ambling past, no longer trying to encourage them to stop. He let out a long, exhausted sigh, tilted his head back, and rested it on the riverstone wall behind him. The brilliance of the sun hanging high in the cloud-dusted sky forced him to shut his eyes.

For at least the fifth time since morningmeal, he wondered if he should just close his stall and go home. The day was too nice to waste being miserable. Summer was almost over; harvest was just around the corner. Perhaps a nice afternoon of fishing would be time better spent. Of course, then his already floundering trading business would spiral even further into obscurity.

Nundle ran both hands through his wild red hair, pulling at it in frustration. He hated what had become of his enterprise.

"Rough day?" asked a friendly voice.

Opening his eyes, Nundle studied the tomble who stood before him. Thick, curly black hair sprung out from a round head, framing rosy cheeks, spring-mud-brown eyes, a bulbous nose, and a mouth much too small for the large face. Most everyone muttered quietly that Bom

Whipplerock was unusual looking. Nundle suspected Bom would agree with them.

Nundle shook his head in dismay as another frustrated sigh seeped from his lips. "So far, I have arranged for a single shipment of Garno's summer squash and two crates of his turnips to an inn just over the border in Cartu."

Bom was quiet for a moment, most likely waiting for the rest of Nundle's sales. When none came, he asked, "That's all?"

Sticking a finger through a hole in his breeches and scratching his knee, Nundle replied, "It's been a very rough day."

Sympathy washed over Bom's face. "I'm sorry, Nundle. Truly, I am."

Nodding his head, Nundle said, "I know you are, Bom." He could not keep his misery from his voice. Nor did he care to try anymore.

Bom took a step closer, nervously inspecting his finely cut, blue vest and fashionable white cotton shirt. "Perhaps I could send a prospective buyer over in your—"

"No," interrupted Nundle with a firm shake of his head. "I will not take charity. Thank you for the offer, though. It is quite kind of you."

Bom was one of the more successful merchants in Deepwell and had been a friend to Nundle the past few years, trying to teach him the intricacies of trading. Either Bom was a bad teacher or Nundle had been a poor student.

Crossing his arms, Bom said, "I know you don't want to hear it, but I will make the proposal again."

Since last harvest, Bom had been making overtures to purchase what remained of the business Nundle had inherited from his great-uncle, even offering Nundle future employment.

Nundle stood from his stool. "Please don't. After today, I might be tempted to accept." Despite his troubles, Nundle could not imagine selling. It would be an admission of his utter failure as a merchant.

Eyeing him carefully, Bom nodded once. "I suppose I understand."

As Nundle started to move past Bom to the front of his booth, he glanced into the crowd and froze upon seeing a familiar figure milling about the market. "Uh-oh…"

Julo Hinglegrog wore a calf-length, sky-blue dress with faded orange bows pinned to her shoulders. She carried a plain satchel with two long loaves of what appeared to be three-grain bread sticking out. Her rich auburn hair was pulled back tight, tied into two long braids that looped back around to the top of her head. She was eyeing the various commodities and items displayed for sale, seemingly oblivious to the wary stares, quiet whispering, and hushed pointing by the local Deepwell citizens. Visitors from afar, however, paid no attention to the pretty tomble female.

Sensing something was wrong, Bom turned to look the direction in which Nundle stared. He let out a low whistle and muttered, "Quite brazen of her to come to town today. With the crowd and all."

Nundle nodded. "Yes, it is. The Custodian will not be pleased." Custodian Cullop obsessed over these market days, trying to ensure nothing would interfere with the commerce.

With his gaze never leaving Julo, Bom muttered, "I wonder if he knows she's here?"

Before Nundle could respond, Julo glanced in their direction. The pretty tomble's lips began to turn up into a smile before she caught herself. The grin arrested and turned wistful as her gaze locked onto Nundle. For a moment, he considered diving for the cover of his stand, but figured hiding was no use. She had already seen him.

A determined expression fixed itself on Julo's face as she turned and began to stride straight toward Bom and Nundle. A flicker of panic danced in Nundle's stomach.

Placing a hand over his mouth to hide his words, Bom mumbled, "Being seen with her is *not* good for business, Nundle."

Covering his own mouth, Nundle hissed, "I know." Unfortunately, short of turning and running down the street, his options were limited.

Julo halted a few paces from the pair, nodded once, and said primly, "Hello, Nundle. It has been a long time." She ignored Bom entirely, which surely made the older tomble happy. Out of the corner of his eye, Nundle saw Bom meander away, pretending to inspect the signs posted on Nundle's stand. At least a dozen nearby vendors and market-goers were staring at him and Julo. Nundle felt every pair of eyes.

Nundle nodded and said evenly, "Hello, Julo. It has been awhile."

Julo eyed him expectantly, waiting, almost yearning, for him to say something more. Regretfully, Nundle did not. And he felt terrible for his silence. He would have preferred to be much more polite, even sociable with her. Julo had once been a close friend. A very close friend. There had even been a time, years past, when he had thought they would marry. That could never happen now.

A small, disappointed frown touched Julo's lips. With a crisp, formal nod, she said softly, "I see the way of things." Her expression danced between melancholy and stubborn pride. "I had hoped you might come to accept me over time." Sorrow beat out her composed dignity as her eyes glistened with unshed tears. "I thought you were different."

While Nundle wanted to say a hundred things, all that felt safe was a quiet, "I'm sorry, Julo. Truly."

"Yes, Nundle Babblebrook, you are." She pressed her lips together and gave him a curt nod. "I'll be on my way, then."

Before he could respond, the auburn tomble turned and started to walk away, her blue dress swishing as she padded down the dirt street. Watching her stride away, Nundle muttered to himself, "Be well, Julo..."

Once she was a dozen paces away, Bom stopped staring at the uninteresting signs, returned to his side, and leaned close. "You would do well to keep her at a great distance. Tombles like her are a bad sort."

Nundle's eyes narrowed at Bom's critical tone. "Tombles 'like her?' What does that mean?"

Eyes darting about the marketplace, Bom whispered, "You know. Mages."

"Why are you whispering? Everyone saw her here."

Bom shrugged his shoulders. "I don't know."

Nundle gave a sad shake of his head and stared back to Julo's retreating form. "Mage or not, Julo is a good soul." He looked over to find Bom gawking at him as if he said the sky was green.

"Nundle, good soul or not—"

Interrupting his friend, Nundle grumbled, "Bom! I don't want to talk about it."

Thankfully, Bom remained quiet as Nundle moved to stand in front of his small booth and stare at the meager presentation. As his dwindling list of suppliers had been reduced to farmers dealing in yet-to-be-harvested produce, his display was embarrassingly bare. Instead, his stand was covered with a number of hand-painted signs proclaiming the future availability of his goods. One read, *"Plump, Tasty, Turnips – Perfect for stews, spicing, or baking – soon!"* while another proclaimed, *"Sugarblue Potatoes! Best in all of Alewold! Soon!"* The only tangible sample he had was a bound bunch of dried smoking-leaf hanging from the sprawling sign that stretched across the two front posts of his booth. Nundle stared at the black sign covered with large, red block letters, trimmed in white, announcing the stand as the *Babblebrook Mercantile Company*. It was all he had left from the two-story shop his great-uncle had left him.

Nundle shook his head, let out a weary sigh, and whispered, "I'm so sorry, Uncle Huber…"

As he stared upward, it seemed as though the sign were mocking him. He had never felt more like a failure than at this exact moment. He had no idea why his great-uncle had left his business to him. Nundle was a terrible merchant.

"I'm done for the day, Bom."

"Done?" Bam moved to stand beside him. "You have the afternoon left, Nundle. Don't give up. Trust me. Huber had periods of trouble, too."

Nundle let a derisive chuckle escape. "Six years of ever-decreasing sales is not a 'period,' Bom."

Bom gave him a sympathetic look, but remained quiet. Nundle supposed he had run out of encouraging things to say.

He listened to the noise of the market behind him, the hum of hectic commerce poking at him, teasing, and jabbing at his ego. A fateful shift in the wind brought with it the heady aroma of savory herbs mingling with some hearty meat stock wafted past. Nundle's stomach gurgled. He huffed, trying to push the odor back out of his nose. As he could not afford to buy any, there was no use in smelling it.

Bom made it difficult to ignore the smell of an excellent meal, however, drawing in a deep breath followed by a satisfied grunt. Swiveling his head in the direction of the Smiling Snake Inn, he exclaimed hungrily, "Gods, that smells good. Smells like Joscoe's rosemary stew."

"I did not notice," lied Nundle.

Bom stared at him with wide, incredulous eyes. "How could you not? Take a deep breath. It is fantastic!"

He shrugged as if to say he could not help it. "I'm getting over an illness. My nose is stuffy." In actuality, he felt fine.

Bom studied him quietly for a moment, before he nodded slowly, accepting Nundle's answer. "Ah…well, then…"

Wanting to forget about the incredibly scrumptious-smelling stew, Nundle began the process of tearing down his stand, reaching up to grab the turnip sign off its hook. As he shuffled over to grab the potato sign, a dark shadow fell over him, accompanied by the sound of boots scuffling the pebbles and dirt behind him.

"Are you closing for the day?" asked an unusually deep voice, too deep for the question to belong to a tomble. Figuring that it was a longleg, Nundle pulled his hand back from the sign and was about to say he most certainly was closed.

Bom, however, whirled around and interjected, "Not at all, good sir. Merchant Babblebrook is most certainly open for business."

Nundle rolled his eyes. He had no interest in negotiating now. He wanted to go fishing and forget today.

"Good," replied the longleg.

With a reluctant sigh, Nundle turned around and stared at the shiny, silver belt buckle of his visitor. Most longlegs —or "men" as they called themselves—towered a few feet over the Boroughs' tombles. This one was no different.

Tilting his head back, Nundle tried to examine the prospective client's face, but was frustrated by the sun's halo of bright light behind the longleg's head. "May I help you?"

"Perhaps," replied the trader. Lifting his arm, he pointed at the hanging bunch of smoking-leaf. "What cut is that?"

A slight tickle of anticipation ran up Nundle's spine. The individual was interested in something he had in stock. Standing up straighter, Nundle said, "Sweetbush, sir. One of the finest in the Five Boroughs."

"Oh, I am quite familiar with Sweetbush, little merchant. How much can you get me?"

As Nundle was about to reply, Bom took a series of quick steps back, away from the stand, saying, "If you will excuse me, I have my own business to attend to." Bowing slightly to the longleg, the tomble said, "Happy travels, sir. Be well." The longleg grunted, more interested in the smoking-leaf than returning a polite farewell. As Bom passed the trader, he turned and gave Nundle a wide, encouraging smile before hurrying east along Merchant's Row.

The trader stepped into the space Bom had occupied and leaned down to sniff the dried bunch of Sweetbush leaf. Nundle studied the longleg closely and concluded his client to be from eastern Cartu. His skin was tan, his features sharp and severe, and he wore his dark brown hair in the manner most Cartusian longlegs did: braided and bound in colorful rope. A dark blue cape hung from his shoulders, almost reaching to the ground and covering simple brown, traveling clothes and metal-studded boots.

After drawing in a lungful of the leaf's pleasantly sweet aroma, the longleg stood tall, with a satisfied expression affixed on his face. As the longleg shifted upright, Nundle caught a glimpse of silver metal beneath the cloak and spotted the hilt of a long dagger. A frown crossed his face.

With a smile, Nundle asked, "Might I have your name, sir?" The question was not borne of politeness. Nundle simply wanted the name of the longleg with the weapon who was wandering around the Deepwell market.

Fingering the smoking-leaf, the tall trader said absentmindedly, "You may call me Ervan."

Nundle figured the chance was slim that was the longleg's true name. Nevertheless, he smiled wide. "A pleasure to meet you, Mr. Ervan, sir. I am Nundle. Nundle Babblebrook."

Ignoring the introduction, Ervan turned an appraising eye to Nundle. "How much of the leaf can you provide?"

The prospect of a sale overrode Nundle's concern about dagger. Trying to beat back the hope threatening to intrude upon his dreary morning, Nundle asked, "By what measure, sir? Cartusian bundles or Borough rolls?" His great-uncle had taught him to open negotiations with such a question in an attempt to gauge the other party's experience in trading.

"Either," replied Ervan with a knowing smirk. "I am quite familiar with both. Ijulan cords work as well. Or perhaps Yutian rings?" He fixed Nundle with a hard gaze and lifted a single eyebrow. "Choose whichever is most convenient for you, Master Merchant."

Nundle's flicker of hope winked out. He had no idea what a Yutian ring was.

With a tiny, resigned sigh, Nundle said, "I have just over fifteen bundles available today. I get another ten next week." It was a significant amount of smoking-leaf. Regular orders typically were for only a bundle at a time. Two weeks ago, Nundle had made the mistake of overbuying an allotment of the Sweetbush cut, committing a large portion of what little he had left in the company's coffers to the purchase. He had expected it to sell better than it had.

The longleg nodded slowly, frowning and pensive. Staring at the bunch hanging from the booth, he said, "Twenty-five, eh? Truthfully, I could use more."

Nundle's eyes grew wide. He was flabbergasted the longleg was willing to buy so much. "I could possibly arrange for more, sir. How much are you looking to acquire?" He did his best to hide his surprise.

"Assuming we can agree on cost, I would take all twenty-five you mentioned. And I'd like another eighty if possible."

"Eighty?" exclaimed Nundle, unable to help himself. "Are you jesting?"

The longleg must be one of the largest dealers in Cartu to want a shipment of such size. Nundle openly gaped at the trader, fully aware that he was giving away his anxious excitement, but he did not care. If Nundle could sell over a hundred bundles of smoking-leaf at any sort of respectable markup, he would make an excellent profit.

Ervan smiled, clearly confident that he had the upper hand now. "I am not jesting, little merchant. Can you meet the order?"

Thinking through his list of potential sources for more Sweetbush, Nundle slowly said, "I believe so, Mr. Ervan." In all honesty, Nundle was not sure. He thought if he called some of the last favors others owed him, it might be possible. "It might take two weeks, though, for the eighty bundles to arrive here."

Nodding, the Cartusian trader said, "I suppose that is an acceptable time. Now, I can offer you..." He paused, seeming to consider a price. Nundle guessed the longleg already knew what his bid was going to be. Giving a firm, decisive nod, Evan said confidently, "Thirty silver rounds per bundle would be a fair rate, I think."

Nundle stared at the merchant, mouth open. Ervan might as well have punched Nundle in the stomach. "Thirty silver?" He had paid forty per for the stock he had now and severely doubted that he could obtain the extra eighty the longleg for anything less than fifty silver rounds per bundle.

"That's my offer, Merchant Bumblebook," replied the longleg firmly. "Take it if you like."

Perturbed, Nundle said, "The name is Babblebrook." He leaned back and pointed to the large and obvious black sign immediately in front of Ervan's face.

The man glanced at the sign. "Oh. So it is."

Nundle waited for an apology or correction, but none came.

Summoning the courage to negotiate a price so he might be able to eat for a few weeks, Nundle said, "I cannot accept anything less than forty-five silver rounds for a bundle. And that price is only good for what I can provide today. The price for any of the rest will be sixty-five per."

Ervan smiled widely at the stated amounts. "You are trying to raid my purse, little merchant." Smirking at the meager stand and Nundle's old, tattered clothes, he added, "I would think you would be anxious for the sale."

Angry at what the man was inferring—no matter how true it was—Nundle declared, "A *sale*, yes. But you are asking me to donate to your enterprise, *Mr. Ervan.*" Nundle twisted the man's name to show he did not believe in the authenticity of the moniker. "I run a business, friend, not a charity."

Holding up his hands in protest, Ervan smiled. "Fair enough. You drive a tough bargain. Your shrewdness had persuaded me to pay a flat rate of forty—for the first hundred bundles of Sweetbush smoking-leaf you could provide. And I expect the last five for free in exchange for the purchase I am making today."

Gritting his teeth, Nundle said sharply, "You, sir, are a highwayman." All politeness was gone from his tone. Six years of ruining his great-uncle's great business weighed heavily on Nundle. One failed venture after another had stacked up over the years. "Should you continue to try to take advantage of me, I will report you *directly* to the Custodian." Leaning forward, he hissed, "Weapons are not allowed within the marketplace, as I am sure you know."

Ervan glared at him with narrowed, critical eyes. "I would advise you do not try to do something so foolish, Master Merchant Rabblebook." He bent over, letting his cloak fall open to reveal the beltknife again, and murmured threateningly, "I am offering you a good deal. I suggest you take it."

Nundle felt a flash of fear, but it was beaten back by his years of frustration. "I will not be bullied into a sale, *sir*."

Ervan frowned and cocked an eyebrow. "Fine, then." Standing tall, he turned to look across the open market, and said, "On my way to your stall, I came across another tomble promising me a good cut of Oldfire Downs leaf for thirty-eight per bundle." He looked back to Nundle. "Forty certainly seems fair to me for your Sweetbush."

Beyond frustrated, Nundle shouted: "You're mad! Oldfire leaf tastes like burnt shoe-leather!" Comparing the two cuts was like comparing a cup of weak, cheap lager to a cool pint of full-bodied, red summer ale.

Nodding in agreement, Ervan said, "Perhaps it does." Crossing his arms, the longleg sighed. "I mean no offense, little merchant. You are a much craftier bargainer than I had assumed you to be."

Nundle bit his lip and said nothing in response. Undercutting had not worked for the longleg. Neither had threats, both personal and business. Here came the flattery.

The trader grinned and said magnanimously, "I will give you, one of the best negotiators I have met in some time, a full forty-four per. Flat rate. You, however, will be responsible for all delivery costs."

Nundle's eyes narrowed in suspicion. "Where is delivery?"

Ervan's confident grin faltered a moment. In a quiet voice, the longleg said, "Harmony."

"Harmony?" laughed Nundle. "The capital of Cartu?" His eyes went wide as he stammered, "It's... you...why, you are...bless the Gods, I should..." What Ervan had offered was worse than his first proposal. It would cost Nundle a fortune to ship the smoking-leaf across the border and to the foothills of the Yaubno Mountains.

Nundle's immense aggravation, held in check for years and hidden behind countless polite smiles, pleading entreaties, and humble apologies, finally burst. Nundle glared at the trader, wishing for once that something would go right for him.

Suddenly, a single, honey-gold string popped into view before Nundle, hovering a few feet before him. Nundle's eyes opened wide as he stared at the long strand of energy, rippling and twisting before him. It glowed and pulsed, beckoning to him. Nundle's eyes went round as he took a single, surprised step back.

The trader stood on the opposite side of the string, continuing to smirk at Nundle, seemingly oblivious to the golden strand hovering between them. Nundle stared up and down at the shimmering gold strand, running his gaze along its length, but never could find an end.

Nundle blinked a few times and rubbed his eyes, convinced he had lost his sense.

Suddenly, more of the additional bright, golden ropes of energy popped into existence and quickly surrounded him, causing him to jump back suddenly and shout, "Ah!" He stared about as each string appeared, spinning around in a frantic circle. By the time he whipped around to find the Cartusian trader gawking at him, he had counted over a dozen strings around him.

Visibly unnerved, Ervan tilted his head forward. "Are feeling all right, little merchant?"

Nundle ignored the longleg's question. He panicked, wanting the little ropes of golden energy to go away. The moment he thought about shoving them away from him, the strands began to move, twisting and twirling together. The more he struggled with them, the more they interwove themselves. Nundle reached out with his arms, physically trying to push the strings away but his hands passed right through them. He tried again and again.

"Go away!"

As he flailed about, trying to force the strings to go away, he realized his panic was causing the strands to fall in upon one another, knitting themselves together into a sort of pattern.

Ervan took a slow step back. "Master Babblebrook…? Are you ill, sir?" There was no tradesman posturing in his voice. The longleg sounded genuinely concerned. Or afraid.

Nundle stared at the strange pattern of gold strings and willed them to go, 'throwing' them away from him. He watched in horror as the bundle of honey-colored strands collided with the trader, sinking into the longleg's chest. Horrified but what he had done, Nundle shouted, "Oh! Gods! I'm so sorry!"

The trader stared at Nundle with worried, guarded eyes. He appeared entirely unaware and unaffected as the weave of gold strands simply faded into his body, slowly disappearing.

Nundle gaped at Ervan, expecting some sort of reaction, violent or otherwise.

Yet nothing happened. Nothing at all.

A long moment of quiet settled between the two even as the quiet bustle of market business continued about them. A few of Nundle's neighboring vendors were left staring at Nundle after his antics.

Clearly nervous, Ervan asked, "Shall I fetch a healer?"

Nundle's eyes darted about, searching for the strings of gold. Spinning around, he looked behind him, up in the sky, and down on the ground. Any evidence of the glowing strands of energy was gone. He was beside himself with bewilderment.

Upon facing the trader, Nundle said carefully, "I...don't think that's...ah...I'm simply a..." He trailed off, shaken by the experience. He did not dare share what he had seen. Others would name him mad. He noticed the tomble at the next stall over—a rude tomble named Doffer, a purveyor of quarry stone and uncut gems—was staring at Nundle with unconcealed disdain. Nundle frowned, knowing that Doffer was sure to tell everyone about his mad behavior.

Ervan took another hesitant step backward. "Perhaps I will go. I can find another to trade with." The Cartusian began to turn, preparing to walk away and take Nundle's best prospect in weeks with him. The threat of more failure trumped his wonder and confusion concerning the strange meshing of strings he had just witnessed.

Staring at the back of the trader's blue coat, Nundle pleaded, "No! Please stop!"

Nundle was stunned when the longleg froze in mid-step, one boot heel off the ground. He waited for Ervan to either continue or turn back, but the longleg simply stayed in the strange position. It looked as if he were posing for a sculptor's statue.

Taking advantage of the longleg's hesitation, Nundle hurried around to stand before Ervan and begged, "Sir, please. I truly would like you to stay. I am sure we can come to an acceptable arrangement for us both."

Ervan nodded and replied immediately, "Of course, little merchant." There was not a hint of dishonesty in the Cartusian's tone.

Nundle blinked a few times and muttered in astonishment, "Truly?"

"If you say we can make a deal, I believe we can. What do you propose?"

"Uh..." Nundle hesitated, caught off guard by the suddenly agreeable Ervan. By all rights, this longleg should be halfway across the marketplace, hurrying away from the mad tomble while quickly trying to forget his name. "Well, to be honest with you, sir, in order for this be worth it to me, I would like to charge you nearly seventy per bundle, but—"

Ervan cut him off, saying decisively, "Done." The longleg extended his arm and offered his palm, offering to seal the deal the in the manner of Cartu.

Nundle stared blankly at the open hand. After a moment, he looked up to study the face of Ervan, wondering if he was the one who had gone mad. "Pardon?"

The trader stood motionless with his arm still outstretched. "I accept your terms, Master Merchant. Clasp my hand and we can arrange details."

The realization that he had just made a very large—and profitable—sale struck Nundle. Not understanding what had happened, he reached out and gripped Ervan's hand. The longleg's large palm engulfed his much smaller hand. Still staring hesitantly at the longleg, he pointed to his stand. "Shall we discuss the intricacies of the contract?"

"That is an excellent idea," replied Ervan.

Nundle moved behind the booth and pulled out his ledger and sheet of new parchment to write the contract. His neighboring vendors gaped in awe at him. Nundle caught Doffer's stare and smiled. Doffer scowled back.

In short order, Nundle and the Cartusian trader worked out the complete terms to the exchange, keeping Nundle's mind busy. He thought he might go and purchase a bowl or two of Joscoe's famous stew shortly.

When it came time to discuss the advance payment, Ervan happily agreed to Nundle's proposal that he pay half of the full amount immediately and handed over thirty seven gold rounds. Nundle took a moment to stare at the heavy coins in his palm. It was more money than he had held in years.

As he finalized the transaction, word spread amongst his neighboring vendors. Two dozen tombles gaped in awe as Ervan and he arranged the details of dates and delivery. The onlookers were surely wondering how Nundle had managed this feat.

Ervan left to discuss specifics with the wagon team Nundle suggested he hire to transport the Sweetbush all the way to Harmony. As blue-cloaked longleg trader strode away, Nundle stared after him, marveling at how quickly his fortunes had turned, trying to figure out what had just happened.

Doffer, the quarry stone supplier, managed to wait only until the Cartusian had walked beyond earshot before stomping over and rudely demanding, "Nundle! How were you able to swing such an impossible deal? He had you at—" Doffer cut off suddenly.

Nundle glanced at the boorish tomble and innocently asked, "What's bothering you? I would think that after all of the…" Nundle trailed off as he realized the tomble was no longer looking at him, but rather over his shoulder and past him.

Wearing an expression of utter distaste, Doffer whirled about and quickly shuffled back to his own stall.

Wondering what had prompted the hurried retreat, Nundle spun around to find Julo Hinglegrog standing a few paces from him. Her sudden reappearance instantly dampened his mood. The auburn-haired beauty stared at him with her head cocked to the side, a tiny frown on her lips, and an unexpected, hopeful glint in her eyes.

Nundle muttered, "I did not hear you approach, Julo."

Julo's frown turned into a thin smile. "You were busy gloating. Which is surprising, actually. It's not like you."

Embarrassed she had seen him act that way, he said quietly, "Yes, well…Doffer deserves it. He rubs every one of his sales under my nose." He gave her a tiny grin. "He's just upset that I made more in that sale than he will in six or seven turns."

Julo nodded once, slowly, and stayed silent, keeping her gaze fixed on him. As a long stretch of quiet grew between them, Nundle quickly grew uncomfortable. He was a little upset that Julo was ruining his moment of triumph. If she kept coming around, people might think he associated with mages.

Finally, she stepped close and leaned in toward him. The intoxicating scent of spring lilacs filled his nose, taking him back a number of years to a happier time. Back to when Julo was a respectable tomble. With her round, sapphire blue eyes fixated on him, she whispered. "You have no idea how you did that, do you?"

Nundle stared at her. "What do you mean?"

Her eyes tightened. "I saw the strings, Nundle. Gold ones only, for sure, but I definitely saw them."

The realization of what had happened hit him with the force of a thousand fists to the gut.

Magic. He had done magic.

For the briefest of moments, he considered turning and running away. Instead, he shook his head and mumbled, "I don't know what you mean."

Julo cocked an eyebrow. "Don't you?"

As the icy fear over the recognition of what he had done spread through him, Nundle stared at Julo. Part of him wanted to shout her down and denounce her accusation. However, as much as he loathed admitting it, something about the strings intrigued him. He was curious. He wanted to know what the strings were.

As he stood there, staring at Julo, the pretty tomble stood tall. "Well, Nundle, it would seem you and I have something to talk about after all."

Nundle swallowed the lump in his throat. His life was about to change.

About the Author

R.T. **Kaelin** is a loving husband, father of two wonderful children, and a lifelong resident of Ohio, currently in Columbus. After graduating from college, for the first twelve years of his career he has worked as a software engineer. After creatively writing a local gaming group, it was suggested he try his hand at writing something more prodigious. Encouraged, he finally committed to the undertaking, writing the first book of his *The Children of the White Lions* series, *Progeny*. When he is not writing, he loves to travel and has a passion for cooking. For more information or stories, visit www.RTKaelin.com.

In the Time of Dragons

Steven Saus

The King bounces the babe on his knee. Her reflection shimmers in the shields along the walls. In the hall's evening quiet—the revelers grumpily dismissed—his grandchild gurgles. She is a solid blond bouncing weight in his arms, giggling toddler gibberish in the torchlight. He feels a smile crinkle the tired, dry skin of his face and shift the shape of his beard. Her pudgy hands reach toward his hair, so he shifts her on the next bounce, keeping his whiskers just out of her hands' reach.

His daughter's still-soft hand rests upon his shoulder. "What, Papa, my daughter doesn't get to tug on the king's beard?"

Brarod's smile grows larger as he tosses his granddaughter full into the air. The child's squeal and his laugh combine as he rises, the girl dropping smooth back into his hands. He turns toward the child's mother.

"Freidi, those days are long past! My old face is too soft and weak now to endure such mighty fists!" He brings his nose close to the girl-child, grin matching grin. "Even her own father shakes in fear at the wrath of my granddaughter's fists!"

The king looks up at his daughter's smile, at the barely-hidden scowl on her husband's face. The king sighs. "Do you need more ale, Hranvir, so that you can tell a joke from a serious insult?"

Freidi turns to her husband, and pokes at Hranvir's shoulder. "Laugh," she says, "unless you want me to loose our daughter against you."

Hranvir brushes a dark lock of hair back, then smiles.

"Close enough for me," Brarod says, handing his granddaughter to Freidi. "Take your daughter away to sleep, so that she may slay a hundred warriors tomorrow."

The king puts his arm around the boy—man, he reminds himself, man—and lets his face fall back into its solid regularity. "Your husband and I have things to speak of, and for once my hall is only crowded by the conquered dead." He waves his hand absently at the mounted parts of foes—a head here, an arm there. He kisses the toddler's head, the left side of his mouth twitching. "Ah, what a playroom for a child."

Freidi nods a short bow, and then with her daughter on her shoulder, leaves the hall. The two men watch her leave. For a moment, Freidi reminds Brarod of her mother. The sway of hips, the easy laugh. The way she was not scared, even as the fever drained her strength.

The king takes a deep breath and shakes his head to clear the memory. He glances at Hranvir and takes another deep sniff. "Has your drink gotten the better of you? Is your mind clear?"

Hranvir blushes, a deep ruddiness against his black beard. "No, my king, though I am Geatish, I –"

"Stop being so grim. I don't give a rat's ass that you're Geatish. I'd be able to outdrink you anywhere." With a quick step, the king stands just a fingerbreadth away from

Hranvir. "I want to know this: Can you think, Hranvir? Are you able to think tonight?"

The younger man does not step back, does not flinch. "Of course, my king."

"Good. Now come along. We're going for a walk."

The lights of the village behind them flicker in the fall wind. Torches, cook fires, all blown in the wind from the sea that crashes at the base of the cliff, far below the two men. Brarod breathes in, saltwater air filling his lungs. "Like Maine," he whispers.

"My king?" Hranvir shufflesteps forward to stand fully beside the king. "Did you say something?"

The king does not reply, staring out at the sky, the sea. The younger man begins to fidget, his feet shuffling back and forth. The king looks out at the moon, still growing in its cycle, covering everything in its silver light. He waits until Hranvir nearly begins pacing.

"Do you know who I am, Hranvir?"

The young man kneels, reciting, head down: "You are Brarod, father of my wife, slayer of monsters, and king of this land, to whom all owe allegiance."

The king snorts. "Get up." When Hranvir does not move, the king cuffs him on the side of the head. "I said, get up. You're wrong." Slowly, the younger man rises. The king notices Hranvir's hand dropping slowly toward his sword. "Relax. I am your king, I am Freidi's father. But my name is not Brarod, and some of those monsters had been my friends. I was born Sergeant Brian Rodham, 93rd Mobile Infantry, Bravo company. I am not from your time, and I have not slain any monsters."

Hranvir backs away from the king, away from the sea and stars. "Why do you tell me this now? You did not slay those monsters?"

Brarod sighs. "He wasn't a monster. Not really. He was a man. Just different, like me."

"My king, you are not differ—" Hranvir stops talking as the king picks him up by the left ankle, holding him free of the ground. Brarod gasps slightly from the effort. "I am three times your age, but can hold you aloft with one hand. Explain that."

"I cannot, my king." Hranvir grunts as Brarod lets him fall to the ground, then rises, his gaze meeting the king's. "Tell me this, promise me this, my lord. Tell me that you do not serve the darkness. Tell me that you will protect my wife, my daughter, and our people."

A streak of light passes across the heavens as the men regard each other under the night sky. The king slowly smiles, then nods, breaking eye contact first. "I do," he says. "I do. No matter the cost."

Hranvir lowers his head. "Then you are still my king, no matter what name you choose. But I still must ask—why tell me this now?"

The king laughs, a deep laugh pushing its way up from somewhere dark. Behind the king, another streak of light flames briefly between the stars. "Because I remembered the whole story, Hranvir. I remember how it ends, and you must care for my granddaughter."

Brian—he still thinks of himself as Brian sometimes—walks away along the cliff edge. Hranvir stays a step behind, talking above the wind and waves. "We all know that you came from far away, to my father's land, to rid Hrothgar's hall of the monster—"

The king stops and whirls toward Hranvir. "Gregory wasn't a monster. We were the same, that monster and I." His voice drops, softens as he continues. "I told him to wear armor when they tested the teleporter. Just an accident, and the field caught us, me with my armor on, him without. That poor bastard."

Hranvir steps back, hand dropping slightly lower toward his sword. "Are you going to become like that mon... like him, my lord?"

The king does not answer, just stares past Hranvir over the water. There is a low rumble, and the king points into the sky. "Do you see it, Hranvir? Do you see?" The sharp line of flame, brighter than the even the brightest during the twice-yearly star-storms, leads the rumble across the heavens.

"I see it, my king."

"It's the seventh one this day. Fire and thunder and scales, falling to earth. They bring my doom."

"Then do not go to it, my lord. Stay here with your people." Hranvir grasps his king's shoulder. "You have fought for us so many times. Let us fight for you."

The king does not answer, just watches the flame curve in a long, slow arc to the north until the fire disappears. Hranvir waits until the king speaks again.

"Hranvir, do you believe in the Aesir?"

"But of cour—"

Brarod turns, grasping both of the Norseman's shoulders tight enough to be uncomfortable under the coat and furs. "No, do you truly believe? Do you believe they care for our people? That they fight to protect us from the forces of the darkness? That there is a purpose?"

Hranvir answers through clenched teeth: "Yes, my king. As do we all." Hranvir's eyebrows narrow. "We do all believe, do we not?"

Brian laughs, another dark deepening laugh, and releases the other warrior. "I don't know anymore."

The king pulls a gold object, slightly larger than his fist, from the pouch at his belt. Several small spots upon it blink, as if reflecting the light from a fire, though the village is far away. "I should have recognized this after my years fighting the wyrms. Gregory would've. He was always better with their tech."

"My king?"

Brian carefully does not look at his son in law. "I realized who I was after I killed Gregory. Your father got his name wrong—did your Hrothgar ever tell you? It's not his fault. The accident did something to Greg, twisted him as it shifted us back to here. Back to now. But I knew who he was. I tore my friend's arm off with my own hands."

"But you saved my father's—"

"Yes. I did. But that's when I knew who I was. Who I had become. And I thought that was it. Defeat the monster, beat its mother, and then relax. I'd forgotten the last part of the story. Probably wouldn't have put it together if I had."

Hranvir's eyes narrow. "You said scales, my lord. Do you mean dragons?" Hranvir scans the horizon, looking for more approaching flame. "Are there dragons coming?"

The king holds up the gold object, examining the engravings and fine lines. The sea breeze whipped around their faces. "When Wiglaf's slave came back with this, I began to remember. I began to understand. Look at the indentations." The king tosses the object to Hranvir.

The younger man turns the object over in his hands, running fingers along it. "There are places for fingers, my king, but they are . . . made poorly. There are too few, and spaced too far apart." He hands the object back to the king.

"They're made to fit a hand perfectly—just not for a human hand." Brarod claps his son-in-law on the back. "Let us return. There will be no more trails of flame, no unnatural shooting stars tonight."

"Were those the wyrms—the dragons—you speak of?"

The king nods. "Those are the wyrms, and this gold object was theirs. Many years from now—many, many years from now—there will be many of them, and they will raid our planet. There will be fierce warriors in those days, with armor like mine, and we will fight back.

"Now, though, there are just a few of the wyrms—perhaps a big drone and a few leaders controlling it. If we did nothing, all would be quiet at first. Then in a few days, we will hear that it ravaged one village. Then another. Then laying waste to the countryside, killing our people. They will be looking for this." With a sharp, fierce contraction of muscle, Brarod throws the gold object out into the air so that it falls into the water far below. "But they will never find it. And I will not wait for them to kill our people. I will go to them, and you will stay."

"My king!"

"You will stay here with my daughter and granddaughter. Listen to my daughter as you would any man. Raise my granddaughter to be fierce. Protect them both from those who would imprison them with looms and cookfires."

The men walked in silence until they reached Brarod's house. "You know my armor. I'm sure it will be damaged. The reactor core will probably—nevermind. Just bury me in it, with all of the dragon's treasure. All of it. Do not distribute the treasure to the people—it will be cursed."

"But my king..." Hranvir's lips are pressed tight as he considers his words. "If you know you will die, why go to your doom?"

The king looks at Hranvir. "Because this will keep the dragons from our world for twenty five hundred generations. Our world is not ready to join in the fight of the Aesir. My sacrifice is already written in the words of bards and sages for generations to come. But for now, it is enough to know that my daughter and grandchild are kept safe from the wyrms. And you will keep our family safe from the enemies of our people."

Brarod clasps Hravnir's shoulder, this time simply with the firmness of friendship. "I will leave tomorrow. Once I am gone, tell my daughter and your child than I love them more than my life. Rule fairly, and listen to the counsel of your wife. Go."

Brian waits for the younger man to leave before opening the door to the armory. The battle armor stands waiting in the moonlight. Upon its left shoulder, his unit insignia—the wolf's head with a berkano—Bravo, he reminds himself, bravo over its shoulder. He steps toward it, and it opens for his approach.

It seals around him and speaks in its carefully gender-neutral tone. "Sergeant, wyrm activity detected approximately 54 kilometers, 657.78 mils."

"Noted," the king says. "Tomorrow."

The battle armor does not respond. He examines the readouts as the suit performs its diagnostics on him. Nanite levels still dropping. Suit power reserves at three percent. No munitions, just the oversized sword he had forged for the suit's powered hand. He takes a deep breath, lets it out slowly.

"They'll remember you. Not me, dammit. They only remember your name."

The suit does not respond.

Sergeant Brian Rodham stands inside Beowulf, and readies himself for his last battle.

About the Author

Steven Saus injects people with radioactivity as his day job, but only to serve the forces of good. His work has appeared in multiple anthologies and magazines both online and off. He also publishes and provides publishing services as Alliteration Ink. You can find him at stevensaus.com and alliterationink.com.

Among The Stars

Sarah Hans

Doctor Fumalatro's Astounding Device lured passersby like a flame lures insects. As night settled over the city, its glow became beacon-like, so bright with electricity that it made the lantern-light from the surrounding shops seem dull and oily. But the groups that clustered around it after dark--mostly orphans and homeless drunkards--never dared to give it a coin, though whether out of poverty, fear, or superstition, no one knew.

Instead the crowd just watched, waiting for someone to give it money and see what predictions it would make.

Colonel Bannister was just the sort of man to try the silly thing. Gwen regretted taking him around Tolliver Street the moment his eyes lit up on sight of the device. He was like a child fixated on a toy. And though Gwen had been known to hold her own in a cat-fight or barroom brawl, the Colonel was a good head taller than she, and drunk to boot, and once he had his mind set on finding out his fortune, she could not hold him back.

The hobos and street-children scrambled out of the Colonel's way as he staggered up to the device. It played a soft, catchy tune while its lights twinkled and danced in time. It appeared to be a fortune-telling automaton, of the sort Gwen had seen at countless fairs and carnivals, seated in a box of red velvet gilded with gold paint and glass gems. "Learn How You Will Meet Your End!" the words beneath the logo promised.

She had to admit: it was unique. She'd never seen a fortune-teller that promised to predict one's demise. *How delightfully morbid.*

As the Colonel stepped up to it, the device flared to life. A spotlight shone down on him, glaring off his bald pate and flushed cheeks. The automaton jerked and tinny words issued from a speaker in its mouth:

> *Present your coins to learn your fate*
> *Don't be afraid, don't hesitate*

The Colonel, quite against the advice of the automaton, jumped back as if spooked, shaking his head. "Gwendolyn, dear, why don't you give it a try?"

Gwen frowned but held out her palm to collect a few pennies from her companion. She thought about teasing the Colonel about his fear--but if his reaction to her teasing was angry, as it so often was, she'd end the night with half as much coin, and with her rent due tomorrow and her need for opium thick and bitter at the back of her throat she needed the money more than she needed to humiliate the fat old fart. *And he'll be gone soon enough--might as well let his last night on Earth be a pleasant one.*

So she took his pennies and made to insert them into the device. She couldn't find a slot. Instead, the automaton's hand swung around and presented her with its palm. The sudden movement was a bit unnerving, but she shrugged and dropped the coins onto the wooden hand anyway. *Not afraid of some mechanized puppet.*

Behind her, she heard the Colonel clicking his watch. *The watch that is not a watch.* The sound made her grind her teeth.

The automaton's hand disappeared with the money. Its button eyes whirled and glowed, and its mouth moved again so that it could recite another poem:

> *Neptune, Jupiter, Venus, Mars*
> *You shall perish among the stars*

When the automaton finished its recitation, a slip of paper slid from its mouth like a flat white tongue. The slip lolled there for a moment before Gwen reached up and tore it away to read it. The poem was printed on the slip in stark black ink beneath Doctor Fumalatro's garish logo.

"But I'm not an aeronaut," she muttered, to nobody in particular.

Colonel Bannister lurched over to her, spinning her around by the shoulders and snatching the fortune from her fingers. "Clearly that one's for me, haha! Must've been because it was my money, don't you know." Before Gwen could protest he had stuffed the slip into his jacket pocket and nodded to the machine. "Give me a few pennies and I'll get your fortune, haha!"

Gwen thought about refusing but again, the promise of the Colonel's extra generosity after a night well spent--or the opportunity to raid his pockets after he'd passed out in the gutter--was too tempting to pass up. She fastened her most winsome smile onto her lips and fished in her reticule for a few coins, passing them obediently to the Colonel.

"There's a girl," the old man cooed, patting her behind as he stepped up to the device. The automaton repeated its routine: hand, pennies, poem. This time the tinny voice announced:

Tea and crumpets, bangers and mash
You shall die in an auto crash

Gwen shuddered as the Colonel presented her with the slip of paper with the demeanor of one issuing an award. "That's much better, much more pedestrian," he mumbled. She wasn't sure what "pedestrian" meant exactly, but she could guess, and she felt the heat of embarrassment and anger rise to her cheeks.

"Did it never occur to you that maybe that fortune was meant for *me*, and you're the one who's to die in the street?" She stormed down the sidewalk, hobos slinking aside to avoid her wrath.

"Oh my dear, don't be silly!" Colonel Bannister called, chasing after her. "I'm going up in the *Daedalus* in only a few hours, so clearly the first fortune was meant for me. And you're never going to the stars, you're just a...a..."

Gwen halted abruptly, then whirled to face him. She was livid, and would have sworn that smoke was streaming from her nostrils. "Say it. I'm just a...a *what*?"

Colonel Bannister had the good sense to look abashed. He swallowed. "Let's just pretend this never happened." He pulled the slip of white paper with Gwen's star-fortune from his pocket and made to tear it up.

The prostitute, more sober than he and therefore quicker, grabbed the piece of paper from his fingers and clutched it to her chest. "This is my fortune, you old fool. And whether I'm a *whore* or not, I'll go to the stars if I like. Just you wait and see!" She knew the words were ridiculous as she said them; preposterous even. She was a woman, a commoner...and worse. *The life of an aeronaut can never be mine.*

"You'd better watch out for autos on the walk back to your spaceship," she spat, turning on her heel and marching away. Behind her, she heard the old man sigh and sink to the curb with a *wuff*. Then she heard the clicking of the not-a-watch, his nervous tic only exacerbating her fury.

The slip of paper seemed small comfort as she stomped down the sidewalk. The anger drained from her, replaced by disappointment, bitterness, sadness, so many emotions that they threatened to overflow her eyes and run down her cheeks. She held in the tears until she made it around the corner, and there she stood on the sidewalk and sobbed.

A loud sound made her look up. An automobile careened around the street corner and into view, charging right toward her, and she only just had time to leap out of the way. The vehicle's driver shrieked something unintelligible and sounded the horn, a loud wailing in the quiet night, before disappearing down Tolliver Street.

Gwen heard the crash: glass shattering and metal tearing. She stood paralyzed for an instant, disbelieving, and then ran toward the wreck. She knew what she would find.

The auto had slammed into a shop window, but not before striking Colonel Bannister. He lay on the sidewalk, broken and bent in unnatural ways. Blood stained the street, rapidly pooling around him. Gwen ran to him, throwing herself down beside him so hard the cobbles bruised her knees. The air smelled of motor oil and blood.

"Tacitus?" It was the first time she'd used his given name, in all their long acquaintance. "Tacitus?" She laid her fingers against his cheek.

His eyelids fluttered and he looked up at her with eyes that were, she noticed for the first time, green. How had she not noticed they were so green? Then the eyes closed and his head lolled to the side, one last gasp of air escaping his lips, ending with a tell-tale rattle that Gwen knew all too well.

In his left hand, flopped against the sidewalk, was the other fortune, the one he had drawn for her--the harbinger of his demise.

When his body stilled, Gwen started to turn away. Though the night was eerily silent in the aftermath of the wreck, there was a great rushing in her ears. A soft metallic click made her turn back. The Colonel's right hand had relaxed, and from his dead fingers had fallen the pocket watch that wasn't a pocket watch, still remarkably intact, gleaming in the dim light of the streetlamps.

Gwen still clutched the fortune about star-travel in her fist. Somewhere, a siren sounded as the constables made their way to the scene of the accident.

Swallowing hard, Gwen picked up the not-a-watch and held it up to the light. She still remembered the codes the Colonel had recited so many times, so eager to impress with his aeronautical genius, in such a drunken stupor that it overwhelmed his better sense. Everyone thought this device was merely the Colonel's favorite and certainly most elaborate watch. But Gwen knew better.

This was the launch key to the *Daedalus*.

In the dimness, the key's brass workings sparkled with stars, and Gwen saw, for a moment, the vastness of space, the incredible possibilities there. She saw in that intricate device the escape from her life as an object of men's use and nothing more. *You're just a whore.*

She turned and ran, gripping the launch key in one hand and her fortune in the other. She ran toward fate.

Neptune, Jupiter, Venus, Mars
You shall perish among the stars

About the Author

Sarah **Hans** is an author, editor, and educator who doesn't let adulthood stop her from playing dress-up. Her most recent project is the anthology *Sidekicks!*, published by Alliteration Ink and featuring stories by Donald J. Bingle, Kelly Swails, and other Origins Library authors. You can read Sarah's fiction and follow her adventures in Steampunk at http://sarahhans.com/.

Parting the Clouds

Bradley P. Beaulieu

Twenty hours, Kinjin thought. Twenty hours from Vegas to L.A. to Tokyo and finally south to Kagoshima, and would his relatives give him one moment's peace?

Fat chance.

A few pleasantries exchanged, but when they got him to the car, the worm turned. How can you fritter away your inheritance like this? Why won't you settle down or go to school? Or even start a company? You must have enough money left for that! Isn't there anything you want to *do*? Your parents would be ashamed!

He did his best to deflect their questions, their concerns, but his aunt was persistent as all get out. She wouldn't leave him alone, even though he'd only come to visit. The urge to skip town bubbled up inside him, but he knew he couldn't leave, not until he'd made his peace with Sakurajima.

Then the news came. Tropical Storm Yomo had found new life in the Pacific and had just reached typhoon status. During the next thirty-six hours it surged up to category 3 and appeared to be heading straight for southern Japan. As the news intensified, so did the mood around Kagoshima. Preparations were made to evacuate should the storm remain on course. Typhoon Yomo reached category 4 the next morning and showed no signs of changing direction.

As the city mobilized, an utter sense of calm came over Kinjin. He had known since he'd first heard word of the storm that he would stay if it headed for Kagoshima, knew he would stand face-to-face with it and see what it had to offer.

When his aunt and cousins left, Kinjin swore he would be right behind them, that he only wished to take a few pictures of the approaching storm from the bay. But when they finally packed up their car and headed north, he abandoned his camera and headed for the waterfront.

Kinjin staked his ground on a grass-covered rise in Kamoike Park, a few dozen feet from Kagoshima's breakwater, where twenty-foot waves crested and collapsed against the piled concrete. The chaos of the charcoal sky turned the once-busy dockside into a colorless menagerie. Against the backdrop of Kagoshima's hotels and office buildings, the wholesale market shivered on the pier as the overspray from the waves pummeled it. Dozens of fishing boats waged a surreal game of king-of-the-mountain in the playground of the harbor.

The raindrops were tacks driven into Kinjin's face and hands and calves. His cutoff jeans and denim jacket did little to protect the skin beneath. Even the piercings over his left eyebrow and the tops of his ears felt sore.

The wind rumbled like a jet engine. The bravado of moments ago ebbed, and he found himself more afraid of the physical act of dying than he had thought he would. From beneath his shirt, he retrieved the one piece of his past he had retained over the years: a brass house key hanging from a dog-tag chain. He shivered and clutched the key. *I need you, Mom and Dad. Please, tell me what to do.*

There was no answer, of course—never had been—but a renewed sense of calm returned, and soon he was able to stare out to sea, ready for the end. He was glad it would come in the form of a force of nature. There would be no questions of morality about drowning in the bay, no right or wrong. It would simply *be*.

A sound like a brick against a block of wood thrummed through Kinjin's head. The rumbling of the wind was replaced instantly with a high-pitched keening.

Moments later, he realized he was lying on the ground in a deep puddle. He coughed from the inhaled water as the rain tried to beat him back down. Every part of him was numb.

As Kinjin staggered to his feet the gash over his ear flared to life, and the sound of the wind returned with renewed fury. He felt warmth in the form of a trickle running down the right side of his face. It tasted of blood. The pain made him cower and shut his eyes tight. His hands shook. But finally, after a dozen shivering breaths, it receded.

The foamy waves—nearly thirty feet high—assaulted the rise Kinjin stood upon, breaking only at the last moment before slipping back under the hungry mass of the next. One wave, over a hundred yards off, strode forward like the general behind the vanguard. Kinjin renewed his grip on the key. The muscle of his arm became so taut that he feared the chain would break, but he couldn't relax. Who knew nature could make something so large!

And then the strangest thing happened. Two faint notes from an instrument—a flute?—intermingled among the locomotive thunder of the wind and rain. How was that possible? Kinjin wrote it off as just the whistling of the wind, but the notes returned a moment later, louder and closer. It *was* a flute. The melody seesawed between wistful and serious.

The mammoth wave sucked the sea back from the breakwater—one deep breath before this grand exhalation. Kinjin could do nothing to ease his grip on the key even though he felt its teeth break the skin of his palm.

The seawater struck like a juggernaut, snatching Kinjin's legs from under him and tossing him backward like a pebble in the surf. As the water receded, Kinjin fought madly, clawing and lunging against the wave's pull. He lost more and more ground. He was going to be sucked out to sea, lost forever.

But finally the wave spat him out. Kinjin coughed and gasped for breath and scrabbled up and over the rise. He stood on shaking legs, mouth agape.

The gale was now little more than a breeze, and only a light rain pattered the ground around him. The clouds seemed beaten, for they gave way and allowed the sun to shine through. Patches of blue sky shone through the maelstrom above. The eye of the typhoon towered miles into the air all around him, as if the entire world was made of roiling clouds save for this one place.

A giggle escaped Kinjin's throat, and he thrust his arms to the sky and laughed and laughed and laughed.

A half-mile east, the wall of the typhoon pulled back further to reveal Kagoshima Bay, and Kinjin's laughter was snuffed like a candle left out in the rain. Beyond the dark, roiling water, the active volcano, Sakurajima, stared angrily down as it spewed ash high into the air.

It was the place he'd been avoiding since he'd arrived in Kagoshima. He hadn't even looked at it until now. It was the reason his parents had died. They had come here on vacation four years ago and chartered a helicopter to tour the mountain. They'd never returned. Hell, they'd never even made it. Their helicopter crashed into the bay a few minutes into the flight.

Kinjin turned when the sound of the flute resumed behind him. Below him lay the debris-riddled soccer field of Tempozan Park. Seven Chinese men—or Mongolian, perhaps —wearing saffron shirts and wheat-colored leggings walked single file toward the center of the field. Braided strips of bamboo wrapped the men's elbows and knees, segmenting them like rag dolls. Each bore a tanned water skin hanging from a thick leather strap over his shoulder. All of them had shaved heads, and the six at the front of the line held wooden bowls. The man at the rear, shorter and older than the rest, played a Japanese flute, a shakuhachi.

When they reached the center, the bowl-carrying monks spread into a rough circle and paced counter-clockwise around the shakuhachi player. Gazing skyward, they held the bowls above their heads as the rain fell. The shakuhachi's song harmonized their movements with those of the storm. It was as if the monks and the typhoon were sharing a communal experience by common agreement. They were obviously collecting rain, but it seemed like they were worshipping the eye as well, for their movements seemed too similar to the spin of the storm to think otherwise.

It was ... beautiful, and so incredibly peaceful. If Kinjin could find that sort of peace, he knew he'd be able to deal with his demons.

With no conscious effort, Kinjin's wobbly legs stepped forward. The monks ignored Kinjin until he came within ten paces, and then the monk playing the shakuhachi lowered his instrument and stared at Kinjin. The monk, now that he'd stopped playing, looked jaundiced and sickly.

Kinjin realized the wind was steadily picking up its pace. It drove harder against his skin, chilled him more hungrily. Kinjin shivered, unsure what to say.

The monk pointed with his shakuhachi toward downtown. "Leave!" he said in Chinese and, when Kinjin didn't respond, "Go!" in Japanese.

Kinjin was so surprised by the monk's vehemence that he replied in English. "I can't."

The man continued to point, his round face rigid, his deep-set eyes angry. "Go, go!"

"I can't!" Kinjin said, switching to Japanese.

The monk's eyes surveyed the area around them, then the sky above. He shook his head ever so slightly and hung the shakuhachi from a loop of twine at his rope belt. He stepped out of the circle and faced Kinjin. "You're lucky to be alive." His Japanese, though clear, had a Mongolian accent.

"Am I?" Kinjin asked, blinking away the rain falling in his face.

The monk's eyes narrowed. There was contempt in that gaze, but also a touch of curiosity. "Yes," he said matter-of-factly, "you are."

"What are you doing here?"

"Our purpose is no concern of yours." The monk coughed and glanced back at his brothers. "And someone like you would never understand. Go back to your world and leave us to ours." A large tattoo marked the inside of the monk's forearm—a rooster, pig, and snake, all three in a circle around a maroon maple tree, each biting the tail of the next. Where had he seen that before?

"I don't have a world to go back to."

The monk looked Kinjin up and down. "Look at you. Pierced eyebrows, Levis, diver's watch. You're probably so buried by your world that you've convinced yourself you can no longer live in it."

Kinjin opened his mouth to speak, but stopped himself. The monk wasn't correct, but he'd struck close enough to the mark. As the silence lengthened, the monk's expression turned to one of embarrassment.

Nearby, what Kinjin had thought to be a rock lying near a rangy bush turned out to be a sea turtle. It tried flipping over several times before finally succeeding and scuffling away as if the typhoon had never passed over. As the light rain continued to settle over the city, a sad laugh escaped Kinjin's throat.

The old man's eyes were hard again as he pointed toward the Sun Royal Hotel. "Find shelter before the eye wall approaches. Do not hide in a cellar or the storm will drown you." Then he pointed to his ear. "And find clean cloth for that wound. You're still bleeding."

He walked back to the center of the circle and began to play the same song as before, though louder.

Kinjin almost turned to follow the monk's advice. It was the smart thing to do. But these men, so heedless of the typhoon, so confident in their dealings with it... He could not simply leave.

Each monk emptied the contents of his wooden bowl into the skin hanging at his side. A day ago Kinjin might have schemed to retrieve one of the skins, to examine the water they had collected. Here, in such divine presence, the mere thought was profane.

The wind howled through the city, louder and louder. Kinjin hadn't realized, but the eastern wall of the eye was nearly upon them. The clouds began to block out the bits of blue sky, the light from the sun.

The monks collected the last of the typhoon's water into their skins and tied the necks securely. They formed a line and returned the way they'd come, the shakuhachi player now leading instead of trailing. Fear surged up in Kinjin like an unholy swell of seawater. It wasn't fear of death that had him in its grip, or even the fear of being left alone. It was the simple act of *not knowing* what they had just done, the feeling that he would *never* know if he didn't do something about it right now.

He ran up to the flutist and paced him. "Please, take me with you."

The old man's only reply was a short coughing fit.

"Please."

The line of monks trudged forward, heedless of the calls, and Kinjin stopped, sure of their determination.

The rain felt colder than before, and the howling wind laughed.

Please.

The monks trudged onward, but then, as if he'd heard Kinjin's unuttered plea, the flutist slowed. He turned, shoulders hunched, and shook his head ever so slightly. He made his way back to Kinjin and held out his shakuhachi.

Kinjin stared at it. "What..."

"You need it more than I do."

"I don't understand."

"No, you wouldn't, would you?" The monk shook the instrument, and Kinjin accepted it reflexively. "But perhaps you will someday." Then the old man turned, jogged back to his brethren, and followed them into the gathering winds.

Kinjin stared at the beautiful color of the bamboo for a long time, even though the speed of the typhoon was rebuilding to deadly proportions.

He made his way into the Sun Royal through its shattered front and hid within an empty banquet hall. As the storm howled its fury and beat against the building, Kinjin huddled in the darkness and listened to the song that still played in his head, still tugged at his soul.

And he smiled.

After the typhoon passed over and continued toward Pusan and the rest of South Korea, Kinjin remained in Kagoshima to do what he could for his mother's relatives. As the city returned to a semblance of order, he tried to find news of the monks, but no one had seen them—no one had even *heard* of such a thing.

The whole time, the shakuhachi's song continued to nip at Kinjin—not the notes themselves, or even the melody, but the sense of balance he'd felt when the monk had played it, the same sense of balance he'd felt from the monk while talking to him.

Kinjin's mother had tried to teach him the shakuhachi when he was young, but he'd been horrible at it. Still, he understood the basics, enough that he could ask his great-uncle to teach him the song. He had little trouble with the song itself, for no matter what he did, it always replayed in his mind as perfectly as when the monk had released it to the wind. But when he finally learned it, he felt none of those emotions he'd felt on the day of the typhoon. It felt every bit as hollow as his life had for the last four years.

A few months after the typhoon, Kinjin knew he had to leave. His relatives were well enough set, and Sakurajima had provided no solace whatsoever. If anything, it only made his memories that much more painful. No, he had to leave. He had to find those monks. They would know how to help him. They'd have to.

He said his goodbyes and flew west to Mongolia. He knew a little Mongolian, and picking up another language had always come to him easily; within the first few months of hiking around the country, he knew enough to get by.

His first hope of finding the monks came in Havirga, where some men at a monastery said they recognized the song. He wandered northwest and took to playing the song on street corners in the cities and villages, hoping someone would recognize it. Most people simply passed on by, pretending he wasn't there, and only three people in four months admitted they'd heard the song, but their recollections of the source contradicted one another.

One day, Kinjin found a fat monk wearing coke-bottle glasses who had the same rooster-pig-snake tattoo as the old man. He asked the monk what it meant.

"It means to take responsibility, young man."

He tried to walk on, but Kinjin had stopped him. "I don't understand."

"Greed, anger, and delusion," he said while pointing in turn to the rooster, the snake, and the pig. "*You alone* reap their fruit; *you alone* control their hold on your heart."

Kinjin considered those words over and over again during the next few months, but they never settled. He wasn't greedy. He admitted to being angry over his parents' deaths, but he never took it out on anybody else. And he was one of the sanest people he knew. If anybody was based in reality, Kinjin was.

After six fruitless months of searching, Kinjin realized he could travel for the rest of his life and still never find the monks. They had *sounded* Mongolian, but he wasn't at all sure they *lived* there.

It was already June, and the new typhoon season had begun to build. He studied the typhoons—their paths, their scales, their births and deaths. Typhoon Yomo had been a Category 4 with winds over two hundred kilometers per hour. He studied its path from inception as a tropical storm to eventual death near Changchun, China.

Kinjin wondered if the monks chose the typhoon for the rain in the eye. Or maybe something about Kagoshima had attracted them, but he soon discovered the storms usually formed further south and struck the Philippines or Vietnam or Malaysia. After debating various possibilities, Kinjin finally settled on the size and limited his search to Category 3s and 4s.

Three weeks later, a tropical storm formed to the east of China and the Philippines. As it trekked westward, it gathered strength and tropical storm Goshen achieved typhoon strength.

After the eye—and the worst of the winds—passed Manila, Kinjin paid through the nose to find a pilot willing to fly him to Kuala Lumpur, where the eye would apparently strike land. From there, he took buses northeast to the coast, using a weather radio to follow the storm's progress, and so, after adjusting several times, Kinjin found himself in Songkhla, Thailand a half-day later.

In the late afternoon, he stood on another rise, taller than the one in Kagoshima, looking down on the shoreline. To the west, nearly colorless under the low-hanging clouds, was Thale Luang, a round lake that drained further north into the South China Sea. The wind rattled the trees as the waves played over the sea's dark green water.

By now the shakuhachi had become an old friend. Kinjin retrieved it from his canvas book bag and began to play, half-expecting another flute to start playing along with his. He almost *felt* the monks walking up behind him. But the only sounds that met his song were those of the oncoming storm.

The high winds would have fouled any normal flute, but Kinjin had long ago realized it was special. It was nearly impossible to play it poorly, and wind, no matter how strong, never seemed to affect it at all. In fact, if anything, it was the *shakuhachi* that affected the *wind*, not the other way around.

He had hoped that playing in the presence of the typhoon would incite the same feelings he'd felt when the monks had played, but that was not the case, so Kinjin decided to incite those same feelings within himself: wonderment, fear, excitement, acceptance. He forced these emotions through the shakuhachi, and it brought him to the proper place; the winds now played among the palm trunks in a different manner. Where it was constant and droning before, it was now fluid and childlike.

And then he heard it. The song of the other flute cut through the chaos of the palm trees and whipping fronds. But the song, Kinjin realized, wasn't the same.

Kinjin stuffed the shakuhachi away and ran headlong over the wooded terrain toward the sound. The winds died down, and he broke through to a small clearing. Atop a swath of moss-infested rock, the monks walked in a circle, holding their begging bowls to the sky, waiting as the rain fell. The flutist stood in the center, playing his altered song.

Kinjin's steps faltered, for the flutist was not the same man. He was taller than the old monk, thinner. His dark-skinned face was gaunt, and he had a mole over one eyebrow. He had carried one of the begging bowls in Kagoshima.

After a sidelong sneer, the flutist stopped and made his way to Kinjin. "You should not have come," the monk said in broken Japanese, his voice forceful and stern.

Kinjin's thoughts tripped over themselves. "Who *are* you?" he blurted in Mongolian.

"Dashiyen," the monk said, a confused expression on his face.

"No." Kinjin shook his head. "I mean, where is he, the one from Kagoshima?"

"He is Manhamha, and our lama is no concern of yours."

"Yes he is. He gave me this," Kinjin dug out the shakuhachi from his bag. "He gave me purpose." Kinjin hadn't realized how true those words were until he'd spoken them. "He saved my life."

The monk stared, utterly serious, but then a sad smile spread over his face. "You gave *yourself* purpose. Now go. Get to safety."

"You don't understand." Kinjin pulled the brass house key from under his black T-shirt and showed it to Dashiyen. "I... My parents. They died, and all I have left is this key."

His face, like so many people when they heard Kinjin's story, went appropriately sad. "I am sorry—"

"No, let me finish. They gave me this before they went to Japan. Twenty-eight years of marriage, and it was their first time away together. Just... Just to spite them, I stayed home, and they died on their *first day* there—some helicopter tour of Sakurajima. I heard the news and—" Kinjin shook the chain, jingling the key beneath his tightened fist, "—the first thing I felt was relief. Relief! How fucked up is that? I had my life and this goddamned key while my parents were being flown home in fucking pine boxes."

"I'm sure your parents meant much—"

Kinjin let the chain fall against his chest and scraped his fingers through his sopping hair. "Don't you get it? I'd been searching for four years for a way to deal with this. When Manhamha gave me the shakuhachi, I found something to..." Kinjin couldn't find the right words. "That could..."

"Lead you away from your guilt?"

Kinjin couldn't find the words to respond around the lump forming in his throat.

Dashiyen replied with a knowing nod, but his eyes were still hard. "Believe me, I understand the search for meaning. Keep the shakuhachi, continue on your path. But do not think of playing it here again; you've already tainted the storm." Dashiyen turned toward the circle.

It took several breaths for the monk's words to sink in. Kinjin grabbed Dashiyen's saffron-robed arm and turned him back around. "I tainted it?"

After pulling his arm away, the monk stood taller. "You twisted the storm for your own purposes. It has turned toward *your* dharma now, not his."

"What is the rain for?"

"Manhamha is dying."

A tingling rush traveled up Kinjin's neck and filled his head. "Dying?"

The monk glanced at his rain-collecting brethren. "It is why we are here."

"Then let me collect rain for you. Let me visit him. I'll do whatever I can."

The monk shook his head. "You cannot help, and your visit would do nothing for him."

"I don't believe that," Kinjin said with all the bravado he could muster.

"I am sorry, but it is true. Now, please, I must complete the song."

"Tell me one last thing," Kinjin said, his vision wavering with tears. "The song. Is it yours or his?"

Dashiyen gripped his shakuhachi in both hands and squeezed it tenderly. "Both." And with that he returned to the circle and resumed his playing.

Kinjin stared as they collected rainwater, as the song played. He let the sounds suffuse his being as he contemplated the monk's answer. *Both.* The song had some of the same feel as Manhamha's, but there were other stanzas as well. Kinjin let it all soak in, trying to understand before it was too late.

After Dashiyen completed his song, the monks formed a line and began walking away, but Dashiyen stopped as he neared Kinjin, thoughts and words warring within his expression. "You can find him in Ulaanbaatar," he said crisply.

And then they left.

Kinjin found shelter in a niche at the base of a cliff. He curled up into a tight ball and considered the monk's words. *You've already tainted the storm.*

Dashiyen had not said so, but he understood it might be disastrous to Manhamha.

It has turned toward your dharma now, not his.

He knew then, knew he would find a way to heal Manhamha.

After the worst of Typhoon Goshen passed over, Kinjin returned to Kuala Lumpur and combed the weather stations and Internet for news of gathering storms. Two tropical storms were warring over the Pacific, and in another few days, Tropical Storm Hagishi achieved typhoon status.

With nearly the last of his dwindling reserves, he flew to Tandag on the Philippines as soon as it became clear it would strike the island. He rented a battered old US Army jeep from the pilot at the airport and rumbled his way north along the coastline to Tigao where a sharp ridge looked down upon the churning sea. After driving the jeep a few hundred yards away, Kinjin took his shakuhachi, a wineskin, and a carved wooden bowl to the edge of the cliff.

Hagishi's winds were already picking up. The bland radio voice from Tandag repeated a message several times. Kinjin knew enough Filipino to tell that Hagishi had achieved Category 4 and might achieve 5. He stared at the storm heading toward him, the heart of it still miles away, and hefted the negligent weight of the shakuhachi in his hand, wondering now that the time had come if he would make it. He could only try, and if the typhoon saw fit to grant him the eye, he would gather the rain and find Manhamha.

The wind's bluster increased, and the rain wrapped Kinjin like smoke from a bonfire enveloping a mosquito. Unsure how to begin, Kinjin played the song he'd first heard from Manhamha. He tried to alter the song, to make it his own, but he could sense his own sour emotions.

Lead you away from your guilt? Dashiyen's words couldn't have been more on the mark. As Kinjin dug deeper, the full weight of the words struck him. He had tried to convince himself that he'd been searching for purpose since they'd died, that his travels to China and Thailand and Mexico and Peru and a dozen others were all about his quest for a goal in life, when really they were about avoiding his guilt. He'd been deluding himself from the very beginning.

The urge to throw the shakuhachi off the cliff and run for the jeep seized him, and the song faltered. The wind laughed at his foolish attempts to control it, swarmed like dragonflies around a hapless gnat.

Shoved by the force of the wind, Kinjin fell and was dragged to the edge of the cliff. His wineskin slipped free of his shoulder and spiraled downward, soon lost in the gray wind and rain. The wooden bowl skittered away and wedged between two stout rocks as the rain pelted Kinjin's face nearly to the point of blindness.

His parents' key, feeling impossibly heavy, hung from his neck and waved before him. A surge of emotion rattled through Kinjin, and he yanked the chain free, heedless of the bite to the back of his neck.

"I'm sorry," he shouted into the wind. "I can't carry you around with me anymore." And with that Kinjin threw the key and chain with all the strength he could muster. The chain caught in the wind and jigged a crazy dance as the rain welcomed it with a howling embrace.

And then it was gone.

Kinjin dragged himself back from the cliff's edge, made it to his knees, and brought the shakuhachi to his lips with shaking hands. He began the song again, no longer attempting to control the storm, merely playing what he felt was *right*. It contained echoes of Manhamha's song, but this one was his too. As his hands steadied, the pace quickened and the tone sharpened. He found surer footing and stood. The wind, so angry with him before, calmed, accepted his presence. The roaring of the wind relaxed, and finally, blessedly, the wall of the eye passed over him.

The center of the storm was huge—nearly twice as large as Yomo's. The rain was cool with the faint taste of salt. It was pure. Kinjin hung the flute from his belt and held the wooden bowl to the sky. He laughed and cried and collected as much as he could. With the wineskin lost, he cradled the brimming bowl back to the jeep, covered it with an old piece of leather, and wrapped it as tight as he could with some twine from the glove box.

After turning back to the storm, Kinjin waited for the opposite side of the eye wall to approach. He feared nothing as he took up his song, but he never felt like he had mastered the typhoon. They had simply come to a mutual understanding.

Kinjin's flights—and the last of his money—took him another forty hours before he reached Ulaanbaatar. Manhamha's temple was the third he called upon. It sat in the northern section of the city along the brown Tuul River, surrounded by green ridges.

Dashiyen approached Kinjin at the gate to the Temple. He noticed the wineskin Kinjin carried, and an embarrassed smile touched his lips. "I didn't believe him when he said you would come," he said. He stepped to one side and motioned Kinjin forward. "Please, he's been waiting for you."

Kinjin bowed, unable to find words to such a greeting.

Dashiyen led him into the cool interior of a two-story temple to a room with sliding wooden doors. Rush mats lay on the floor, and a wide bed lay in the center of the room. Manhamha, covered by a saffron blanket with a maroon tree stitched into it, was propped up on a small pile of embroidered pillows. He stared through listless eyes as Kinjin approached.

Kinjin waited for a long time, so long that he feared he was too late.

Manhamha's eyes finally gained coherence and fixed upon him.

Kinjin held his wine skin and showed it to Manhamha. "I've brought you rain."

Manhamha frowned as he stared at the skin.

"From another typhoon. I knew you needed more."

Manhamha forced a smile onto his round face. "We can all use help," he said, his voice a thin thread, "but I wonder if you know what help you've brought."

"Typhoon rain. Healing rain."

Manhamha smiled again. It was genuine but very, very sad. "Those drops do not heal."

Heart beating faster, Kinjin stared at the old man, then at his wineskin. "Yes, they do. Dashiyen told me."

"No, they do not. They are used to ease the path to the next life."

Hot blood rushed to his face. *Ease the path?*

"Do not be troubled. There are others here to guide you."

Kinjin stared around the room, struggling to bring some sense of meaning. "But I just found you."

"That may be." Manhamha's eyes went distant, then refocused. "But we will find each other again. I am sure of it."

Kinjin hefted the wineskin. The weight of it, so slight, felt repulsive. How could he give it to Manhamha? But as he stared at the smiling, round face of the man before him, he realized how selfish he was being. He didn't understand, wasn't sure that he ever would, but Manhamha did—how could he *not* give him the rain?

He forced a smile and stepped to the side of the bed, feeling like he was about to cut the rope that held him to a savior ship in the middle of a raging ocean. He unscrewed the cap and handed the wineskin to Manhamha.

"Go well," Kinjin said.

"*Learn* well," Manhamha replied. And then he took the wineskin and drank the handfuls of liquid. The wheezing in his lungs vanished, and the pained look in his eyes relaxed.

He stared out through the window toward the setting sun which had just reached the ridge to the west.

Kinjin waited, hands folded, feeling lost.

He looked to Dashiyen, who bowed his head, and then recorded where Manhamha watched so they could begin the search for their newly birthed lama.

Despite the feelings of loss, a small bit of pride blossomed within Kinjin. He had helped the lama, and that was enough.

He turned to Dashiyen. "Is there room here? For someone like me?"

The smile on Dashiyen's face warmed Kinjin's heart. "We may be able to find room, young novice."

About the Author

Bradley P. Beaulieu is the author of *The Winds of Khalakovo*, the book Pat's Fantasy Hotlist named the Debut of the Year for 2011. The follow-up is *The Straits of Galahesh*. In addition to being an L. Ron Hubbard Writers of the Future Award winner, Brad's stories have appeared in various other publications, including *Realms of Fantasy Magazine, Orson Scott Card's Intergalactic Medicine Show, Writers of the Future 20*, and several anthologies from DAW Books. His story, "In the Eyes of the Empress's Cat," was voted a Notable Story of 2006 in the Million Writers Award. Visit his website at www.quillings.com.

Protection

Timothy Zahn

The small flock of sheep had settled into the meadow alongside Boone Creek, and Jeff Harfeld was all the way across on the far side of it, when Maizie decided to make her break.

She did it subtly, of course, or at least as subtly as a sheep could do anything. She started by angling away from the rest of the animals, as if she was merely following a particularly tasty stand of grass. Then she veered a little farther.

The next thing Jeff knew, she was waddling directly away and straight for the woods, moving as fast as her stubby little legs would take her.

Jeff shook his head, wondering yet again how some of these creatures managed to survive. The grass in the meadow was far superior to anything Maizie would find in the woods, and there was the creek for water, and there were no predators. Yet Maizie had somehow gotten it into her woolly head that life would be better in the forest, so off she took.

Jeff had been herding sheep ever since he was a teenager, and he knew they weren't exactly brilliant. But even with that standard, Jake Thompson's flock had to be one of the dumbest and most stubborn collection of mammals in the state.

Maizie was nearly to the first line of trees now, her backside waggling as she trundled along. For most herders, this would be the time to whistle up one of their border collies or German Shepherds to go round up the critter and get it back.

But Jeff didn't have any dogs. For one thing, working dog upkeep was expensive, and he couldn't afford it.

For another, he had something better.

He took a moment first to carefully scan the edges of the meadow. Not too many people came to this part of Rilling Lake, but he couldn't afford to take any chances. Satisfying himself that there was no one else around, he threw himself toward the ground, shapeshifted into his wolf form, and headed off around the edge of the flock.

A couple of the sheep lifted their heads as he loped by, but most of them just ignored him. His first couple of days with a new flock were usually pretty tense, but he'd been with Thompson's sheep long enough that they mostly saw him now as just another big, gray dog.

Maizie had made it to the woods by the time Jeff reached her. Planting himself directly in front of her, he gave a little warning growl. She replied with an indignant bleat and tried to go around him. He sidestepped back into her path, and they did their usual brief two-step until she gave up and headed back. Jeff stayed right behind her the whole way, nudging her with his snout a couple of times to keep her moving. She reached the flock, and Jeff shifted back to human.

For a long minute he gazed at the animals, a trickle of mixed emotions coloring his mood. Back in his childhood, before his parents had been killed in that accident, he'd dreamed about the kind of exciting life he would have one day. Instead, here he was, herding another man's sheep.

But at least it was work. With the economy in Travis County the way it was, he was lucky to have any job at all.

The sun had passed the top of the sky and disappeared behind some fluffy afternoon clouds by the time they reached the edge of the lake.

The sheep had already had a good drink from the stream, and none of them seemed interested in sampling lake water today. They weren't all that interested in walking any farther, either, and Jeff was kept busy as he nudged them along the shore toward the gravel road that led back to the Highway 46 in one direction and around the south end of the lake in the other.

The road wasn't the only way back to the Thompson ranch. It wasn't even the most direct route, actually. But Jeff always tried to come this way, because right where the road turned to follow the lake was a mostly unused boat dock called Perkins Pier.

And the only true friend he had in the entire county always saw him coming in time to be waiting under that dock when he and the sheep reached it.

She was waiting there now, he saw as he approached with his charges. The top of her head, from the eyes up, was just visible in the shadows beneath the rough wood, her shimmering, green-gray hair a perfect match for the lake grasses and long strands of algae riding the gentle waves.

Again, Jeff looked carefully around. Again, there was no one else in sight. A quarter mile away across the lake, O'Reilly's fishing shack was visible amid the reeds, but O'Reilly never visited the place except on weekends. "Hey, Tressla," he called softly, working his way through the sheep toward the dock. "How's the water today?"

Tressla bobbed up a little higher, bringing the rest of her face into view. Normally, her lips would be open in a smile by now, her sharp, pointed white teeth in contrast to the textured tan-brown of her face.

But today there was no smile on the mermaid's face. Instead, as Jeff got closer, he could see that there were deep tension lines.

He grimaced. Had she run into another of the lost fishhooks that years of sport fishing had left on the lake bottom? "Hey," he said again as he walked out to the end of the dock and lay down with his head hanging over the edge so that he could see her. "Is something wrong?"

"Something is very wrong," she said, her usually pleasant voice as harsh and grim as her face. "MacAvoy's boat was out on the lake last night. Very late, after moonset."

"Okay," Jeff said, frowning. An odd time to go fishing, but there were lots of strange characters in and around Dapper's Hollow, and Frank MacAvoy was no more or less strange than anyone else. "Did he see you or something?"

Tressla shook her head, her hair making little ripples in the water. "He dropped something into the water. Two things. This was the first." She lifted her right hand out of the water.

To reveal a small gun clutched in her fingers.

"What in the *world*?" Jeff breathed, leaning over the dock for a closer look. It was a semiautomatic, smaller than the guns Sheriff Daniels and Deputy Stadler wore on their belts. It was made of a darker metal, too, something he vaguely remembered hearing once was called bluing.

And fastened to its muzzle was a long, fat cylinder. A gadget Jeff knew from the movies and TV cop shows was called a silencer.

He tore his gaze away from the gun and looked at Tressla. She was looking back at him, her expression even tauter than it had been before. "This was the second," she said.

And to Jeff's stunned horror, she lifted the collar of a fancy suit jacket above the water's surface.

With the body of a dead man still wearing it.

It was just as well, he reflected distantly, that he was already lying down. "What in the name of—?" He strangled back the curse. Tressla didn't like it when he swore. "Who—what—?" With an effort, he strangled off the useless question and clamped his mouth shut. If he wasn't going to swear, he certainly wasn't going to babble. "Do you know who he is?"

"No," Tressla said. "But I only know people who come to the lake."

"Right." Jeff set his teeth firmly together. "Right. Okay. Go ahead and turn him over."

Jeff didn't socialize all that much with the people of Dapper's Hollow and the others who lived in the hills around the lake. But he knew most of them by sight, and the dead man was definitely not one of them. "I don't suppose he had a wallet, did he?"

"A what?"

"One of these," Jeff said, pulling out his own wallet and showing it to her. "Check his pants pockets. Actually, you should probably check <u>all</u> his pockets. The ones in his jacket, too.

"All right." She held the gun up toward him.

Gingerly, he took it. She slipped below the surface again, taking the body down with her.

He shifted his attention to the gun, wondering why in the world Mac would even have something like this. The man liked to hunt even more than he liked to fish, but that was all rifle and shotgun stuff.

And where in the world could he have gotten hold of a silencer? Jeff was no expert, but the things surely weren't available just by walking into Crow's Tackle and Hardware store. Not even by special order.

There was a soft splash, and Tressla's head appeared again above the water. "This was all he carried," she said, lifting her tail out of the water. Arrayed neatly across the dark gray of her flukes were a handkerchief, a few coins, a comb, a small flashlight, a wallet, and a thick envelope.

Laying the gun on the fluke beside the coins, Jeff picked up the wallet. There was a grand total of fifty-five dollars in it, plus a driver's license and credit card made out to a Jano Kostava. The address on the license, he noted, was in the city. Returning the wallet to Tressla's fluke, he picked up the envelope and opened it.

And nearly had a heart attack right there on the dock. The envelope contained money. A lot of money. Probably ten thousand dollars, he estimated as he thumbed through it. "What do you find?" Tressla asked.

"Nothing useful," Jeff said, carefully closing the envelope again and setting it beside the gun. "You said all this came from MacAvoy's boat. Are you sure MacAvoy was the one driving it?"

Tressla twitched her tail, the mermaid equivalent of a shrug. "It smelled like him."

Which meant that it definitely had been him. Tressla had an extraordinary sense of smell, both in and out of the water. "I guess I'm going to have to have a talk with him."

"Will that be safe?" Tressla asked anxiously.

"Don't worry, I'll be fine," Jeff assured her. "Can you keep an eye on the sheep for me? They've been well fed, and I'll get them into that little grassy pocket over there before I go. Just give them one of your eel-chaser screeches if they start to wander away—that ought to keep them there until I get back."

"I can try," Tressla said, eyeing the sheep doubtfully. "You won't be long, will you?"

"I'll be as fast as I can," Jeff promised. "It's mostly woods between here and Mac's house—I can wolf it over there in five minutes. Even if he's not home and I have to go into town, I shouldn't be more than an hour."

He gestured to the items still spread across her flukes. "Better put all this stuff back in the pockets where you found it. And whatever you do, don't let anyone else see the body."

MacAvoy lived just off Highway 46, in an eighty-year-old stick-built house on three heavily wooded acres. Jeff loped around the edge of the lake in wolf form, noting with some relief as he reached Mac's land that the other's boat was still tied to the dock. At least he wasn't out dumping any more bodies. He reached the homestead clearing, shifted back to human, and walked up to the house.

There was no answer when he tried the bell, and a peek into the garage showed that Mac's truck was gone. Returning to the woods, he shifted back to wolf and headed toward town.

He stopped first at the feed shop where Mac worked, where he learned that Mac had called in sick that day with a bad back. Wondering uneasily if Mac might have skipped town, he tried the final place on his mental list.

Which was, naturally, where he should have started in the first place.

Otto's was just starting to fill up as men and women got off work and dropped in for a couple of drinks before heading home. Mac was sitting alone at one of the tables in back, staring moodily into the half-full whisky glass in front of him.

Jeff could feel his pulse throbbing in his neck as he worked his way through the maze of tables. The bar wasn't all that crowded, but there ought to be enough witnesses to keep Mac from trying anything.

Unless he'd gone completely insane, of course. In that case, Jeff could very easily wind up in a position where he would have no choice but to shift to wolf and defend himself.

At which point the long, dark Harfeld family secret would be blown open in about as spectacular a way as anyone could ever want.

Mac looked up as Jeff sat down across from him. "Go away, Harfeld," he growled.

"In a minute," Jeff said. "I came by to talk about your boat."

Mac's forehead wrinkled. "My <u>boat</u>?"

"And," Jeff said, lowering his voice, "what you used it for last night."

For a couple of seconds Mac just stared at him, his face utterly expressionless. Jeff braced himself, wondering how fast he could shift if the man had another of those nasty little pistols tucked away under his jacket.

Then, to his relief, Mac lowered his gaze. "So you saw," he said, his voice dead.

Jeff inclined his head, an ambiguous gesture that kept him from having to lie outright. Tressla hated lying even more than she hated swearing. "You want to tell me about it?"

"What's the point?" Mac muttered. "Sheriff's going to bust in any second now and arrest me anyway, right?"

"Actually, I haven't told him about it yet," Jeff said, watching the other closely.

Mac looked up again, a spark of wary hope in his eyes. "You haven't?" he asked. "Look, it was an accident—I swear to God. He was there, and he had that gun, and—"

"Easy," Jeff soothed, holding up a hand. He'd never seen Mac babble before, and it was a little unnerving. "Start at the beginning. Who was he?"

Mac glanced furtively around the room. "It's about my brother. You knew he moved to the city right after the Fourth, right?"

"Yes," Jeff said, trying to remember the details of Billy MacAvoy's move. "He was opening a restaurant, right?"

"A coffee shop," Mac corrected. "Anyway, he's been working real hard, and it's finally starting to pay off. Then, a week ago, a couple of guys came to see him."

"What kind of guys?"

"The kind who wanted some of the money he was making," Mac said contemptuously. "Or something bad was going to happen to the place."

Jeff grimaced. "A protection racket."

"Yeah," Mac said grimly. "Damn them, anyway. A little hole-in-the-wall coffee shop, and these lousy—"

"I get the picture," Jeff said. "So what did he do?"

"The only thing he could," Mac said. "He stalled them, and when they left he went straight to the cops."

"Who said they couldn't do anything without proof?"

"Yeah, they said that," Mac confirmed. "Only he *had* proof: a security camera videotape. Picture <u>and</u> sound, so it caught everything."

"Beautiful," Jeff said. He'd never pegged the MacAvoys as being mental giants, but in this case Billy had definitely been thinking ahead. "I'll bet the thugs weren't happy about that."

"Happier than you think," Mac said coldly, his grin fading. "The tape Billy gave the cops disappeared."

Jeff stared. "You mean the cops are *in* on it?"

"Well, *one* of them is, anyway," Mac said heavily. "The guy I—the guy you saw—he was one of the gang."

"And he came all the way out *here*?" Jeff asked, frowning. "What in the world for?"

"Because it turns out there were *two* cameras," Mac said, smiling coldly. "Billy's still got the other tape."

Jeff glanced over his shoulder. "And he's *here*?"

"Naw, he's off in hiding somewhere," Mac said. "He's trying to find someone in the FBI to talk to about this. You know, with that cop involved. But I guess the thugs did their homework and figured out this was where he came from. So they sent this guy to find Billy or the tape."

"Only he found you instead."

Mac leaned over the table, his expression suddenly intense. "I swear to God it was an accident, Harfeld," he said tightly. "He was threatening me, pointing that damn gun in my face. I just...I don't even know how I did it, but I got to the gun and...I swear to God, I was just trying to take it away from him and not get shot." He swallowed hard. "And it just went off."

"And he happened to be in the way," Jeff said, a trickle of relief rippling over him. He should have guessed it would be something like that. The MacAvoys had gotten into more than their fair share of fist fights over the years, but he'd never heard of either Mac or Billy ever taking a gun to anyone. "So why didn't you just call Sheriff Daniel?"

" 'Cause I—" Mac broke off, lowering his gaze to the table again. " 'Cause I was scared," he said, almost too quietly for Jeff to hear. "And I...I panicked."

"Yeah," Jeff said, momentarily at a loss for words. This was a side of Frank MacAvoy most people never saw. Jeff certainly never had. "It happens, I guess."

"Not to me it doesn't," Mac growled. He looked up suddenly. "And if you ever tell anyone what I just said—" He broke off, rubbing his hand nervously across his mouth. "What am I *saying*?" he muttered. "Forget that. Just forget it. Anyway, I saw that he was...that calling a doctor wouldn't do any good. So I took him down to my boat, tied his feet to one of those big paving stones that Dad bought twenty years ago and never put in and...well, you know the rest."

"Right," Jeff said, nodding. "So when in all of that that did he try to buy you off?"

Mac's eyes narrowed suddenly. "How did you know about that? Damn it, Harfeld, were you outside my house?"

"No, no," Jeff said hastily, wincing. He'd forgotten he wasn't supposed to have actually seen the body up close. "I just assumed he'd try to buy his way out of this mess before he started making threats."

"Yeah, he did that, all right," Mac said, subsiding again. "Said he could give me ten grand now and another twenty when I gave him the tape. I told him to go to hell. That's when he pulled the gun." He seemed to brace himself. "Are you going to tell Sheriff Daniels?"

"There's a dead body in the lake," Jeff reminded him. "Eventually, we'll have to tell <u>someone</u>."

Mac hissed between his teeth. "Yeah, I know."

"But that doesn't mean we have to tell anyone right away," Jeff went on, an odd thought suddenly striking him. The one thing Jano Kostava should have been carrying, but hadn't, was a cell phone. "Did he happen to leave you a contact number for his boss?" he asked. "I mean, when he was trying to bribe you?"

"Not really," Mac said sourly. "But it wouldn't be hard to find one. I've got the guy's phone—took it before I dumped him. I thought...I don't know what I thought. Anyway, the damn thing's been ringing every two hours since breakfast."

"What are you telling him?"

"Nothing," Mac said with a snort. "You think I'm *answering* the damn thing?"

"No, of course not," Jeff said, drumming his fingers gently on the table. The beginnings of an idea were starting to pull together in the back of his mind. The kind of gang that would target a hole-in-the-wall coffee shop probably wouldn't be very big... "Let me make sure I've got this straight. No one saw you shoot the guy."

"Right," Mac said. "Probably didn't hear it, either—it had one of those silencers you see on cop shows. Lot louder than it sounds on TV, though. But no one came running, so I guess no one figured out it was a shot."

"And no one—except me—saw you dump the body," Jeff continued. "So Kostava's boss doesn't know what happened to him."

"Yeah, well, that won't last long," Mac said grimly. "I've been wondering if I should make a run for it."

"Not with a dead body in the lake," Jeff said. "But you shouldn't go back to your house, either. Let me think... how about O'Reilly's fishing shack? It's vacant right now, and the only way to get there is Old Rillside Road. You'd see anyone coming a mile away."

"I suppose I could do that," Mac said doubtfully. "You think I should do that?"

"Definitely," Jeff said, holding out his hand. "Let me have that phone first."

Mac's face suddenly darkened. "Why?" he asked suspiciously. "You going to call him?"

"Text him, actually," Jeff said calmly. "I'm pretty sure he'd recognize that my voice wasn't Kostava's."

"Harfeld—"

"And we don't have time to argue," Jeff interrupted. "You've basically got three choices here: turn yourself in to Sheriff Daniels, wait for Kostava's boss to show up on his own, or trust me."

For a moment Mac continued to glare. Then his lip twitched, and he dug into his side jacket pocket and pulled out a small phone. "I hope you know what you're doing," he muttered as he pushed it across the table.

"Don't worry," Jeff said, wishing those didn't sound so much like famous last words. "Now get going—I need you inside that shack and out of sight before it gets dark. Oh, and I'll need to borrow your boat, too."

"Yeah, whatever," Mac said, standing up. "You'll let me know what happens, right?

"You'll be the first," Jeff promised. "Go on."

With a final grimace, Mac strode across the bar and out into the late afternoon sunlight.

Jeff watched until he was gone, then turned his attention to the cell phone. It was one of those cheap, prepaid jobs that criminals on cop shows always used. A check of the call history gave him the number that Mac had been ducking all day, and a search through the menu gave him the text options.

And as for the message itself…

This really *was* crazy, Jeff knew as he laboriously thumbed out his message to Kostava's distant boss. Crazy, dangerous, and probably extremely stupid.

But still, even as his pulse continued its low-level pounding, one fact overlaid all of the fear and uncertainty.

The fact that this beat the heck out of herding sheep.

His first task was to get Mac's boat away from his private dock and move it to Perkins Pier.

Tressla was waiting when he arrived, her head half above water, her eyes on the sheep Jeff had left under her care. The sheep themselves, to Jeff's mild surprise, were also waiting. Even Maizie, who by all past history should be halfway down the gravel road by now. Apparently, Tressla's eel-chaser screech, designed to startle back underwater predators, was effective on land herbivores, too.

Nevertheless, the mermaid was clearly relieved to have Jeff back.

Her relief vanished as he laid out the plan he'd concocted.

But the alternative was for Mac to go to prison, or worse, and some bad people to get away with their badness. Jeff kept at her, and in the end she reluctantly agreed.

It was just after sunset by the time Jeff got back to Mac's house. Pulling Mac's ladder out of the tool shed, he propped it up against the side of the house and climbed up to the second-floor eaves. He didn't know if Kostava's people would be coming tonight or whether they would wait until tomorrow, but he needed to be ready.

It was just as well that he was. He'd barely begun scooping the handfuls of leaves and twigs out of Mac's gutters when a fancy car came smoothly up the drive and stopped a few feet from the foot of the ladder. The car's glass was heavily tinted, but Jeff could make out four shadowy figures inside.

The front passenger door opened and a smooth-faced man in a dark suit stepped out. "Evening," he said politely. "Are you Frank MacAvoy?"

"No, Mac's gone fishing," Jeff told him, putting on his most innocent country-boy expression as he looked down from his ladder. "Can I help you?"

"My name's Bronson," the man said. "I'm a lawyer from the city. I don't know if you knew, but Mr. MacAvoy's uncle Charles passed away three months ago."

"No, I hadn't heard that," Jeff said, wondering if Mac even had an Uncle Charles. "Real sorry to hear that."

"Well, he'd been ill for quite awhile," Bronson said. "At any rate, the will has now been probated, and Mr. MacAvoy has come into a small legacy."

"Hey, that's great," Jeff said brightening. "He'll be glad to hear that."

"Not a very big legacy, I'm afraid," Bronson conceded. "Still, I daresay that with the economy the way it is around here every bit helps. At any rate, I'm here with the legacy and the necessary papers for him to sigh. But you say he's gone fishing?"

"Yeah, but he's not <u>gone</u> or anything," Jeff said. "He's out on the lake, in one of the old fishing shacks that don't get used much once the season's over. Likes to get away from things sometimes, you know. Says he likes to think things over, though just between us I don't know if Mac's really got much equipment in the thinking-over department."

"I wouldn't know about that," Bronson said diplomatically, the way a good lawyer should. "Is the place he's currently staying hard to get to?"

"Oh, shoot, no," Jeff said, pointing over the other's head. "You make a left at the end of the driveway and go back to the highway. Turn right there and go about, oh, three miles to Old Rillside Road—it's a new sign; it used to be just Rillside Road until the *new* Rillside Road opened up through town—"

"Yes, we saw the turnoff for the new road," Bronson interrupted. "And then?"

"About two miles down Old Rillside you'll reach the lake," Jeff said. "The shack's right across the water—in fact, Perkins Pier points practically straight at it. Turn left and follow the road for another couple-three miles around the end of the lake, and it'll run you right up to the cabin."

"Sounds very rustic," Bronson said.

"You don't have any noisy neighbors dropping by, that's for sure," Jeff said. "I can go along and show you if you want."

He held his breath. The last thing he wanted was to be stuck in a car with these people when he had a bunch of jobs to do elsewhere. But it might look suspicious if he didn't at least offer.

Fortunately, the last thing *they* apparently wanted was to be saddled with an unwanted witness. "No, that's all right," Bronson assured him. "We can find it. Are you Mr. MacAvoy's handyman?"

Jeff snorted. "I wish," he growled. "Probably pay better than what I'm getting now. No, I'm just a neighbor who lost a bet and has to clean his damn gutters."

"Ah," Bronson said nodding. "Well, thank you for your help."

"Sure," Jeff said, waving cheerfully and turning back to the gutter.

"By the way," Bronson said, "is your name Wade, by any chance?"

Jeff turned back, frowning. "No, Jenkins," he said. "Pete Jenkins. Don't think I know anyone named Wade."

"Or Wired, or Weird, or something like that?" Bronson persisted. "I received a strange text message from someone in town that simply said 'weird happen.' Any idea what that might mean?"

"Not really," Jeff said, frowning harder. Actually, the message he'd sent had also included the words *need help need help*, but he wasn't surprised that Bronson hadn't mentioned that part. "We've got our share of campfire ghost stories around here. But no one really believes them. Probably someone just pulling your leg."

"Probably," Bronson said. "Good luck with the gutters."

Jeff turned back to the house, watching out of the corner of his eye while he scooped out leaves. He waited until the car had disappeared down the drive and he could tell from the engine and road sounds that it was headed back toward the highway. Then, climbing down, he hurried along the path toward Mac's dock and the lake.

Halfway there, concealed again by the woods, he shifted to wolf and broke into a flat-out run. He had to get to the lake end of Old Rillside Road before Bronson.

He needn't have worried. Whether Bronson's driver got lost or, more likely, slowed to a leisurely pace so as to give their planned activities a more complete cover of darkness, Jeff was in place and ready by the time he heard the crunch of leaves and stones under automobile tires. Making sure the hood of the sweatshirt he'd borrowed from Mac's boat was obscuring his face, he turned his back to the approaching car and nudged his flock of sheep onto the road.

The glow of the headlights lit up the ground and the sheep, sending bouncing shadows across the ground all the way to Perkins Pier. There was an extra-loud crunch of gravel, and the light washing over them steadied as the car came to a halt. "Hey!" a gruff voice called. "Move it, will you?"

Keeping his face turned away, Jeff waved a hand in acknowledgment. Giving the nearest sheep an encouraging nudge, he looked toward the rear of the flock. Waving his arms as if beckoning to some stragglers, he headed that direction.

A few steps away, out of the glare of the headlights and obscured by a stand of bushes, he shifted to wolf. Circling quietly around through the trees, he came up behind the car.

Possibly the occupants' full attention was on the flock of sheep milling past in front of them. More likely, whoever was watching the mirrors saw nothing menacing about a vague dog shape wandering around the woods at dusk. Whichever it was, Jeff made it to his chosen spot directly behind the trunk without sparking any reaction from Bronson or his associates. Dropping flat onto his belly, he shifted to human and slithered far enough beneath the car to reach the valve stem cap on the right rear tire. He got it off, then shifted back to wolf and pressed one of his claws firmly into the valve, listening tensely as the tire slowly hissed itself flat.

Again, there was no reaction from inside. For a moment he considered flattening the other rear tire as well, decided he didn't have time, and backed his way carefully out from under the car. Crouching down, making sure to stay out of sight of all the mirrors, he shifted to human and carefully slid the small flat pebble he'd prepared into the trunk lock. He made sure it was wedged tightly, then again shifted to wolf and retraced his steps through to the trees to the rear of the flock.

A minute later, once again in human form, he guided the last of the sheep across the road. "There you go," he called back over his shoulder to the car, using an old man's wheezy voice. "Sorry about that."

There was a subtle change in engine pitch, and with a crunch of gravel the car started forward again. Jeff had made it another twenty feet with the flock when the crunching stopped, the engine shifted back to park, and there was the sound of a door opening. By the time he'd gotten the sheep gathered into the grassy pocket where he'd left them earlier, there were more doors opening and closing, and the car engine had been shut off. Jeff made sure the sheep were settled, then shifted to wolf and padded quietly back to the road.

There were four of them, all right, Bronson plus three others. All four were gathered at the rear of the vehicle, and one of them was trying vainly to get the trunk open.

"—something in there," the man was saying as Jeff arrived at the edge of the woods. "Feels like—I don't know —like a stone or something."

"How the hell could a stone get in there?" one of the others growled. "It just bounced in off the road and stuck? Huh?"

Bronson stirred. "Calm yourself," he said.

Jeff bared his teeth, his fur standing momentarily on end. Back at Mac's house, Bronson had been all smooth and pleasant, a civilized man on an honest errand.

Now, suddenly, that voice had gone cold and ruthless and utterly evil. Bronson wasn't another errand boy, Jeff realized suddenly. Bronson was the protection racket boss himself.

"How it got there isn't important," Bronson continued. "Keep yourselves focused. Chinks, is that a boat I see by the pier?"

"Yeah, I think so," one of the men said, peering toward the lake.

"Go check it out," Bronson ordered. "See if it's got oars or a motor."

"Right." Chinks headed off toward the boat at a fast jog.

"We're going to take a *boat*?" one of the others asked, sounding surprised.

"The cabin's right there," Bronson said, pointing toward O'Reilly's cabin. "The DMV says Frank MacAvoy drives a '95 Bronco. That's a '95 Bronco parked there."

"Yeah, but a *boat*?" the man repeated, more plaintively this time. "I don't like boats."

"Would you rather walk?" Bronson countered. "Because if Stojan can't get into the trunk for the spare, that's the only other way."

From the dock came the sound of Mac's trolling motor. "Boat looks good," Chinks called softly. "Motor's all gassed up, too."

"Good," Bronson said calmly, stepping away from the car. "You going to walk it, Gav? If not, everyone in."

"Oh, hell," Stojan said suddenly, pointing at Jeff. "Look."

The others turned. "Damn," Gav breathed. "That's a *wolf*."

"Don't panic," Bronson said, glacially calm. "Wolves don't attack people like they do in books. It's probably just curious."

That was, Jeff decided, as good an exit cue as any. Giving a small snuff, he turned around and headed as nonchalantly as he could deeper into the woods.

"See?" he heard Bronson say from behind him. "All right, everyone in the boat. Let's do this."

By the time Jeff returned to his sheep the four men were in the boat and the craft was moving slowly but steadily away from the dock, heading toward the cabin on the far side. Jeff let them get a couple hundred feet from shore, and then shifted back to human. Pulling out Kostava's cell phone, he punched in 911.

"This is Jeff Harfeld," he said softly when the dispatcher answered. "I'm out by Perkins Pier on Old Rillside Road. There's four strangers out here with guns, and I think they're stealing Frank MacAvoy's boat. You'd better get Sheriff Daniels out here right away."

He got an acknowledgment and hung up. Moving closer to the road, where he could listen for the sheriff's approach, he sat with his back to one of the trees and settled in to wait.

It began as a quick but sharp splash from about fifty feet to the boat's right, a small circular burst of whitewater bouncing up in the fading light. One of the men in the boat looked in that direction. The other three didn't bother. A few seconds later came a louder splash, this one from the same distance on the other side of the boat. This time two of the men looked. They looked again a few seconds later when another, louder splash came from directly behind the boat.

A sudden idea struck Jeff—a little extra window dressing to help set the proper mood. Shifting to wolf, he gave a long, mournful howl.

All four men looked back at the trees on that one. Jeff gave another howl, this one punctuated by another splash from the right side of the boat. Two of the men looked over at the splash area, and Jeff could hear low, nervous-sounding voices coming from the boat. He heard Bronson say something sharp, and with clear reluctance all but one of the men turned their attention forward again. The last man was slower, or else more nervous, his gaze lingering another second on the splash area.

Which was why he was the only one of the four who saw the head and shoulders of the dead Jano Kostava rise dramatically above the water.

The man yelped a startled curse, jerking so violently that he sent the boat rocking. The other three grabbed the gunwales for balance, and while they did so Kostava's body slipped back out of sight. For a few seconds Jeff could hear the man's panic-stricken voice as he tried to explain what he'd seen. The other three clearly thought he was nuts, and again it took Bronson's sharp voice to quiet them down.

And then, on the opposite side of the boat, the body again rose into view.

All four of them saw it this time. They sat frozen, staring at the corpse as it floated impossibly upright in the rippling water. Tentatively, suspiciously, Bronson called Kostava's name; the body's response was to slide back down out of sight.

Jeff smiled grimly as a fresh round of edgy chatter broke out in the boat. Tressla was playing it perfectly, keeping them swimming in confusion as she ratcheted up the primal fear of death and the unknown. With men like these, Jeff knew, that fear could lead to only one response.

For a few taut seconds nothing happened. Bronson gave an order, and the man in the stern reluctantly fed power to the motor again. The others sat stiffly in their seats, looking back and forth through the gathering gloom.

Then, fifty feet to the right, the body once again rose into view.

Only this time, instead of just floating in place, it began moving slowly but steadily toward the boat.

It took a few seconds for the situation to fully sink in. Bronson gave a sharp order, and the man in the stern twisted the throttle arm hard over, sending the boat arcing away from the approaching corpse.

The body responded by picking up speed. The boat was driving desperately away from it now, but it was clear that the pursuer was closing the distance.

It was no more than ten feet away when it abruptly sank again beneath the water.

And with that, even Bronson had clearly had enough. He gave another sharp order, his voice shaking now as badly as those of his men. The boat turned again, this time toward shore, and made for the dock as fast as the straining trolling motor could take it.

They were fifty feet from safety when the body rose for the last time from the water behind them and once again headed toward them.

Only this time, it was moving with the speed of an avenging angel, a white-topped wake streaming behind it.

The men in the boat didn't even hesitate. Almost in unison, all four of them snatched guns from beneath their jackets and opened fire.

Jeff tensed. But Tressla was well protected as she pushed Kostava along, both by the body itself and the foot or so of water between her and the guns. The corpse didn't slow down as the desperate thunderclaps split the quiet of the evening, sending birds streaming into the air from the shoreline trees. The men continued firing as the body caught up with the boat—

And with a sudden heaving lunge threw itself high over the side and into the bottom of the boat.

Someone screamed in terror, the sound audible even over the suddenly intensified gunfire. The boat rocked back and forth, nearly capsizing, as the four living occupants scrambled violently away from the body now sprawled in their midst.

And with every eye pointed at Kostava's body, none of them saw the slender mermaid hand dart up from the water at the bow and slip Kostava's gun over the side into the boat.

It took a few seconds for the men to realize that the body had stopped moving and for the gunfire to fade away. It took a few seconds more for them to realize just who it was. "It's Kos!" someone gasped. "Mr. Finch, it's <u>Kos</u>."

"What do we do?" someone else said, his voice still bubbling at the edge of panic.

But Bronson, at least, was back on balance. "We dump him," he said, his voice icy calm again.

"But—"

"It was a trick," Bronson cut him off harshly. "I don't know how MacAvoy pulled it off. But I'm very much looking forward to asking him. Come on—grab his arms."

"We're just going to *dump* him?" someone asked.

"Would you rather give him a ride?" Bronson shot back. "Come <u>on</u>, damn you—grab his arms."

"Don't even think about it," an electronically enhanced voice boomed suddenly from Jeff's left.

He started, twisting his head around to look. Sheriff Daniels was standing at the treeline by the road, a small megaphone raised to his lips. Behind him, Deputy Stadler was getting the shotgun out of the police car that was now parked behind Bronson's car. "Bring the boat in, nice and easy," Daniels continued, striding forward with his hand resting on his holstered gun. "I see anything go in the water, you're going in after it."

Both cops were waiting on the dock when the boat arrived. "Well, well," Daniels said, craning his neck. "What have we here?"

"It wasn't us," one of the men insisted, his voice still shaking. "He was already dead. I swear."

"He was coming toward us," another added tautly. "He was in the water and coming right toward us."

"Sure," Daniels said. "Why don't we all get out, and we'll go down to the station and sort all this out. Rick, better call Claire and have her bring her car, too—we've kind of got a crowd here. And you four boys can just set your guns right here on the dock, if you don't mind."

Silently, they complied. Then, one by one, they climbed up out of the boat, where Stadler was waiting with handcuffs. Bronson was the last, glowering silently as he put his hands behind his back and let the deputy cuff him. Jeff held his breath...

"Hold it—looks like we forgot one," Daniels said suddenly, peering into the boat. Kneeling down, he reached in and retrieved Kostava's silenced gun.

Bronson inhaled sharply. "That's not ours," he said quickly. "It must belong to the boat's owner."

Stadler snorted. "Who, Frank MacAvoy? You're kidding, right?"

"No, really," Bronson insisted. "It's not ours."

"I don't know what you're used to in the city," Daniels said, his voice gone cold and professional. "But people in these parts don't have much use for guns with suppressors." He gestured. "And we *sure* as hell know better than to leave our guns in the water at the bottom of a boat. Deputy Stadler, I think it's time we read these folks their rights."

It took another hour for Jeff to get the sheep back to their barn at the Thompson ranch and then go give the sheriff a somewhat edited version of his side of the day's events.

After that, he hung around the station for awhile, staying out of the way of the crowd of state police who were suddenly arriving on the scene as he engaged in a bit of eavesdropping.

It was full dark, and Tressla was waiting, when he finally made it back to Perkins Pier. "You were gone a long time," she said as he leaned down over the edge of the dock. "I was getting worried."

"Sorry," Jeff apologized. "But I wanted to make sure the investigation was going in the right direction."

"Is it?"

"I think so," Jeff said. "The whole thing's tangled enough that Bronson and his men should still be in jail by the time Billy MacAvoy finds someone in the FBI to talk to about their little protection racket."

"Even though none of those men actually killed anyone?"

Jeff shrugged. "The gun that *did* kill Kostava was found in their boat," he reminded her. "And the way Bronson tried to bluster himself and the gun out from under all this tells me that the thing's probably going to have an interesting history once they start looking into it. Bronson's actually a city cop named Finch, by the way. Probably the one Billy MacAvoy went to and who destroyed the first security tape.

I'm guessing he got Kostava's gun out of the police evidence locker or something. But they'll figure it out."

"I see," Tressla said, in a tone that told Jeff that she didn't really see at all. But then, swimming peacefully through Rilling Lake, Tressla never got to watch TV cop shows. "The town and the people are safe?"

"Looks that way," Jeff said. "More importantly, you and the lake are safe."

"Thank you," Tressla said quietly.

"I couldn't have done it without you," Jeff said. Reaching beneath the dock, he found her hand and squeezed it. "See you tomorrow?"

She squeezed his hand back. "I'll be here."

About the Author

Timothy Zahn has been writing science fiction for more than thirty years. In that time he has published forty-two novels, nearly ninety short stories and novelettes, and four collections of short fiction. Best known for his nine *Star Wars* novels, he is also the author of the Quadrail series, the Cobra series, the Conquerors Trilogy, and the young-adult Dragonback series. Recent books include *Cobra Guardian* and *Cobra Gamble*, the second and third books of the Cobra War Trilogy, *Star Wars: Choices of One,* and the 20th Anniversary edition of his first Star Wars novel, *Heir to the Empire.*

Upcoming books include *Judgment at Proteus*, the final book of the Quadrail series, and *Pawn*, the first of the Sibyl's War series. You can contact him at facebook.com/ TimothyZahn. "Protection" first appeared in the DAW Books anthology *Boondocks Fantasy*.

The Price of Fame

Brian E. Shaw

May 23, 2044

Dr. Eoin Littlefield was exhausted. But planning a man's demise is not an affair to be undertaken lightly. And planning a man's death two-thousand years in the past while on camera, without getting caught, required a degree of dedication and brilliance that few men possessed.

Fortunately, he had both.

Unfortunately, Eoin's back and eyes ached terribly from a night of non-stop research, and his stomach growled ominously from a long night of no food and too much coffee. Frankly, pure rage and humiliation had been his primary fuel.

So, he stepped out of the museum and onto Constitution Avenue. He made for the closest food truck he could find. It was only just past 6 a.m., but in the most ambitious and powerful city on the planet, there were already people in line.

Finally making his way to the front, he purchased two breakfast burritos and a bottle of imported milk. He was old enough to remember real milk, back before the Bovine Fevers of the 20s, and he had never developed a taste for the synthetic stuff. But he drank it anyway.

Wolfing the food down as he walked, Eoin's stride grew faster and stronger as he approached the closest green-

271

glowing Hop Portal. He stepped through the tingly energy field and instantly emerged eighty feet below, inside the Smithsonian Metro station.

It was a strange twist of scientific evolution that humans could move great distances through space and time, as long as one element was temporal; but they could not yet move and reestablish a living creature more than a mile away.

But he wasn't a physicist or an engineer, nor would he want to be. In fact, his head hurt just thinking about the math involved. No, he was a serious student of humanity, its ancient history, and of the science and art of time-travel filmmaking. Those pursuits in turn allowed him to bring the results of his research to the world.

So as long as he could travel back in time and hide in the bush to watch Aztec rituals be performed in person, he'd happily keep taking trains to move about his adopted city like some old-timer who kept talking about the days before cars drove themselves.

On the train ride out to Maryland, Eoin quickly accessed the address of his closest rival, Simon Linux.

The man lived near a Hop Portal, so Eoin used his contact lenses to communicate his required destination to the train's digital controller. A few minutes later, a blue light began to flash across his lenses and he stood to wait in the aisle. Thirty seconds later, a green portal opened at the front of the car and he quickly moved down the empty aisle and through the portal which deposited him on a tree-lined sidewalk above without the train ever slowing.

Eoin took several deep breaths. Then he accessed the map and strode purposefully down the sidewalk, following the translucent green dots that showed him the quickest route to Linux's home.

A former and reputably honorable Marine officer, Simon Linux had used his chiseled jaw and baritone voice to help launch the *History Extreme! Channel* into instant financial success; success that came directly at a cost to Eoin and his cash-strapped benefactors at the Smithsonian.

Eoin would never forgive or forget the number of humiliations and setbacks he'd experienced at their hands, but one always stood out in his mind.

It had taken him two years of research, a geologic and hydrologic study, and four significant grants to fund an expedition to film Ghengis Khan and the Mongol Horde as it swept across the steppes of Central Asia. Eoin had laid still and silent in sweltering heat, pissing on himself, and getting gnawed on by ants for two days. All so he could avoid detection by the Khan's scouts.

And finally he had his shot.

It was the great man himself. And he was riding at the front of his main column, laughing and joking. It was as good a shot as Eoin could have hoped for. So he settled his body, checked his comms link back to the Smithsonian and zoomed in.

Eoin didn't want to rush the shot. He loved the art. So Eoin had painstakingly panned his Koshari Contact-lens Cam up through the dust swirling around the horse's hooves, taken in the stitching of the Khan's boots and saddle and finally, dramatically, he had panned up to the man's face. The Khan had a hard face and dark, intelligent eyes.

Eyes that were locked on Simon Linux who rode next to the Khan, laughing and smiling as he gestured wildly with his strong hands, trying to communicate with the man that had once ruled most of the known world as if they were engaged in a game of charades.

That humiliation had cost Eoin the Academy Award that year, and because of the politics involved probably the next as well. It had even cost him the Muldrow Award which was supposed to go to academics, like him. *For God's sake, he had two PhDs!*

He didn't even know if Linux could read.

Eoin's face and neck burned as he swam in a temporary miasma of loathing and bitter regret over what might have been. Then his lenses triggered a rapid beeping inside his head.

Three blocks from his arrival above ground and removed from the crush of traffic back on Georgia Avenue, Eoin stood on the sun-dappled sidewalk in front of a beautiful Georgian home with two books tucked tightly under his arm.

Besides whiskey, books were Eoin's only true luxury. Since they had stopped being printed around 2035, physical books were considered an affectation only for the wealthy or eccentric academics. But to Eoin they were something more. His books represented a physical connection to the past, the times he so painstakingly researched and documented. And besides his videos, they were the only part of the past he owned, as he strictly adhered to the Covenants of Non-Interference and Exploitation that were required of any time-traveling researcher worth his salt.

Men worthy of fame and respect. Men like him.

Eoin's face felt cool and his back straightened. And then, nodding to himself, he strode up the walk and faced the home's automated greeting system.

"Dr. Eoin Littlefield to see Mr. Linux," he said stiffly.

"One moment please," came the automated and oddly sultry reply.

What kind of home-control system did Linux own?

As he waited, Eoin became uncomfortably aware that the home bothered him. Not the house itself, it was gorgeous. But the fact that Simon Linux owned it. It wasn't his style. The man should live in something more akin to the Playboy Mansion crossed with a trailer park than this place. This place was genteel and classic. Second, it was too quiet.

Simon was loud. He was brash. But the home had a tranquility that seemed to ooze out of the white rocking chairs and honeysuckle bushes that entwined the porch railing. It defied everything Simon knew about the man. And then the door opened.

Eoin was surprised to see that Simon had not only answered the door himself, but that he appeared awake and alert. Eoin had deliberately picked the early morning hour in the hope of gaining an upper-hand on a man he assumed partied until close to sunrise on most days. But there Simon was, dressed in a gray Marines T-shirt, black workout shorts, and bathed in a light sweat. And if he was surprised to see Eoin, he didn't show it.

That annoyed the hell out of Eoin, whose own eyebrows knit together in consternation.

"Eoin! Jesus, how are you? "

"I'm fine."

"Well, I'm glad to hear it. Please, come on in. I don't want to be rude, even though I am surprised to see you. What brings you to my neighborhood?" Linux led the way deeper into the house and motioned for Eoin to take a seat on a bar stool in his well-appointed kitchen.

Eoin suddenly discovered that he was at a loss for words, so he made a show of setting down his books on the blue-granite counter and taking in his surroundings as he pulled out a leather journal and a small antique map.

Linux's eyes darted to the map immediately, a fact Eoin did not miss. But he didn't stare or invite any questions. Instead, Eoin remained nonchalant. He let his eyes roam, taking in the chef's kitchen and paired oil paintings of revolutionary naval battles that flanked the breakfast nook behind him. It was entirely incongruous. But it didn't do one damn thing to change Eoin's plan, so he gathered his thoughts and sat down.

"I have a proposition for you," Eoin began as Simon crossed his muscled arms and arched an eyebrow in his direction.

"What kind of proposition?"

"The kind to make and record history neither of us has ever dreamed of. The kind that will raise the bar for generations. That kind."

Simon's quizzical eyebrows dropped and settled over blue eyes that had turned calculating and intense. Eyes that didn't belong on a man that had once rode dirt bikes and hover-boards for a living.

Simon uncrossed his arms and leaned against the counter, his eyes boring into Eoin's.

"Tell me more. And let me see that map please."

Hook. Line. And sinker. Eoin almost exhaled in relief. But instead he maintained his game-face and asked one off topic question. He just couldn't help himself.

"Alright, but first tell me about this house. You make a good living. But is it that good?"

"This?" Simon gestured around with open palms. "My Dad left me this house and his company when he died. I was deployed when it happened. So, when I got out of the Corps, I sold the company to fund my businesses. But my wife adored the house and when I lost her too, I just couldn't part with it. It's my only real connection left to either of them. Why do you ask?"

Eoin searched for a response as several competing thoughts and emotions danced through his consciousness.

Linux had been married? It didn't matter.

An inheritance. Of course. The home, the money, the lifestyle were all part of an inheritance. Simon hadn't worked for any of it. He hadn't lived, crushed under a mountain of student loans.

And what legacy had Eoin's father left him? Nothing.

The un-ambitious clod had left his mother with a minor pension from the former US Postal Service and a son with memories of an empty chair next to his mother at science fairs, spelling bees, and anything else that wasn't an athletic event. Eoin's first real home, the first place he'd ever felt accepted and respected had been the halls of his universities. Places dedicated to furthering knowledge.

What about his wife? Was Simon Linux capable of love? It was a revelation. But it wasn't germane to his decision to proceed.

"I just want to understand your motivations. I want to understand why you do what you do."

Simon laughed at this. The sound made Eoin's chest tight and his fingers curl. But he forced himself to be calm.

"That's the easiest question of all," Simon replied. "I do it because nobody else has. I do it because I have nothing to lose. I want to climb new mountains. I want to push limits. I want to advance…everything…anything. Now, are you gonna let me in on your plan or keep playing twenty questions?"

Only slightly mollified, Eoin swallowed his pride and began to lay out his plan. At least, the parts Simon needed to know about.

An hour later neither man had moved much, though Simon had pulled up a chair next to Eoin at the bar.

"So, your plan is for us to get captured by the Legionnaire son of a slave merchant as the Roman army returns from the conquest of Dacia in AD 109 and hope *really* hard things go right from that point on?"

Eoin shook his head. "Luck has little to do with it. First off, if things go badly, we simply open a gate and come home. Emergency extraction is allowed for in the Protocols. But they won't go badly. Flavius kept a precise journal of the Dacian campaign."

"And his father's business records are among the best documented in any collection. It was the year 109 and Octavian could have stood up to an IRS audit," Eoin said, tapping a red-leather bound journal. "And from these records we know that he was tasked personally by Emporer Trajan with buying slaves. All we need to do is fall into his lap and make the greatest first person documentary experience ever."

And then it hit him. "How did you know about Dacia? I never mentioned that."

"I majored in History at the Naval Academy," Simon answered nonchalantly. "As you might imagine, military history makes up a lot of the required credit hours."

Not wanting to press his luck, Eoin returned his notes and the map to his books and turned to face the enigma that sat next to him.

"Do we have a deal?"

"Damn right we do," Simon said extending one of his large hands. "I just hope you know how to fight."

Eoin just shook his hand in return. He knew Simon had seen action during his time in the service, but the closest Eoin had come to a fight was when he ran from one is sixth grade. He liked to joke that all the running he'd done as a child was what had turned him into a triathlete later in life. But he didn't think Simon would find that amusing given the circumstances. So he just nodded and smiled, knowing it wasn't going to matter anyway.

May 24, 2044 and AD 109 – Day 0

Dressed in the best ancient Germanic attire the *History Extreme!* costume shop could make on short order, Eoin and Simon adjusted their contacts and performed audio and video checks with the channel's technicians.

When everything checked out they stepped onto the time-transfer platform and waited.

It didn't take long. But as always, the gut wrenching sensation of being sucked backwards through a vacuum at a thousand miles an hour, made it feel like an eternity. When Eoin felt his feet touch hard-packed earth, he opened his eyes.

Just in time to see a horse bearing down on him.

Eoin rolled to the side, aided by the added momentum from a kick in his ribs. He landed roughly and lay motionless for a second as he caught his breath.

Simon rushed to his side and helped him stand. Opening his eyes, Eoin became the first man in history to find himself pleased to be facing a very surprised and stern looking Roman officer on horseback and a dozen of his men. All of whom held swords or spears pointed at him and Simon.

Apparently Eoin's research and calculations had been accurate. So in his best classical Latin, he demanded to know why the officer had attacked him.

The officer didn't respond directly. He simply barked out orders for his men to seize the 'barbarians.' Eoin quickly reminded Simon of their plan in a stage whisper. "Fight back, but just enough for pride. Don't let an unarmed man take you."

"I remember," the former leatherneck said as an armored soldier strode over. The Roman's lips were curled back under his scarred and bearded face.

Simon waited casually until the man seized him by the wrist. Then, taking advantage of an extra sixty pounds of muscle and centuries of martial science, he grabbed the man's arm, flipped his wrist over, and sent the man head over heels into the dirt with a sickening popping sound.

Eoin barely had time to register the impressive counter before another man rushed him from his right. But using the skills he'd learned in a campus sponsored self-defense class he met the charge head on, placed his hands on the man's shoulders and drove his knee into the man's stomach just above his groin. Had Eoin been a woman and had his attacker been a modern sized man, it would have hurt worse. But it did the trick.

Turning back to face their enemies Eoin saw that his first goal had been achieved. They had earned a modicum of respect. Of course, it was demonstrated by a dozen spears and swords now fanned out around them, motioning them to lie down on the dirt road.

As more soldiers emerged from the darkness, Eoin heard the metallic clanking of chains and allowed himself a small smile.

Next to him, their faces just a few feet apart in the darkness, Simon asked him if the plan had worked.

"So far, so good," he answered, not willing to get overly optimistic just yet.

AD 109, Day +1

After being chained together and kicked and punched for good measure, Eoin and Simon were led back down the road to the back of the column of tired-looking Roman soldiers. They were settled in with a group of men of all races and ages. It was dark, and the exhaustion of marching was still evident in their shuffling footsteps. But it was the bend of these men's backs that told the real story. They were slaves. And he and Simon were now among them.

Eoin couldn't imagine why the army was marching through the night south of the Rubicon, especially so close to Rome. But then came sunrise and from the top of a hill he saw the Imperial city spread out before them like an old lover inviting him into her arms. He'd recognize her anywhere, at any time. Eoin loved Rome. And so did her soldiers.

A throaty cheer went up from the massed columns of warriors, and a short time later, officers on horseback began riding up and down the column barking short orders, tightening the ranks, and ensuring a more professional appearance.

Eoin did his best to capture all of it.

A few hours later the army actually arrived at the wide section of road just outside the gates of the city. The arches were tantalizingly close and Eoin marveled at them in wonder.

And then he and Simon, along with three other men were yanked roughly out of line and pushed across an open field toward a series of tents set up around a packed-earth market that operated in the shadows of Rome's walls.

Four soldiers with spears at their backs poked and prodded them forward until a large man with tanned skin and a full black beard approached them, shaking hands and smiling warmly at the officer with them.

Eoin held his breath.

And then the young Legionnaire dismounted and let the older man take him in a great bear hug, clapping him heartily on the back. Eoin exhaled in relief and tried to listen in as the men spoke.

It was difficult for Eoin to understand everything being said, even with the aid of his implanted translation software, but body language counts for a lot. And there was no mistaking the officer reenacting their fight the night before as he gestured toward the two time-travelers.

Finally, the older man he could only assume was Octavian called out to one of his workers and pointed at the group of slaves. He pointed at the city, gave some instructions, and then led his son into the shade of a large open tent where fruit and large comfortable pillows waited for them.

Eoin and Simon were not shown any such hospitality. They were taken away by a large man with a shaved head and a missing ear. The brute didn't talk much, but he didn't need to. His cudgel proved adequate to his needs for communication as Simon and later Eoin were to learn as they were led down back alleys and into the dusty, foul underbelly of the most idealized of Roman venues. The Coliseum.

AD 109, Day +5

Their confinement had been more horrifying than Eoin had imagined. Despite his expertise, his senses were simply not prepared for the shock of sharing a dark confined space with men that looked like ghouls and who shit on themselves in their sleep when they weren't screaming themselves awake at night.

But the days, the days were much worse. As he knew would happen, Emporer Trajan had ordered the most tremendous gladiatorial games in Roman history be held in honor of the victorious army. And every day Eoin and Simon watched from their cell as men who were there before them were led out of the cell block, sometimes screaming and wailing like children, but never to return.

The entire time they could hear the screams of the populace and feel the stomping of their feet through the earth as the people of Rome called for blood time and time again. It was an abattoir of sport and Eoin had a front row seat to the trembling, horrifying splendor.

And then their turn arrived.

There was no notice. Just the shouts and muted calls for blood that announced the end of every battle, followed by the jingling of keys and the presence of five malicious eyed guards behind the sadistic slave-master. There was no Spartacus-like glory. There was no speechmaking or dignified ritual. They were simply human chattel to be slaughtered for entertainment. Which ironically would probably play a big role in how the *History Extreme! Channel* chose to market the event.

He chuckled at that as their cell door was opened and he and Simon shared a knowing look. They had prepared for this. They had designed this moment.

None of which made it less horrific.

But they got to their feet and were led away without a fuss. The group walked through two heavy, iron-bonded doors and into a long tunnel with daylight at the end.

His eyes took a moment to adjust, but once they did, Eoin realized they had reached the point of no return. Behind them a heavy iron gate slammed shut and the guard with the key backed away from it, far out of reach, his cracked, yellowed teeth and mad eyes fading away into the darkness.

Ahead and above them he could clearly hear the crowds and see the dirt floor of the Coliseum lit brightly and baking in the mid-summer sun. His lenses told him it was close to 100 degrees Fahrenheit and he believed it.

Next to them, laid out on a crumbling table, were an assortment of weapons in various stages of quality and decay. Eoin paused to look at it all, carefully panning across the table, knowing the techs back home were already using the images he was transmitting to identify the arsenal. Axes. Swords. Spears. Nets. Daggers. Anything you could imagine, and some still sporting fresh blood.

Simon didn't pause at all. He moved in quickly and belted one of the better looking swords around his waist. Then he stuck a dagger in the belt and picked up a spear, a net, and a large two-headed axe.

Eoin tried to follow suit but could only lay his hands on a spear and a heavy headed mace before the crowd let out a thunderous roar and the bulbous thug behind them began ushering them up the tunnel's ramp.

Linux never looked at Eoin and he only spoke two words. "Stay close." Then he began to stride purposefully into the arena, his face a mask of stone. His back straight and his shoulders and chest spread wide. He was an intimidating man.

Eoin did his best to imitate it, but he had to draw hard on his belief in what was to be achieved just to keep his feet moving in step with Simon's.

But the cameras wouldn't know any of that. They would just see two men stalking heroically toward the battle. Only Eoin knew that one of them wouldn't be leaving.

Emerging into the Coliseum, a chorus of boos went up from the crowd of thousands gathered around them. But it wasn't the thousands that concerned Eoin. It was the four men standing between them and a gaudily decorated balcony in the shade at one end of the Coliseum.

Seeing they had some distance between them and their opponents, Eoin took a moment to turn around slowly and capture the Coliseum in all its undulating, seething grandeur.

And in that moment he was infinitely thankful that his audio and video equipment could not read his mind.

What the hell am I doing?

Eoin finished his turn and came to stand at Simon's shoulder. In front of them, the four athletic looking warriors, each outfitted in gleaming, exotic armor, raised their weapons in salute to the balcony above them. Next, they turned and gave a much less hearty salute to the pair of counterfeit gladiators.

Eoin tried to soak up the moment, zooming in on each of his enemies.

Simon just rushed to his right, taking up position where the wall and tunnel met. Eoin immediately realized his strategy.

He had stone to his right and a twelve foot fall at his back, leaving him with only two sides to defend. Eoin swiftly took up his position on Simon's left as the four men spread out. Simon arrayed his arsenal about him, starting with the net in his left hand and spear in his right.

Taking his cue from the former Marine, Eoin laid his mace at his feet and took the spear up in both hands as a man in creased bronze armor and wielding a wicked trident separated himself from the pack and began stalking forward toward the pair, his eyes staring death at them with every inch his sandaled feet covered in their direction.

In his head, Eoin heard the calm voice of Captain Stephanie Drumm, their mission controller.

"We can pull you boys out anytime. Just say the word,"

Seizing the moment to build the drama and story, Eoin replied. "Roger that, but we want to take this as far as possible. Don't get trigger happy on us. We'll call for extraction if we need it."

"It's your life," the former Navy pilot and astronaut said back.

Simon crouched and began lightly twirling the net in front of him. His face betrayed no emotion or sign that he had even heard the conversation with their mission controller. "When I move, guard my flank."

"Got it," Eoin replied with more conviction than he felt.

The trident wielding gladiator was now less than ten feet away. Simon feinted with the net, testing him. He didn't budge.

He came two steps closer, his armored companions a few paces behind him.

Simon took a step forward. Eoin did likewise with feet that felt like lead.

In a flash, Simon sprang forward, eating up the distance between himself and surprising Trident. Simon's arm snapped out. The net flew high and sailed just over the head of the gladiator.

Eoin groaned at the obvious miss. But Simon was already moving. His legs propelled him forward inside the trident's reach and he stabbed with his long arms, burying his spear in the distracted man's belly.

Blood splattered and the man screamed. It was a choked and terrible sound, half sob and half pain. It was the scream of a man dying suddenly and violently, and it was a sound Eoin prayed never to hear again.

A threat emerged to Simon's left. A short, dark-skinned man in helmet and loincloth sprinted at Simon's exposed side with two swords leading his charge.

Eoin didn't think. He didn't have time. He just lunged with his spear hoping to stop the man's momentum before an inescapable disaster occurred.

He succeeded. The man was forced to halt his charge and spin away to avoid impalement.

Simon came up to his side. "They won't make the mistake of attacking alone again. I need you to keep the little guy off my back. I'm going to try and take out the guy with the axe first. Then things will probably get ugly quick. You ready?"

"No."

"Good." Simon even smiled. Eoin just shook his head and began circling with Simon until they had closed the distance to a medium built man wielding a very large axe. Eoin immediately understood why Simon had picked him. The gladiator wasn't strong enough to properly wield his own weapon. And he proved it as he raised it laboriously in a two handed swing back above and behind his head.

A swing that ended with Simon's thrown spear buried in the man's chest, toppling him over, following his axe to the ground.

Simon drew his sword and fast-stepped backward to their starting position. "Two-on-two. I like these odds."

Eoin didn't have time to tell him not to jinx them. But when he heard the sound of a cage opening back down the tunnel they'd came from he knew it was too late. They were the barbarian slaves. They were the villains in this bloody play. They weren't supposed to win.

And as if reading his mind, the roar of a large cat of some sort tore through the noise of the crowd as it leaped up on its hind paws to swipe at them from its chained position. It was a large, emaciated male lion. And it was probably very hungry.

Their static defensive position was gone.

Eoin made a quick stab at the lion and scored a glancing wound on one of its paws, causing it to pull back. But it wouldn't last. And it had been exactly the distraction the short man had been waiting for.

Eoin turned and saw that they were being rushed by both remaining gladiators. Simon sprang forward, meeting his opponent head-on and locking sword blades in a battle of strength and iron. But Eoin was on his heels and had no time. The best he could manage was a half-hearted throw of his spear that barely slowed down his attacker.

To his right, Simon kicked his opponent in the stomach and lunged at Eoin's attacker, causing the man to stop in his tracks. But it also left the former Marine's back open as he hacked and slashed furiously at the little man, trying to keep him distracted long enough for Eoin to get back in the fight.

Eoin dove and grabbed his mace. Standing, he raised it back above his head as he sprinted around Simon's backside. The original swordsman was there, standing up and charging at Simon. Now with a weapon in each hand and one arm cocked above his head.

Eoin let the twenty pound weapon fly. End-over-end it soared until it crashed into the man's armor like an old VW beetle from the movies, shattering his sternum and collar bone in a sickening crunch and dropping the man on his back.

Then Simon screamed.

Turning around he saw a dagger lodged in Simon's hip. He knew the man he'd just bludgeoned must have thrown it. But Eoin was now weaponless and Simon was doing all he could to fend off the attack.

It was a moment legends were made of. It was a moment men sang about in bygone eras.

It was precisely the moment Eoin had been waiting for. The moment when all his planning, research, and dreaming would come together in one glorious moment, the moment that Dr. Eoin Littleton's legacy would be cemented—permanently and in a way no individual award could ever match.

He did not miss it.

With all the speed of a racer Eoin dashed six steps and launched himself like a spear into the much smaller man. They rolled. They clawed and bit. They punched and kicked. And then with Eoin's legs wrapped tightly around the smaller man's legs, they rolled off the main floor of the coliseum and onto the ramp where the wounded lion waited.

Eoin heard Simon call out to him. He heard the anguish in the man's voice. But he also saw the fear in his opponent's eyes as his leverage drove the two of them inexorably into the lion's range.

The gladiator screamed and writhed.

Eoin looked up, making sure his final moments would be captured for eternity.

He saw a massive paw and large cracked claws descend toward his face.

May 27, 2045

Simon Linux still walked with slight limp, but as always his back was straight and his chin was held high.

He had an important duty to perform that night and was determined to carry it out with the dignity the moment deserved. So he took a moment backstage to get his bearing in check. Then he strode out to the podium and the packed house of celebrities and dignitaries beyond to honor his fallen friend and colleague. A man he knew too little about and for too little time.

"Good evening Ladies and Gentlemen, tonight I have the great privilege and sacred honor of awarding the first Dr. Eoin Littleton Award for Exceptional Bravery in Documentary Filmmaking . . ."

About the Author

Brian **E. Shaw** burst onto the scene with his first story, The Defense of Dupont Circle, in 2012. Since then he has been hard at work on two novels and surviving parenthood. When not facing down these dangers he is a professional intelligence officer, Marine combat veteran, and a former Senate staffer. He hopes to bring these unique experiences at the nexus of power and secrecy to craft some amazing stories in the coming years. In the meantime he will continue to chase his brood, love his wife, and attempt to confine the chewing of his golden retriever to the less expensive furniture. You can follow Brian on Twitter at @BrianEShaw, Facebook at www.facebook.com/BrianShawWrites and the soon to be launched BrianShawWrites.com.

Collide-o-Scope

A Timekeepers Story

Aaron Allston

One: Name Games

I was slipping the key card into the hotel room's door lock when I heard his voice—*my* voice—sounding very surprised: "Crap, I *am* sequelling."

Startled, I turned to look. A few feet back along the corridor stood, well, me. Same lanky build, same bald head and too-big nose, same facial features that my wife used to described as a bald eagle trying to smile but failing tragically.

This me wore cargo pants, khaki slacks with extra pockets on the legs, the same pair I had briefly considered in the store yesterday, and the black T-shirt with a rearing bronco logo on it that I'd looked at but dismissed in the same shopping run. As for me, I was in tan slacks and a tan windbreaker over a black T-shirt with no art or logo on it. We both wore the same black billed cap featuring a big yellow smiley face. We had the same cheap-ass green backpack slung across one shoulder.

I didn't freak out. In my business, you run into yourself from time to time.

I slid the key card in. "We're not sequelling. I don't remember this encounter. And if you don't, either..."

He made my I-just-bit-into-an-anchovy face. "Then meeting one another isn't in our respective histories. So we're splintered instead."

"Looks that way." I pulled the card out. The little light on the lock gleamed green. I opened the door and stepped in. Beyond was a little nook—bathroom door left, closet right, a section of wall straight ahead, something to keep people at the front door from seeing what was going on in the suite. We had to step around the wall to fully enter the main room.

The other me followed, shutting the door behind us. And as I stepped around the visual-block wall, I came within sight of two more people.

One of them was another me. But this time the sight stopped me cold.

The third me lay stretched out face-up on the suite's dining table, unmoving, eyes open. And when I say unmoving, I mean unbreathing, unblinking. It took a few seconds to be sure of that, but I knew it from the first second I saw him—he, I, was dead.

The room was dominated by a big picture window on the far wall. Its drapes open, it showed downtown Los Angeles in all its semi-skyscrapery glory, and let in daylight that fell across the face of the dead me. On the left wall was a big flat-screen TV in a sort of armoire with a mini-bar in its base. Beside the armoire was a half-open door, darkness beyond, which I assumed led to the suite's bedroom. A couch straight ahead faced the TV with big stuffed chairs at either end of it. The dining table, with straight-backed chairs around it, was between the back of the couch and the right wall, with a little kitchenette beyond a doorway in that wall. The room's dull white walls were decorated with flea-market art prints. The carpet, an indescribably average brown, looked like it was as hard to stain as a Teflon toilet.

In the stuffed chair closest to the picture window sat a young woman. She had on the innocuous dark blue dress that all the female members of this hotel's housekeeping staff wore, and her hair was up in a bun like most of them. A little plastic nameplate on her chest read CAROLINA. Her arms were twisted behind her, suggesting her wrists were bound. Green-and-white nylon cord, identical to a roll in my backpack, bound her ankles, and a length of the same stuff ran up behind her legs, probably to her wrists, keeping her knees a little bent, hobbling her. She was blindfolded and gagged with strips of white cloth that looked like the remains of a towel. Her light brown skin tone and what I could see of her features spoke of mixed-race ancestry. She knew we'd come in, was turning her head back and forth to listen to us. But she didn't make a noise.

The dead me was too tall to fit comfortably on the table, so his legs from the knees down hung off the near edge of the table. He wore dark polyester department-store slacks and a touristy black T-shirt with "New York" on it in gold. I'd considered that shirt, too, in the previous day's shopping expedition.

The dead me showed no sign of violence. I saw another billed cap with a smiley face lying on the couch, beside a green backpack identical to mine.

I had to pause for a moment. I'd seen other dead guys and had manufactured a couple, but had never seen myself that way.

The me in the bronco shirt and I looked at each other. With the same motion, we unslung our backpacks and set them on the couch, flanking the one already there. Each of us tossed our smiley caps on top of the one already on the cushion.

I stepped through the door beside the TV armoire. It did lead to a bedroom. I saw two queen beds, another big TV, table and chairs, a window with drapes pulled, doors into a bathroom and out the front... no other people. I heard no people noises.

I looked in the bathroom. On the sink counter was a brown suede toilet kit identical to the one in my backpack.

As I emerged from the bedroom, I saw Bronco Dave coming out of the kitchenette. He made an all-clear gesture. I replied with the same motion.

We convened beside the table and bent over the corpse. Bronco Dave looked him over for signs of violence, shook his head. "Looks like he's been—"

I put my finger to my lips, then pointed to the housekeeper. It wouldn't do to let her overhear too much Timekeepers jargon.

So instead of saying "jellied," Bronco Dave finished, "laid out for a buffet."

We heard the door lock cycle. Bronco Dave and I turned toward the entry and drew sidearms from the holsters in our waistbands. These handguns were small, flat, easily concealed, lethal... and *quiet*. They used compressed-air cartridges to fire lead shot. The results, at close range, were wounds indistinguishable from those made by a 20-gauge shotgun.

Two more Daves walked in, staring at each other as if they were the strangest things they'd seen all day. Then they caught sight of us and the weapons pointed at them.

They didn't register any alarm. We pretty much knew that no Dave was going to kill another Dave. They looked at the woman and Dead Dave.

One of them, in electric-blue shorts, a black T-shirt showing a stylized trumpet advertising a major jazz festival, and the same damned smiley-face cap, looked very put-upon. "Oh, great. This just gets better and better."

The other Dave didn't say anything. His attention was fixed on the dead me. He looked more dismayed than his companion. He also had a full head of hair and a trim little mustache and beard, all salon stylish, all darker than my hair was back when I had some. His skin was a shade darker than mine and his eyes brown instead of blue, meaning he'd been through a thorough makeup effort including spray-tan and contact lenses. The whole effect combined to make him look younger than I actually was. Instead of some T-shirt with a distracting logo, he wore a black, lightweight overcoat belted at the waist. He had the same cap the rest of us did, and carried a soft-sided briefcase instead of a green backpack. There was a red plastic toothpick in his mouth, and its tip transcribed a slow arc as if he were using it to draw a circle around a mistake on a test paper.

He tucked something into his outer coat pocket—a Master Pass, a credit card-sized gizmo that gets Timekeepers past electronic door locks, causes ATMs to spit up money, and does all sorts of good things for us. It was probably how he'd gotten the door open.

I frowned at him. I didn't remember seeing anything like his coat on my shopping trip. He must have shopped longer than I had, just as I'd shopped longer than Bronco Dave had.

Bronco Dave and I tucked our weapons away. I gave the two newcomers a palms-up "Hell, I don't know" gesture.

Bronco Dave pointed at the housekeeper, then at the door into the bedroom. We all headed that way. The Dave with the jazz-festival shirt dropped his smiley cap and backpack on the couch as he passed. The one with the toothpick deposited his cap and briefcase.

Two: Each One in Turn

Once we were in the bedroom, Bronco Dave closed the door most of the way, keeping his eye at the crack to watch the housekeeper. We hadn't latched the suite's door to the hallway—we didn't want to alert someone, such as a returning murderer, that things had changed—so Bronco would also have to keep an ear out for someone coming in that door.

We didn't talk at first. We spread out. Toothpick Dave went through the bathroom and the micro-closet beyond it, just on this side of the bedroom's door into the hall. Jazzy Dave took the bed on that side of the room and all furnishings around it; I took the other bed and all furnishings over to the window. In a couple of minutes, we were pretty sure the room had no eavesdropping devices installed.

I sat on the office-style swivel chair at the table and started. "Okay, I have *never* seen this many splinters on an operation."

Bronco Dave glared at me. He spoke with his mouth beside the door so his voice would not carry into the other room. "None of us has, idiot. Clearly we splintered only minutes apart. No need to tell us what we all know."

I ignored him. "Let me make sure we're all on the same page. Anybody with a variance, speak up."

The other three nodded. Toothpick Dave settled down on the corner of the bed nearest the bathroom and kept the exterior door in his peripheral vision. Jazzy Dave remained standing, began pacing.

I took a deep breath. Even though I was talking to me, the subject was going to be painful. "Two days ago our time, Katee says it's over, she's moving out, there's no way to patch things up, it's been coming for a long time." Saying those words was like coughing up recently-chewed, recently-swallowed bits of glass. "She says things turned a corner on the first of July a year ago, when I was out of town. We all experienced that, right?"

"All congruent." Jazzy Dave didn't stop pacing. He looked as uncomfortable as I felt.

I kept going. "So she packs a suitcase and leaves. Yesterday morning, after a bender I'm still feeling hung over from, I decide to beg a favor of Zach the Whack, tech specialist of the gods—"

The others all chimed in, "—who owes me more than he can ever repay."

I glanced at the door, then glared at the other three, willing them to keep it down. "He agrees to send me back on an undocumented, unauthorized launch to July the first. Today." I tried, semi-successfully, not to glance at Jazzy Dave's blue shorts. "Then I do some research, find out Katee had a hotel room here on that date. Yesterday afternoon, I go shopping for clothes, stuff where eyewitnesses will remember distinctive logos instead of my face."

Toothpick Dave didn't turn, but he nodded. "Because if there are witnesses, they'll be witnesses to a crime. Maybe a murder. But why aren't we all in the same set of clothes?"

I thought about it. "Because we splintered during that shopping trip. As we were deciding what to do. Stress fractures in time. But we made different decisions at different moments—so we got different outcomes."

Bronco Dave glanced at me, then returned his attention to the door. "We all bought the same stupid hat. So our timelines didn't start splintering until we'd grabbed it." He turned his head a little, looking away from the housekeeper and toward the table with the body. "I remember seeing the New York shirt that the dead us is wearing. But I decided against buying it, moved on and bought this." He gestured at his own shirt and cargo pants. "I checked out right after that. Never saw what the rest of you are wearing."

Toothpick Dave, looking uncomfortable, cleared his throat. "And what was in your *head* at the point you checked out?"

Bronco Dave scowled at him. "You remember. It was only yesterday. Don't make me say it."

"I *don't* remember. I remember what I decided. My memories of my thoughts at the point *you* decided are kind of jumbled up."

Bronco Dave sighed. "When I was considering the New York shirt, I figured out that Katee would never jump ship without a place to land. Meaning she's got another lover. I got pretty mad. I was sure I was going to kill the guy."

Toothpick Dave made his toothpick dance around for a moment. "And?"

"And... kill Katee too." Bronco Dave didn't look abashed. If anything, he looked stone-faced and resolute.

I'd have been startled, except, of course, his decision had been mine, too, at least for a while.

Toothpick Dave didn't let up. "So let's say that deciding to kill Katee and her new guy was one stress point. The point where the first splinter took place. He," Toothpick gestured at the door and implicitly at the dead me beyond, "picked up that shirt and the first pair of slacks he saw, checked out, and went home... knowing that he was getting ready for a double homicide. But along proximate timelines, the rest of us, still one guy, kept shopping. At some point you found the horsey shirt and the cargo pants, and *you* checked out. What did *you* decide?"

Bronco Dave glowered at him. "All that time, I was kind of listening to this little voice in my head saying, 'Don't do it, you could never come back from that.' So, yeah, I came to a different conclusion. I decided to kill Katee's guy and then listen to what she had to say before I decided whether or not to kill her, too. That's what was on my mind when I checked out."

I did a slow spin in my swivel chair, chiefly so that I could look away from Bronco Dave. I wanted to pound his face in. He'd been willing to kill Katee. *Katee.*

Of course, so had I, for a while. I wanted to pound *my* face in.

I finished my spin and looked at Bronco again. "Then you went home and prepped for today's launch."

"Yeah." Bronco Dave returned his attention to the door.

I looked over at Jazzy Dave. "If I remember right, you're next."

"I think so." He stopped pacing for a minute. He slumped a little, his posture not as ramrod-straight as Bronco's. "I didn't buy anything but the smiley-face cap. I drove around for a while, debating whether the launch was a good idea. I decided to go through with it. Went to a discount clothing store. That stupid voice came back, telling me, 'Don't do it, Dave. Just let her go.' But I couldn't. I grabbed the first things that looked like they'd fit me, and checked out." He indicated his eye-hurting blue shorts and the jazz festival shirt.

I asked the next question before Toothpick Dave could: "And what decision did you come to?"

"I was going to throw Katee's boyfriend out a window." Jazzy glanced at the bedroom window. "But in the unlikely event that he survived eleven stories of drop, I wasn't going to cap him. And I wasn't going to hurt Katee."

I rubbed my jaw. "So we have a gradual decision trend away from violence."

Toothpick Dave glanced at me. "With you, too?"

"Yeah... I didn't check out when Jazzy Dave did. I just told the stupid voice in my head to shut up so I could think, and it did. I went back to shopping, which saved me from Jazzy Dave's clothing tragedy."

Jazzy glared at me.

I went on, "I found what I wanted to buy, and decided that Katee's boyfriend probably needed a good beating, which I'll be happy to administer. But I'm not going to kill him. Not going to do more to Katee than ask her for the *whole* truth. I'm not going to hurt her. I still love her."

"*Hey.*" That was Bronco, too loud. "*I* love her. I just haven't ruled out killing her."

Toothpick Dave looked worried. "Even now?"

I saw a flicker of surprise cross Bronco's eyes. He thought about it for a second. "Not even now. I'm not sure I can live without her. I'm not sure she should live without me." Seeing the expressions the rest of me turned on him, he got defensive. "We made promises to each other. Promises for life. You make a promise, even just to yourself, you stick by it. For better or worse."

Well, yeah, I'd lived by that rule for a good many years. But him saying those words caused a little metaphoric light bulb to flare up over my head. "That's it."

They all looked at me with my curious expression. Bronco was the first to speak. *"What's it?"*

"Never back away from a promise. Yesterday, during our shopping, we each promised ourselves what we were going to do. Dead Dave first—he promised to kill both of them. Bronco Dave next—"

"Don't call me that, shithead."

"Whatever. You promised to kill the guy but to give Katee a chance to talk her way out of it. And so on. The moment we promised, we stopped... stopped..." I struggled for the right word.

"Reasoning." Toothpick Dave waved his toothpick around like it was being held by a little orchestra conductor in his mouth. "Learning. It became a frozen decision point. A stress fracture in time."

I sighed. "Killing Katee... And here I thought I was past all the 'borderline sociopathic tendencies' stuff."

Jazzy gave me a look of near contempt. "We can't be, not completely. Not and be good at our job. What's your story, Toothpick?"

Toothpick Dave shrugged. "Didn't buy anything at the discount store. Went driving and thought some more about not performing this launch at all. But I decided to do it. Saw a little clothing boutique where I picked up the coat and the briefcase. Speaking of which..." He unbelted his coat and shrugged out of it, laying it over his arm. Under it he wore a plain black shirt like mine. "But I decided to get a full makeover instead of relying on clothes for my disguise."

Jazzy snorted. "You're obviously the thoughtful, sensitive one."

Toothpick Dave glared at him. "Shut up, prick."

I rubbed my temples—the arguing was threatening to set

off my hangover headache again. "Jesus, it's no wonder Katee left us. What a bunch of assholes. Toothpick, it looks like you got some chair time with Makeover Molly."

He nodded. "I headed over to the office and asked Molly about a complete color job. She was game." He switched the red toothpick in his mouth from one side to the other, a nimble move.

I frowned at him. "Molly teach you that, too?"

"Huh?"

"The toothpick stuff."

"Oh. No." He looked a bit startled. "Molly had a box of the things on her desk. I was bored waiting. I just started practicing while I was in the makeup chair. Looks like we're a natural at toothpick wrangling."

"And what did you decide about Katee?"

He grimaced. "It's going to sound stupid."

Now he had all our attention. It's okay to watch yourself acting stupid or vulnerable when it's not actually you. I gave him what I hoped was an encouraging look.

He gave in. "I'm not going to hurt her, man. Or her boyfriend, if she has one. Or girlfriend, for that matter. I'm just hoping to see what makes her happy. In case I can learn something to make her, or someone else, happy in the future."

Bronco's scowl didn't abate. "So you gave up on her."

Toothpick Dave shot him an angry look. "Jackass. I gave up on *murder*."

Bronco decided not to pursue the argument. He returned his attention to the door crack, looking once again at our dead self. "One of us *didn't* give up on murder."

"Maybe not one of us." I shrugged. "Jury's still out. Besides, we're all missing something important. We splintered a year from now, and the splinter followed us back in time. I've never heard of that before. Something big is going on here—and we're not even on an official op. We might not be able to report it."

We fell silent for a moment.

Jazzy Dave snorted. "I have it. We come back in time and find Katee shacked up with another guy. We heave him out a window. But he's supposed to find the cure for the common stupid. Our little spy operation dooms humanity to another century of reality shows."

I ignored him. I sometimes go sarcastic and passive-aggressive when hurt. That was obviously his situation. The best response was not to notice. "All right. So this morning, we launch. Zach the Whack's randomizer puts us in slightly different arrival spots, probably a few minutes apart. We make our way here. I try to check in, but the room isn't made up, so I have to wait. I wait in the bar."

"I heard the desk clerk telling someone—maybe you—that no suites would be available until three. So I waited in the gift shop." That was Bronco.

Jazzy resumed his pacing. "I didn't even come in to the lobby before three. I went for a walk."

"Restaurant." Toothpick shrugged. "They do a good bacon, lettuce, and tomato."

I suppressed a sigh. "But Dead Dave didn't wait at all. He must have come straight up, let himself in with his Master Pass. And grabbed the housekeeper, and got himself killed." Himself. Myself. That was *me* lying dead on the table.

Bronco Dave nodded. "And then the rest of us made our way up here. I didn't try to check in again because I saw you," he indicated me, "getting on the elevator. I took the next one up."

"I saw Bronco and followed *him*. And Toothpick caught up to me." Jazzy looked thoughtful. "Which is probably good, because then we didn't have a five-man unit of identical dumbasses confusing and being memorable for the front desk staff."

Toothpick Dave looked toward Bronco and the room beyond. "We need to find out who killed him, and why."

None of us had really brought up the point, but Dead Dave being dead was the spookiest part of the equation. Splintered timelines tend to recombine—at the point no one alive could sort out the 'true facts' of a splintered event, the timelines have reconverged. In this case, there was a possibility, one in five, that when we got back to our normal time frame and our timelines recombined, Dead Dave would be the Ur—the basis for our mutual reality. Meaning we'd all be dead. Odds favored our survival, but a 20% random chance of suddenly, inescapably being dead was spooky even for someone used to bathing in the time stream.

"I didn't do it." Toothpick Dave reached into one of his coat's outer pockets. "I've still got my Jellifier." He pulled out a flat, gleaming plastic disk about as big across as his palm. On top was a little LED glowing green.

Each of us pulled our Jellifiers out from other pockets, showed off their green lights, and put them away again.

Place a Jellifier against someone's biceps and trigger it, and you get a deep muscle injury with unblemished skin on top. The wound is painful, even debilitating, but not fatal. But put the device against a victim's head and set it off, and you get a fatal aneurism that medical science can't yet distinguish from a natural one. Jellifiers are one-shot weapons, though, their LEDs switching to red when they've been discharged.

I nodded toward the door. "We need to find out what happened to Dead Dave and the housekeeper. We also need to send one of us down to Katee's room, assuming she's not there, and plant the cameras. We'll learn what we came here to learn, dispose of Dead Dave's body, and go home. Nobody kills anybody else. Agreed?"

Most of the rest nodded. Bronco Dave didn't look too happy. He gave us a grudging, "Maybe."

Jazzy Dave glanced between us. "Who's doing the questioning—Bronco, Toothpick, Jazzy, or Generic?"

I scowled at him. "Don't call me that. I'm Dave Prime."

He gave me a look of mock surprise. "What makes *you* Prime?"

"I rented the room. I have the keys."

Jazzy Dave's condescending expression didn't change. "Okay, you can be Dave Prime. If it's that important to you."

I glared at him. "And I'll do the questioning."

Three: Playing House

The woman heard us approach and tilted her head, clearly trying to get a sense of us.

The gag was tight across her mouth. I leaned around to look at the knot. It was a tight square knot and would take some time to undo.

I pulled out my knife, a black tactical folder, and one-handed it open. The woman jerked when she heard the blade click home. I told her, "No worries, I'm not going to hurt you. Hold still." Carefully, I cut the gag away.

Her captor had additionally plugged her mouth with more rolled-up cloth. She didn't exactly spit it out, but she did ease it from her mouth. It dropped into her lap, then rolled onto the floor. She took a few deep breaths, working her jaw.

"Your name is Carolina, right?" I pronounced it like the state, North or South.

She corrected me, "Carolina," pronounced Spanish style, "Caw-row-LEE-na." But she nodded.

I closed the knife and put it away. "I need to know what happened to you."

"That's a joke, right?" Her voice was raspy. Her mouth was probably dry. There was a little Spanish flavor to her words—Cuban, I thought.

"No joke. Tell us what happened."

"Just let me go. Or get it over with." She sounded resigned, like she expected getting-it-over-with to be my preference.

"Get *what* over with?"

"You're not fooling me. You choked me. And when I woke up tied like this, I knew you were going to play some sort of sick game with me."

"I didn't attack you."

"Bullshit." The word sounded more sorrowful than angry. "I know your voice. I know your *smell*."

I looked at the other Daves. Jazzy and Bronco shrugged. Toothpick made his toothpick dance around in his mouth like it was trying out for the Rockettes, but his face stayed impassive.

Well... hell.

Every so often a field agent is confronted with a civilian who sees way too much. That civilian either gets convinced to stay quiet, or gets discredited so nobody ever believes him again, or, in the rare cases when he is determined to screw up history and cause untold deaths, gets killed. I'd prided myself that I'd never had to kill a civilian, but I never enjoyed coping with one of the troublemakers. Now I found myself looking at one, a civilian who knew too much and had extra reason to be uncooperative.

I put my hands on either side of her face. She flinched at the contact. I got my thumbs under her blindfold and pulled it up and off.

Hers was a round face with pretty features and chocolate-colored eyes. They were a little teary at the corners. She looked at me, then at the other Daves, and those eyes got really wide. "What the *hell*."

Jazzy Dave gave her a slightly superior smile. "I'm sure you've heard of us. We're the Albert DeSalvo Quintuplets."

She looked at him, suspicious. "Quintuplets means five. There are only four of you."

Jazzy nodded. "Number Five was crazy. He's the one who tried to kill you." He gestured toward the table.

She looked that way. Dead Dave was still sprawled there. The way his head had lolled, he was kind of looking back at her. She shuddered and looked away.

I managed to get her attention back on me. "And now we need to know why. Give us the whole story. *We're* not here to hurt you."

She looked between us and deliberated a moment before she started talking. "I came in to clean up. They wanted it done fast because a guest wanted this exact suite. But when I came in, the bathroom door was closed and I could hear water running in there. I thought maybe the new occupant was already here. The teevee was showing a hotel room, one of ours, with a man and woman making out in bed."

We looked among ourselves. I felt the blood drain from my face. Jazzy and Bronco looked pale, too.

Toothpick Dave moved to the big-screen TV and looked it over front and back. "It's been set up for an additional feed." He glanced over his shoulder at the rest of us. "From one of our receivers. It's already in place." From the armoire shelf under the TV, he picked up and displayed two remote controls. One was small, black, cheap, clearly the one that came with the room. The other was very familiar to me, a silver universal remote—unlabelled, but definitely Timekeepers issue. I knew the gal who had designed it, in fact. Anyone opening the battery compartment the most obvious way would cause caustic fluid, battery acid with some additional ingredients, to leak through the device, destroying all the special circuitry in it. There was a remote identical to it in my backpack.

Toothpick Dave used the remote to turn on the TV. The picture that came into focus was a split screen, four camera views.

The upper left quarter of the screen showed a hotel bed, now being straightened by another hotel housekeeper, an Asian teenager. I heard Carolina murmur "Hien" like maybe she hoped the girl would hear her, recognize her distress. But Hien just kept making the bed.

The upper right quadrant displayed another angle on that same room, showing the easy chair, the table and its office chair, the window with its view of downtown L.A. We could occasionally glimpse Hien's movements at the bottom of that view.

Lower left showed a fish-eye view of a hotel door from out in the hall; the little plaque beside it read 1122, so it was Katee's room. The door was open, a housekeeper's cart parked in front of it.

The fourth view, lower right, was a similar view of a closed hotel room door. Its plaque read 1224, so it was my, our, suite. Standard operating procedure—pointing a camera at your own hotel door made it harder for people to sneak up on you.

I turned back to Carolina. "Tell me about the man and the woman on the teevee." I didn't want to hear the answer, since the woman was probably Katee, but I had to know.

"They were under the sheets. They were talking and messing around. Like they were..."

Jazzy supplied the term. "Post-coital?" He didn't sound happy to be saying it. Then he added, "That means 'after sex.'"

Now, finally, Carolina got mad. "I know what post-coital means, you Neanderthal. I'll stack my vocabulary up against yours any day."

Jazzy's eyebrows rose. He didn't answer.

Bronco Dave moved a backpack off the couch, onto the floor to the side, and sat where it had rested. He looked like he'd been hit by a truck and just hadn't started to bleed yet. "The woman—blond, beautiful, nice rack?"

Carolina nodded.

I made an effort to keep my breakfast from rising. *My wife*, having sex with some other guy, a year before I even understood that we were in trouble. "And the guy?"

"Black guy. Really cut. Good-looking enough to be a movie star, except his lips were kind of too full."

"Murphy. Oh, God, it had to be Murphy." Bronco Dave hammered his fists into the sides of his head like maybe the pain would drive out the image that had just popped into all our minds. "Is there any woman, anywhere, the son of a bitch can't bag?"

"Okay, he goes out the window." Jazzy Dave sounded calm. "Or maybe I'll make it look like an accident. But a really stupid accident so everyone will think he was a moron."

Carolina tried not to show her alarm. I saw her attention flit from Dave to Dave, saw her starting to add things up.

I raised my voice. "Guys. Focus." Then I turned back to Carolina. "What were they talking about?"

"He was trying to get her to come work for his company. As a scriptwriter, I think. Except he didn't say scriptwriter. He kept saying 'scenarist.'"

Bronco Dave stared at her. "Holy shit, he was *recruiting* her."

Jazzy Dave was more analytical about it. "A year ago. So the new job she got, the personal assistant job—"

I nodded. "That was a cover. She was really with the—with *us*. And she never told me. Clearly, she didn't know I was with the same firm."

But in the last year, why hadn't I even suspected?

Because, like she'd told me a million times, I didn't pay attention to her.

Toothpick Dave took over while I was distracted. "What happened then?"

Carolina looked over at Dead Dave. "I didn't hear him come out of the bathroom, but suddenly I was lying across the chair and he was standing over me. Wide-eyed and crazy. He told me not to move or he might have to hurt me. He started walking back and forth, arguing with himself. About what I'd seen. He kept looking at the teevee and getting crazier and crazier. The man and woman kept talking about her problems with some guy, and how she didn't know who she was anymore, and about... time travel." She paused as if waiting to gauge our reaction when she said those last two words. I don't think our stony faces gave her too much to work with. "And then he, the guy who looks like you, said he was sorry for scaring me. He said I could go. But when I got up and moved past him... he grabbed me." Her voice broke on the last two words. "His arm went around my neck. I fought him, but... that's the last I remember. Before I woke up tied in the chair. With a headache."

I stood, getting a little distance between me and Carolina, and tried to absorb it all. Bad enough to discover that Katee was cheating on me. But the idea that discovering this could drive me to an act of murder...

Yeah, I know. Carolina's story hadn't mentioned murder. But Dead Dave's tactic was obvious to me, because I'd used it in the past. Employ a choke hold on a target until he passes out. Then use the Jellifier. Dead Dave had intended to kill Carolina.

Granted, catching Katee in bed with some other guy might have made me willing to beat the crap out of the guy. But to try to kill this woman—that wasn't *me*.

Was it?

I felt for Dead Dave. I really did. But I was ashamed of him, too. Of me.

I looked at the other Daves. Toothpick was stone-faced, making his toothpick dance around. Bronco stared at Carolina as if wondering where to bury her body. Jazzy glanced my way, offered a mocking little grin as though he was enjoying Bronco's and my consternation.

I decided I was starting to hate Jazzy Dave. I wondered if Katee had mostly been dealing with him.

I returned my attention to Carolina. "Like I said. Your attacker was psycho."

"You didn't say that." She looked at Jazzy. "*He* said that."

"Yeah, whatever. It sounded a lot like me." I breathed a heavy sigh. "So you blacked out."

"Yeah. And woke up tied and blindfolded. I heard you, one of you, tell me not to make a noise. You'd be right back. Then you left. A little while later, you all came in."

I moved over to the corpse and began rifling his left-side pockets. Toothpick got to work on his right side.

Neither of us found a Jellifier. It looked like maybe he'd been killed with his own weapon. Or maybe his killer used the killer's own Jellifier, disposed of it, took Dead Dave's. Carolina's story made it pretty certain that one of us had killed Dead Dave.

I had a hard time believing that one of me would kill another one of me. The risk to my survival was alarmingly high. I tended to think I could have reasoned with myself. What had the killer known or seen to make him think otherwise?

Jazzy Dave frowned and glanced at Carolina. "Hey, where's your cart?"

"Right outside."

Jazzy pointed to the TV. The exterior image of our room door showed no housekeeper's cart.

Carolina shook her head. "I don't know."

Bronco Dave looked even more frustrated. "We need to get a forensics team in here."

Jazzy Dave rolled his eyes. "This isn't an authorized op, asshole. We can't send for a forensics team."

"Don't call me asshole, asshole."

I resisted the urge to bury my face in my hands. "Guys, back it down a notch." Dealing with myself was starting to make me very tired. "We need to dispose of the body."

Bronco Dave turned away, sulky "So do it."

"Random choice." I pulled a deck of cards from my back pocket. "Low cards do the disposal."

Jazzy Dave pulled out his own deck, identical to mine— same view of the Taj Mahal on the box and the backs of the cards. "Lowest *hands*."

We gathered around a puffy footstool. Toothpick Dave shuffled atop it. "Five cards, no draw, no wild cards, best two hands stay here and enjoy the air conditioning." He dealt.

With no draw to contend with, we each just flipped our cards face-up as they landed. Toothpick Dave dealt himself a pair of kings. I ended up with a pair of threes and cursed my luck. But Bronco Dave received a nothing hand, and Jazzy Dave got a pair of twos.

Disgruntled, Jazzy and Bronco headed out to find a bellman's cart and a bag or box for the body. I hoped they'd find a container large enough—I'd hate to have to participate in cutting up my own corpse.

Four: Confidence Games

I sat in the stuffed chair opposite Carolina. "You understand that nobody will ever find that body. You try to tell the police you're aware of a murder, you'll end up with the cops thinking you're crazy."

She thought about it. "I don't need justice for the guy who attacked me. What I need is to pee." She did look uncomfortable.

"Okay, here's how we do it. The bathroom in the bedroom doesn't share a wall with the corridor, so you can't make a noise that'll be heard outside without alerting us. I stay outside the bathroom, but you only close the door enough for minimal privacy. Talk to me throughout. Got it?"

She nodded.

I got up, pulled out the knife again, cut her ankle bonds, got to work on her wrists. "You can call me Prime."

"But your name is Dave, isn't it?"

I froze for a split-second. Fortunately, since I was leaning around her, she couldn't see my expression. I got my face back into order and finished the cut, then straightened. "Yeah. I'm Dave. Where'd you hear that name?"

"On the teevee." She rubbed her wrists for a moment, then stood—or tried to. Wobbly, she dropped right back into her chair. After being bound for a while, she was finding that her limbs didn't work too well. I helped her up.

And she finished answering. "Before the other guy grabbed me, the girl on the teevee was talking about having trouble with the guy she was involved with. Dave. You've been acting like someone involved with her."

"Fair enough." I gestured toward the bedroom door.

She did head that way, but didn't stop talking. "You *are* the dead guy." She glanced back at Toothpick, who now sat in a chair near Dead Dave's legs. "Both of you are. Somehow."

I put on my cold killer face. "The more you know, the more some of the other *Daves* are going to want to sanitize you."

"Sanitize—kill?" She sounded more thoughtful than frightened.

In the bedroom, I gestured for Carolina to go into the bathroom. "Yeah. Kill you."

She went in. "But you don't want to, do you?" She sounded pretty confident. She partially closed the bathroom door, enough that I couldn't see the commode.

I didn't answer. I spent those seconds puzzling out what she was doing. My best guess was that she wasn't taking it on faith that I didn't want to kill her. She was establishing a connection with me through conversation, making herself more real. And the only thing we had to talk about was the current situation. I nodded to myself. It was a smart tactic— smart so long as she didn't aggravate any of the Daves.

She went on, "What's it like, being a time traveler?"

I resisted the urge to grind my teeth. It would have been much better if she hadn't believed any part of the time travel talk she'd heard. "What convinced you?"

"Oh, come *on*. Five identical guys, all of you crazy in love with the same woman? You should have seen all your faces every time someone mentioned Katee. That and all the other weird stuff you've been saying... what am I supposed to think? And I know who Albert DeSalvo was. The Boston Strangler. That was a sick joke."

I frowned. "How do you know that?'

"History major. Specializing in modern American history." She flushed. A moment later, she opened the door again, but didn't immediately move out into the bedroom. She turned to the sink and washed her hands.

A handful of details clicked into place in my head. "History major... with a minor in psychology."

Startled, she looked at me over her shoulder. "Psych was my first major, before I switched. My minor's in education. How did you know?"

"Just a guess."

She dried her hands on a bathroom towel. "You take hostages a lot?"

"Not really, but I've been doing this a long time. Done?"

"I suppose." She preceded me back into the main room.

Dead Dave was gone. Toothpick still sat at the table. With the corpse gone, he seemed just a touch less tense than before.

I pointed for Carolina to take her original chair, but when she sat, I didn't tie her up again. I just sat in the chair opposite her. "To answer your question, being a time traveler is a job." I didn't look at Toothpick Dave, but I could feel him tense up. I ignored him and kept going. "You get an assignment, you carry it out. Sometimes you do good, sometimes you limit the bad being done, sometimes you screw up. You deal with middle management and jockey for pay raises. A job. Except you don't want to leave traces of yourself. Anomalies. They can cause variances in history. Little inconsistencies that might confuse a history major with a minor in education."

She shook her head. "So what are your assignments like —do you hop back in time to kill Hitler or stop President Kennedy from being shot?"

I grimaced. "It's not like that. We don't try to *change* history. That's not really a good idea, or effective."

"Why not?"

I struggled with metaphors they'd run past me when I was undergoing my first Timekeepers orientation, fifteen years before. "Think of time as an animal. You injure it, it heals after a while. Say you go back in time and kill Hitler. The timeline you're already familiar with doesn't just go away—it runs along in parallel to the new line or lines you've created. We call them splinters. And they all run toward a reunification point, so that at some time in the future, they all look the same. This might happen because, right after you kill Hitler, his double, who's just as crazy, takes over, and most people never find out the difference. Or the German High Command keeps issuing orders in his name and pretends that he's in hiding. Fifty years later, everyone who knew the truth is dead, it all looks the same, with a bunch of 'I don't knows' and 'some people claims' in the history books. But the timelines have recombined."

She didn't look confused by my explanation. "So what do you *do*?"

"We mostly just record. Uncover secrets. Solve mysteries." I shrugged and looked at Toothpick Dave.

He was staring at me as though he couldn't believe I was telling her all of this. His toothpick was motionless in his mouth, like it had been stunned.

I turned back to Carolina. "For instance, President Kennedy. It would mess things up to save him... but we do know who killed him and why. We have it all on tape."

She leaned forward, suddenly wide-eyed. "Who?"

"Not going to tell you. But we're building up a historical record that, some day, will demystify the past."

She blinked at that. "You're not secret agents. You're *academics*. You don't actually *do* anything."

I fidgeted. "Just because you have a technology doesn't mean it's a good idea to use it." This was a lie on my part, a lie of omission. We *were* secret agents. There were others out there with the technology, people who profited, built up personal power, by manipulating events of the past. From time to time we ran into them, and whenever that happened, people on one side or the other, or both, died. But Carolina didn't need to know that. I didn't want her romanticizing, investigating what we did. I wanted her to lose interest.

Toothpick Dave finally got his toothpick moving again. "Atom bombs."

"Yeah, atom bombs." I turned back to Carolina. "Are you suggesting that since we know how to make atom bombs, we should use them all the time?"

She was saved from having to answer. We heard the door open. Bronco and Jazzy walked in.

Bronco stopped and looked at Carolina. "What's she doing loose?"

"Behaving herself." I shrugged. "Besides, she's figured out that we're all Daves. That Katee and Murphy talking about time travel wasn't just for a script."

"Grrrrreat." Bronco moved over to his spot on the couch and flopped down, putting him halfway between me and Carolina. "You should have kept her tied up. And especially gagged."

"Why are you being such a prick?" I glared at him.

He shrugged. "More to the point, why aren't we all identical pricks?"

"I know why." Jazzy sat at the table to the left of Toothpick. He stretched, pretending to be unconcerned. "It's roles, man. Modality. I walk into a party, I see who's assumed what roles in the night's entertainment, and I assume one that isn't yet filled. I'd bet my left nut that Prime was the first one to see Carolina. He instantly became the Protector of the Weak, and it's colored his perceptions ever since. Bronco saw him take on that role and knew the situation still needed a war chief, an aggressor. Or 'prick,' in common parlance. Which he's been since that moment. I come in, I see the Defender of Damsels and the war chief, I know the situation needs an analyst."

I nodded. "Also 'prick' in common parlance." What I didn't say, though, was that while Jazzy's analysis was good, I didn't think it was the only factor. The day before, the decisions we'd made in the various clothing stores... I thought maybe they had changed us, each different decision yielding a different Dave. Maybe for good.

Jazzy grinned. "Atta boy. And Toothpick here..." Jazzy glanced at Toothpick Dave. "He's been grim and quiet since he saw Dead Dave. Maybe he's our emotional touchstone. Let's call him Emo Dave from now on."

Toothpick caused his piece of red plastic to stand straight up, as though he were extending a middle finger. "Screw you."

"That idea makes sense a bunch of ways." Carolina spoke in such a quiet tone that I barely heard her.

But Jazzy heard it too. "What do you mean?"

Carolina shrugged. "Katee saying she doesn't know who she is. How can she, when her guy becomes a different person each time the situation changes?"

Bronco ignored her, kept his attention on me. "Okay, fearless leader, the dead guy is disposed of. What's next?"

I pondered that. "Well, since we don't know where Katee and Murphy went, we don't have much to do until they come back. And since the table's cleared off... I suggest poker."

Bronco stood. "I'm in."

All the Daves congregated at the table. I waved Carolina over and pointed her toward the end where Dead Dave's head had once rested. She sat, a little uncomfortable.

We all pulled out our wallets and dropped money on the table, the $1,000 in mixed bills we'd supplied ourselves with for this operation.

Toothpick had an extra wallet. He set the money from it in front of Carolina.

I stared at him. "Where'd that come from?"

"That's my wallet. I'm playing with Dead Dave's money."

"Oh, right." I shuffled my deck and dealt. "Five card draw, one-eyed jacks are wild." Then I dealt and it got quiet for a moment.

The four Daves eyed one another. It was weird, playing people with the exact same tells you have. Except Carolina was an unknown. She had a good poker face, though, and she didn't waste time with coy protests that she wasn't very good at cards.

On the other hand, when the deal passed to her, she switched to Texas Hold 'Em. Jazzy, Bronco, and I groaned, but dutifully went along.

It was Jazzy who got the conversation going again. He looked up at Carolina. "So you've obviously been thinking about what you heard Katee say. Give me the woman's perspective. What do you think I need to do to get her back?"

Carolina concentrated on her cards. "Tell me what she's been saying to you. The things she's said so often you're sick of hearing them. I'll translate her words from woman into dude."

I started. "Like you saw on the teevee, she talks a lot about not knowing who she is any more."

Carolina looked at me over the tops of her cards. "Did she ever know who she was?"

I nodded. "I think so. When we met. When we were first married."

"So what are some of the differences in what she does or says now? Even the little changes."

Jazzy looked reflective. "I've got one. She never talks about her boobs anymore."

We all nodded.

Carolina gave him a curious look. "She used to?"

Bronco shrugged. "It was kind of a joke. She had small boobs. She used to talk about being with the Itty-Bitty Titty Committee. She didn't seem sad about it or anything."

I nodded. "But she did keep mentioning it. One day I said I could afford implants for her. She kind of stopped talking about her boobs then."

That hand went to Carolina, and deal passed to Toothpick. He shuffled, announced seven-card draw, and dealt.

Carolina picked up and regarded her hand. "But she got the boob job. The girl I saw on the teevee had large boobs."

Bronco smiled, visualizing them, as we all were. "Thirty-six cees. Yeah, I brought up the subject again, looking for a clear yes or no. She'd been kind of evasive on the subject. Then she started asking what *I* wanted. It was like what she wanted didn't matter to her anymore, or she didn't have an opinion."

Carolina looked thoughtful. "Her hair color's out of a bottle. What's her real color?"

I regarded my cards with distaste. "Blond. But a darker blond."

"One day she asked if you thought she ought to go lighter? You told her yes?"

I gave her a little frown. "I told her she should *try* lighter. For a while. Now it's been two years."

"When she's bundled up in a coat or she's just worked out, does she ever freak out, say that she feels like she's smothering? Anything like—"

Bronco slammed his cards down. He looked for a moment like he was thinking about going across the tabletop at Carolina. His voice actually shook. "She said that while you were watching her and Murphy. Didn't she?"

Caroline had pulled back when he slammed the cards. Now she leaned forward again, tentative, and put her elbows back on the table. She shook her head. "No, it's... not uncommon. A woman in a suffocating relationship. She'll feel like she's being buried, can't breathe. But it's really the relationship." She gave each of me a sympathetic look. "Just as a guess, I'd say she's been desperate to please you all this time. She might be feeling intimidated by you. You're kind of domineering. And trying so hard to please you, she's been abandoning little pieces of her real self."

"Plus there's the fact that it turns out I'm a prick." Suddenly tired, I set my cards on the table. "Fold." I got up, moved over to the stuffed chair, and sat. I just stared at the four unmoving views on the TV.

"I can fix this." That was Jazzy.

Carolina sounded dubious. "All by yourself?"

"Yeah... yeah. Now it's clear she knows about the Timekeepers. I'll tell her I'm a field agent. She'll have to reevaluate me, our whole relationship. I'll be more supportive. I'll pay more attention to what she tells me."

I shifted, uncomfortable. The pain in his/my voice was starting to get to me.

There was movement on the TV. I turned to address the table. "They're back."

Five: Endgame

On the TV screen, Katee and Murphy were now at the door to her room. He wore casual slacks and a pullover shirt; she was in her floral print, yellow on blue summer dress. Even in the slightly grainy image of the spy camera, she was gorgeous, all long blond hair and classic California beach-girl features. Interestingly, neither of them looked happy. That made my heart jump with a little spike of hope.

Jazzy took the couch; Bronco took Carolina's former chair. Toothpick stayed at the table, probably to keep an eye on Carolina.

Katee and Murphy entered the room, moving into the view showing the bed. I handled the remote and the other three video images went away.

But Katee and Murphy moved past the bed. I felt another stab of hope. I pressed a button and the image switched to the view of the stuffed chair and table. Katee sat on the office chair and Murphy relaxed into the stuffed chair.

He was first, his somber tone making his words sound like a sad confession. "You're right. We have to approach it as two subjects. My fault—my bad." He was so movie-star serious and believable, handsome and forthcoming, that I just wanted to race downstairs and throw him through the window behind him.

"Thanks." Katee's fingernails, pink, plucked at the desktop, a nervous habit she wasn't even aware of. "The job thing. I *want* it. I want to make a difference. At something."

He nodded. "So it's a yes?"

"It's a yes."

"Okay. I'll put in the paperwork. We'll bring you in next week for orientation, tests, evaluations. I'm sure you'll do great." He fell silent.

The silence hung between them. It seemed to radiate out from the TV screen to envelop the Daves.

Finally she broke it. "Yes, I want to see you again. But I'm not going to. I'm going to make things work with Dave. He deserves that. He's my *husband*."

"Yeah." Murphy drew the word out like it was a slow, mournful curse word. "I get that, Katee. And you may want to keep in mind that a field agent like Dave has to be a certain way so he can go out and keep coming back alive. Maybe it will help to understand that. But I just... If it doesn't work out..."

"If it doesn't work out, you'll be the first one I run to."

"I'm glad." Moving like he was suddenly hauling around three hundred extra pounds, he stood. "I'd better go."

"Yeah. But... listen. Today, for the first time in, I don't know, forever, I felt like myself. Like I could say what I thought and the guy I was with wouldn't look at me like I was retarded. You wouldn't give me one of those Dave stares that wrap me up in a straightjacket and jams a gag in my mouth. That meant a *lot* to me. Today was really, really important to me."

"To me, too." Awkward, he remained there a second more as if deciding whether to try to embrace her. Then he blew her a kiss and moved out of the camera frame. We heard the door of Katee's room open and close.

Katee watched him go. And her expression... open, vulnerable, Katee as I hadn't seen her for a couple of years, a lifetime. It was a look she never directed at me anymore. A look I knew she never would turn my way again.

She'd been trying for this whole last year to make things work. I hadn't noticed.

She'd known for this whole year that I was a Timekeepers field agent. I couldn't play that card to make her think things over again. She'd been thinking about them from this day forward. She'd *known*.

I'd failed. Katee and I were done.

I didn't have to look at the other Daves. I could feel the stiffness in their postures. I could hear the pain in their silence.

I pointed the remote at Katee. Katee, who smashed grown men flat with nothing more than a look of hope directed at another guy. I pressed a button and her image faded to nothingness.

I looked around. Carolina was staring at me, sympathy on her face, maybe even a little glisten of tears at the corners of her eyes.

"Okay." Jazzy couldn't keep a sudden raspiness out of his voice. "That's settled. Now we have to figure out who killed Dead Dave, and then we can leave."

But no one moved. A silence fell across us.

Toothpick Dave gathered up the cards at the table, slid them back into my card box. "I did it."

We all looked at him. Bronco, all his anger squeezed out of his voice and gone, asked the question. "Why?"

It took Toothpick a few moments to answer. He set the cards in front of the chair where I'd been playing. "I came in, found him standing over Carolina with the Jellifier. Years ago—you remember—I'd made a promise to myself. Never, ever hurt an innocent if it could possibly be avoided. Carolina dying could be avoided. The me I was looking at didn't just need to be stopped. He needed to be expunged."

"That's a first." Glum as I was, I actually saw the tiniest trace of humor in the confession. "A murder-suicide with only one victim."

"I'm sorry, guys." Toothpick shrugged. "Sorry for putting us all at risk. But I couldn't live with... with *that*."

"Yeah, I get it." Jazzy stood. He looked at the array of identical backpacks on the couch. "Which one is mine?"

I shook my head. "They all are."

He picked up the closest one. He also picked up one of the smiley-face caps. He regarded the stupid grin in the stupid yellow circle, then flipped the cap into the trash can beside the armoire. "See you all at home. In my skull." He slung the pack and, stone-faced, headed for the door. "Last one out, turn off the lights."

Bronco got up a moment later. His movements were less angry than before, more heavy. He took a backpack and flipped another cap into the trash. He headed out without saying a word.

That left me, Toothpick, and Carolina staring at one another.

Toothpick looked more relieved than crushed. "You want to retrieve Dead Dave's cameras?"

"No, I'll just burn them out. Don't want to risk Katee seeing me." I entered a series of numbers on the remote control. Transmitted, they'd instruct the cameras' circuitry to burn out. Anyone finding them would discover only innocuous strips of burned plastic and some fiberoptics that looked like spider webs.

I looked back at Toothpick, jerked my head toward the door. "Go ahead, clear out. I'll clean up. My room, after all."

He just shook his head. He glanced at Carolina, then back at me.

"Oh, come on, Toothpick. I'm not going to do her any harm. You've known that from the start."

He shrugged. "Same back at you. You go first."

"We'll go together."

He made his toothpick dance around a little. "Okay."

I looked at Carolina. "While my dumbass doppelganger and I stare at each other, you should take off. I think you can figure out that it won't do you any good to tell anybody about what you've seen."

She stood. "Yeah."

"Will the time you were missing from work count against you?"

She nodded. "The manager, she's... strict. And there's some competition for the job. I'll be fired. But it's better than being dead."

"True. But hold on." I grabbed a backpack and moved over to the table. From the pack, I pulled out my slate—a tablet computer lots more capable than the commercial model it was disguised to look like.

I set it down, brought it to life with a button-press, and pulled up a file wrangler, then went wandering through the slate's storage memory.

Toothpick moved to stare over my shoulder. "What are you doing?"

"Don't you know? You're slipping, Toothpick." In moments, I found my file named Anomalies_Resources. I entered an elaborate password to open it.

Mind you, when I'm not going batshit crazy because my life is falling apart, I'm pretty good at my job. One thing I do is keep meticulous track of little historical anomalies I can exploit if I'm trapped at a landing zone longer than I expect to be. In the Anomalies_Resources file, I scrolled down to find the block of entries closest to this date and location.

I found an entry that looked promising. "Toothpick, get me a notepad and pen, would you?"

He did. When he handed them to me, I scribbled a few notes from the slate's screen onto the notepad. Then I tore the sheet free and handed it to Carolina.

She glanced at it, trying to make sense of my handwriting, then gave me a confused look. "What is it?"

"On the first of August, there's going to be a news story. A set of gang-bangers will make a hit on a meth lab belonging to another gang. They'll leave with a lot of drugs and cash. But they'll be spotted leaving by members of the rival gang and by the cops. There'll be a lot of driving and shooting and wrapping of cars around concrete pillars. Before being arrested, one of the gang-bangers will stash a bag full of money in the trunk of an abandoned car. When he goes back for it after getting out on bail, the bag will be gone." I pointed at the note. "That's where the car is. August the first, wee hours, you take a crowbar to the brown Intrepid parked at that address. And have someone with you so you don't get mugged. You'll see a black zippered duffel with pink stripes. In the pocket where shoes go, you'll find enough money to live on for, well, long enough to finish college. It'll pay your college expenses and get your career started."

She looked at the note again, then at me. "You're kidding."

"Nope. Consider it an apology. I really am sorry about what you had to go through."

She tucked the note away under the neck of her blouse, in her bra, I assumed.

She moved cautiously past me, watching me, as if assuming I'd choke her again. Then she gave me a quick embrace. "Thank you."

"Good luck."

Toothpick added something in Spanish. Drawing back from me, Carolina smiled at him. And then she left.

Leaving only me and Toothpick Dave.

I let the silence linger for a moment. Then: "What did you tell her?"

"I suggested she go for a doctorate. I said she certainly had the brains for it."

"Yeah, she does. Hey, Toothpick?"

"Yeah?"

"I don't speak Spanish."

"*Shit.*" He slammed his fist down on the table. "Shit, shit, shit. Yes, you do. But *later*. Stupid, stupid, stupid." Finally he was showing a lot of emotion, self-directed anger and dismay, so cartoony it was funny.

But it wasn't the kind of face I'd ever made.

I gave him a little grin. "Later, huh. So you're not a splinter from a year from now. You're from farther down my timeline. And you're not really a Dave."

He sighed and looked toward heaven. Then he looked back at me. "I'm from about thirty years on. Yeah, I'm a Timekeeper. A cleaner, actually."

"And, whatever you look like in real life, you've got some magical far-future gizmo that lets you look just like me." Then I frowned. "No, that doesn't make sense. If you had something like that, you'd have looked *just* like me. Without all that hair. What the hell are you?"

He paused, considering whether to answer.

But I started to add it up without his help. He sounded just like me, looked a lot like me, but maybe the differences in our skin tone and eye color were not from makeup and contact lenses. My knees went a little wobbly. "Dammit. You're my *kid*."

He made a disgusted face. "One of the problems with having smart parents is that you can't get away with *anything*. You're a pain in the ass, Pop."

His light, matter-of-fact tone had to be covering up a crazy range of emotions. He'd had to kill his *dad* — one iteration of his dad, anyway. I wondered what being forced into such an action had done to him, was probably still doing to him. I shoved that question to the side, just as I assumed he was having to shove his own feelings to the side.

"Pop. But who's your mother? Do Katee and I get back together?" No, that didn't make sense. I'm good at reading people. Katee had moved on.

Then more evidence clicked into place. Dark complexion. Spanish. He'd killed his father, risked his own existence, to protect *her*... I think my mouth fell open. "Carolina?"

Toothpick just stared at me. "It always sucked to play guessing games with you."

Questions about two women both tried to spill out of my mouth simultaneously. I tried to stick with one at a time. "Does she... does Katee at least forgive me?"

"Yeah. You and Mom, Katee and her husband, you all still get together Fridays for poker."

"Not Texas Hold 'Em, I pray to God."

"In dealer rotation, yeah."

"Okay. I guess I'll learn to live with it." I sighed. "I can't even gripe at you for making an unauthorized jump to save your mom."

"Oh, this was an *authorized* mission to save Mom. The office has been prepping for this operation for six months. Trying to keep it from even being necessary, in fact. I followed you around two stores broadcasting a tight isolation recording of your own voice saying, 'Don't do it, don't do it,' hoping you'd wise up. But why did I think you'd listen to yourself when you didn't listen to *anybody* back now?"

"The whole op was about saving Carolina?" I shook my head, confused. "Why?"

"If she'd died here, today, she'd never have—" Toothpick shut up quick.

"What?"

"Can't say. Hang around twenty-five years or so and you'll know." He managed a little smile. "But I learned something today. Just what it was you'd done so that, years later, when she bumped into you again, she didn't run screaming. You paid for her education. Neither of you ever told me that."

"Unexpected dividends..."

"You'd better scram, Pop. Leave the rest to me. I'm the cleaner in the family, after all."

"Okay." I stowed my slate and zipped the backpack shut. "What's your name, Toothpick?"

"Andy."

"Andrew. My middle name."

"Yeah, well. Hand-me-downs are okay sometimes."

I moved over to the couch, picked up one of the smiley caps. I glanced at the trash can, but I put the cap on. Then I returned to the table. Awkward, I hugged Andy.

He hugged me back. "Don't worry, Pop. You get better. You even turn into a pretty good guy eventually."

"Wiseass. Consider yourself grounded." I picked up and slung my pack. Then I moved to the entryway. Before

I lost sight of him, I told him, "I look forward to seeing you again."

"You say that now. Wait until I prang your Harley."

I shook my head and left.

So there it was, the story of how I lost my first wife, met my second wife, met my son years before he was born, argued with myself, became just a bit more self-aware, and saw myself dead.

It mostly sucked at the time. Now, well, I think of it as a pretty good day's work.

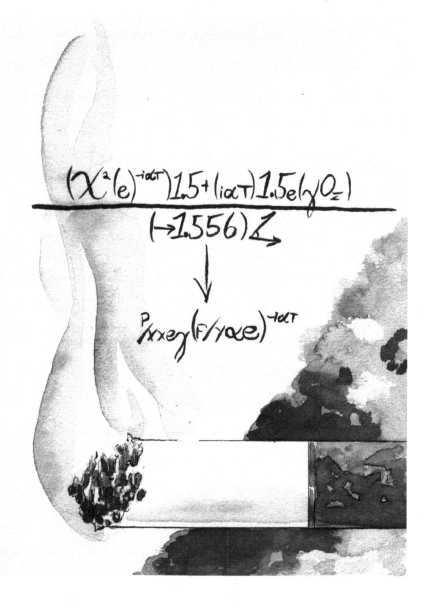

Time Bomb

Timothy Zahn

Introduction

The year was 1988. Life was simpler then. People were happier. Birds sang louder. Peanut butter was more spreadable.

Well, no, not really. None of them, in fact. Except it being 1988.

But things *were* different.

For starters, my family and I were living in Champaign, Illinois. Following the traditional dictum of writing what you know, I set "Time Bomb" in the Central Illinois region that I was familiar with. Champaign, Mahomet, Rantoul, and Springfield were all places I'd spent time in. I had friends from Chanute Air Force Base. I knew about the University of Illinois' Beckman Institute for Advanced Science and Technology, which would officially open in 1989. All of those places and institutions ended up in the story.

The path to that story, like some of the country roads I'd driven around Champaign-Urbana, was a bit bumpy. I'd written at least three other versions of the same idea over the years, none of which had quite jelled. (And by "jelled" I mean "sold.") I liked the idea, though, and I was determined to keep going until I got it right.

Finally, I found a version that worked. A few years earlier Jim Baen had revived his idea of "bookazines," quarterly magazines of fiction and non-fiction in paperback-size format, starting with *Far Frontiers* and later adding *New Destinies*. I was able to sell him this latest version of "Time Bomb" for *New Destinies Volume IV* (summer 1988), and we then went on to reprint the story later that year in my second single-author collection, *Time Bomb and Zahndry Others*. For the record, that was *not* my preferred title. *I* wanted to go with the much more dignified *Hot Fudge Zahnday*.

(As a side note, my editor on the project was a wonderful lady and terrific editor named Betsy Mitchell. A little over a year later, she and I would both find ourselves at a new publisher, Bantam Books, working together on this little media tie-in called *Heir to the Empire*.)

As for the story itself…well, the cities and interstate highways are still there. But a few other things have changed in the past quarter century.

Chanute AFB closed in 1993. Smoking is no longer allowed by ticket sellers in bus stations. There aren't any smoking sections in the busses themselves either, of course. The bus route between Springfield and Champaign still exists, and the fare has actually gone *down* a bit. (Bet you didn't see *that* one coming.) The bus no longer stops at Mahomet, though.

Tape recorders and modems are still around, but they're fading away rapidly. The Cray Y-MP supercomputer was introduced in 1988 and did some impressive work, though its powerhouse design would subsequently be overtaken by the massively parallel approach to computational power.

Aside from those minor details, I think the story itself has aged well. But I guess you'll be the judge of that.

Timothy Zahn,
July 2013

I

The bus station was stiflingly hot, despite the light evening breeze drifting in through the open door and windows. In a way the heat was almost comforting to Garwood as he stood at the ticket window; it proved the air conditioning had broken down much earlier in the day, long before he'd come anywhere near the place.

Puffing on a particularly pungent cigar—the smoke of which made Garwood's eyes water—the clerk looked down at the bills in front of him and shook his head. "Costs forty-one sixty to Champaign now," he said around his cigar.

Garwood frowned. "The schedule says thirty-eight," he pointed out.

"You gotta old one, prob'ly." The clerk ran a stubby finger down a list in front of him. "Prices went up 'bout a week ago. Yep—forty-one sixty."

A fresh trickle of sweat ran down the side of Garwood's face. "May I see that?" he asked.

The clerk's cigar shifted to the other side of his mouth and his eyes flicked to Garwood's slightly threadbare sport coat and the considerably classier leather suitcase at his side. "If you got proper ident'fication I can take a check or card," he offered.

"May I see the schedule, please?" Garwood repeated.

The cigar shifted again, and Garwood could almost see the wheels spinning behind the other's eyes as he swiveled the card and pushed it slowly under the old-fashioned grille. Getting suspicious; but there wasn't anything

Garwood could do about it. Even if he'd been willing to risk using one, all his credit cards had fallen apart in his wallet nearly a month ago. With the rising interest rates of the past two years and the record number of bankruptcies it had triggered, there were more people than ever roundly damning the American credit system and its excesses. And on top of that, the cards were made of plastic, based on a resource the world was rapidly running out of and still desperately needed. A double whammy. "Okay," he said, scanning the rate listing. "I'll go to Mahomet instead—what's that, about ten miles this side of Champaign?"

"Closer t' seven." The clerk took the card back, eying Garwood through a freshly replenished cloud of smoke. "Be thirty-six seventy-five."

Garwood handed over thirty-seven of his forty dollars, silently cursing his out-of-date schedule. He'd cut things a little too fine, and now he was going to look exactly like what he was: a man on the run. For a moment he debated simply turning around and leaving, trying it again tomorrow on someone else's shift.

But that would mean spending another night in Springfield. And with all the Lincoln memorabilia so close at hand…

"Bus's boarding now," the clerk told him, choosing one of the preprinted tickets and pushing it under the grille. "Out that door; be leavin' 'bout five minutes."

Gritting his teeth, Garwood picked up the ticket…and as he withdrew his hand, there was a sudden *crack*, as if someone had fired a cap pistol.

"Damn kids," the clerk growled, craning his neck to peer out his side window.

Garwood looked down, his eyes searching the ledge inside the ticket window grille. He'd heard that particular sound before…and just inside the grille, near where his hand had twice reached, he saw it.

The clerk's ashtray. An ashtray once made of clear glass…now shot through by a thousand hairline fractures.

The clerk was still looking through his window for the kid with the cap pistol as Garwood left, forcing himself to walk.

He half expected the police to show up before the bus could leave, but to his mild surprise the vehicle wheezed leisurely out of the lot on time and headed a few minutes later onto the eastbound interstate. For the first few miles Garwood gave his full attention to his ears, straining tensely for the first faint sound of pursuing sirens. But as the minutes crawled by and no one showed up to pull them over, he was forced to the conclusion that the clerk had decided it wasn't any of his business.

The thought was strangely depressing. To realize that the latest upswing in the "not-me" noninvolvement philosophy had spread its rot from the polarized coasts into America's heartland bothered Garwood far more than it should have. Perhaps it was all the learned opinions he'd read weighing upon him; all the doomsayings about how such a national malaise could foreshadow the end of democracy.

Or perhaps it was simply the realization that even a nation full of selfish people didn't make a shred of difference to the cloud of destruction surrounding him.

Stop it! he ordered himself silently. *Self-pity…* Taking a deep breath, he looked around him.

He'd chosen his third-row seat carefully—as far from the bus's rear-mounted engine as he could reasonably get without sitting in the driver's lap, and well within the non-smoking section. His seatmate… He threw the kid a surreptitious look, confirmed that his first-glance analysis had been correct. Faded denim jeans and an old cotton shirt. That was good; natural fibers held up much better than synthetic ones, for the same reason that plastic had a tendency to disintegrate in his presence. Reaching a hand under his jacket, Garwood checked his own sweat-soaked polyester shirt for new tears. A rip at his right shoulder lengthened as he did so, and he muttered a curse.

"Don't make 'em like they use'ta, do they?"

Startled, Garwood turned to see his seatmate's smile. "What?" he asked.

"Your shirt," the kid explained. "I heard it rip. Guys who make 'em just get away with crapzi, don't they?"

"Um," Garwood grunted, turning away again.

"You headed for Champaign?" the kid persisted.

Garwood sighed. "Mahomet."

"No kidding! I grew up there. You, too, or are you just visiting?"

"Just visiting."

"You'll like it. Small place, but friendly. Speaking of which—" he stuck out his hand. "Name's Tom Arnold. Tom *Benedict* Arnold, actually."

Automatically, Garwood shook the proffered hand. Somewhere in the back of his head the alarm bells were going off… "Not, uh, any relation to…?"

"Benedict Arnold?" The kid grinned widely. "Sure am. Direct descendent, in fact."

An icy shiver ran up Garwood's back, a shiver having nothing to do with the bus's air conditioning. "You mean... *really* direct?" he asked, dropping the other's hand. "Not from a cousin or anything?"

"Straight shot line," Arnold nodded, the grin still in place. He was watching Garwood's face closely, and Garwood got the distinct impression the kid liked shocking people this way. "It's nothin' to be 'shamed of, you know—he did America a lot more good than he did bad. Whipped the Brits at Saratoga 'fore goin' over on their side—"

"Yes, I know," Garwood said, interrupting the impromptu history lesson. "Excuse me a second—washroom."

Stepping into the aisle, he went to the small cubicle at the rear of the bus. He waited a few minutes, then emerged and found an empty seat four rows behind the kid. He hoped Arnold wouldn't take it too personally, though he rather thought the other would. But he couldn't afford to take the chance. Benedict Arnold's victory at Saratoga had been a pivotal factor in persuading France to enter the war on the rebels' side, and Garwood had no desire to see if he had the same effect on living beings that he had on history's more inanimate descendants.

The afterglow in the sky behind them slowly faded, and as the sky darkened Garwood drifted in and out of sleep. The thought of the boy four seats ahead troubled his rest, filling his dreams with broken ashtrays and TV sets, half-melted-looking car engines and statues. After a while the bus stopped in Decatur, taking half an hour to trade a handful of passengers for an equally small number of others. Eventually they left; and back out in the dark of the prairie again, with the stars visible above, he again drifted to sleep...

The sound of the bus driver's voice jolted him awake. "...and gentlemen, I'm afraid we're having some trouble with the engine. Rather than take a chance on it quitting straight out before we get to Champaign, we're going to ask you to transfer to a bus that's being sent up from Decatur. It ought to be here in just a few minutes."

Blinking in the relative brightness of the overhead lights, Garwood joined the line of grumbling passengers moving down the aisle, a familiar knot wrenching at his stomach. Had it been him? He'd been far enough away from the engine—surely he had. Unless the effective distance was increasing with time... Forcing his jaw to unclench, he stepped carefully down the bus's steps, hoping desperately it was just a coincidence.

Outside, the only light came from a small building the bus had pulled alongside and from one or two dim streetlights. Half blind as his eyes again adjusted, Garwood took two tentative steps forward—

And came to an abrupt halt as strong hands slipped smoothly around each arm.

"Dr. James Garwood?" a shadowy figure before him asked quietly.

Garwood opened his mouth to deny it...but even as he did so he knew it would be useless. "Yes," he sighed. "And you?"

"Major Alan Davidson; Combined Services Intelligence. They miss you back at your lab, Doctor."

Garwood glanced past the husky man holding his right arm, saw the line of passengers goggling at him. "So it was all a set-up?" he asked. "The bus is okay?"

Davidson nodded. "A suspicious clerk in Springfield thought you might be a fugitive. From your description and something about a broken ashtray my superiors thought it might be you. Come with me, please."

Garwood didn't have much choice. Propelled gently along by the hands still holding his arms, he followed Davidson toward the lighted building and a long car parked in the shadows there. "Where are you taking me?" he asked, trying to keep his voice steady.

Davidson reached the car and opened the back door; and it wasn't until he and Garwood were in the back seat and the other two soldiers in front that the major answered the question. "Chanute AFB, about fifteen miles north of Champaign," he told Garwood as the car pulled back onto the interstate and headed east. "We'll be transferring you to a special plane there for the trip back to the Project."

Garwood licked his lips. A plane. How many people, he wondered, wished that mankind had never learned to fly? There was only one way to know for sure…and that way might wind up killing him. "You put me on that plane and it could be the last anyone ever sees of me," he told Davidson.

"Really?" the major asked politely.

"Did they tell you why I ran out on the Project? That the place was falling down around my ears?"

"They mentioned something about that, yes," Davidson nodded. "I really don't think you have anything to worry about, though. The people in charge of security on this one are all top notch."

Garwood snorted. "You're missing the point, Major. The lab wasn't under any kind of attack from outside agents. It was falling apart because *I* was in it."

Davidson nodded. "And as I said, we're going to have you under complete protection—"

"No!" Garwood snapped. "I'm not talking about someone out there gunning for me or the Project. It's my presence there—my *physical* presence inside Backdrop— that was causing all the destruction."

Davidson's dimly visible expression didn't change. "How do you figure that?"

Garwood hesitated, glancing at the front seat and the two silhouettes there listening into the conversation. Major Davidson might possibly be cleared for something this sensitive; the others almost certainly weren't. "I can't tell you the details," he said, turning back to Davidson. "I—look, you said your superiors nailed me because of a broken ashtray in Springfield, right? Did they tell you anything more?"

Davidson hesitated, then shook his head. "No."

"It broke because I came too close to it," Garwood told him. "There's a—oh, an aura, I guess you could call it, of destruction surrounding me. Certain types of items are especially susceptible, including internal combustion engines. That's why I don't want to be put on any plane."

"Uh-huh," Davidson nodded. "West, you having any trouble with the car?"

"No, sir," the driver said promptly. "Running real smooth."

Garwood took a deep breath. "It doesn't always happen right away," he said through clenched teeth. "I rode the bus for over an hour without anything happening, remember? But if it *does* happen with a plane, we can't just pull off the road and stop."

Davidson sighed. "Look, Dr. Garwood, just relax, okay? Trust me, the plane will run just fine."

Garwood glared through the gloom at him. "You want some proof?—is that what it'll take? Fine. Do you have any cigarettes?"

For a moment Davidson regarded him in silence. Then, flicking on a dim overhead dome light, he dug a crumpled pack from his pocket.

"Put a couple in my hand," Garwood instructed him, extending a palm, "and leave the light on."

Davidson complied with the cautious air of a man at a magic show. "Now what?"

"Just keep an eye on them. Tell me, do you *like* smoking?"

The other snorted. "Hell, no. Tried to give the damn things up at least twenty times. I'm hooked pretty good, I guess."

"You like being hooked?"

"That's a stupid question."

Garwood nodded. "Sorry. So, now...how many other people, do you suppose, hate being hooked by tobacco?"

Davidson gave him a look that was half frown, half glare. "What's your point, Doctor?"

Garwood hesitated. "Consider it as a sort of subconscious democracy. You don't like smoking, and a whole lot of other people in this country don't like smoking. A lot of them wish there weren't any cigarettes—wish *these* cigarettes didn't exist."

"And if wishes were horses, beggars would ride," Davidson quoted. He reached over, to close his fingers on the cigarettes in Garwood's palm—

And jerked his hand back as they crumpled into shreds at his touch.

"What the *hell*?" he snapped, practically in Garwood's ear. "What did you *do*?"

"I was near them," Garwood said simply. "I was near them, and a lot of people don't like smoking. That's all there is to it."

Davidson was still staring at the mess in Garwood's palm. "It's a trick. You switched cigarettes on me."

"While you watched?" Garwood snorted. "All right, fine, let's do it again. You can write your initials on them this time."

Slowly, Davidson raised his eyes to Garwood's face. "Why *you?*"

Garwood brushed the bits of paper and tobacco off his hand with a shudder. Even after all these months it still scared him spitless to watch something disintegrate like that. "I know…something. I can't tell you just what."

"Okay, you know something. And?"

"No ands about it. It's the knowledge alone that does it."

Davidson's eyes were steady on his face. "Knowledge. Knowledge that shreds cigarettes all by itself."

"That, combined with the way a lot of people feel about smoking. Look, I know it's hard to believe—"

"Skip that point for now," Davidson cut him off. "Assume you're right, that it's pure knowledge that somehow does all this. Is it something connected with the Backdrop Project?"

"Yes."

"They know about it? And know what it does?"

"Yes, to both."

"And they still want you back?"

Garwood thought about Saunders. The long discussions he'd had with the other. The even longer arguments. "Dr. Saunders doesn't really understand."

For a moment Davidson was silent. "What else does this aura affect besides cigarettes?" he asked at last. "You mentioned car engines?"

"Engines, plastics, televisions—modern conveniences of all kinds, mainly, though there are other things in danger as well. Literally *anything* that someone doesn't like can be a target." He thought about the bus and Tom Benedict Arnold. "It might work on people, too," he added, shivering. "That one I haven't had to find out about for sure."

"And all that this...destructive wishing...needs to come out is for you to be there?"

Garwood licked his lips. "So far, yes. But if Backdrop ever finishes its work—"

"In other words, you're a walking time bomb."

Garwood winced at the harshness in Davidson's voice. "I suppose you could put it that way, yes. That's why I didn't want to risk staying at Backdrop. Why I don't want to risk riding in that plane."

The major nodded. "The second part we can do something about, anyway. We'll scrap the plane and keep you on the ground. You want to tell us where this Backdrop Project is, or would you rather I get the directions through channels?"

Garwood felt a trickle of sweat run between his shoulder blades. "Major, I can't go back there. I'm one man, and it's bad enough that I can wreck things the way I do. But if Backdrop finishes its work, the effect will spread a million-fold."

Davidson eyed him warily. "You mean it's contagious? Like a virus or something?"

"Well...not exactly."

"Not exactly," Davidson repeated with a snort. "All right, then, try this one: do the people at Backdrop know what it is about you that does this?"

"To some extent," Garwood admitted. "But as I said, they don't grasp all the implications—"

"Then you'd agree that there's no place better equipped to deal with you than Backdrop?"

Garwood took a deep breath. "Major, I can't go back to Backdrop. Either the project will disintegrate around me and someone will get killed, or else it'll succeed and what happened to your cigarettes will start happening all over the world. Can't you understand that?"

"What I understand isn't the issue here, Doctor," Davidson growled. "My orders were very specific: to deliver you to Chanute AFB and from there to Backdrop. You've convinced me you're dangerous; you *haven't* convinced me it would be safer to keep you anywhere else."

"Major—"

"And you can damn well shut up now, too." He turned his face toward the front of the car.

Garwood took a shuddering breath, let it out in a sigh of defeat as he slumped back into the cushions. It had been a waste of time and energy—he'd known it would be right from the start. Even if he could have told Davidson everything, it wouldn't have made any difference. Davidson was part of the "not-me" generation, and he had his orders, and all the logic and reason in the world wouldn't have moved him into taking such a chance.

And now it was over…because logic and reason were the only weapons Garwood had.

Unless….

He licked his lips. Maybe he *did* have one other weapon. Closing his eyes, he began to concentrate on his formulae.

Contrary to what he'd told Saunders, there were only four truly fundamental equations, plus a handful of others needed to define the various quantities. One of the equations was given in the notes he hadn't been able to destroy; the other three were still exclusively his. Squeezing his eyelids tightly together, he listened to the hum of the car's engine and tried to visualize the equations exactly as they'd looked in his notebook…

But it was no use, and ten minutes later he finally admitted defeat. The engine hadn't even misfired, let alone failed. The first time the curse might actually have been useful, and he was apparently too far away for it to take effect. Too far away, and no way to get closer without crawling into the front seat with the soldiers.

The soldiers…

He opened his eyes. Davidson was watching him narrowly; ahead, through the windshield, the lights of a city were throwing a glow onto the low clouds overhead. "Coming up on I-57, Major," the driver said over his shoulder. "You want to take that or the back door to Chanute?"

"Back door," Davidson said, keeping his eyes on Garwood.

"Yes, sir."

Back door? Garwood licked his lips in a mixture of sudden hope and sudden dread. The only reasonable back door was Route 45 north…and on the way to that exit they would pass through the northern end of Champaign.

Which meant he had one last chance to escape…and one last chance to let the genie so far out of the bottle that he'd never get it back in.

But he had to risk it. "All right, Major," he said through dry lips, making sure he was loud enough to be heard in the front seat as well. "Chi square e to the minus i alpha t to the three-halves, plus i alpha t to the three-halves e to the gamma zero z. Sum over all momentum states and do a rotation transformation of one point five five six radians. Energy transfer equation: first tensor is—"

"What the hell are you talking about?" Davidson snarled. But there was a growing note of uneasiness in his voice.

"You wanted proof that what I know was too dangerous to be given to Saunders and Backdrop?" Garwood asked. "Fine; here it is. First tensor is p sub xx e to the gamma—"

Davidson swore suddenly and lunged at him. But Garwood was ready for the move and got there first, throwing his arms around the other in an imprisoning bear hug. "—times p sub y alpha e to the minus i alpha t—"

Davidson threw off the grip, aiming a punch for Garwood's stomach. But the bouncing car ruined his aim and Garwood took the blow on his ribs instead. Again he threw his arms around Davidson. "—plus four pi sigma chi over gamma one z—"

A hand grabbed at Garwood's hair: the soldier in the front seat, leaning over to assist in the fray. Garwood ducked under the hand and kept shouting equations. The lack of space was on his side, hampering the other two as they tried to subdue him. Dimly, Garwood wondered why the driver hadn't stopped, realized that the car *was* now slowing down. There was a bump as they dropped onto the shoulder—

And with a loud staccato crackle from the front, the engine suddenly died.

The driver tried hard, but it was obvious that the car's abrupt failure had taken him completely by surprise. For a handful of wild heartbeats the vehicle careened wildly, dropping down off the shoulder into the ditch and then up the other side. A pair of close-spaced trees loomed ahead— the driver managed to steer between them—and an instant later the car slammed to a halt against the rear fence of a used car lot.

Garwood was the first to recover. Yanking on the handle, he threw the door open and scrambled out. The car had knocked a section of the fence part way over; climbing onto the hood, he gripped the chain links and pulled himself up and over.

He'd made it nearly halfway across the lot when the voice came from far behind him. "Okay, Garwood, that's far enough," Davidson called sharply. "Freeze or I shoot."

Garwood half turned, to see Davidson's silhouette drop over the fence and bring his arms up into a two-handed marksman's stance. Instinctively, Garwood ducked, trying to speed up a little. Ahead of him, the lines of cars lit up with the reflected flash; behind came the crack of an explosion—

And a yelp of pain.

Garwood braked to a halt and turned. Davidson was on the pavement twenty yards back of him, curled onto his side. A few feet in front of him was his gun. Or, rather, what had once been his gun…

Garwood looked around, eyes trying to pierce the shadows outside the fence. Neither of the other soldiers was anywhere in sight. Still in the car, or moving to flank him? Whichever, the best thing he could do right now was to forget Davidson and get moving.

The not-me generation. "Damn," Garwood muttered to himself. "Davidson?" he called tentatively. "You all right?"

"I'm alive," the other's voice bit back.

"Where did you get hit?"

There was a short pause. "Right calf. Doesn't seem too bad."

"Probably took a chunk of your gun. You shouldn't have tried to shoot me—there are just as many people out there who hate guns as hate smoking." A truck with its brights on swept uncaringly past on the interstate behind Davidson, and Garwood got a glimpse of two figures inside the wrecked car. Moving sluggishly, which took at least a little of the load off Garwood's conscience. At least his little stratagem hadn't gotten anyone killed outright. "Are your men okay?"

"Do you care?" the other shot back.

Garwood grimaced. "Look, I'm sorry, Davidson, but I had no choice."

"Sure. What do a few lives matter, anyway?"

"Davidson—"

"Especially when your personal freedom's at stake. You know, I have to say you really did a marvelous job of it. Now, instead of your colleagues hounding *you* for whatever it is those equations are, all they have to do is hound *us*. All that crap about the dangers of this stuff getting out—that's all it was, wasn't it? Just crap."

Garwood gritted his teeth. He knew full well that Davidson was playing a game here, deliberately trying to enmesh him in conversation until reinforcements could arrive. But he might never see this man again... "I wasn't trying to saddle you with this mess, Davidson—really I wasn't. I needed to strengthen the effect enough to stop the car, but it wasn't a tradeoff between my freedom and all hell breaking loose. You and your men can't possibly retain the equations I was calling out—you don't have the necessary mathematical background, for one thing. They'll be gone from your mind within minutes, if they aren't already."

"I'm so pleased to hear it," Davidson said, heavily sarcastic. "Well, *I'm* certainly convinced. How about you?"

To that Garwood had no answer...and it was long past time for him to get out of here. "I've got to go, now. Please—tell them to leave me alone. What they want just isn't possible."

Davidson didn't reply. With a sigh, Garwood turned his back and hurried toward the other end of the car lot and the street beyond it. Soon, he knew, the soldiers would be coming.

II

"...One...two...*three*."

Davidson opened his eyes, blinking for a minute as they adjusted to the room's light. He swallowed experimentally, glancing at the clock on the desk to his left. Just after three-thirty in the morning, which meant he'd been under for nearly an hour…and from the way his throat felt, he'd apparently been talking for most of that time. "How'd it go?" he asked the man seated beyond the microphone that had been set up in front of him.

Dr. Hamish nodded, the standard medical professional's neutral expression pasted across his face. "Quite well, Major. At least once we got you started."

"Sorry. I *did* warn you I've never been good at being hypnotized." A slight scraping of feet to his right made Davidson turn, to find a distinguished-looking middle-aged man who'd been seated just outside his field of view. On the other's lap was a pad and pencil; beside him on another chair was a tape recorder connected to the microphone. "Dr. Saunders," Davidson nodded in greeting, vaguely surprised to see Backdrop's director looking so alert at such an ungodly hour. "I didn't hear you come in."

"Dr. Hamish was having enough trouble putting you under," Saunders shrugged. "I didn't think it would help for me to be here, too, during the process."

Davidson's eyes flicked to the notepad. "Did you get what you wanted?"

Saunders shrugged again, his neutral expression almost as good as Hamish's. "We'll know soon enough," he said. "It'll take awhile to run the equations you gave us past our various experts, of course."

"Of course," Davidson nodded. "I hope whatever you got doesn't make things worse, the way Garwood thought it would."

"Dr. Garwood is a pessimist," Saunders said shortly.

"Maybe," Davidson said, knowing better than to start an argument. "Has there been any word about him?"

"From the searchers, you mean?" Saunders shook his head. "Not yet. Though that's hardly surprising—he had over half an hour to find a hole to hide in, after all."

Davidson winced at the implied accusation in the other's tone. It wasn't *his* fault, after all, that none of the damned "not-me" generation drivers on the interstate had bothered to stop. "Men with mild concussions aren't usually up to using car radios," he said, perhaps more tartly than was called for.

"I know, Major." Saunders sighed. "And I'm sorry we couldn't prepare you better for handling him. But—well, you understand."

"I understand that your security wound up working against you, yes," Davidson said. "If a fugitive is carrying a weapon, we're supposed to know that in advance. If the fugitive *is* a weapon, we ought to know *that*, too."

"Dr. Garwood as walking time bomb?" Saunders's lip twitched. "Yes, you mentioned that characterization of him a few minutes ago, during your debriefing."

Davidson only vaguely remembered calling Garwood that. "You disagree?"

"On the contrary, it's an uncomfortably vivid description of the situation," Saunders said grimly.

"Yeah." Davidson braced himself. "And now my men and I are in the same boat, aren't we?"

"Hardly," Saunders shook his head. The neutral expression, Davidson noted, was back in place. "We're going to keep the three of you here for awhile, just to be on the safe side, but I'm ninety-nine percent certain there's no danger of the same effect developing."

"I hope you're right," Davidson said. Perhaps a gentle probe… "Seems to me, though, that if there's even a chance it'll show up, we deserve to know what it is we've got. And how it works."

"Sorry, Major," Saunders said, with a quickness that showed he'd been expecting the question. "Until an updated security check's been done on you, we can't consider telling you anything else. You already know more than I'm really comfortable with."

Which was undoubtedly the *real* reason Saunders was keeping them here. "And if my security comes through clean?" he asked, passing up the cheap-shot reminder of what Saunders's overtight security had already cost him tonight.

"We'll see," Saunders said shortly, getting to his feet and sliding the pad into his pocket. "The guard will escort you to your quarters, Major. Good-night."

He left the room, taking the tape recorder with him, and Davidson turned his attention back to Hamish. "Any post-hypnotic side effects I should watch out for, Doctor?" he asked, reaching down for his crutches and carefully standing up. He winced as he put a shade too much weight on his injured leg.

Hamish shook his head. "No, nothing like that."

"Good." Davidson eyed the other. "I don't suppose *you* could give me any hints as to my prognosis here, could you?"

"You mean as regards the—ah—problem with Dr. Garwood?" Hamish shook his head, too quickly. "I really don't think you're in any danger, Major. Really I don't. The room here didn't suffer any damage while Dr. Saunders was writing down the equations you gave him, which implies you don't know enough to bother you."

Davidson felt the skin on the back of his neck crawl. So Garwood had been telling the truth, after all. It was indeed pure knowledge alone that was behind his walking jinx effect.

He shook his head. No, that was utterly impossible. Much easier to believe that whatever scam Garwood was running, he'd managed to take in Backdrop's heads with it, too.

Either way, of course, it made Garwood one hell of a dangerous man. "I see," he said through stiff lips. "Thank you, Doctor. Good-night."

A Marine guard, dressed in one of Backdrop's oddly nonstandard jumpsuit outfits, was waiting outside the door as Davidson emerged. "If you'll follow me, Major," he said, and led the way to an undistinguished door a couple of corridors away. Behind the door, Davidson found a compact dorm-style apartment, minimally furnished with writing desk, chair, and fold-down bed, with a closet and bathroom tucked into opposite corners. Through the open closet door a half dozen orange jumpsuits could be seen hanging; laid out on the bed was a set of underwear and a large paper bag. "You'll need to put your clothing into the bag," the guard explained after showing Davidson around the room. "Your watch and other personal effects, too, if you would."

"Can I keep my cigarettes?"

"No, sir. Cigarettes are especially forbidden."

Davidson thought back to the car ride, and Garwood's disintegrating trick. "Because that effect of Garwood's destroys them?" he hazarded.

The Marine's face might have twitched, but Davidson wouldn't have sworn to it. "I'll wait outside, sir, while you change."

He retired to the hallway, shutting the door behind him. Grimacing, Davidson stripped and put on the underwear, wondering if it would help to tell Saunders that he'd already seen what the Garwood Effect did to cigarettes. The thought of spending however many days or weeks here without nicotine… Preoccupied, it was only as he was stuffing his clothes into it that his mind registered the oddity of using a *paper* bag instead of the usual plastic. A minor mystery, to go with all the major ones.

The Marine was waiting to accept the bag when he opened the door a minute later. Tucking it under his arm, he gave Davidson directions to the mess hall, wished him good-night, and left. Closing the door and locking it, Davidson limped his way back to the bed and shut off the nightstand light.

Lying there, eyes closed, he tried to think; but it had been a long day, and between fatigue and the medication he'd been given for his leg he found he couldn't hold onto a coherent train of thought. Two minutes after hitting the pillow he gave up the effort. A minute after that, he was fast asleep.

The jumpsuits hanging in the closet were the first surprise of the new day.

Not their color. Davidson hadn't seen any other orange outfits in his brief walk through Backdrop the previous night, but he'd rather expected to be given something distinctive as long as he was effectively on security probation here. But it was something else that caught his attention, some oddity in the feel of the material as he pulled it off its wooden hanger. Examining the label, he quickly found the reason: the jumpsuit was one hundred percent linen.

Davidson frowned, trying to remember what Garwood had said about the potential targets of his strange destructive power. *Engines, plastics, televisions,* had been on the list; *modern conveniences* had also been there. Did synthetic fibers come under the latter heading? Apparently so. He pulled the jumpsuit on, fingers brushing something thin but solid in the left breast pocket as he did so. He finished dressing, then dug the object out.

It was a plastic card.

Frowning, Davidson studied it. It wasn't an ID, at least not a very sophisticated one. His name was impressed into it, but there was no photo, thumbprint, or even a description. It wasn't a digital key, or a radiation dosimeter, or a coded info plate, or anything else he could think of.

Unless...

He licked his lips, a sudden chill running up his back. *Engines, plastics, televisions...* He'd been wrong; the card *was* a dosimeter. A dosimeter for the Garwood Effect.

Whatever the hell the Garwood Effect was.

He gritted his teeth. *All right, let's take this in a logical manner.* The Garwood Effect destroyed plastics; okay. It also ruined car engines and pistols...and cigarettes and ash trays. What did all of those have in common?

He puzzled at it for a few more minutes before giving up the effort. Without more information he wasn't going to get anywhere. Besides, a persistent growling in his stomach was reminding him he was overdue for a meal. *No one thinks well on an empty stomach,* he silently quoted his grandfather's favorite admonition. Retrieving his crutches from the floor by his bed, he clumped off to the mess hall.

After the linen jumpsuit, he half expected breakfast to consist of nuts and berries served in coconut shells, but fortunately Backdrop hadn't gone quite that far overboard. The dishware was a somewhat nonstandard heavy ceramic, but the meal itself was all too military standard: nutritious and filling without bothering as much with flavor as one might like. He ate quickly, swearing to himself afterward at the lack of a cigarette to help bury the taste. Manhandling his tray to the conveyer, he headed off to try and find some answers.

And ran immediately into a brick wall.

"Sorry, Major, but you're not authorized for entry," the Marine guard outside the Backdrop garage said apologetically.

"Not even to see my own car?" Davidson growled, waving past the Marine at the double doors behind him. "Come on, now—what kind of secrets does anybody keep in a garage?"

"You might be surprised, sir," the guard said. "I suggest you check with Colonel Bidwell and see if he'll authorize you to get in."

Davidson gritted his teeth. "I suppose I'll have to. Where's his office?"

Colonel Bidwell was a lean, weathered man with gray hair and eyes that seemed to be in a perpetual squint. "Major,"

he said, nodding in greeting as Davidson was ushered into his office. "Sit down. Come to apply for a job?"

"More or less, sir," Davidson said, easing gratefully into the proffered chair. "I thought I could lend a hand in hunting down Dr. Garwood. Unless you've already found him, that is."

Bidwell gave him a hard look. "No, not yet. But he's in the Champaign-Urbana area—that's for damn sure. It's only a matter of time."

Automatically, Davidson reached for a cigarette, dropping his hand to his lap halfway through the motion. "Yes, sir. I'd still like to help."

For a long moment Bidwell eyed him. "Uh-huh," he grunted. "Well, I'll tell you something, Major. Your file came through about an hour ago...and there are things there I really don't like."

"I'm sorry to hear that, sir," Davidson said evenly.

Bidwell's expression tightened a bit. "Your record shows a lot of bulldog, Major. You get hold of something and you won't let go until you've torn it apart."

"My superiors generally consider that an asset, sir."

"It usually is. But not if it gets you personally involved with your quarry. Like it might now."

Davidson pursed his lips. "Has the colonel had a chance to look over the rest of my file? Including my success rate?"

Bidwell grimaced. "I have. And I still don't want you. Unfortunately, that decision's been taken away from me. You're already here, and it's been decided that there's no point in letting you just spin your wheels. So. Effective immediately, you're assigned to hunter duty. Long-range duty, of course—we can't let you leave Backdrop until your updated security check is finished. You'll have a desk and computer in Room 138, with access to everything we know about Dr. Garwood."

Davidson nodded. Computer analysis was a highly impersonal way to track down a quarry, but he knew from long experience that it could be as effective as actually getting into the field and beating the bushes. "Understood, sir. Can I also have access to the less secure areas of Backdrop?"

Bidwell frowned. "Why?"

"I'd like to get into the garage to look at my car, for one thing. Garwood may have left a clue there as to where he was headed."

"The car's already been checked over," Bidwell told him. "They didn't find anything."

Davidson remained silent, his eyes holding Bidwell's, and eventually the colonel snorted. "Oh, all right." Reaching into his desk, he withdrew a small card and scribbled on it. "Just to get you off my back. Here—a Level One security pass. And that's it, so don't try to badger me for anything higher."

"Yes, sir." The card, Davidson noted as he took it, was a thickened cardboard instead of standard passcard plastic. Not really surprising. "With your permission, then, I'll get straight to work."

"Be my guest," Bidwell grunted, turning back to his paperwork. "Dismissed."

"**W**hat in blazes happened to it?" Davidson asked, frowning into the open engine compartment. After what had happened to his cigarettes and gun, he'd rather expected to find a mess of shattered metal and disintegrated plastic under the hood of his car. But *this*—

"It's what happens to engines," the mechanic across the hood said vaguely, his eyes flicking to Davidson's orange jumpsuit.

Davidson gingerly reached in to touch the mass of metal. "It looks half melted."

"Yeah, it does," the mechanic agreed. "Uh…if that's all, Major, I have work to get to."

All right, Davidson thought grimly to himself as he clumped his way back down the corridor. *So this Garwood Effect doesn't affect everything the same way. No big deal—it just means it'll take a little more work to track down whatever the hell is going on here, that's all.*

What it *didn't* mean was that he was going to toss in the towel and give up. Colonel Bidwell had been right on that count, at least; he did indeed have a lot of bulldog in him.

Dr. James Garwood was one of that vanishingly rare breed of scientist who was equally at home with scientific hardware as he was with scientific theory. A triple-threat man with advanced degrees in theoretical physics, applied physics, and electrical engineering, he was a certified genius with a proven knack for visualizing the real-world results of even the most esoteric mathematical theory. He'd been a highly-paid member of a highly respected research group until two years previously, when he'd taken a leave of absence to join the fledgling Backdrop Project. From almost the beginning, it seemed, he'd disagreed with Saunders's policies and procedures until, three months ago, he'd suddenly disappeared.

And that was the entire synopsis of Garwood's life since coming to Backdrop. Seated before the computer terminal, Davidson permitted himself an annoyed scowl. So much for having access to everything that was known about Dr. Garwood.

Of Garwood since his break there was, of course, nothing; but the files did contain a full report of the efforts to find him. The FBI had been called in early on, after which the National Security Agency had gotten involved and quickly pulled the rest of the country's intelligence services onto the case. In spite of it all, Garwood had managed to remain completely hidden until the report of yesterday's incident at the Springfield bus station had happened to catch the proper eye.

After three months he'd been caught. And promptly lost again.

Davidson clenched his teeth, forcing himself not to dwell on his failure. Bidwell had been right: too much emotional involvement had a bad tendency to cloud the thinking.

But then, there was more than one form of emotional involvement. Leaning back in his seat, stretching his injured leg out beneath the desk, he closed his eyes and tried to become Dr. James Garwood.

For whatever reason, he'd decided to quit Backdrop. Perhaps he and Saunders had argued one too many times; perhaps the presence of the Garwood Effect had finally gotten too much for him to take. Perhaps—as he'd claimed on the ride last night—he truly felt that Backdrop was a danger and that the best thing for him to do was to abandon it.

So all right. He'd left, and managed to remain hidden from practically everybody for a solid three months. Which implied money. Which usually implied friends or relatives.

Opening his eyes, Davidson attacked the keyboard again. Family…? Negative—all members already interviewed or under quiet surveillance. Ditto for relatives. Ditto for friends.

Fine. Where else, then, could he have gotten money from? His own bank accounts? It was too obvious a possibility to have been missed, but Davidson keyed for it anyway. Sure enough, there was no evidence of large withdrawals in the months previous to his abrupt departure from Backdrop. He went back another year, just to be sure. Nothing.

Behind him, the door squeaked open, and Davidson turned to see a young man with major's oak leaves on his jumpsuit step into the room. "Major Davidson, I presume," the other nodded in greeting. "I'm Major Lyman, data coordinator for Backdrop Security."

"Nice to meet you," Davidson nodded, reaching back to shake hands.

"Colonel Bidwell told me you've been co-opted for the Garwood bird hunt," Lyman continued, looking over Davidson's shoulder at the computer screen. "How's it going?"

"It might go better if I had more information on Garwood's activities at Backdrop," Davidson told him. "As it is, I've got barely one paragraph to cover two years out of the man's life. The two most important years, yet."

Lyman nodded. "I sympathize, but I'm afraid that's per the colonel's direct order. Apparently he thinks the full records would give you more information about what Backdrop is doing than he wants you to have."

"And Backdrop is doing something he doesn't want anyone to know about?" Davidson asked.

Lyman's face hardened a bit. "I wouldn't make vague inferences like that if I were you, Major," he said darkly. "You wouldn't have been allowed to just waltz into the Manhattan Project and get the whole story, either, and Backdrop is at least as sensitive as that was."

"As destructive, too." Davidson held a hand up before Lyman could reply. "Sorry—didn't mean it that way. Remember that all I know about this whole thing is that Garwood can use it to wreck cars and cigarettes."

"Yeah—the walking time bomb, I hear you dubbed him." Lyman snorted under his breath. "It's hoped that that... side effect, as it were...can be eliminated. Hoped a *lot*."

"Can't argue with that one," Davidson agreed. So his description of Garwood as a walking time bomb was being circulated around Backdrop. Interesting that what had been essentially a throwaway line would be so widely picked up on. He filed the datum away for possible future reference. "You think Garwood can help get rid of it if we find him?"

Lyman shrugged. "All I know is that my orders are to find him and get him back. What happens after that is someone else's problem. Anyway, my office is down the hall in Room One Fifty—let me know if you need anything."

"Thanks."

Lyman turned to go, then paused. "Oh, by the way...if your computer seems to go on the blink, don't waste time fiddling with it. Just call Maintenance and they'll take care of it."

Davidson frowned. "Computers go on the blink a lot around here?"

The other hesitated. "Often enough," he said vaguely. "The point is, just tell Maintenance and let them figure out whether to fix or replace."

"Right."

Lyman nodded and left, and Davidson turned back to his terminal. So computers were among the modern conveniences subject to attack by the Garwood Effect...and it reminded Davidson of something else he'd planned to try.

It took a few minutes of searching, but eventually he found what he was looking for: a list of maintenance records, going all the way back to Backdrop's inception two years ago. Now, with a little analysis...

An hour later he straightened up in his chair, trying to work the cramps out of his fingers and the knot out of his stomach. If ever he'd needed confirmation of Garwood's story, he had it now. The amount of wrecked equipment coming up from the offices and experimental areas to Maintenance was simply staggering: computers, all kinds of electronic equipment, plastic-based items—the list went on and on. Even the physical structure of Backdrop itself was affected; a long report detailed instance after instance of walls that had been replastered and ceilings that had had to be shored up. That it was a result of Backdrop's work was beyond doubt: a simple analysis of the areas where damage had occurred showed steadily increasing frequency the closer to the experimental areas one got. To the experimental areas, and to Garwood's office.

And the analysis had yielded one other fact. The damage had been slowly increasing in frequency over the two years Garwood had been with Backdrop...until the point three months back when he'd left. After that, it had dropped nearly to zero.

Which meant that Garwood hadn't been lying. He was indeed at the center of what was happening.

A walking time bomb. Davidson felt a shiver run up his back. If Garwood remained at large, and if the Garwood Effect continued to increase in strength as it had over the past two years…

With a conscious effort he forced the thought from his mind. Worry of that sort would gain him nothing. Somewhere, somehow, Garwood had to have left a trail of some sort. It was up to Davidson to find it.

He fumbled for a cigarette, swore under his breath. Leaning back in his seat again, he closed his eyes. *I am James Garwood,* he told himself, dragging his mind away from the irritations of nicotine withdrawal and willing his thoughts to drift. *I'm in hiding from the whole world. How exactly—exactly—have I pulled it off?*

III

…T*imes e to the gamma one t.*

Garwood circled the last equation and laid down the pencil, and for a minute he gazed at the set of equations he'd derived. It was progress of a sort, he supposed; he *had* gotten rid of the gamma zero factor this time, and that was the one the computer had been having its latest conniption fits over. Maybe this time the run would yield something useful.

Or maybe this time the damn machine would just find something else to trip over.

Stop it! he ordered himself darkly. Self-pity was for children, or for failures. Not for him.

Across the tiny efficiency apartment, the computer terminal was humming patiently as it sat on the floor in the corner. Easing down into a cross-legged sitting position on the floor, Garwood consulted his paper and maneuvered his remote arm into position. The arm was pretty crude, as such things went: a long dowel rod reaching across the room to the terminal with a shorter one fastened to it at a right angle for actually hitting the keys, the whole contraption resting on a universal pivot about its center. But crude or not, it enabled him to enter data without getting anywhere near the terminal, with the result that this terminal had already outlasted all the others he'd used since fleeing Backdrop. He only wished he'd thought of this trick sooner.

Entering the equations was a long, painstaking job, made all the more difficult by having to watch what he was doing through a small set of opera glasses. But finally he hit the return key for the last time, keying in the simultaneous-solutions program already loaded. The terminal beeped acknowledgment, and with a grunt Garwood got stiffly back into his chair. His stomach growled as he did so, and with a mild shock he saw that it was ten-thirty. No wonder his stomach had been growling for the past hour or so. Getting up, rubbing at the cramps in his legs, he went over to the kitchen alcove.

To find that he'd once again let his supplies run below acceptable levels. "Blast," he muttered under his breath, and snared his wallet from the top of the dresser. There was a burger place a few blocks away that might still be open...but on the other hand, his wad of bills was getting dangerously thin, and when this batch was gone there wouldn't be any more. For a moment he studied the terminal's display with his opera glasses, but the lack of diagnostic messages implied that nothing immediate and obvious had tripped it up. Which meant that it would probably be chugging away happily on the equations for at least another half hour. Which meant there was plenty of time for him to skip the fast food and walk instead to the grocery store.

The overhead lights were humming loudly as Garwood started across the store's parking lot, and for a moment he fantasized that that he was out in some exotic wilderness, circled by giant insects made of equal parts firefly and cicada. Out in the wilderness, away from Backdrop and the curse that hounded him.

It might come to that eventually, he knew. Even if he was able to continue eluding the searchers Saunders had scouring the area, he still couldn't stay here. His carefully engineered sublet would last only another five weeks, his dwindling bankroll dropping near zero at about the same time. Leaving him a choice between surrender and finding a job.

Both of which, he knew, really boiled down to the same thing. Any job paying enough for him to live on would leave a trail of paper that would bring Saunders's people down on him in double-quick time. Not to mention the risk he would present to the people he'd be working with.

He grimaced. A walking time bomb, that Intelligence major—Davidson—had dubbed him. A part of Garwood's mind appreciated the unintended irony of such a characterization. The rest of it winced at the truth also there.

The grocery store, not surprisingly, was quiet. Wrestling a cart that seemed determined to veer to the left, he went up and down the aisles, picking out his usual selection of convenience foods and allowing his nerves to relax as much as they could. There were probably some people somewhere who truly disliked supermarkets and the efficient long-term storage of food that made them possible; but if there were, the number must be vanishingly small. As a result, grocery stores were near the top of the short list of places where Garwood could feel fairly safe. As long as he stayed away from the cigarettes and smoking paraphernalia, he could be reasonably certain that nothing would break or crumble around him.

He collected as many packages as he estimated would fit into two bags and headed for the checkout. There, the teenage girl manning the register—or possibly she was a college student; they all looked equally young to him these days—gave him a pleasant smile and got to work unloading his cart. Listening to the familiar beep of the laser scanner, Garwood pulled out his wallet and watched the march of prices across the display.

The cart was still half full when a jar of instant coffee failed to register. The girl tried scanning it four times, then gave up and manually keyed the UPC code into her register. The next item, a frozen dinner, was similarly ignored. As was the next item…and the next…and the next…

"Trouble?" Garwood asked, his mouth going dry.

"Scanner seems to have quit," she frowned, tapping the glass slits as if trying to get the machine's attention. "Funny—they're supposed to last longer than this."

"Well, you know how these things are," Garwood said, striving for nonchalance even as his heart began to pound in his ears.

"Yeah, but this one was just replaced Saturday. Oh, well, that's progress for you." She picked up the next item and turned back to her register.

Almost unwillingly, Garwood bent over and peered into the glass. Behind it, the laser scanner was dimly visible. Looking perfectly normal... *No*, he told himself firmly. *No, it's just coincidence. It has to be. Nobody hates laser grocery scanners, for God's sake.* But even as he fought to convince himself of that, a horrible thought occurred to him.

Perhaps it was no longer necessary for anyone to hate laser grocery scanners directly. Perhaps all it took now was enough people hating the lasers in self-guided weapons systems.

A dark haze seemed to settle across his vision. It had started, then; the beginning of the end. If a concerted desire to eliminate one incarnation of a given technology could spill over onto another, then there was literally nothing on the face of the earth that could resist Garwood's influence. His eyes fell on the packages of frozen food before him on the counter, and a dimly remembered television program came to mind. A program that had showed how the root invention of refrigeration had led to both frozen foods and ICBMs.

The girl finished packing the two paper bags and read off the total for him. Garwood pulled out the requisite number of bills, accepted his change, and left. Outside, the parking lot lights were still humming their cicada/firefly song. Still beckoning him to the safety of the wilderness.

A wilderness, he knew, which didn't exist.

The bags, light enough at the beginning of the walk, got progressively heavier as the blocks went by, and by the time he reached the door to his apartment house his arms were starting to tremble with the strain. Working the outside door open with his fingertips, he let it close behind him and started up the stairs. A young woman was starting down at the same time, and for an instant, just as they passed, their eyes met. But only for an instant. The woman broke the contact almost at once, her face the neutral inward-looking expression that everyone seemed to be wearing these days.

Garwood continued up the stairs, feeling a dull ache in the center of his chest. The "not-me" generation. Everyone encased in his or her own little bubble of space. *So why should I care, either?* he thought morosely. *Let it all fall apart around me. Why am I killing myself trying to take on decisions like this, anyway? Saunders is the one in charge, and if he says it'll work, then whatever happens is his responsibility. Right?*

The computer had finished its work. Setting the bags down, Garwood dug out his opera glasses again and studied the display. The machine had found three solutions to his coupled equations. The first was the one he'd already come up with, the one that had started this whole mess in the first place. The second was also one he'd seen before, and found to be mathematically correct but non-physical. The third solution...

Heart thudding in his ears, Garwood stepped to the table and reached to the ashtray for one of the loose cigarettes lying there. The third solution was new. And if it contained the build-in safeguard he was hoping to find...

He picked up one of the cigarettes. Squeezing it gently between thumb and fingertips, he gazed at the formula through his opera glasses, letting his eyes and thoughts linger on each symbol as he ticked off the seconds in his mind. At a count of *ten* he thought he felt a softness in the cigarette paper; at *twenty-two*, it crumbled to powder.

Wearily, he brushed the pieces from his hand into the garbage. Twenty-two seconds. The same length of time it had taken the last time. It wasn't getting any worse, but it wasn't getting any better, either.

Which probably implied this was yet another walk down a blind alley.

For a moment he gazed down at the cigarettes. A long time ago he'd believed that this field contained nothing but blind alleys—had believed it, and had done all he could to persuade Saunders of it, too. But Saunders hadn't believed...and now, Garwood couldn't afford to, either. Because if there weren't any stable solutions, then this curse would be with him forever.

Stepping over to the counter, he began unloading his groceries. Of course there was a stable solution. There *had* to be.

The only trick would be finding it before his time ran out.

IV

"**W**ell," Davidson said, "at least he's staying put. I suppose that's *something*."

"Maybe," Lyman said, reaching over Davidson's shoulder to drop the report back onto his desk. "A broken laser scanner is hardly conclusive evidence, though."

"Oh, he's there, all right," Davidson growled, glaring at the paper. His fingertips rubbed restlessly at the edge of his desk, itching to be holding a cigarette. Damn Saunders's stupid rule, anyway. "He's there. Somewhere."

Lyman shrugged. "Well, he's not at any hotel or motel in the area—that much is for sure. We've got taps on all his friends around the country, checking for any calls he might make to them, but so far that's come up dry, too."

"Which means either he's somehow getting cash despite the net, or else he's been holed up for nearly three weeks without any money. How?"

"You got me," Lyman sighed. "Maybe he had a wad of cash buried in a safe deposit box somewhere in town."

"I'd bet a couple of days' salary on that," Davidson agreed. "But any such cash had to *come* from somewhere. I've been over his finances four times. His accounts have long since been frozen, and every cent he's made since coming to Backdrop has been accounted for."

Lyman grimaced. "Yeah, I know—I ran my own check on that a month ago. You think he could be working transient jobs or something? Maybe even at that supermarket where the laser scanner broke?"

Davidson shook his head. "I tend to doubt it. I can't see someone like Garwood taking the kind of underground job that doesn't leave a paper trail. On the other hand...do we know if he was ever in Champaign before?"

"Oh, sure." Lyman stepped around to Davidson's terminal, punched some keys. "He was there—yeah, there it is," he said over his shoulder. "A little over two and a half years ago, on a seminar tour."

Davidson frowned at the screen. Princeton, Ohio State, Illinois, Cal Tech—there were over a dozen others on the list. Silently, he cursed the bureaucratic foot-dragging that was still keeping his full security clearance from coming through. If he'd had access to all this data three weeks ago... "Did it occur to anyone that Garwood *might* have made some friends during that trip that he's now turning to for help?

"Of course it did," Lyman said, a bit tartly. "We've spent the last three weeks checking out all the people he met at that particular seminar. So far he hasn't contacted any of them."

"Or so they say." Davidson chewed at his lip. "Why a seminar tour, anyway? I thought that sort of thing was reserved for the really big names."

"Garwood is big enough in his field," Lyman said. "Besides, with him about to drop behind Backdrop's security screen, it was his last chance to get out and around—"

"Wait a second," Davidson interrupted him. "He was already scheduled to come to Backdrop? I thought he came here only two years ago."

Lyman gave him an odd look. "Yes, but Backdrop didn't even exist until his paper got the ball rolling. I thought you knew that."

"No, I did not," Davidson said through clenched teeth. "You mean to tell me Backdrop was *Garwood's* idea?"

"No, the project was Saunders's brainchild. It was simply Garwood's paper on—" he broke off. "On the appropriate subject," he continued more cautiously, "that gave Saunders the idea. And that made Backdrop possible, for that matter."

"So Garwood did the original paper," Davidson said slowly. "Saunders then saw it and convinced someone in the government to create and fund Backdrop. Then... what? He went to Garwood and recruited him?"

"More or less. Though I understand Garwood wasn't all that enthusiastic about coming."

"Philosophical conflicts?"

"Or else he thought he knew what would happen when Backdrop got going."

The Garwood Effect. Had Garwood really foreseen that fate coming at him? The thought made Davidson shiver. "So what it boils down to is that Saunders approached Garwood half a year before he actually came to Backdrop?"

"Probably closer to a year. It takes a fair amount of time to build and equip a place like this—"

"Or put another way," Davidson cut him off, "Garwood knew a year in advance that he was coming here. And had that same year to quietly siphon enough money out of his salary to live on if he decided to cut and run."

Lyman's face seemed to tighten, his eyes slightly unfocused. "But we checked his pre-Backdrop finances. I'm sure we did."

"How sure? And how well?"

Lyman swore under his breath. "Hang on. I'll go get another chair."

It took them six hours. But by the end of that time, they'd found it.

"I'll be damned," Lyman growled, shutting off the microfiche record of Garwood's checking account and calling up the last set of numbers on the computer. "Fifteen thousand dollars. Enough for a year of running if he was careful with it."

Davidson nodded grimly. "And don't forget the per diem he would have gotten while he was on that seminar tour," he reminded the other. "If he skimped on meals he could have put away another couple of thousand."

Lyman stood up. "I'm going to go talk to the Colonel," he said, moving toward the door. "At least we know now how he's doing it. We can start hitting all the local landlords again and see which of them has a new tenant who paid in cash."

He left. *Great idea*, Davidson thought after him. *It assumes, of course, that Garwood didn't find a sublet that he could get into totally independently of the landlords. In a college town like Champaign that would be easy enough to do.*

The financial data was still on the display, and Davidson reached over to cancel it. The screen blanked; and for a long moment he just stared at the flashing cursor. "All right," he said out loud. "But why pick Champaign as a hideout in the first place?"

Because his seminar tour had taken him through there, giving him the chance to rent a safety deposit box? But the same tour had also taken him to universities in Chicago and Seattle, and either one of those metro areas would have provided him a far bigger haystack to hide in.

So why Champaign?

Garwood was running—that much was clear. But was he running *away* from something, or running *toward* something? Away from his problems at Backdrop, or toward—

Or toward a solution to those problems?

His fingers wanted a cigarette. Instead, he reached back to the keyboard. Everything about the Champaign area had, not surprisingly, been loaded into the computer's main database in the past three weeks. Now if he could just find the right question to ask the machine.

Five minutes later, on his second try, he found it.

There were men, Davidson had long ago learned, who could be put at a psychological disadvantage simply by standing over them while they sat. Colonel Bidwell, clearly, wasn't one of them. "Yes, I just got finished talking to Major Lyman," he said, looking up at Davidson from behind his desk. "Nice bit of work, if a little late in the day. You here to make sure you get proper credit?"

"No, sir," Davidson said. "I'm here to ask for permission to go back to Champaign to pick up Dr. Garwood."

Bidwell's eyebrows lifted politely. "Isn't that a little premature, Major? We haven't even really gotten a handle on him yet."

"And we may not, either, sir, at least not the way Major Lyman thinks we will. There are at least two ways Garwood could have covered his trail well enough for us not to find it without tipping him off. But I think I know another way to track him down."

"Which is...?"

Davidson hesitated. "I'd like to be there at the arrest, sir."

"You bargaining with me, Major?" Bidwell's voice remained glacially calm, but there was an unpleasant fire kindling in his eyes.

"No, sir, not really," Davidson said, mentally bracing himself against the force of the other's will. "But I submit to you that Garwood's arrest is unfinished business, and that I deserve the chance to rectify my earlier failure."

Bidwell snorted. "As I said when you first came in, Major, you have a bad tendency to get personally involved with your cases."

"And if I've really found the way to track Garwood down?"

Bidwell shook his head. "Worth a commendation in my report. Not worth letting you gad about central Illinois."

Davidson took a deep breath. "All right, then, sir, try this: if you don't let *me* go get him, someone else will have to do it. Someone who doesn't already know about the Garwood Effect...but who'll have to be told."

Bidwell glared up at him, a faintly disgusted expression on his face. Clearly, he was a man who hated being maneuvered. But he was also a man who knew better than to let emotional reactions cloud his logic.

And for once, the logic was on Davidson's side. Eventually, Bidwell gave in.

He stood at the door for a minute, listening. No voices; nothing but the occasional creaking of floorboards. Taking a deep breath, preparing himself for possible action, he knocked.

For a moment there was no answer. Then more creaking, and a set of footsteps approached the door. "Who is it?" a familiar voice called.

"It's Major Davidson. Please open the door, Dr. Garwood."

He rather expected Garwood to refuse. But the man was intelligent enough not to bother with useless gestures. There was the click of a lock, the more elongated tinkle of a chain being removed, and the door swung slowly open.

Garwood looked about the same as the last time Davidson had seen him, though perhaps a bit wearier. Hardly surprising, under the circumstances. "I'm impressed," he said.

"That I found you?" Davidson shrugged. "Finding people on the run is largely a matter of learning to think the way they do. I seem to have that knack. May I come in?"

Garwood's lip twisted. "Do I have a choice?" he asked, taking a step backwards.

"Not really." Davidson walked inside, eyes automatically sweeping for possible danger. Across the room a computer terminal was sitting on the floor, humming to itself. "Rented?" he asked, nodding toward it.

"Purchased. They're not that expensive, really, and renting them usually requires a major credit card and more scrutiny than I could afford. Is that how you traced me?"

"Indirectly. It struck me that this was a pretty unlikely town for someone to try and hide out in...unless there was something here that you needed. The Beckman Institute's fancy computer system was the obvious candidate. Once we had that figured out, all we had to do was backtrack all the incoming modem links. Something of a risk for you, wasn't it?"

Garwood shook his head. "I didn't have any choice. I needed the use of a Cray Y-MP, and there aren't a lot of them around that the average citizen can get access to."

"Besides the ones at Stanford and Minneapolis, that is?"

Garwood grimaced. "I don't seem to have any secrets left, do I? I'd hoped I'd covered my trail a little better than that."

"Oh, we only got the high points," Davidson assured him. "And only after the fact. Once we knew you were here for the Beckman supercomputer it was just a matter of checking on which others around the country had had more than their share of breakdowns since you left Backdrop."

Garwood's lips compressed into a tight line, and something like pain flitted across his eyes. "My fault?"

"I don't know. Saunders said he'd look into it, see if there might have been other causes. He may have something by the time we get you back."

Garwood snorted. "So Saunders in his infinite wisdom is determined to keep going with it," he said bitterly. "He hasn't learned anything at all in the past four months, has he?"

"I guess not." Davidson nodded again at the terminal. "Have *you*?" he asked pointedly.

Garwood shook his head. "Only that the universe is full of blind alleys."

"Um." Stepping past Garwood, Davidson sat down at the table. "Well, I guess we can make that unanimous," he told the other. "I haven't learned much lately, either. Certainly not as much as I'd like."

He looked up, to find Garwood frowning at him with surprise. Surprise, and a suddenly nervous indecision… "No, don't try it, Doctor," Davidson told him. "Running won't help —I have men covering all the exits. Sit down, please."

Slowly, Garwood stepped forward to sink into the chair across from Davidson. "What do you want?" he asked carefully, resting his hands in front of him on the table.

"I want you to tell me what's going on," Davidson said bluntly. He glanced down at the table, noting both the equation-filled papers and the loose cigarettes scattered about. "I want to know what Backdrop's purpose is, why you left it—" he raised his eyes again "—and how this voodoo effect of yours works."

Garwood licked his lips, a quick slash of the tongue tip. "Major…if you had the proper clearance—"

"Then Saunders would have told me everything?" Davidson shrugged. "Maybe. But he's had three weeks to do so, and I'm not sure he's ever going to."

"So why should I?"

Davidson let his face harden just a bit. "Because if Backdrop is a danger to my country, I want to know about it."

Garwood matched his gaze for a second, then dropped his eyes to the table, his fingers interlacing themselves into a tight double fist there. Then he took a deep breath. "You don't play fair, Major," he sighed. "But I suppose it doesn't really matter anymore. Besides, what's Saunders going to do, lock me up? He plans to do that anyway."

"So what is it you know that has them so nervous?" Davidson prompted.

Garwood visibly braced himself. "I know how to make a time machine."

For a long moment the only sound in the room was the hum of the terminal in the corner. That, and the hazy buzzing of Garwood's words spinning over and over in Davidson's brain. "You *what*?" he whispered at last.

Garwood's shoulders heaved fractionally. "Sounds impossible, doesn't it? But it's true. And it's because of that..." he trailed off, reached over to flick one of the loose cigarettes a few inches further away from him.

"Dr. Garwood—" Davidson worked moisture into his mouth, tried again. "Doctor, that doesn't make any sense.

Why should a....a time machine—?" He faltered, his tongue balking at even suggesting such a ridiculous thing.

"Make things disintegrate?" Garwood sighed. "Saunders didn't believe it, either. Not even after I explained what my paper really said."

The shock was slowly fading from Davidson's brain. "So what *did* it say?" he demanded.

"That the uncertainty factor in quantum mechanics didn't necessarily arise from the observer/universe interaction," Garwood said. "At least not in the usual sense. What I found was a set of self-consistent equations that showed the same effect would arise from the universe allowing for the possibility of time travel."

"And these equations of yours are the ones you recited to me when you wrecked my car and gun?"

Garwood shook his head. "No, those came later. Those were the equations that actually show how time travel is possible." His fingers moved restlessly, worrying at another of the cigarettes. "You know, Major, it would be almost funny if it weren't so deadly serious. Even after Backdrop started to fall apart around us Saunders refused to admit the possibility that it was our research that was causing it. That trying to build a time travel from my equations was by its very nature a self-defeating exercise."

"A long time ago," Davidson said slowly, "on that car ride from Springfield, you called it subconscious democracy. That cigarettes disintegrated in your hand because some people didn't like smoking."

Garwood nodded. "It happens to cigarettes, plastics—"

"How? How can peoples' opinions affect the universe that way?"

Garwood sighed. "Look. Quantum mechanics says that everything around us is made up of atoms, each of which is a sort of cloudy particle with a very high mathematical probability of staying where it's supposed to. In particular, it's the atom's electron cloud that shows the most mathematical fuzziness; and it's the electron clouds that interact with each other to form molecules."

Davidson nodded. That much he remembered from college physics.

"Okay," Garwood continued. "Now, you told me once that you hated being hooked by cigarettes, right? Suppose you had the chance—right now—to wipe out the tobacco industry and force yourself out of that addiction. Would you do it?"

"With North Carolina's economy on the line?" Davidson retorted. "Of course not."

Garwood lips compressed. "You're more ethical than most," he acknowledged. "A lot of the 'not-me' generation wouldn't even bother to consider that particular consequence. Of course, it's a moot question anyway—we both know the industry is too well established for anyone to get rid of it now.

"But what if you could wipe it out in, say, 1750?"

Davidson opened his mouth. Closed it again. Slowly, it was starting to become clear... "All right," he said at last. "Let's say I'd like to do that. What then?"

Garwood picked up one of the cigarettes. "Remember what I said about atoms—the atoms in this cigarette are only *probably* there. Think of it as a given atom being in its proper place ninety-nine point nine nine nine nine percent of the time and somewhere else the rest of it. Of course, it's never gone long enough to really affect the atomic bonds, which is why the whole cigarette normally holds together.

"But now *I* know how to make a time machine; and *you* want to eliminate the tobacco industry in 1750. *If* I build my machine, and *if* you get hold of it, and *if* you succeed in stamping out smoking, then this cigarette would never have been made and all of its atoms *would* be somewhere else."

Davidson's mouth seemed abnormally dry. "That's a lot of *ifs*," he managed.

"True, and that's probably why the cigarette doesn't simply disappear. But if enough of the electron clouds are affected—if they start being *gone* long enough to strain their bonds with the other atoms—then eventually the cigarette will fall apart." He held out his palm toward Davidson.

Davidson looked at the cigarette, kept his hands where they were. "I've seen the demo before, thanks."

Garwood nodded soberly. "It's scary, isn't it?"

"Yeah," Davidson admitted. "And all because I don't like smoking?"

"Oh, it's not just you," Garwood sighed. He turned his hand over, dropping the cigarette onto the table, where it burst into a little puddle of powder. "You could be president of Philip Morris and the same thing would happen. Remember that if a time machine is built from my equations, literally *everyone* from now until the end of time has access to the 1750 tobacco crop. And to the start of the computer age; and the inception of the credit card; and the invention of plastic." He rubbed his forehead wearily. "The list goes on and on. Maybe forever."

Davidson nodded, his stomach feeling strangely hollow. A *walking time bomb*, he'd called Garwood. *A time bomb*. No wonder everyone at Backdrop had been so quick to latch onto that particular epithet. "What about my car?" he asked. "Surely no one seriously wants to go back to the horse and buggy."

"Probably not," Garwood shook his head. "But the internal combustion engine is both more complicated and less efficient than several alternatives that were stamped out early in the century. If you could go back and nurture the steam engine, for instance—"

"Which is why the engine seemed to be trying to flow into a new shape, instead of just falling apart?" Davidson frowned. "It was starting to change into a steam engine?"

Garwood shrugged. "Possibly. I really don't know for sure why engines behave the way they do."

Almost unwillingly, Davidson reached out to touch what was left of the cigarette. "Why you?" he asked. "If your time machine is built, then everything in the world ought to be equally fair game. So why don't things disintegrate in *my* hands, too?"

"Again, I don't know for sure. I suspect the probability shifts cluster around me because I'm the only one who knows how to make the machine." Garwood seemed to brace himself. "But you're right. If the machine is actually made, then it's all out of my hands. And at that point, I can't see any reason why the effect wouldn't mushroom into something worldwide."

A brief mental image flashed through Davidson's mind: a black vision of the whole of advanced technology falling to pieces, rapidly followed by society itself. If a superpower war of suspicion didn't end things even quicker. "My God," he murmured. "You can't let that happen, Doctor."

Garwood locked eyes with him. "I agree. At the moment, though, you have more power over that than I do."

For a long minute Davidson returned the other's gaze, torn by indecision. He could do it—he *could* simply let Garwood walk. It would mean his career, possibly, but the stakes here made such considerations trivial. Another possibility occurred briefly to him— "Why did you need the computer?" he asked. "What were you trying to do?"

"Find a solution to my equations that would allow for a safer form of time travel," Garwood said. "Something that would allow us to observe events, perhaps, without interacting with them."

"Did you have any luck?"

"No. But I'm not ready to give up the search, either. If you let me go, I'll keep at it."

Davidson clenched his jaw tightly enough to hurt. "I know that, Doctor," he said quietly. "But you'll have to continue your search at Backdrop."

Garwood sighed. "I should have known you wouldn't buck your orders," he said bitterly.

"And leave you out here, threatening a community of innocent bystanders?" Davidson retorted, feeling oddly stung by the accusation. "I have a working conscience, Doctor, but I also have a working brain. Backdrop is still the safest place for you to be, and you're going back there. End of argument." Abruptly, he got to his feet. "Come on. I'll have some of my people pack up your stuff and bring it to Backdrop behind us."

Reluctantly, Garwood also stood up. "Can I at least ask a favor?"

"Shoot."

"Can we drive instead of flying? I'm still afraid of what influence I might have on a plane's engines."

"If you can sit this close to that terminal without killing it, the engines should be perfectly safe," Davidson told him.

"Under the circumstances, 'should' is hardly adequate—"

"You're arguing in circles," Davidson pointed out. "If you get killed in a plane crash, how is anyone going to use your equations be used to build a time machine?"

Garwood blinked, then frowned. "Well...maybe I wouldn't actually die in the wreck."

"All right, fine," Davidson snapped, suddenly tired of the whole debate. "We'll put an impact bomb under your seat to make sure you'll die if we crash. Okay?"

Garwood's face reddened, and for a second Davidson thought he would explode with anger of his own. But he didn't. "I see," he said stiffly. "Very well, then, let's find a phone booth and see what Saunders says. You *will* accept suggestions from Saunders, won't you?"

Davidson gritted his teeth. "Never mind. You want to sit in a car for fourteen hours, fine. Let's go; we'll radio Chanute from the car and have them call in the change of schedule to Backdrop. And arrange for a quiet escort."

V

"**I** hope you realize," Garwood said heavily, "that by bringing me back you're putting everyone in Backdrop at risk."

Saunders raised polite eyebrows. Polite, stupidly unconcerned eyebrows. "Perhaps," he said. "But at least here we understand what's going on and can take the appropriate precautions. Unlike the nation at large, I may add, which you've just spent nearly four months putting at similar risk. Under the circumstances, I'm sure you'd agree that one of our concerns now has to be to keep you as isolated from the rest of the country as possible." He shrugged. "And as long as you have to be here anyway, you might as well keep busy."

"Oh, of course," Garwood snorted. "I might as well help Backdrop to fall apart that much soo—"

He broke off as a muffled cracking sound drifted into the room. "More of the plaster going," Saunders identified it off-handedly. "Nice to hear again after so long."

Garwood felt like hitting the man. "Damn it all, Saunders," he snarled. "Why won't you listen to reason? A working time machine *cannot be made.* The very fact that Backdrop is falling apart around me—"

"Proves that the machine *can* be made," Saunders cut him off. "If you'd stop thinking emotionally for a minute and track through the logic you'd realize that." Abruptly, all the vaguely amused patience vanished from his face, and his eyes hardened as they bored into Garwood's with an unexpected intensity. "Don't you understand?" he continued quietly. "When you left, the probability-shift damage to Backdrop dropped off to near zero. Now that you're back, the destruction is on the increase again."

"Which is my point—"

"No, which is *my* point," Saunders snapped. "The probability-shift effect cannot exist if a working time machine isn't possible."

"And yet that same effect precludes the manufacture of any such machine," Garwood pointed out. "As I've explained to you at least a hundred times."

"Perhaps. But perhaps not. Even given that the concept of time-travel generates circular arguments in the first place, has it occurred to you that a working time machine might actually prove to be a *stabilizing* factor?"

Garwood frowned. "You mean that if we have the theoretical capability of going back and correcting all these alterations of history then the wild fluctuations will subside of their own accord?"

"Something like that," Saunders nodded. "I did some preliminary mathematics on that question while you were gone and it looks promising. Of course, we won't know for sure until I have all the equations to work with."

"And what if you're wrong?" Garwood countered. "What if a working time machine would simply destabilize things further?"

A flicker of Saunders's old innocent expression crossed the man's face. "Why, then, we won't be able to make one, will we? The components will fall apart faster than we can replace them."

"In which event, we're back to the probability-shift effect being a circular paradox," Garwood sighed. "If it prevents us from building a time machine, there's no time travel. If there's no time travel, there's no change in probabilities and hence no probability-shift effect."

"As I said, time travel tends to generate paradoxes like that." Saunders pursed his lips. "There's one other possibility that's occurred to me, though. The man who brought you back from Champaign—Major Davidson— said in his report that you'd been trying to find an alternative solution to the time travel equations. Any luck?"

Garwood shook his head. "All I found was blind alleys."

"Maybe you just didn't get to look long enough."

Garwood eyed him. "Meaning...?"

"Meaning that one other possible explanation of the probability-shift effect is that there is indeed another set of solutions. A set that will let us build the machine and still be able to go back and change things."

Garwood sighed. "Saunders, don't you see that all you're doing is just making things worse? Isn't it bad enough that things fall apart around *me*? Do you want to see it happening on a global scale? Stabilization be damned: a time machine—a real, functional time machine —would be the worst instrument of destruction ever created. *Ever* created."

"All I know," Saunders said softly, "is that anything the universe allows us to do *will* eventually be done. If *we* don't build the machine, someone else will. Someone who might not hesitate to use it for the mass destruction you're so worried about."

Garwood shook his head tiredly. The discussion was finally turning, as he'd known it eventually would, onto all-too familiar territory: the question of whether or not the fruits of Backdrop's labor would be used responsibly by the politicians who would inherit it. "We've gone round and round on this one," he said with a sigh as he got to his feet. "Neither of us is likely to change the other's mind this time, either. So if you don't mind, it's been a long drive and I'd like to get some rest."

"Fine." Saunders stood, too. "Tomorrow is soon enough to get back to work."

In the distance, the sound of more cracking plaster underlined his last word. "And if I refuse?" Garwood asked.

"You won't."

"Suppose I do?" Garwood persisted.

Saunders smiled lopsidedly and waved a hand in an all-encompassing gesture. "You talk too contemptuously about the 'not-me' generation to adopt their philosophy. You won't turn your back on a problem this serious. Especially given that it's a problem partially of your own creation."

For a long moment Garwood considered arguing the latter point. It had been Saunders, after all, who'd pushed Backdrop into existence and then dragged him into it.

But on the other hand, it wasn't Saunders who knew how to build the damn time machine.

Wordlessly, he turned his back on the other and headed for the door. "Rest well," Saunders called after him.

His office, when he arrived there the next morning, was almost unrecognizable.

Two pieces of brand-new equipment had been shoehorned into the already cramped space, for starters: a terminal with what turned out to be a direct line to the Minneapolis Cray III supercomputer lab, and an expensive optical scanner that seemed set up to read typewritten equations directly onto the line. *So Saunders is capable of learning,* Garwood thought sardonically, careful not to touch either instrument as he gave them a brief examination. The electronic blackboard that had fallen apart shortly before he left Backdrop was gone, replaced by an old-fashioned chalk-on-slate type, and his steel-and-plastic chair had been replaced by a steel-and-wood one. Even his desk looked somehow different, though it took him a long minute to realize why.

All the piles of papers had been changed.

Silently, he mouthed a curse. He hadn't expected the papers to remain untouched—Saunders would certainly have ransacked his desk in hopes of finding the rest of his time-travel equations—but he hadn't expected everything to get so thoroughly shuffled in the process. Clearly, Saunders had gone about his task with a will and to hell with neatness. Just as clearly, it was going to take most of the day to put things back where he could find them again. With a sigh, he sank gingerly into his new chair and started restacking.

It was two hours later, and he was not quite halfway through the task, when there was a knock on the door. "Come in, Saunders," he called.

It wasn't Saunders. "Hello, Dr. Garwood," Major Davidson nodded, throwing a glance around the room. "You busy?"

"Not especially." Garwood looked up at him. "Checking to make sure I'm still here?"

Davidson shrugged fractionally, his gaze steady on Garwood. "Not really. I believe Colonel Bidwell has been able to plug the hole you got out by the last time."

"I'm not surprised." The look in Davidson's eyes was becoming just the least bit unnerving. "May I ask why you're here, then?"

Davidson pursed his lips. "The random destruction has started up again since we got in last night."

"This surprises you?"

Davidson opened his mouth. Closed it. Tried again. "I'd rather hoped you weren't so clearly the pivotal point of the effect."

"I thought we'd discussed all that back in Champaign," Garwood reminded him. "I'm the only one who knows how to build the machine, so of course the probability-shift effect centers around me."

Davidson's eyes flicked to the computer terminal/optical scanner setup. "And Saunders wants you to let him in on the secret."

"Naturally. I don't intend to, of course."

"And if he doesn't give you that choice?"

"Meaning?"

"Meaning he tried to use hypnosis to get your equations out of me. With you, the method would probably work."

Garwood's mouth felt dry. "He knows better than to try something that blatant," he said. Even to himself the words didn't sound very convincing.

"I hope so. But if he doesn't...I trust you'll always remember that there's at least one other person in Backdrop who recognizes the danger your knowledge poses."

Garwood nodded, wishing he knew exactly what the man was saying. Was he offering to help Garwood escape again should that become necessary? "I'll remember," he promised. "You're going to be here for awhile, then?"

Davidson smiled wryly. "They let me out on a tight rein to go after you, Doctor. That doesn't mean they want me running around loose with what I know about Backdrop. I'll be on temporary duty with the security office, at least for the foreseeable future." He paused halfway through the act of turning back toward the door. "Though I don't suppose the term 'foreseeable future' has quite the same meaning as it used to, does it?"

Without waiting for an answer, he nodded and left. *No, it doesn't,* Garwood agreed silently at the closed door. *It really doesn't.*

He thought about it for a long minute. Then, with a shiver, he turned back to his papers.

One by one, the leads faded into blind alleys. Two months later, Garwood finally admitted defeat.

"Damn you," he muttered aloud, slouching wearily in his chair as far away from his terminal as space permitted. "Damn you." An impotent curse hurled at the terminal, at the program, at the universe itself. "There has to be a way. There *has* to be."

His only answer was the vague and distant crash of something heavy, the sound muffled and unidentifiable. A piece of I-beam from the ceiling, he rather thought—the basic infrastructure of Backdrop had started to go the way of the more fragile plaster and electronics over the past couple of weeks. Saunders had spent much of that time trying to invent correlations between the increase in the destruction with some supposed progress in Garwood's mathematical work, and he'd come up with some highly imaginative ones.

But imaginative was all they were. Because Garwood knew what was really happening.

Perversely, even as it blocked his attempts to find a safe method of time travel, the universe had been busily showing him exactly how to transform his original equations into actual real-world hardware.

It was, on one level, maddening. He would be sitting at his typewriter, preparing a new set of equations for the optical scanner to feed into the computer, when suddenly he would have a flash of insight as to how a properly tuned set of asynchronous drivers could handle the multiple timing pulses. Or he'd be waiting for the computer to chew through a tensor calculation and suddenly recognize that an extra coil winding superimposed on a standard transformer system could create both the power and the odd voltage patterns his equations implied. Or he'd even be trying to fall asleep at night, head throbbing with the day's frustrations, and practically see a vision of the mu-metal molding that would distort a pulsed magnetic field by just the right amount to create the necessary envelope for radiating plasma bursts.

And as the insights came more and more frequently—as a working time machine came closer and closer to reality— the environment inside Backdrop came to look more and more like a war zone.

Across the room the terminal emitted a raucous beep, signaling the possibility of parity error in its buffer memory. "Damn," Garwood muttered again and dragged himself to his feet. Eventually, he would have to tell Saunders that his last attempts had gone up in the same black smoke as all the previous ones. There was, he decided, nothing to be gained by putting it off. Picking up his hardhat, he put it on and stepped out of his office.

The corridor outside had changed dramatically in the past weeks, its soothing pastel walls giving way to the stark metallic glitter of steel shoring columns. Senses alert for new ripples in the floor beneath him as well as for falling objects from above, he set off toward Saunders's office.

Luck was with him. The passages were relatively clear, with only the minor challenge of maneuvering past shoring and other travelers to require his attention. He was nearly to Saunders's office, in fact, before he hit the first real roadblock.

And it was a good one. He'd been right about the sound earlier: one of the steel I-beams from the ceiling had indeed broken free, creating a somewhat bowed diagonal across the hallway. A team of men armed with acetylene torches were cutting carefully across the beam, trying to free it without bringing more down.

"Dr. Garwood?"

Garwood focused on the burly man stepping toward him, an engineer's insignia glittering amid the plaster dust on his jumpsuit collar. "Yes, Captain?"

"If you don't mind, sir," the other said in a gravelly voice, "we'd appreciate it if you wouldn't hang around here any longer than necessary. There may be more waiting to come down."

Garwood glanced at the ceiling, stomach tightening within him as he recognized the all-too familiar message beneath the other's words. It wasn't so much interest in his, Garwood's, safety as it was concern that the cloud of destruction around him might wind up killing one of the workers. Briefly, bitterly, Garwood wondered if this was how Jonah had felt during the shipboard storm. Before he'd been thrown overboard to the whale.... "I understand," he sighed. "Would you mind passing a message on to Dr. Saunders when you have the chance, then, asking him to meet me at my office? My phone's gone out again."

"A lot of 'em have, Doctor," the engineer nodded. "I'll give him the message."

Garwood nodded back and turned to go—

And nearly bumped into Major Davidson, standing quietly behind him.

"Major," Garwood managed, feeling his heart settle down again. "You startled me."

Davidson nodded, a simple acknowledgment of Garwood's statement. "Haven't seen you in a while, Dr. Garwood," he said, his voice the same neutral as his face. "How's it going?"

Garwood's usual vague deflection to that question came to his lips. "I have to get back to my office," he said instead. "The workmen are worried about another collapse."

"I'll walk with you," Davidson offered, falling into step beside him.

Davidson waited until they were out of sight of the workers before speaking again. "I've been keeping an eye on the damage reports," he commented in that same neutral tone. "You been following them?"

"Not really," Garwood replied through dry lips. Suddenly there was something about Davidson that frightened him. "I can usually see the most immediate consequences in and around my office."

"Been some extra problems cropping up in the various machine and electronic fabrication shops, too," Davidson told him, almost off-handedly. "As if there's been some work going on there that's particularly susceptible to the Garwood Effect."

Garwood winced. The Garwood Effect. An appropriate, if painful, name for it. "Saunders has had some people trying to translate what little he and the rest of the team know into practical hardware terms," he said.

"But they don't yet know how to build a time machine?"

"No. They don't."

"Do you?"

Again, Garwood's reflex was to lie. "I think so," he admitted instead. "I'm pretty close, anyway."

They walked on in silence for a few more paces. "I'm sure you realize," Davidson said at last, "the implications of what you're saying."

Garwood sighed. "Do try to remember, Major, that I was worrying about all this long before you were even on the scene."

"Perhaps. But my experience with scientists has been that you often have a tendency toward tunnel vision, so it never hurts to check. Have you told anyone yet? Or left any hard copies of the technique?"

"No, to both."

"Well, that's a start." Davidson threw him a sideways look. "Unfortunately, it won't hold anyone for long. If *I'm* smart enough to figure out what the increase in the Garwood Effect implies, Saunders is certainly smart enough to do likewise."

Garwood looked over at Davidson's face, and the knot in his stomach tightened further as he remembered what the other had once said about Saunders using hypnosis against him. "Then I have to get away again before that happens," he said in a quiet voice.

Davidson shook his head. "That won't be easy to do a second time."

"Then I'll need help, won't I?"

Davidson didn't reply for several seconds. "Perhaps," he said at last. "But bear in mind that above everything else I have my duty to consider."

"I understand," Garwood nodded.

Davidson eyed him. "Do you, Doctor? Do you really?"

Garwood met his eyes…and at long last, he really *did* understand.

Davidson wasn't offering him safe passage to that mythical wilderness Garwood had so often longed for. He was offering only to help Garwood keep the secret of time travel out of Saunders's grasp. To keep it away from a world that such a secret would surely destroy.

Offering the only way out that was guaranteed to be permanent.

Garwood's heart was thudding in his ears, and he could feel sweat gathering on his upper lip. "And when," he heard himself say, "would your duty require you to take that action?"

"When it was clear there was no longer any choice," Davidson said evenly. "When you finally proved safe time travel was impossible, for instance. Or perhaps when you showed a working time machine could be built."

They'd reached the door to Garwood's office now. "But if I instead proved that the probability-shift effect would in fact keep a working time machine from actually being built?" Garwood asked, turning to face the other. "What then?"

"Then it's not a working time machine, is it?" Davidson countered.

Garwood took a deep breath. "Major...I want a working time machine built even less than you do. Believe me."

"I hope so," Davidson nodded, his eyes steady on Garwood's. "Because you and I may be the only ones here who feel that way. And speaking for myself, I know only one way to keep your equations from bringing chaos onto the world. I hope I don't have to use it."

A violent shiver ran up Garwood's back. "I do, too," he managed. Turning the doorknob with a shaking hand, he fled from Davidson's eyes to the safety of his office.

To the relative safety, anyway, of his office.

For several minutes he paced the room, his pounding heart only gradually calming down. A long time ago, before his break from Backdrop, he'd contemplated suicide as the only sure way to escape the cloud of destruction around him. But it had never been a serious consideration, and he'd turned instead to his escape-and-research plan.

A plan which had eventually ended in failure. And now, with the stakes even higher than they'd been back then, death was once again being presented to him as the only sure way to keep the genie in the bottle.

Only this time the decision wasn't necessarily going to be his. And to add irony to the whole thing, Davidson's presence here was ultimately his own fault. If he hadn't skipped out of Backdrop six months ago, the major would never even have come onto the scene.

Or maybe he would have. With the contorted circular logic that seemed to drive the probability-shift effect nothing could be taken for granted. Besides, if Davidson hadn't caught him, perhaps someone less intelligent would have. Someone who might have brushed aside his fears and forced him onto that airplane at Chanute AFB. If that had happened—if the effect had then precipitated a crash—

He shook his head to clear it. It was, he thought bitterly, like the old college bull sessions about free will versus predestination. There were no answers, ever, and you could go around in circles all night chasing after them. On one hand, the probability-shift effect could destroy engines; on the other, as Davidson himself had pointed out, it logically shouldn't be able to crash a plane that Garwood himself was on…

Garwood frowned, his train of thought breaking as a wisp of something brushed past his mind. *Davidson…airplane…?*

And with a sudden flood of adrenaline, the answer came to him.

Maybe.

Deep in thought, he barely noticed the knock at the door. "Who is it?" he called mechanically.

"Saunders," the other's familiar voice came through the panel.

Garwood licked his lips, shifting his mind as best he could back to the real world. The next few minutes could be crucial ones indeed. "Come in," he called.

"I got a message that you wanted to see me," Saunders said, glancing toward the terminal as he came into the room. "More equipment trouble?"

"Always," Garwood nodded, waving him to a chair. "But that's not why I called you here. I think I may have some good news."

Saunders's eyes probed Garwood's face as he sank into the proffered seat. "Oh? What kind?"

Garwood hesitated. "It'll depend, of course, on just what kind of latitude you're willing to allow me—how much control I'll have on this. And I'll tell you up front that if you buck me you'll wind up with nothing. Understand?"

"It would be hard not to," Saunders said dryly, "considering that you've been making these same demands since you got here. What am I promising not to interfere with this time?"

Garwood took a deep breath. "I'm ready," he said, "to build you a time machine."

VI

Within a few days the Garwood Effect damage that had been occurring sporadically throughout Backdrop's several fabrication areas jumped nearly eight hundred percent. A few days after that, repair and replacement equipment began to be shipped into the complex at a correspondingly increased rate, almost—but not quite—masking the even more dramatic flood of non-damage-control shipping also entering Backdrop. The invoice lists for the latter made for interesting reading: esoteric electronic and mechanical equipment, exotic metals, specialized machine tools for both macro and micro work, odd power supplies—it ran the entire gamut.

And for Davidson, the invoices combined with the damage reports were all the proof he needed.

Garwood had figured out how to build his time machine.

And was building it.

Damn him. Hissing between his teeth, Davidson leaned wearily back into his chair and blanked the last of the invoices from his terminal screen. So Garwood had been lying through his teeth all along. Lying about his fears concerning time travel; lying about his disagreements with Dr. Saunders; lying about how noble and self-sacrificing he was willing to be to keep the world safe from the wildfire Garwood Effect a time machine would create.

And Davidson, that supposedly expert reader of people, had fallen for the whole act like a novice investigator.

Firmly, he shook the thought away. Bruised pride was far and away the least of his considerations at the moment. If Garwood was building a time machine...

But *could* he in fact build it?

Davidson gnawed at the inside of his cheek, listening to the logic spin in circles in his head. Garwood had suggested more than once that the Garwood Effect would destroy a time machine piecemeal before it could even be assembled. Had he been lying about that, too? It had seemed reasonable enough at the time...but then why would he and Saunders even bother trying? No, there had to be something else happening, something Garwood had managed to leave out of his argument and which Davidson hadn't caught on his own.

But whatever it was he'd missed, circumstances still left him no choice. Garwood had to be stopped.

Taking a deep breath, Davidson leaned forward to the terminal again and called up Backdrop's cafeteria records. If Garwood was working around the clock, as Davidson certainly would be doing in his place...and after a few tries he found what he was looking for: the records of the meals delivered to the main assembly area at the end of Backdrop's security tunnel. Scanning them, he found there had been between three and twelve meals going into the tunnel each mealtime since two days before the dramatic upsurge in Garwood Effect damage.

And Garwood's ordering number was on each one of the meal lists.

Davidson swore again, under his breath. Of course Garwood would be spending all his time down the tunnel —after their last conversation a couple of weeks ago the man would be crazy to stay anywhere that Davidson's security clearance would let him get to. And he'd chosen his sanctuary well. Down the security tunnel, buried beneath the assembly area's artificial hill, it would take either a company of Marines or a medium-sized tactical nuke to get to him now.

Or maybe—just maybe—all it would take would be a single man with a computer terminal. A man with some knowledge of security systems, some patience, and some time.

Davidson chewed his lip. The terminal he had; and the knowledge, and the patience. But as for the time...he would know in a few days.

If the world still existed by then.

VII

The five techs were still going strong as the clocks reached midnight, but Garwood called a halt anyway. "We'll be doing the final wiring assembly and checkout tomorrow," he reminded them. "I don't want people falling asleep over their voltmeters while they're doing that."

"You really expect any of us to *sleep*?" one of the techs grumbled half-seriously.

"Well, *I* sure will," Garwood told him lightly, hooking a thumb toward the door. "Come on, everybody out. See you at eight tomorrow morning. Pleasant dreams."

The tech had been right, Garwood realized as he watched them empty their tool pouches onto an already cluttered work table: with the project so close to completion they *were* indeed going to be too wired up for easy sleep. But fortunately they were as obedient as they were competent, and they filed out without any real protest.

And Garwood was alone.

Exhaling tiredly, he locked the double doors and made his way back to the center of the huge shored-up fabrication dome and the lopsided monstrosity looming there. Beyond it across the dome was his cot, beckoning temptingly to him...

Stepping instead to the cluttered work table, he picked up a screwdriver set and climbed up through the tangle of equipment into the seat at its center. Fifteen minutes later, the final connections were complete.

It was finished.

For a long minute he just sat there, eyes gazing unseeingly at the simple control/indicator panel before him. It was finished. After all the blood, sweat, and tears— after all the arguments with Saunders—after the total disruption of his life, it was done.

He had created a time machine.

Sighing, he climbed stiffly down from the seat and returned the screwdrivers to their place on the work table. The next table over was covered with various papers;

snaring a wastebasket, he began pushing the papers into it, tamping them down as necessary until the table was clear. A length of electrical cable secured the wastebasket to a protruding metal plate at the back of the time machine's seat, leaving enough room for the suitcase and survival pack he retrieved from beneath his cot. Two more lengths of cable to secure them…and then there was just one more chore to do. A set of three video cameras stood spaced around the room, silent on their tripods. Stepping to each in turn, he turned all of them on.

He was just starting back to the time machine when there was a faint sound from the double doors.

He turned, stomach tightening into a knot. It could only be Saunders, here for a late-night briefing on the day's progress. If he noticed that the cameras were running—realized what that meant—

The doors swung open, and Major Davidson stepped in.

Garwood felt an instantaneous burst of relief…followed by an equally instantaneous burst of fear. He'd specifically requested that Davidson not be cleared for this part of Backdrop. "Major," he managed to say between suddenly dry lips. "Up—ah, rather late, aren't you?"

Davidson closed the doors, his eyes never leaving Garwood's face. "I only hope I'm *not* here too late," he said in a quiet voice. "You've done it, haven't you?"

Garwood licked his lips, nodded his head fractionally toward the machine beside him. "Here it is."

For a long moment neither man spoke. "I misjudged you," Davidson said at last, and to Garwood's ears there was more sorrow than anger in the words. "You talked a lot about responsibility to the world. But in the end you backed down and did what they told you to do."

"And you?" Garwood asked softly, the tightness in his stomach beginning to unknot. If Davidson was willing to talk first; to talk, and to listen... "Have you thought through the consequences of *your* actions? You went to a lot of illegal trouble to get in here. If you kill me on top of that, your own life's effectively over."

A muscle in Davidson's cheek twitched. "Unlike you, Doctor, I don't just talk about responsibility. And there *are* things worth dying for."

Unbidden, a smile twitched at Garwood's lips. "You know, Major, I'm glad you came. It gives me a measure of hope to know that even in the midst of the 'not-me' generation there are still people willing to look beyond their own selfish interests."

Davidson snorted. "Doctor, I'll remind you that I've seen this nobility act of yours before. I'm not buying it this time."

"Good. Then just listen."

Davidson frowned. "To what?"

"To the silence."

"The—?" Davidson stopped abruptly. And then, all at once, he seemed to get it. "It's *quiet*," he almost whispered, his eyes darting around the room and then coming to rest on the machine beside Garwood. "But—the Garwood Effect—you've found a way to stop it?"

Garwood shook his head. "No, not really. Though I think I may understand it a bit better now." He waved a hand around the room. "In a sense, the trouble is merely that I was born at the wrong time. If I'd lived a hundred years earlier the culture wouldn't have had the technological base to do anything with my equations. If I'd been born a hundred years later, perhaps I'd have had the time and necessary mathematics to work out a safe method of time travel, leaving my current equations as nothing more than useless curiosities to be forgotten."

"I'd hardly call them useless," Davidson interjected.

"Oh, but they are. Or didn't you notice how much trouble the various fabrication shops had in constructing the modules for this machine?"

"Of course I did," Davidson nodded, a frown still hovering across his eyes. "But if the modules themselves were falling apart...?"

"How was I able to assemble a working machine?" Garwood reached up to touch one of the machine's supports. "To be blunt, I cheated. And as it happens, *you* were the one who showed me how to do it."

Davidson's eyes locked with his. "Me?"

"You," Garwood nodded. "With a simple, rather sarcastic remark you made to me back in my Champaign apartment. Tell me, what's the underlying force that drives the Garwood Effect?"

Davidson hesitated, as if looking for a verbal trap. "You told me it was the possibility that someone would use time travel to change the past—" He broke off, head jerking with sudden insight. "Are you saying...?"

"Exactly," Garwood nodded. "There's no possibility of changing the past *if my machine can only take me into the future.*"

Davidson looked up at the machine. "How did you manage that?"

"As I said, it was your idea. Remember when I balked at flying back here and you suggested putting a bomb under my seat to make sure a crash would be fatal?" Garwood pointed upwards. "If you'll look under the seat there you'll see three full tanks of acetylene, rigged to incinerate both the rider and the machine if the 'reverse' setting is connected and used."

Davidson looked at the machine for a long moment, eyes flicking across the tanks and the mechanism for igniting them. "And that was really all it took?" he asked.

"That's all. Before I installed the system we couldn't even load the modules into their racks without them coming apart in our hands. Afterwards, they were still touchy to make, but once they were in place they were completely stable. Though if I disconnected the suicide system they'd probably fall apart en masse."

Slowly, Davidson nodded. "All right. So that covers the machine. It still doesn't explain what's happened to your own personal Garwood Effect."

"Do you really need an explanation for that?" Garwood asked.

Davidson's eyes searched his. "But you don't even know how well it'll work," he reminded Garwood. "Or if there are any dangerous side effects."

That thought had occurred to Garwood, too. "Ultimately, it doesn't matter. One way or another, this is my final ticket out of Backdrop. My equations go with me, of course—" he pointed at the secured wastebasket— "and all the evidence to date indicates Saunders and his team could work till Doomsday without being able to reproduce them."

"They know how to make the modules for this machine," Davidson pointed out.

"Only some of them. None of the really vital ones—I made those myself, and I'm taking all the documentation with me. And even if they somehow reconstructed them, I'm still convinced that assembling a fully operational machine based on my equations will be impossible." He paused, focused his attention on the cameras silently recording the scene. "You hear that, Saunders? Drop it.

Drop it, unless and until you can find equations that lead to a safer means of time travel. You'll just be wasting your own time and the taxpayer's money if you don't."

Turning his back on the cameras, he climbed once again up into the seat. "Well, Major," he said, looking down, "I guess this is good-bye. I've enjoyed knowing you."

"That's crap, Doctor," Davidson said softly. "But good luck anyway."

"Thanks." There were a handful of switches to be thrown —a dozen strokes on each of three keypads—and amid the quiet hum and vibration of the machine he reached for the trigger lever—

"Doctor?"

He paused. "Yes, Major?"

"Thanks," Davidson said, a faint smile on his lips, "for helping me quit smoking."

Garwood smiled back. "You're welcome."

Grasping the trigger lever, he pulled it.

Up and Down the Line

Aaron Rosenberg

"Awright, you primitive screwheads! Get ready to jump!"

Awg looked up. He didn't understand the words the little metal-headed man was shouting, but he recognized the tone. Time to fight. Awg smiled. He liked to fight.

Behind him came grunts and growls as the others stood. So did Awg. He was the first because he was the strongest, so he was right next to the place where the metal bird opened. Next to his head was the little fire-cage. Right now the fire in it burned red. The little man shouted something else, and Awg nodded. That, he had learned, was the right response when the metal-heads squawked at him.

After a second the red fire winked out. Awg heard a massive grinding sound all around him, and the metal bird split open. The sky outside was a clear blue, and he could see the ground just below. It was almost time.

A green flame appeared inside the fire-cage, and Awg grunted. Good. Now he could go. He hefted his club, took two steps forward, and jumped down. The wind rushed past him as he fell, and the ground raced up to meet him.

Wham!

Awg hit hard, absorbing the impact on bent legs, then straightened. All around him were little men, some metal-headed and others fuzzy-headed. It didn't matter. They were all the same to him. He laid about him with his club, the chipped stone head striking two men at once and crushing them to the side. A sweep in the other direction cleared three more. The others were falling to earth all around him, and soon Awg was the tip of a moving wall as they lumbered forward, smashing the little men out of their way. Their little metal tubes spat small pointy rocks, but they tapped against his chest with all the force of an angry insect and Awg bareley noticed.

It was good.

Then the ground rumbled. Awg looked up as something rolled toward him. What was this? It was big and metal, like the bird that had carried them here but without wings. It had a long tube like the men's but much larger, almost like the beak of a squat bird, and that swiveled toward Awg as he closed distance with the monster. He didn't really care what it was. It was here and he was here, so he would fight it.

Awg struck the beast with his club, a heavy overhand blow, and the impact shuddered up his arm. This thing was tough! Its hide bore a deep dent where he'd struck so he raised his club to hit that spot again, but now the beak swung and slammed into the side of his head. Awg felt a blinding pain, and toppled to the side and back. He had never been hit like that, not even when battling old Orf for control of their tribe!

Awg spit out blood and a few teeth—and grinned. So the metal beast could fight. Good. He liked a challenge.

He rose to his feet again and raised his club once more—but the beak was now right in his face. Awg saw fire within it, and heard a mighty roar—

—and the world exploded around and through him. Awg crumpled, his club falling from his hand. He was dead long before it hit the ground.

"**D**amn! Who knew they had a tank battalion over the ridge?"

Major Will Statton shook his head. "Our intel didn't mention that, sir. They must have been under cover somehow."

"Cover. Great." Colonel Al Garner slammed a fist down on the desk, just shy of the surveillance monitor. "So we got sloppy intel and it costs us the entire unit!"

"They were doing great until the tanks," Statton pointed out. "Excellent against the ground troops, just as we'd hoped."

But Garner wasn't soothed. "Yeah, but now we're back to square one. Even if we can get another unit together, it'll take us time to train them all over again. And we don't have that kind of time."

The two of them studied the monitor, where the tanks were now rolling unopposed across that region. Beside the monitor were their tactical maps, which showed the full scope of the war. Their forces were marked in blue, the enemy's in red.

They were losing.

Garner sighed. "All right, let's go tell the eggheads we need more cavemen."

As they left the command tent and headed toward the science complex, Statton wondered if anyone had ever uttered that exact sentence before. Probably not. They certainly hadn't, and never would have considered it, before the eggheads' big breakthrough a month ago.

They had been working on a matter translation device. Doctor Ferrin, the lead scientist—Chief Egghead, as everyone called him behind his back—had assured them he could successfully transfer not only inorganic matter but living people up to a hundred miles away, sending them through safely and almost instantaneously. And he could recall them just as quickly. If true, the device would allow them to move their troops into a region, strike, and disappear before the enemy could respond. They could end this war in a matter of days.

But things hadn't exactly gone according to plan.

"Aw, hell! Command, the egghead screwed us! This ain't the rendezvous point!" Even over the helmet mike Lieutenant Grant Card, the head of their scouts and the point man on this test run, managed to express his disgust for all things scientific, and for their science team in particular. At least his voice was coming through loud and clear. The same couldn't be said for his transponder, unfortunately.

"Negative on the transponder, sir," one of the techs reported. "We don't have a lock on their location."

"I don't understand," Doctor Ferrin muttered, staring at the little screens arrayed before him. "It should have worked perfectly! Lieutenant Card and his team should be at the rendezvous point with Doctor Pavel and the others."

"Well, 'should' doesn't do me a whole lot of good, doctor," Garner growled at him. "Now figure out where you sent my boys and get 'em back here, ASAP!"

"Yes, of course." Ferrin stepped up to the central monitor and picked up the mike sitting there. "Lieutenant Card, this is Doctor Ferrin," he shouted into it, in the time-honored form of a brilliant man who doesn't understand just how well electronics carry sound. "Can you hear me?"

"I think the entire landscape heard you, doc," Card snapped. "Where the hell am I?"

"What do you see?" Ferrin countered. "Describe your surroundings."

"Heavy foliage," Card answered. "Big plants, and lots of 'em. Kinda like elephant plants, or ferns, but huge. It's cool here but moist, humid. Lots of insect sounds. The ground's soggy and covered in vegetation. What'd you do, send me to the Amazon by mistake? And if so, Colonel, can I consider myself on leave?"

"Not bloody likely, soldier," Garner barked, but Statton could hear the affection in his voice, and knew Card could as well. "You're still on active duty, so get your butt back here right now! That's an order!"

"Happy to oblige, sir, if someone can just point me toward the exit." Statton could hear Card's men laughing at the exchange—Card was only a first lieutenant but he'd served under Garner for years and could get away with a little lip now and then.

Then Statton heard something else in the background. Something low and rumbling. Like thunder. Or—growling?

"Something's out here," Card stated, confirming his assessment. "A big cat, maybe. It's nearby, and getting closer. Fast. Team, fan out and ready weapons!"

There were a few seconds of clicks and clacks as the soldiers raised their rifles.

"Whatever it is, it's almost on top of us," Card announced. "Just southeast of us, I'd say, though these damn plants make it hard to judge. Wait, there—something moved! Get ready!"

The growling returned, louder, then was replaced by shouts and screams. Some of them were Card and his men:

"What the hell?"

"Holy crap!"

"Shoot it! Fast!"

"Look out!"

But there was another scream, something loud and angry and almost but not quite human. And mixed in with it all was the loud report of repeated gunfire, and the sharp crunch of breaking bone. And more screams of pain.

"What's happening out there? Damnit, Card, report!" Garner was clenching the mike so hard Statton was surprised it hadn't snapped yet.

"Card here, sir," came the weary reply finally, and everyone in the command tent cheered. "We got it, sir, but you're not going to believe it. I'm down two men—Kowalski and Nicholls—Adams and Reynolds are badly wounded, and we all need medical attention stat. We also need to get out of here ASAP, before more of them show up."

"More of what?" Garner demanded at the same time as Ferrin shouted "Where is here? I need to know your location before I can pull you back!"

"Cavemen." The flat tone made it clear Card wasn't even remotely kidding. "We got attacked by a freaking caveman. Figure that one out, doc—and hurry it up, wouldya?"

"Cavemen?" Ferrin looked stunned, then excited. "Wait, of course! I didn't account for the quantum irregularities in the matrix, that would have . . ." he muttered off into geek-speak as Statton and Garner stared at each other, trying to figure out if this was real. But after a minute, Ferrin glanced up. "Yes, I have it now," he assured them. He sat himself at the operations panel and rapidly typed in several commands, glancing repeatedly at some notes he had just scribbled on the logbook before the monitor. "Lieutenant, prepare for translation," he told Card. "And please stand around the, uh, caveman, with your hands on him—that should let us bring him across as well. Transfer in three, two, one—now!" And he flipped a switch.

There was a flash of light, gone so fast Statton barely had time to blink, and then several figures resolved themselves on the transfer pad at the center of the tent. As his eyes recovered he recognized Card, Adams, and the others.

But his gaze was drawn to the massive figure in their midst. Clearly humanoid but easily two feet taller and broader, with massive limbs, huge hands and feet, and a large, craggy-featured head. It wore animal skins, and an enormous stone club was still clutched in one fist. Statton counted over two dozen wounds on the creature's torso and head.

There was no doubt he was looking at a real caveman. A dead one, but recently dead. And he had no doubt the blood still on its club belonged to Kowalski, Nicholls, and the rest of the scout team.

Beside him, Garner was staring as well. "Good lord, he's huge," the major whispered. "Our boys didn't stand a chance." Then, as if completing the thought: "What a soldier he'd make!"

Statton met the major's eye, and realized he'd been thinking the same thing. He just hadn't wanted to say it out loud. It was ludicrous, after all.

Wasn't it?

"We're gonna need some more cavemen, Ferrin," Garner announced as they entered the camp's science complex. One of the other eggheads—Statton thought his name was Kaldost but wasn't really sure, since all the scientists seemed interchangeable to him—groaned. Statton didn't blame him. After Garner's plan had been given the go-ahead and they had been sure using the hastily renamed temporal transfer device wouldn't cause other problems (Ferrin had yammered on about causalities and parallel universes and butterflies and other things but the upshot had been that they could steal from the past with impunity), it had taken them a week to find a tribe of cavemen, tranquilize them, and drag them into the present. That had been the easy part. Training the cavemen to attack upon command—or rather, to wait until the command (and thus let their own people get clear) —had taken another three weeks. The flak jackets, at least, had been surprisingly easy. The cavemen had loved the sturdy oversized jackets and never took them off, though they steadfastly refused to wear the helmets. The idea of having to find, capture, and train another tribe was a nightmare.

Surprisingly, Ferrin wasn't fazed. "Never mind those primordial thugs," he replied, glancing up from the controls of the device. "I may have something far, far better."

"Better?" Garner's eyes lit up. "Dinosaurs?"

But Ferrin tsked. "Utterly uncontrollable," he pointed out. "No, I have deduced how to reset the device to pierce the temporal barriers blocking probable outcomes." The chief scientist must have noticed the major's blank look—Statton suspected his own matched—because he sighed. "We can travel to the future as well as the past," he explained.

"The future?" Statton grinned. "So we could send a scout forward to tell us exactly where and when the enemy's troops will move!"

"Not quite," Ferrin corrected. "The probabilities are too diverse—you would be able to see one possible future but would have no guarantee that the future in question would ever become our reality."

"So what can we do with it, exactly?"

But the major already had the answer. "Weapons!" He shouted. "Weapons from the future! Tanks and planes from the future! Soldiers from the future!"

"Precisely!"

Statton nodded. "How soon can you bring someone through?" he asked.

"Another hour to make the final adjustments," Ferrin replied. "Then we can send someone through, and they can bring back whomever—and whatever—they find."

"Excellent!" Garner was clearly pleased. "Forget the cavemen —we'll have an army of laser rifles and jetpacks instead!"

Three hours later—not surprisingly the scientists had taken longer than predicted to finish their work—Statton and Garner stood beside Ferrin, watching as Lieutenant

Card led his team onto the transfer platform. One of the techs flipped the switch and the scout team vanished.

"Safe arrival," Card reported almost immediately. "Strange place. No buildings, no vegetation, no ground cover at all. Sky's got a shimmer like a heat trail but all over. Ground's springy but firm. Everything's fluid, shifting, not quite solid. Colors, too. Hard on the eyes and havoc with the depth perception."

"How far ahead did you send him?" Statton asked the scientists.

"It's difficult to say precisely," Ferrin replied absently, studying the monitors. "But according to my calculations, roughly ten thousand years. Give or take an epoch or two."

"Something's coming," Card called out. "Team at the ready! It's moving fast, completely silent. Here it comes!"

There was a faint whoosh over the mikes. Then a voice speaking a mixture of numbers and what sounded like gibberish.

"I don't understand," Card replied. "Sorry. Do you speak English?"

"Twentieth to twenty-first century Earth colloquial," the voice responded. "Downloading translation matrix. Yes, I speak English. Who are you and what do you want here?"

"Lieutenant Grant Card, United States Army," Card answered. "We're here to ask your assistance in resolving a major conflict in my time, early twenty-first century."

"You have a way to move from your time to this one?" the voice asked.

"Yes."

A moment's pause. Then, "My family and I will accompany you."

"Roger that. Control, prepare to activate return."

"Excellent work, Card," Garner called out. "Just let us know when you're ready."

A few minutes later Card's new companion had gathered his family, and the techs reversed the transfer process. There was the almost-familiar flash, and then Lieutenant Card and his team were back on the transfer pad. And they were not alone.

At first Statton thought he was looking at small ships instead of people. Then he realized they were both. Each one was no larger than a small car and hovered silently a few feet above the platform. They were silvery-gray and had mirrored surfaces, but above the spherical bases were triangular torsos, cylindrical arms, and diamond-shaped heads. The eyes were hidden by—or were—gleaming mirrored orbs. They had only bumps to indicate ears noses, but the mouths looked surprisingly normal. So did the hands, which seemed oddly delicate against the gleaming bodies.

"Welcome to the twenty-first century," Garner announced, stepping forward. "I'm Colonel Garner and I'm in charge of this operation. I'd like to start by—"

"What is the date?" One of the future-men interrupted. Garner told him. "Man has not yet traveled to Venus, then?" When he was told no, the creature's face split in a wide, slightly predatory smile. "Excellent!" He turned and said something in his own language, and the others responded. Then he led them off the platform and toward the tent flap.

"Wait!" Garner called out. "We need to get you oriented, find out your weapons capabilities, and prepare strategies!" The future-men ignored him. "How are you going to fight for us if you don't even know the enemy's location?"

That made the leader stop. "Fight for you?" he asked. "We did not come here to be involved in your petty land conflicts! We have a far greater objective."

"Wait, you didn't come here to help us?" Statton stepped up beside the major. "Then why did you come?"

"Venus," the future-man replied. "In our time, we battle the Venusians incessantly. In your time, we have yet to encounter them, which suggests several of their greatest military advances have also not yet occurred. We can rout them easily, and conquer their planet now, preventing centuries of conflict."

"That won't exactly work," Ferrin warned, approaching the leader. "You'll wind up creating a new future rather than overwriting the old one."

"The result for us will be the same," the future-man pointed out. "And that will be enough." He pushed through the tent flap, leading his people outside. Statton followed quickly, with Garner and Ferrin beside him, and was in time to see the future-men shoot up into the sky. They quickly dwindled to tiny dots, and then vanished completely.

For a minute the three men simply stood there, staring up at the empty sky. Finally Garner sighed.

"Right," he said. "No more far-future men, doc."

"Back to the cavemen?" Statton asked.

But Garner shook his head. "Naw, future tech is still the answer," he decided. "We'll just aim a little closer to home."

"**P**repare to activate return," Card informed them, and Statton tensed. He hoped this foray went better than the last one. Still, this time Card's team had suffered no difficulties in locating suitable military figures, communicating the situation, and securing their aid. The interaction had been far more promising than with those far-future men, which made sense. Ferrin had only sent the team a century or so into the future this time. He and Garner had agreed that a hundred years of military advancement should still be more than enough to win the war for them.

"Return activated," one of the techs announced, and Statton squinted reflexively. The tent interior flared and he let his eyes open fully again as Card stepped down from the platform, another man right behind him. Statton was relieved to see that the newcomer looked completely normal. True, his one-piece uniform was made of some silvery material, very sleek and smooth, and rippled almost like water as he walked, and his face was a bit angular, his features sharp and straight, but he had normal limbs, hair, ears, etc. It was surprising how comforting the presence of a normal nose could be.

"Colonel Al Garner, United States Army," Garner introduced himself, stepping forward to shake the stranger's hand. "My second, Major Will Statton."

"Combat Master Res Nemberg, Allied Forces, Northern Division," the newcomer replied. His grip was firm. "Your man here said you could use our help." His eyes, a clear, cold blue, skipped past them and took in the tent, the monitors, and the situation board in back. "Yes, I see you can." He brushed by and strode to the board, examining the troop deployments. "Ah, the Great Land War!" He sounded excited, almost thrilled, Statton thought, like a little boy finally allowed to play with a new toy. "One of the last of the traditionally designated conflicts before the Great Amalgamation! And I will be a part of it!" Nemberg turned back to them, rubbing his hands together. "Permission to bring through my troops?"

Garner nodded eagerly. "By all means!"

"Excellent!" A second stranger had accompanied the scout team back, Statton realized now, and while they had followed Nemberg over to the board this other newcomer had been conferring with Doctor Ferrin. Now he glanced up and nodded to Nemberg.

"Internal transponders cued in to translational matrix signal," the man reported. "Units ready to deploy."

"Activate translation," Nemberg commanded. The man nodded, saluted—Statton was pleased to see that gesture hadn't changed, at least—and muttered something. Then the air above the translation platform shimmered.

There was no flare this time, just that shimmer, and from it stepped men. Men dressed like Nemberg and his subordinate. Men carrying streamlined silvery rifles of some sort—the laser rifles Garner had hoped for, no doubt. Men who saluted Nemberg and then marched off the platform in perfect formation.

"Combat squad ready, sir," the man in front announced.

"Very good, Combat Chief," Nemberg replied. He gestured toward a spot on the board, the heaviest concentration of enemy troops. "Full strike, that location, at best speed. Move out!" The soldier saluted and began barking orders to his men, who turned as one and followed him from the tent. Statton and Garner were on their heels, as were Ferrin, Nemberg, and Nemberg's nameless associate.

Once outside, the future-soldiers formed up again. The Combat Chief shouted "aerogear, activate!" and flat silvery ovals rose across the men's backs and shoulders, as if they were sprouting wings. Then the bottoms of those ovals began to glow, and the entire unit rose in the air. They hovered for a few seconds, the flight packs emitting only a faint hum, then accelerated, zooming across the plain like a swarm of angry insects. They were, as near as Statton could tell, heading straight for the enemy encampment.

"They will reach the location in less than a minute," Nemberg informed him and Garner. "That is the command tent, I presume?" They nodded and mutely followed him into it. Within seconds the monitors showing long-range surveillance of the enemy's location were alight with activity as the combat squad descended upon the soldiers there, laser rifles blazing. The enemy never stood a chance.

Two minutes later Nemberg nodded. "Very good, Combat Chief," he stated. "Return to base and await further instructions."

"That's amazing!" Garner admitted, still staring at the screen. "Their largest force and your men wiped them out in minutes!" He turned and grinned at Statton. "We'll have this war won by the end of the day!"

"Hours, actually," Nemberg corrected. "It's simply a matter of applying appropriate force at the critical juncture points." His tone became disapproving. "You have used your men and other resources carelessly, Colonel. That simply won't do. Best you sit back and leave the fighting to the professionals."

"Professionals?" Garner bristled. "I'll have you know, sir, I've been in this army more than twenty years! I'm a full colonel! And while I appreciate the assist, this is my command and my war!"

"Not anymore," their visitor corrected. He smiled. It was not a friendly smile. "I recognize your rank, Colonel, though we abolished those grades when we merged the various nations' militaries into a single cohesive force. My own rank, Combat Master, is equivalent to your army's major general." His smile grew sharper. "I outrank you, sir. And I am officially relieving you and your subordinate of command, effective immediately. You may remain as observers, but do not interfere or I will have you detained." Then he turned away, clearly dismissing them.

Garner wandered out of the command tent, stunned. Statton followed him. For a moment they stood outside, staring at the desert beyond, unable to speak.

"I can't believe it," Garner said finally. "Cashiered out of my own command! By some yahoo in a jumpsuit!"

"You brought him in," Statton couldn't help pointing out. "And he does outrank us." And, he thought to himself, he's winning the war for us. Our war. Only it isn't ours anymore. It's his.

"Well, we'll just see what the Joint Chiefs have to say about all this," Garner blustered, but Statton could hear the defeat in the colonel's voice. They both knew their own bosses wouldn't care. As long as they had a victory, they would be happy. And he suspected they would welcome Combat Master Nemberg with open arms, eager to gain his advanced weaponry and knowledge.

"We wanted help," Statton said softly. "And we got it. Exactly the help we needed to win this thing." He shook his head. He didn't mind that Nemberg had taken command, not really, not if it would end the conflict quickly and with no further losses on their side. No, what bothered him was something else. Something that hadn't entirely sunk in until now.

They had traveled through time in search of help. And they had found it, all too easily. The cavemen had been more than willing to fight anything in front of them. The far-future men had not helped but only because they were too occupied with their own interplanetary conflict. And Nemberg had been eager to get involved in what he had called "the last traditionally designated conflict." Warriors, one and all. Fighters. Soldiers. All through human history.

Was that all they were? Clearly mankind never outgrew its violent instincts. Clearly they never stopped fighting. One war grew into the next, on down the line into infinity.

It was a sobering thought.

"Well, let's go see how it ends," Garner told him. He patted Statton on the shoulder, turned, and headed slowly back toward the command tent. Statton followed. Where else was there to go? But it wasn't an end—they'd already seen that much. It wasn't even a beginning. It was just another bump in the road.

With a sigh he lifted the tent flap, preparing himself. He was about to watch the future conquer the present, but in the end it was all one. The war never ended. And he was a soldier. That was all he knew. If he couldn't fight the battle himself, the least he could do was watch and appreciate the skills of those directly involved.

He wondered if he could talk Ferrin into sending him backward in time. One-way. Then, perhaps, he could do what Nemberg was doing here. He, Major Will Statton, could pre-empt some earlier military commander, awe them with his skills and his weaponry, and end a historic conflict almost before it began. But would it make any difference except to his own ego? In his mind's eye he pictured a series of dominos, each one an earlier battle, each one toppling the one after it. How far back could he go? How much would history be changed? Would men still be fighting each other, no matter what he did?

Yes. Yes they would. There was no way to avoid that, he thought, stepping into the relative darkness of the tent. It was all they knew. No matter what point in human history they were at.

It was all they knew.

Statton let the tent flap fall behind him, and focused on the monitors. The battles they displayed were a testament to Man, to his true nature.

He had a duty to at least observe and acknowledge those events. War didn't exist in a vacuum, after all. Conflict would never occur without other people. They all had a part to play. Right now, his part was to observe. Perhaps that would change again at some point. If it did, Statton would be ready. But if not, he would still do his best.

That was all any of them could do, no matter what time they came from, no matter where they found themselves. They could only do their best with what they had. The rest would resolve itself. Apparently, it always did. All the way down the line.

About the Author

Aaron **Rosenberg** is an award-winning, bestselling novelist, children's book author, and game designer. He's written original fiction (including the NOOK-bestselling

humorous science fiction novel *No Small Bills*, the Dread
Remora space-opera series, and the O.C.L.T. supernatural
thriller series), tie-in novels (including the PsiPhi winner
Collective Hindsight for Star Trek: SCE, the Daemon Gates
trilogy for Warhammer, *Tides of Darkness* and the Scribe-
nominated *Beyond the Dark Portal* for WarCraft, *Hunt and
Run* for Stargate: Atlantis, and *Substitution Method* and *Road
Less Traveled* for Eureka), young adult novels (including the
Scribe-winning *Bandslam: The Novel* and books for iCarly
and Ben10), children's books (including an original
Scholastic Bestseller series, *Pete and Penny's Pizza Puzzles*,
and work for PowerPuff Girls and Transformers Animated),
roleplaying games (including original games like Asylum
and Spookshow, the Origins Award-winning Gamemastering
Secrets, and sections of The Supernatural Roleplaying Game,
Warhammer Fantasy Roleplay, and The Deryni Roleplaying
Game), short stories, webcomics, essays, and educational
books. He has ranged from mystery to speculative fiction to
drama to comedy, always with the same intent—to tell a
good story. You can visit him online at gryphonrose.com or
follow him on Twitter @gryphonrose.

Timeslip

Maggie Allen

Kat felt the bass drum before she could hear it, like an insistent heartbeat. Standing at the back of the small, deserted, semi-dark concert hall, she could see the stage at the front was equally empty. She was totally alone, and yet… there was music here.

With a quick, nervous look behind her, Kat moved toward the stage. The air was still as she walked past rows of vacant chairs to stand at the edge of what was clearly intended as a dance floor. As Kat stepped forward onto it, she felt a slight resistance to the air, as if she pushed her way through invisible dancers. The drumbeat thudded louder in her ears.

Kat stopped and covered her eyes with her hands, straining to listen, willing the musicians and their audience into existence. She imagined how strange she would look to someone walking in off the street, a lone teenager in the middle of an empty room listening intently to nothing. They might have thought her crazy. Kat might have questioned her own sanity too, except this wasn't the first time something like this had happened.

Something bumped Kat from behind and startled her into dropping her hands. The instant she did, the sound burst into life. All around her, teenagers jostled into each other, dancing and jumping. Another push came from behind. Kat turned her head to glare, but the boy there gave her an apologetic smile. He wore a suit jacket, and though his tie was coming undone, she couldn't help by feel underdressed in her faded skinny jeans and Chuck Taylor sneakers. The boy didn't seem to notice or mind, and Kat's smile at him, tentative though it was, must have been encouragement enough for him. He grabbed her hand and twirled her.

Kat couldn't focus on dancing—she was too distracted by what felt like sensory overload. The dance floor was crowded with other boys in suits, and girls who twisted and spun, skirts swirling out. Kat was sure that someone would notice that her wardrobe, not to mention the blue streaks in her dirty blonde hair, clearly marked her as an outsider, but no one spoke to her. Not even her dance partner.

Then there was the music. The beat was driving, but Kat recognized it as old-fashioned rock and roll, the kind of twelve bar blues that was popular long before she was born. Despite its age, rock and roll music from that era still thrilled Kat and spoke to her in a way modern music didn't. Her very favorite band had started out playing music just like this in small clubs and auditoriums all over the U.K. more than fifty years ago. Small venues like this one. That was why she had come here in the first place today, wasn't it?

Being able to explore places like this was one of the few benefits of being torn away from her home and her friends, and having to move to a foreign country for her father's job. Kat would be spending her final year of high school in a strange, new place, but at least she had a few precious weeks to herself before that began.

Her days were spent wandering the older parts of town, and when she'd learned that the band had once played here, she had to see it for herself. To experience it. Kat wasn't sure if it would work, wasn't sure if she could make the place come alive once more, even for a few brief moments.

But she had done it.

Kat suddenly realized the spell could break at any moment. Giving the boy she was dancing with a wink, she broke away from him and pushed through the crowd. She had to make it to the stage and get a glimpse of the band, of *him*, before it all went away. And suddenly, there he was in front of her. She dared not even breath his name for fear that doing so would break the spell and cause him to vanish.

Feet planted apart, aggressively strumming rhythm on his guitar, he was every bit the rebel despite his dark suit. Kat watched fascinated as he sang, punctuating the verses now and then with a whoop or a scream.

To the non-discerning eye, all four young men on stage would have looked identical, not only because of their matching dress, but because they all had the shaggy dark hair of '60s rockers. Kat had always laughed at the thought that their appearance could ever have been shocking. But here, now, in front of them, she finally understood. The experience of seeing them play live was visceral.

Entranced, she stood watching them, not even bothering to dance, ignoring everyone around her, taking in every detail. The way the bass player bobbed his head in time with the music, the drummer's intensity, the way the lead guitarist leaped all over the stage. And the way the rhythm guitarist squinted into the crowd.

Kat froze when his gaze fell on her. Mentally she again catalogued the wrongness of her being here. Her hair was wrong, her clothes were wrong. She had no idea how well he could even see her, since she knew his eyesight was bad, but surely even he could tell that she was way more interested in the band than in dancing to their music. Though the crowd was enjoying their playing, she was the only one that knew who they were and what they would become. He couldn't know any of that, of course, but Kat felt like it was written all over her face.

Yet she couldn't withdraw or even look away. This whole room, teeming with life, could vanish in an instant. She had to soak it all in while she still could. And so Kat met his stare.

They stayed locked that way for the rest of the song. He struck the final chord and let it ring. When the distorted sound finally died, he blinked nearsightedly and looked away.

"We'll be taking a ten minute break, then," he said in a strongly accented voice into the microphone. He slung the guitar carelessly over his head and leaned it against his amplifier. The rest of the band followed his lead, and Kat watched them all jump off the side of the stage. The dancers swarmed around her; some of them went up to the band, and others went off to use the restrooms or to buy Cokes or beers. Unsure of what to do, she just stayed where she was, watching the group laughing and joking with their friends and fans. Kat again felt she stuck out like sore thumb, and wondered that no one but the guitarist had seemed to notice that she was different. In fact, no one else seemed to notice her at all anymore.

Maybe that meant the tableau around her was starting to fade. Though Kat could sometimes will a scene from the past into existence, she couldn't control how long she was in it. Worried, she looked around her for signs of transparency. *Did that girl talking to the bass player look solid enough? Were the guitars paler than they were before?* She strained her eyes staring at the black guitar sitting on the stage, but the lighting was dim in the hall and it was hard to tell.

Kat turned to peek back at the band, and was startled when she found her view blocked by him. Her favorite. He squinted down at her, as if he were studying her now that he could see her more closely, just as she had studied him while he was on stage.

He leaned over. "Come with me," he said softly into her ear.

"Where?" she tried to ask, but it was too late, he had hold of her hand and was towing her through the crowd.

The two of them spilled through the side door of the concert hall into an empty alley. Though it was dark, a single streetlight illuminated them and made the damp pavement that was not in shadow sparkle as though it were full of stars.

He reached into his pocket and drew out a pair of black, heavy-rimmed glasses. Putting them on he said, "Now I can see you proper. Didn't want to put these on out there, though," he said, gesturing toward the building. "No one needs to know about these." He wrinkled his nose, which made her laugh.

"It'll be our secret."

"You're not like them, are you?" he asked suddenly. "Not one of them."

"No, I'm not," she admitted.

"To tell the truth, I don't think I'm one of them either."

"What are you then?" she asked, curious.

"I don't know yet, do I? But whatever it is, it's going to be more than them. Than this." He waved his arms around him. Kat wasn't sure if he meant the small venue, the small town, or his small country, but now, standing in front of him, she knew that none of it seemed big enough to contain him. She nodded, not sure what to say to him, not wanting to give away the enormity of his future. "You understand, don't you? Somehow, I can feel you do."

She nodded again.

"I like your hair. It's different." He reached out and gently tugged at a blue strand.

"Thank you." She shivered suddenly. Was it his touch or the feel of the chilly night air on her bare arms?

"Cold, are you?"

"Just a bit," Kat struggled to keep her teeth from chattering.

"Here, take this," he said, shrugging out of his jacket and draping it over her shoulders.

"Oh, I couldn't..." she protested weakly.

"It's my fault, isn't it? Dragging you out here..." He gave her a grin that made her face flush. Between that and the jacket, she was now quite warm. "That's all right, it suits you." He grasped the lapels of the jacket and straightened them and the collar, tugging her hair out from under it, his fingers lingering slightly in its tangles.

She looked up at him to see that he was once again gazing intently back, as if he could see through her. And perhaps he could.

"You're fading," he said, puzzled.

No, it couldn't be ending already, Kat thought, panicked. He still looked solid to her, but who was to say whose time they were in? Maybe he now was temporarily in hers, and soon it would all disappear, her with it, leaving him back where he belonged.

"We don't have long," Kat whispered. "I'm sorry."

"I don't understand."

"I don't fully either. But I will remember you for the rest of my life."

"I'll never see you again?" A hint of regret was visible in his eyes. Though they'd only had a few minutes together, she could tell that talking to someone from outside of his life had meant something to him. If nothing else, it had shown him that there was more out there, things outside the narrow world in which he'd been raised.

"I don't know. Maybe. But I don't think so," Kat shook her head, trying to keep tears from forming.

"I can almost see through you. Please, don't go." The jacket she was wearing was evidently still solid because he used it to pull her close to him. And before the chance was gone, he touched his lips to hers. Eyes closed, Kat could feel his warmth and the softness of his mouth, but she had no idea if he could feel her, or whether he was kissing a ghost. She put her hands over his, which were still clinging to the jacket and gripped them as tightly as she could. He squeezed her fingers back. Once, twice, and then... his touch was gone.

Kat opened her eyes. Weak daylight spilt into the alley between the buildings where she was standing. Alone. Closing her eyes again, she tried to will him back into existence, even if just for a moment. And briefly, it was as though she could still feel his arms wrapped around her. She stood still as long as she could, trying to hold onto him, but eventually she felt his lingering presence slip away.

Ephemeral though the experience had proven, Kat knew that the things that had drawn them together, like a love of music and a rebellious spirit, were real, and she was certain that their connection had meant something to both of them. For a time at least, maybe they had each felt a little less alone in the world. Kat thrilled in this, despite knowing that he was gone, perhaps for good. Though, perhaps not... They had come together once; it might not be outside the realm of possibility that their paths could overlap again someday. Or some time.

About the Author

Maggie Allen is new to the publishing world, but not new to writing. By day, Maggie writes about non-fictional topics in astronomy and astrophysics - and at night she spends time in other creative pursuits. These include writing short stories, sewing (mostly historical) costumes, and playing guitar in a rock band, which just came out with it's first album of original music. She is married and lives with her husband (and a fluffy white cat) in the Washington, D.C. area.

The Crossed-wires Adventure

Michael A. Stackpole

Jack Card—safely ensconced in his room cataloguing the latest addition to his coin collection—heard Aunt Flora well before he saw her. His mom had greeted the old woman at the front door, which was a straight shot down the stairs from Jack's room. Though he couldn't make out any of the words spoken, Aunt Flora's high-pitched tone meant only one thing: adventure was afoot.

"Jack, Aunt Flora is here to see you." His mom's voice had a note of urgency. Jack hurried getting his sneakers on. "She needs your help."

He took the stairs two at a time, pausing near the bottom. "Hi, Aunt Flora."

"There you are, Master John." The elderly woman—who was really his great grand-aunt—cupped his face in her boney hands. "Mina, dear, you will let me borrow him? Atrocious manners, short notice and all, I do apologize, dear, but I need your bright boy."

"Is your homework done, Jack?"

"Finished an hour ago."

445

Jack's mother nodded, then gave him *the look*. Aunt Flora had taken a small fortune left to her by her father and turned it into a large fortune through shrewd investments. Because she was known as the richest person in North Greenvale, lots of people came to her with investment ideas. As his mother had done when she was his age, Jack was given the duty of protecting Aunt Flora against swindlers.

"Of course, Aunt Flora. Jack should be out and about on a nice afternoon like this anyway, shouldn't you, Jack?"

He nodded. "Yes."

Aunt Flora smiled. "You're very kind."

Jack raised an eyebrow. "What do you need me for?"

"Well, John, I have been given a most wonderful opportunity to invest in a treasure hunt. You'll get the details when we make it to the old Appleby farm. Suffice it to say, an experience treasure-finder has been brought to town, and he is going to make us all rich!"

"Treasure-finder?"

The older woman's smile shifted from pride to indulgence. "Well, when I was a girl we called them water-witches. Dowsers. They'd tell you where to sink a well to get water. But this one can find *gold*, Master John. He'll prove it this afternoon. I want you there to see."

Jack and his mom exchanged a quick glance. "I would love to go, Aunt Flora. Can we ask my friend Henry Lee to come, too?"

"The young man from the Shippington mansion? Yes, of course, by all means."

"Great. I'll call him." Jack shifted on the stairs. "I'll get my phone and a few other things. Just to be sure."

"Splendid, splendid." Flora clapped her hands. "I do believe, Mina, your boy enjoys these adventures more than you ever did!"

Aunt Flora had her limousine driver stop by Henry Lee's place on the way out to the Appleby farm. Henry had moved to North Greenvale in the summer. Jack had seen the Asian-American boy at the YMCA. They both attended sixth grade at Erik Weisz Middle School. They were lab partners in science class and geeked out over science fiction, games, and science in general.

Jack briefed Henry on the Appleby farm. "Horace Appleby owned most of North Greenvale at one time. He made money off logging, farming and some manufacturing. He made a fortune during the Civil War— some folks said by cheating on government contracts. He worried about the Confederate Army coming north to steal his fortune. Local legend has it that he buried a bunch of strongboxes full of gold throughout the area. He died without revealing where any of them were."

Henry frowned. "Lots of folks must have looked for them."

Aunt Flora laughed. "For year and years, Master Henry. The Appleby family fell on hard times after Horace died. They sold off great portions of the estates, but not before having dug up every inch of the plots. During the Depression treasure hunters poured over what was left. Eventually the last of the Applebys moved away and the town took over the farm for taxes."

The limo pulled onto a dirt road that wound its way up a low hill. At the top stood the ruins of what had once been a proud stone house. The roof had long since sagged in, and trees thrust branches through the windows from the inside. A number of other people—potential investors—stood on an area of lawn that had been raggedly cut back. A dozen post-holes had been dug in a circle roughly thirty feet in diameter.

A young man with thinning blond hair, wearing a gray suit and red tie over white shirt, smiled as he walked toward the limo. The driver helped Aunt Flora from the car. Jack and Henry piled out behind her. "Miss Williams, so happy you were able to come."

"My pleasure, Mr. Boyer." Aunt Flora waved a gloved hand toward the boys. "This is my nephew John, and his friend Henry. They're clever boys."

"Good, I might need some assistants." Boyer shook each boy's hand. Jack didn't like the man's soft grip, or the way his nostrils had flared when Aunt Flora said they were clever. "Please, if you would join the rest of us."

Boyer led the way to the center of the circle. "Gather round, please. I want to thank you all for joining me here. This is a great opportunity for your town, to enrich it not only in monetary terms, but historical terms. You're all aware of the Appleby family contribution to North Greenvale. The endeavor we begin today will not only refurbish their reputation, but allow North Greenvale to place itself on the map as a tourist destination. I have drawn up some plans that will make this a reality, and if all goes well here today, I'll be speaking with your mayor very soon."

Boyer opened his arms and turned toward the ruins. "However, I am not the man whom you have come to see. I do not have the gift that will locate the Appleby treasure. For that we need an expert, and I present to you Augustus Fitch."

A man came around the corner of the house. He wore a red union-suit stained black around the cuffs and neck, with soiled overalls over. One pant leg had been tucked into a half-laced, battered brown boot. The other boot was black and in not much better shape. Dirt made a thick, black line under the man's fingernails. He hadn't shaved in at least a week. What little hair he had on top of his head hadn't felt a comb or brush in forever. His icy blue eyes— one appearing bigger than the other—moved more quickly than the rest of him. The way he staggered, Jack thought the man might have been drinking.

As unsteady as he was, however, the divining rods in his calloused hands swung smoothly and fluidly back and forth. As Fitch entered the circle, he half-turned and his hands extended. The silvery rods, bent at the bottom to form grips, swung together and pointed at the thick, gold chain Aunt Flora wore. Fitch tugged hard at the rods, as if they were resisting him. He pulled them free of their attraction to gold, staggering back as he did so. The rods swung apart as he passed them over each boy, then he curled in toward the middle of the circle and Boyer.

"You'll be a-forgiving me, I hope." He scratched his unshaven throat with filthy nails. "There's times, you see, when there's so many riches, that I am just a-feeling them hither and yon. This is such a place. But I ain't a-specting you to be taking my word for it. No sir or ma'am."

Mr. Boyer, with some apparent reluctance, rested a hand on Fitch's shoulder. "You're asking yourselves, I'm sure, why, if there is so much treasure here as to make Mr. Fitch take notice, we don't just go out, dig it up and be done with it?"

Fitch shrugged Boyer's hand off his shoulder. "Well now, it's this way. I is the seventh son of a seventh son. Y'all know what that means. I have the Second Sight and the power. My granddaddy did, too, and he done tolt me how it works. This here power, it only works for good, and greed ain't good. So I go around and find lost things for people, returning good to them, see. I done found millions, and will take my reward in God's Heaven."

Boyer smiled. "As Mr. Fitch has so succinctly put it, he cannot use his powers to enrich himself. Our preliminary survey indicates that the majority of the Appleby treasure is located here, on the farm. We need to buy the farm from the city, then we will own the treasure. I have contracts that will sell you shares in our company. Fifty percent of the recovered treasure will be sold on the open market to repay you, and the other half will be donated to North Greenvale; along with enough money to create a museum and a visitors' center for all those who will come to see this location."

Aunt Flora nodded. "Very civic-minded of you."

"As Mr. Fitch said, he returns the lost to those who deserve it, and North Greenvale is very deserving." Boyer pointed over toward the corner of the building from where Fitch had appeared. "Augustus, if you don't mind."

The dowser nodded and headed off, fighting to keep his dowsing rods from drawing him to Aunt Flora again. Jack watched him, making sure the man disappeared from sight.

Boyer pointed toward the nearest of the holes. "I don't expect you to invest in supposition, so I propose a test of Mr. Fitch's ability." He dug into his pocket and produced a small golden coin in a plastic coin case. Jack recognized it easily since many of the coins in his collection came similarly packaged from the United States Mint. "Here I have this year's dollar coin. It's Ulysses S. Grant—fitting since he was the president when Horace Appleby died. I will have one of you place it in a hole. I have eleven more coins—quarters also encased in plastic—which will go into the other holes. You'll fill them in, then Mr. Fitch will find the gold coin. His random chance of being correct is one in twelve, and we can run multiple tests, if you wish. I assure you, he will always find the gold coin."

Jack raised a hand. "Excuse me."

"Yes?"

"Just to make the test scientific, shouldn't anyone wearing gold put their gold back in their cars?"

Boyer smiled. "My, you are clever, aren't you? Perhaps a couple of you would also like to go keep an eye on Mr. Fitch to make sure he's not watching?"

Two of the men appointed themselves to that committee, while everyone else, including Aunt Flora, returned to their cars to get rid of their jewelry.

Henry glanced over at Jack. "You know..."

"I do." Jack nodded confidently. "You'll need to get pictures of each hole. Make north equal twelve o'clock, then work around clockwise."

"Got it."

When people returned from their cars, Boyer directed them to pick a hole. Aunt Flora and Jack had number four. Boyer went around the circle, handing people coins. Flora got a quarter, but before she could bend down to drop it in the hole, Jack took it from her.

"You don't want to get dirty, Aunt Flora."

"Thank you, Master John."

"Now, if you all will put your coin in the bottom of the hole and scoop the dirt back on top of it, please." Boyer nodded as Kenny Erickson—the owner of the Jack & Sons Burgers chain—dragged the small mound of dirt into his hole. "And when you're done, just tamp it down good with your foot.

Jack laid his coin in the bottom of the hole, then dumped handfuls of dirt on it. It mounded up just a little bit, so he stood and stomped it down good and hard. Boyer came along, inspected his work, then added one final stamp to seal the hole.

"Well done, son. Thank you."

Henry, who had been following behind Boyer taking pictures, gave Jack a nod. He flashed him some fingers. The gold coin was in hole number nine—Erickson's hole.

"Gentlemen, if you would bring Mr. Fitch back, please." Boyer lowered his voice again. "And you, ladies and gentlemen, if you don't mind, please turn away from the circle. We don't want anyone suspecting that a stray glance might influence Mr. Fitch."

Boyer dutifully turned away from the circle and Jack did as well. Mostly. He actually kept looking at Boyer out of the corner of his eye and watched Fitch as he approached the circle. The man staggered as before. The dowsing rods swung wildly back and forth until Fitch entered the circle near hole six. Then they quieted down. Jack lost sight of him as he headed toward seven, then found him again as he came back to hole five.

Fitch approached hole four. Jack couldn't see him, but he could hear the dowser. The man was sniffing like a hound dog. He mumbled under his breath. The only words Jack actually understood were, "Nope, ain't here." Then Fitch came into view to his left and continued on around the circle.

Jack half-turned. The man moved slowly, the rods held steady. They didn't so much as twitch until he got around to hole number ten. Both of them skewed toward nine. Fitch snarled, which brought everyone around. He fought the rods, but then they fairly well yanked him off his feet toward number nine. Fitch dropped to a knee. The rods crossed and stabbed at the hole.

Kenny Erickson gasped.

Fitch ignored him and got to his feet like a man trying to haul an anchor from the river. He pulled back, staggered, then tried to go on to hole eight, but the rods plunged back toward hole nine.

Fitch surrendered to the rods and landed on his knees. "Praise the Lord. If this ain't the hole, I'm beat."

"But it is!" Erickson sank to his knees and scooped the dirt away. He reached down into the hole and pulled the coin out. He cleaned the dirt off and held it up. "See, there it is!"

Boyer plucked it from his hand and lifted it higher. "He found it, just as he'll find the Appleby treasure!"

Kenny Erickson stood and brushed dirt off his knees. He glanced at his wife. "Honey, get me my check book."

"I wouldn't do that, Mr. Erickson." Jack pointed a finger at Boyer and Fitch. "These two can't find gold."

Erickson shook his head. "I've seen them do it with my own eyes, son."

"Sir, you saw no such thing." Jack pointed to the coin in Boyer's hand. "One dollar coins in the United States look gold, but there's not a speck of gold in them. Anyone with a smart phone can look at the US Mint website and read that."

One of the men who'd kept an eye on Fitch pulled his phone out. He touched the screen several times, then looked up. "The boy's right."

Erickson shook his head. "Doesn't matter. He found the gold colored coin out of all the others. Hit it right off."

Henry held his camera up. "I took pictures of all the holes. Mr. Boyer stomped on each one. You can see his footprint on top. And on eleven of the twelve, it's his right foot. On number nine, he used his left foot. If you look at his left shoe, it has a line carved down the center of the heel. He tipped Fitch off."

Erickson's face flushed red.

Jack smiled and walked back over to hole number four. He dug down and pulled the coin from the bottom of it. "In case that's not enough for you, I didn't put a quarter in the bottom of my hole. This is the latest addition to my collection: a five dollar, Medal of Honor commemorative coin, straight from the mint. It's ninety percent pure gold. It was the only treasure in this field, and Mr. Fitch passed it by."

Fitch sprang to his feet and dashed off, looking a lot more spry than he ever had before. Unfortunately for him, the half-laced boots that made up part of his costume came loose and tripped him up. He sprawled face-first and Aunt Flora's driver pounced on him.

Boyer looked as if he wanted to run, but the circle of investors closed around him.

Erickson pulled out his cell phone. "I'm calling the police."

The police responded quickly enough, including Henry's mom, who was a detective with the North Greenvale fraud squad. Jack and Henry got to watch the crime scene investigators dig up the other coins for evidence. Henry turned his camera over so his mother could copy the pictures.

Finally, as the sun began to set and the police started to pack up, Aunt Flora bundled the boys into her car. "I'd still like to believe that Horace Appleby's treasure is out there somewhere, boys, because it is fun to dream. But..." She winked at them, "I think the true treasure in North Greenvale is the pair of young men seated right here with me. And that makes us all very rich indeed."

To Our Many Contributors:

Silence in the Library Publishing and the authors and artist of *Time Traveled Tales* would like to say thank you to the backers of our Kickstarter funding initiative. Without you, this project would never have come to life.

We have identified many of you by name in the following pages, but all 742 of you are the true force behind *Time Traveled Tales*, and your efforts stand as a testament to the power of readers to shape publishing.

Patrons

Benefactors

Masters of Time

Allen and Brenda Jellison	Curtis H. Steinhour
Elizabeth Dibble	Olivia the time traveling ninja
Janine Martinez	T.M. 'Pirate Ted' Crim
Zak	Heather Wilke
Jonathan You	Richard Hannon
Allen Wold	Christopher Miller
David Galbis-Reig	David Murray Solomon
Kelly Adams	Max Meltser
Michael F. Hampton-Fitzgerald	Paul McMullen
Stefan Gore	Y.M. Rivadeneira
Bob Michiels	Lucas K. Law
Marc Wydler	Ty Hooge
James Crouch	David Chase
Jennifer	Jim Bernheimer
Ronald R. Richter	Marc Winkelmann
Zach Murray	Adrienne Romani
Cliff Winnig	Bert 'LW' Sanders
Jason Flanders	Kat Sharp
Michael Stim	Kent Yausie
Josh Short	Erica Deel
Scott Skene	Jeff
Jim Silva	Abilash Sarhadi
Travis Skinner	Myles C. Allen
Launi L. Purcell	Kevin Luman
Molli P. Barnes	Abraham M. Denmark

Champions of Horology

Allen Cheesman
Rob Carome
Paul Canolesio
R.B. Wood
Kevin Eaves
Jonathan Clift
Rob
Ryan Leduc
Cole Peel
Ashleigh King
Mike Tripicco
Steven Petrovski
Jenny O'Callaghan
Christopher J. Northern
Noah Jellison
Rick Reischman
Eva Guest Blum
Alex CJ
Pepita Hogg-Sonnenberg
Steven Mentzel
Amanda Johnson
Heather Guillette
The Tandy Family
Mark Bennett
Amber Biles

A HERO
By Any Other Name
Edited by Jean Rabe
With Stories by:
Aaron Allston
Janine K. Spendlove
Michael A. Stackpole
Bryan Young
and more...